How to Lose the Lottery

Jay McKenzie grew up in the North East surrounded by storytellers and Catherine Cookson novels. She has worked as a holiday rep, a performing arts teacher, a life model and a street theatre performer in Greece, Indonesia, Singapore, South Korea and Australia, as well as appearing in *Byker Grove* for four years. Jay also writes short fiction and has received publication and recognition in a number of literary magazines. She has a penchant for knitwear and lives in the North East with her husband, daughter and too many cardigans.

Keep in touch with Jay:

www.jaymckenzieauthor.com
@jay_writes_books

How to Lose the Lottery

Jay McKenzie

HarperCollins*Publishers*

HarperCollins*Publishers* Ltd
1 London Bridge Street
London SE1 9GF

www.harpercollins.co.uk

HarperCollins*Publishers*
Macken House, 39/40 Mayor Street Upper
Dublin 1, D01 C9W8, Ireland

First published by HarperCollins*Publishers* Ltd 2026

1

Copyright © Jay McKenzie 2026

Jay McKenzie asserts the moral right to be identified as the author of this work.

A catalogue record for this book is available from the British Library.

ISBN: 978-0-00-876525-5 (HB)
ISBN: 978-0-00-876527-9 (TPB)

This novel is entirely a work of fiction. The names, characters and incidents portrayed in it are the work of the author's imagination. Any resemblance to actual persons, living or dead, events or localities is entirely coincidental.

Set in Adobe Caslon Pro by HarperCollins*Publishers* India

Printed and bound in the UK using 100% Renewable Electricity at CPI Group (UK) Ltd

All rights reserved. No part of this publication may be reproduced, stored in a retrieval system, or transmitted, in any form or by any means, electronic, mechanical, photocopying, recording or otherwise, without the prior written permission of the publishers.

Without limiting the exclusive rights of any author, contributor or the publisher of this publication, any unauthorised use of this publication to train generative artificial intelligence (AI) technologies is expressly prohibited. HarperCollins also exercise their rights under Article 4(3) of the Digital Single Market Directive 2019/790 and expressly reserve this publication from the text and data mining exception.

*To Carol McKenzie and Abigail Kranicz who both
showed me how to be a mother.*

Ladybird, ladybird, fly away home
Your house is on fire and your children are gone
— traditional nursery rhyme

The cars came before anything else. Before the new-build in Darras Hall had been discussed, or the theatre weekend in London booked, the cars appeared like a pair of sapphire earrings at a church hall jumble sale. They came even before Edie had the opportunity to talk to her friends.

Carol said that Gary saw it on the internet.

When your neighbours win the lottery, it read, accompanied by a photo of their street, the cars gleaming rudely. Moira Kirby's rusting Cortina was in the shot behind them looking like an undernourished old donkey in a thoroughbred racehorse compound.

The vehicles had only been there a few hours when the neighbours started to gather.

'Don't think I've seen one of those before.'

'I think that dude that plays for Newcastle's got one.'

'They're a bit fancy.'

'Do they cost more than a Volvo, Margaret?'

Edie lurked behind the curtain in the living room, peeking out. They were all there: neighbours, friends and acquaintances she'd known for thirty years, but she wanted nothing more than to disappear into the wallpaper. Ron and Colin were out in the thick of it. Ron was more animated than she'd seen him in years. Colin had a light flush in his cheeks. They were presidential amongst their friends.

Edie sighed. It wasn't that she was unhappy, as such – how could someone be unhappy when all of their dreams could now become a reality? It was more that she'd hoped to discuss it first. Make some proper plans. This felt like too much of a whim.

Of course, they weren't whims: her husband and son had endlessly discussed their ideal cars in great detail. So much so, that even non-driving, non-interested Edie knew a little bit about them. *If money was no object*, they'd say.

For Ron, the Jaguar XKS. Coupe, not convertible. He ran a little cold and didn't like the idea of being windswept. Not that he had enough hair to become windswept, but he seemed curiously oblivious to his balding pate. And red. Bright, gleaming, pillar-box red. *'You don't want a dark car, Edie,'* he'd tell her, wagging a finger. *'Too dangerous at night.'*

Colin's choice was a hulking great Mustang convertible. In his fantasy musings, it was a sleek black. The real-life one was prison-jumpsuit orange. *'I couldn't resist!'*

The two men in her life presided over their treasures as Edie filled the kettle to make a cup of tea. She ran a finger across the window ledge to see if it needed a clean. Not that it would matter. Ron would have them sold up and in a new house pronto. She sighed and tried to remember where she'd stashed her secret packet of Party Rings.

Part 1

Ball Number 5: Ron's Birthday

1

After

Edie swears that the thing falls off spontaneously whenever she walks past it. Not every time, but at least three or four times in the last three months, their framed winning lottery ticket has launched itself off the wall and crash-landed at her feet. This time, however, it has broken. Usually, the thick carpet cushions the blow, but today, it hit the stepstool she'd put below it so she could give it a proper clean.

The glass has splintered into six spears, one for each of their winning numbers, and they remind Edie of icicles. She sighs.

'It's almost like you know how much you've messed with the order of things,' she tells it as she picks up the shards and examines the frame to see whether it can be saved or not.

In the big sitting room, Colin is in one of the armchairs eating Ritz crackers directly from the box. *Top Gear* blares from the massive TV. She's not sure why they need more than one sitting room – how much sitting can three people do? – but Ron and Colin were adamant that the more sitting rooms, the better.

'Where's your dad?'

Colin shrugs, eyes not leaving the screen. 'Gone for a drive, I reckon. Or he might still be in bed.'

He's got cracker crumbs on his chin and cheeks. Edie marvels that they are the same pillowy baby cheeks that made her cry with love every time she kissed them. They're still chubby, his cheeks, but somehow they are much less endearing on a thirty-three-year-old man. She fights the urge to lick a tissue and clean his face.

'Look,' she says, waving the broken frame. 'The ticket attacked me again. Maybe it's telling me it wanted someone else to win.' She's joking, of course, but Colin gives her a pointed look.

'Or maybe it's telling you to get out and start enjoying yourself with the money.' He points at her in a *gotcha!* kind of way, nods, and goes back to the TV.

Edie examines the ticket again, then looks back to her son. 'What are you going to do today?'

He shrugs again and pushes another cracker in his mouth. He guffaws at something one of the presenters has said. Edie can never remember which one is which. She finds them all obnoxious.

'Which one's he again?'

Colin tears his eyes from the TV. 'What?'

'The presenter man. Him in the jeans. Is he the one that had the nasty accident?'

A small grin tugs at the edge of Colin's lips. 'No, Mam. That was Richard. That one.' He points at the screen, crunching another cracker.

'Right. And he's okay now, is he?'

A nod. He sticks his hand into the box and rummages, then peers inside before shaking it upside down. 'We're out of crackers.'

'I only bought them on Wednesday!'

'Mam, you can buy more than one, you know.' He grins. 'It's

not like we can't afford it.' He looks hopefully into the box again, sighs and puts it on the floor. 'You know, some of the big guns at my old work used Tesco Direct. You get your groceries delivered. It's great. Means you wouldn't have to go down the shops.'

'I like going down to the shops!'

He frowns. 'Bit far from here though. And why won't you let Dad or me drive you?'

'I like to walk.'

She doesn't really like to walk. She misses getting the bus with Carol and Brenda, rolling their eyes at the boys with their underpants on show and the girls with fake eyelashes that look like severed bird wings stuck to their faces.

She closes her eyes. She'd phoned them both last week. Brenda had sounded distracted. Carol had sounded guilty.

Colin snorts. For a moment, it seems that he's laughing at something on the TV, then she spots his eyes shut, his jaw hanging open. She's briefly furious, though isn't sure whether it is the ease with which he can fall asleep, or the realization that her baby is a fully grown man now with a divorce and the beginnings of a receding hairline behind him. She teeters for a second between dropping something with a crash so she can watch him wake with a start, or the motherly desire to tiptoe out of the room when your child is sleeping. She stifles a sigh, then gently tugs the charcoal boucle scatter throw over her boy. She directs an air kiss at his cheek and slinks off to do some sitting elsewhere. Or perhaps see if Ron is somewhere.

Ron's room smells like worn socks and furniture polish. She wishes he'd let a breeze in from time to time – waft some of the foost away – but his extremities are always cold, so he won't have a bar of it.

He insisted on total blackout curtains when Delph was here sorting out the interior design, but she's yet to see him close them.

Outside, their garden is a neatly manicured ode to greenery, resplendent in the morning light with hedges trimmed into neat globes. Garden ornaments carved to look like a who's who of Greek mythology are dotted across the landscape, though Edie is fairly certain that neither Ron nor Colin could tell their Zeus from their Odysseus. Edie would have preferred somewhere to plant crocuses so that she could spend her springs remembering the purple and yellows of the Marine Park in May.

A super-king size bed with grey velvet headboard lies opposite the window, but there's an expanse the length of a bus between them. There's a plush armchair with a footstool in the corner with a reading lamp bending nosily over it, and a display case with all of Ron's *Top Gear* and *What Car?* lined up as though they are first edition Brontës.

He's snoring, lips flapping out horsily when he exhales. One arm has escaped the warmth. 'Let's get ones like they have in hotels,' he'd said of the bedding, as though they were people who stayed in hotels. 'You know, the kind of crispy ones.'

The sleeve of his T-shirt has ridden up, revealing the blurry indigo outline of a tattoo.

'Morning pet,' she whispers.

He slaps his lips together and blinks. 'Ah, Edie,' he pushes himself up.

'How did you sleep?'

'Terrible! My bloody bladder had me up about five times. I swear Edie, these *en suites* are a godsend. What about you? I bet you're sleeping like a baby now without my snoring?'

Edie sighs. 'I'm not sleeping all that well, actually. It just feels a bit . . . weird.'

'You'll soon be used to it, love.' He nods approvingly. 'What's the point in having five bedrooms if we're going to share? Besides, you're always hot these days, I'm always cold.' He shrugs. 'Makes sense.'

'I suppose.' She rescues a fallen cushion from the floor. 'So, I was thinking we could try that bakery I was on about. See what their scones are like.'

Ron grins. 'Can't today, love. It's perfect driving conditions. I want to do Buttertubs Pass.'

'You've been there loads of times!'

'Yes, but not in the Jag!' Ron pats her hand. 'Oh Edie! The bakery will still be there tomorrow!'

So will the road. She doesn't want to be petulant, so she doesn't say it.

There's a chirp from his mobile phone, and he wipes his fingers on his pyjamas before flipping up the lid and squinting at it.

'You should get your eyes checked again, Ron.'

'What? My eyes are perfect! Forty-forty vision, me.' He squints harder, tuts. 'That bloody cleaner.'

'What about her?'

Edie hadn't wanted a cleaner, but Ron had insisted.

'Called in sick. Again.' He shakes his head. 'Honestly, youngsters have got no work ethic these days.'

'She's forty-three!'

'Still.' He contemplates the duvet sadly, as though the cleaner's illness is a personal conspiracy against him.

'I told you before, we don't need a cleaner,' says Edie.

'Of course we do. Everyone's got a cleaner.' He nods at the window, where Edie can just make out the eaves of another sprawling abode. 'All of them.'

'Not everyone's got a cleaner. Some of us *were* cleaners.' She picks a lint ball from the duvet and rolls it between her fingers. 'Besides, it'd be nice to have something to do while you're off driving places.'

He sighs. 'There's lots you can do, Edie. You could have a swim like you used to at the leisure centre.'

'That was aqua aerobics.'

'Great! Do that.' He pats her knee. 'Lovely.'

And just like that, Edie is dismissed. Dismissed from her husband's bedroom in their rambling Darras Hall villa that has more toilets than people, in favour of the fancy racing cars Ron only thought he'd drive in his dreams. Returning to the hallway, she picks up the broken frame with the ticket and carries it to the kitchen. *Maybe I'll go out and get a new frame.* For some unknown reason, the thought depresses her.

Looking across the back garden studded with triads and dyads and villains and warriors in blank-eyed stone judgement, she tries out the belly breathing that Judy, her old aqua aerobics teacher, said they should do every now and then. 'Check in with how you are feeling,' she used to say. Edie checks in with how she's feeling and is alarmed to find a gaping hole where her feelings should be.

They, whoever they are, always say that money doesn't buy happiness, but surely a freshly minted multi-millionaire who grew up begging the grocer for just one more chicken neck on credit could find some joy in it? Surely there must be more pleasure in a lottery win than finding a replacement grey ash frame for a ticket to a life she wasn't ready for?

2

Before

Patricia leans against the wall wriggling her feet back into her shoes. 'Ooof!' she says. 'Who'd have thought these sandals would be this painful?'

Edie hears her own voice floating back to her: *'You'll never be able to dance in those, Pats. You can't even walk in them!'*

'Why did I think I could dance in these things? I can't even walk in them!' She waggles one foot, striped with angry blood where the line-thin straps have cut into her. They are leaning against the front entrance of the Golden Slipper, two streets from where the bus spat them out and one metre from where a bouncer with shoulders the size of a truck told Pats that no, she absolutely could not come in with no shoes on.

The Yella Welly. The Golden Slipper, as it is actually called, might be located in a frilly little sister town to Newcastle, but it has a reputation for being the place to be on a Friday, and people will even travel the twelve miles from the regional capital to shimmy to Annie Nightingale spinning tunes by the sea until dawn.

Edie surveys the queue of the young and the well-heeled and

shakes her head. The women are in mini-skirts and platform shoes, dresses printed with flowers and stars and swirls. Their hair is ironed mirror-flat, and though they are all different, there's something slightly uniform in them, like a dancing troupe or a fashionable choir. The men are in suits and brightly coloured shirts reminding her of a flock of exotic birds.

Edie glances down her own dress. It was her mother's, and although she has removed the bow from the nape, the ribbon from the waist and washed the starchy skirts so that they swing, she still looks as though somebody has vomited up a taffeta woman. She reminds herself of the doll with the hoop skirt hiding the immodest new toilet rolls in Patricia's bathroom.

'I can't go in there,' says Edie. 'Look at me. I look like I've been in stasis since 1943.'

Patricia waves a dismissive hand. 'You look fine, Edie. Classic. We need to start living, dancing, singing these songs.' She winks at a well-cut gent in a green jacket, whose friends respond with a round of raucous 'Wahey!'s. 'Besides,' she grins, 'this place is packed with men.'

'Men who won't look twice at a girl wearing a granny outfit.' Edie steps away from the building. 'Look, I'm not really in the mood. I should get home. Check on Mam.'

'Your mam is asleep, Edie. We saw her twenty minutes ago.' Pats folds her arms. 'What are you going to do? Spend all night trying to guess what she's dreaming about?'

'I don't know,' she says half-heartedly. 'I just don't think I'm a dancing kind of woman. You'll be fine on your own.' Even as she says it, she feels guilty.

Patricia gazes longingly at the door. It is the first time both of them have been, and Edie suspects that it may be the last. She only came because Patricia is desperate to capitalize on the changes that the Sixties are bringing, in music, in fashion, all the way from the vibrant streets of London to their breezy little corner of the North East, and Edie worries that having a burdensome best friend like her is holding the vibrant Pats back. She's lost count of the times she's let her down over the past eight years: a cinema trip derailed because they have been hunting through bins to find Edie's mam's handbag, a walk to the shops on a nice day cancelled because Edie has woken to an unlocked door and a missing mother. Patricia is the sister Edie has always needed, and she burns with shame when she pictures her mother crying in an armchair while Pats gently slips off her shoes and says, *There, there, Cynthia. It's going to be all right.* Surely the least she can do is dance to a couple of songs with her friend and be ready to reassure her that her clumsy courtship attempts are in fact 'witty and attractive'.

'Come on, Edes. I'll buy you a soda.'

Edie pushes away the odd fluttering sensation in her belly and loops her arm through Patricia's.

'Okay,' she says. 'Just for a bit.'

Inside, the room is sweaty. Not just the people, but the actual room. A teardrop of condensation lands with a plop on Edie's collarbone. Girls in brightly coloured dresses are wiggling to 'Ya Ya Twist' while boys stand stiffly around the perimeter. A couple of brave chaps jiggle hopelessly beside girls who pointedly ignore them.

In the middle of the dance floor there's a woman dancing like she hasn't got any bones, as though she's composed entirely of liquid. Edie squints, but can't make out anything that resembles a joint or a hinge on her compact little body. A man nearby is moving side to side like a crab, all angles next to the woman's ribbony flow. *Where did they all learn how to dance like that?* Even if she knew how, she's not sure she'd want to have all eyes on her while she did.

Edie follows Patricia to the bar, conscious of her awkward gait. Years of gymnastics had trickled out of her body when adolescence crept in and did odd things to her joints and muscles, the willowy fluid of her limbs stiffening like drying concrete.

Patricia thrusts a thin plastic cup brimming with soda into Edie's hand. There's a tinny smell to the drink, and the cup is warm and wet on the outside, like it's just been washed in a bath. A jiggling man hits her elbow with a loose hip and the liquid splashes onto Edie's shoes.

'Sorry,' he says, then grins. 'You getting your groove on?' He smells like unwashed socks and three of his four front teeth are grey. Edie coughs and angles her body away from his.

'What do you think of him?' asks Patricia, nodding unsubtly at Grey Teeth.

When Edie glances over her shoulder, he's still grinning at her. She leans into Patricia. 'He smells like he's got trench foot,' she whispers but Patricia is already looking elsewhere.

'Ooh, look, the boys from Marsden!'

Edie follows Patricia's nod to a group of young men jostling each other by the disc jockey. They're smartly dressed with well-trimmed hair, but there's something a little roguish in their roughhousing. A man with a ramrod-straight back stands on the outskirts of the group, clutching his cup. Strands of rusty-brown hair are plastered across his forehead and his sleeves are rolled up to the elbow, revealing smooth, muscled forearms. His eyes scan the room, settling back on his friends to smile politely every so often.

'Who's the tall one?'

Patricia frowns. 'Mac something? McDonald? No, McVey. That's it. Jimmy McVey.' She grins. 'Why? Do you like him?'

'I like his posture. Very . . . noble.'

'Playing a brand-new record for you now, kids.' The disc jockey's voice comes tinnily out of a large speaker. 'From the lovely Martha and the Vandellas.'

'Oh Edie! It's a sign!'

The opening 'Jimmy's of 'Jimmy Mack' ring through the hall as the jiggling dancers seamlessly transition into fluid sways.

'Come on. We have to dance.' Before she can protest, Edie finds herself being dragged by Patricia to an empty spot by the boys. 'Don't just stand there Edie, dance!'

Edie sways, her whole body moving as one solid lump. Her face burns when the real-life Jimmy Mack lets his eyes linger on her for a moment.

'Pats,' she hisses, 'I feel like a cactus.'

Patricia throws back her head and laughs, throwing the tail end of it at the Marsden boys. She starts swaying her hips like a pendulum, dropping her chin and pushing her lips out. Their attention fully captured, Patricia turns her body to face the nearest of the boys.

Edie is horrified that she's now dancing alone and immediately stops moving.

'You don't really like dancing?'

Jimmy McVey is standing beside her, a human giraffe grinning a slightly lopsided grin from all the way up there. 'Oh, yes, I just don't know . . . or at least I feel a bit . . .' Under the flash of the disco lights, his skin cycles through red and blue and green and yellow, coming back to red again, and they all suit him, somehow. There's a light smattering of freckles across the bridge of his nose. Angel kisses, her mother used to call them. She blushes. 'I feel a bit shy.'

He nods. He's about a head-and-shoulder taller than her, and she has to lift her chin to look at him.

'I'm no good at dancing. I just come to watch these lunatics bobbing about and trying it on with girls. If I was any good, I'd ask you to dance though.' Edie's neck flushes hotly. There's a slight frown in his eyebrows, as though he's concentrating really hard, but his dark eyes and lips are smiling. It's at once comical and endearing and Edie can feel the pulse in her wrists like a small bird trying to get out. Over his shoulder, she sees Patricia being flung like a bag of potatoes onto a man's shoulder. 'Maybe you'd like to sit over there with me to drink our . . .' he gives her a knowing nod 'soda.'

Edie nods shyly and follows him to a row of plastic seats. Jimmy glances furtively at the tank-shaped bouncer by the door before pulling a small silver flask out of his trouser pocket and tipping liquid into both of their cups. Edie gives her drink a subtle sniff.

'One day they'll get a proper licence,' he says. 'Then it really will be the best place in the north.'

They talk without running headlong into an awkward pause, and Jimmy's soda is making her feel warm and happy.

She's told him about her gymnastic past and her cleaning job present. He's shared details of his mechanical apprenticeship at his uncle's garage in Hull that keeps him away from home for weeks at a time. And they've both rolled their eyes at Patricia who is waggling like a wet dog in the middle of a circle of Jimmy's friends in a strange courtship dance.

While he's talking, she can't stop staring at his lips, his nose, his fingers. Away from the lights and the music and his friends, he's looser and softer than he first appeared like he's liquefying. *I like him.* She watches his fingers animate a story about a seagull he and his uncle call Winston and shivers at a sudden mental image of those slightly rough fingertips touching her cheek.

After the thought appears, it keeps buzzing around and won't go away, until it is all she can think about.

At 9:43 p.m. Patricia catches her eye and taps her wrist, even though she isn't wearing a watch. She has promised her parents they'll be on the ten o'clock bus, and neither of them like giving Patricia's parents a worry by being late. Besides, the next bus after that isn't until 10:45 p.m. and Patricia's sore feet don't have another hour in them. Plus, she hates leaving her own mam alone for this long.

'I've got to go,' she tells him. She holds her cup out for him to take, but he grabs her hand, mistaking it for a handshake, and sloshes the dregs of her drink all over her dress.

He leaps up dramatically. 'Crumbs! Sorry.' He flaps a hand down her dress to flick the liquid off, but brushes her chest. 'Oh god!' He covers his face with his hands. 'I'm such an idiot.'

Edie can still feel the part of her breast that his fingers touched. Suddenly bold, she reaches for his arm.

'It's okay,' she says, and leaves her hand there. His skin is warm as though he's been sitting out in the sun, and she suddenly wonders what he'd look like in just a pair of swimming shorts reclining on a beach. She blushes again.

He peeps from between his fingers, grinning. 'Well, it's been great getting to know you.'

Edie is very aware of her hand on his arm and suddenly jerks away. 'Bye then,' she says, turning to look for Patricia. She hopes that he can't see the disappointment she is definitely wearing on her face.

'Wait!' he says. 'I need to know when I'll see you again!' Edie's pulse speeds up and she looks over her shoulder as casually as she can manage. He pulls a scrap of paper out of his pocket and studies it. 'I'm back on the fifteenth of next month. We could go for tea on the sixteenth if you like?'

Edie does a quick mental calculation. *That's six weeks away. He'll have forgotten me by then. Or be snapped up by some glamorous Hull girl.*

'I won't forget.' He grins. Edie flames, cursing her face for always saying exactly what she is thinking. 'Two o'clock? On the sixteenth? At Minchella's?'

Edie shrugs. 'I'd like that.'

'Splendid! I'll see you there . . .?'

'Eva.' The lie is out of her mouth before she can think about what she is doing.

'Lovely name Eva. I'm . . .'

'Oh, I know who you are!' She blushes again.

He smiles, walking backwards to rejoin his friends, blowing her a kiss and tripping over someone's extended, twisting leg. There's a warm spread stretching from Edie's head to her belly. Patricia laces her arm through hers as Edie tries to quell the fluttering in her tummy. And they hobble like that arm in arm, shoes swung over their shoulders, to catch the ten o'clock bus home.

3

After

As Edie turns the corner, she sees Carol trotting up the street towards Brenda's house. Carol clocks Edie and slows down, looking everywhere but at Edie. They arrive at the gate together, Edie waits for Carol to step through, while Carol waits for Edie to do the same. Then they both step together. For a moment, they're hip to hip, two fillings in a pensioner sandwich, before Edie pops out first. *Like a cork*. She wants to giggle and say it aloud, but Carol's cheeks are pink and it all feels a bit off.

'Edie! We weren't expecting you.'

'I phoned Brenda last night.' Edie recalls her stuttery message on Brenda's answering machine last night.

'Right!'

The door clicks open and there's Brenda in her blue velour aqua aerobics day tracksuit. 'Edie! What a lovely surprise.' Her mouth is stretched into a rigor mortis smile and she's blinking a lot considering that the grey clouds are trying to smuggle the sun away.

'I phoned you last night, Brenda. Left a message. Said I was going to come today.'

Brenda taps at her chin with a busy finger. 'Oh dear. I don't think I got that message.' Edie frowns. Carol's eyes volley back and forth between the two women as Brenda shrugs. 'Perhaps that answering machine is playing up again.'

'Technology,' tuts Carol, shaking her head.

'Well.' Edie holds out the nice Marks & Spencer's holdall that Colin had bought her when she first started aqua aerobics. 'I'm here now! And with my swimsuit. You know, I'm so looking forward to this. It's been ages!'

Brenda and Carol shoot each other a weird glance.

'What? What is it?'

Carol suddenly seems extremely interested in the hanging basket by the door with a few spindly shoots poking out. Brenda straightens up.

'It's just, well, there's not space in the car any more.'

'Oh?'

'Since you moved away, we asked Sue if she wanted to go with us.'

'Sue?'

'Yes, Sue.'

'Which Sue? Sue with the hydrangeas?'

'No,' Carol interjects. 'Sue with the hair thing.'

'Hair thing Sue? She goes to aqua aerobics with you now?'

'She's not that bad actually. Not once you get past the hair thing.' Carol nods sagely.

Brenda shrugs. 'So there's not really space.'

Edie looks at the ground.

Carol says, 'I mean, could we . . .'

Brenda snaps, 'No, Carol. I have told you before, I can't take Dexter's baby seat out because I won't be able to put it back in when they have another baby.'

Edie tries to catch Carol's attention so they can roll their eyes about the mythical future baby that Brenda's daughter won't be having, but Carol is still examining the forlorn basket.

'I took three buses to get here . . .' Edie hears the tremor of a pathetic old woman and hates herself for it.

'I'm sorry, Edie. That's just the way it is.'

'Hiiiiiiiyyyyaaaaaaaaa!'

Edie turns to see Sue with the hair thing pushing her way through the gate. Her huge bag gets wedged behind her and her skirt catches on the broken post, tethering her between the pavement and the garden path. 'I'm trapped,' she says. 'Trapped like that Carrel Folin in *Phone Booth*.'

Horrified, Brenda charges over to release the billowing picnic blanket of a skirt, Sue's hair thing quivering like a frightened squirrel.

'Eee Sue, looks like I'm going to have to snap a thread.'

Sue sighs. 'You've got to do what you've got to do, Bren. I can't be a prisoner forever.'

Edie leaves them to their tussle and turns to her old friend. 'What's going on, Carol?'

Carol looks at the ground. 'Nothing. I mean, Brenda said . . . It's just the space.' Edie raises her eyebrows. 'Honest to god, Edie!'

Sue, finally free, saunters towards the house. 'Hiya, Edie. How's the mansion? Did you come here by limousine today?' Sue chortles. 'Bet it's like *Downton Abbey* at your place. You've got a servant, haven't you?'

Edie brushes past them all and heads for the gate.

'Maybe next week, Edie!' she hears Carol shout. 'Maybe Ron can bring you in his nice car?'

'Or you can come in your private jet like Peas Diddy,' adds Sue.

Edie's aiming for a dignified exit, but a fluttering web of thread left behind from Sue's entrapment wraps around her wrist. She drops her keys with a clatter and when she reaches for them, her trapped arm won't go where she tries to direct it. She gives a forceful yank and she's free. The other women are staring, but Edie pushes her lips into a solid line and searches for a profound way to punctuate the moment, but instead, all she can see is an image of her mother outside the Post Office, a line of cross-armed women glaring at her. Edie can't remember what the infraction was, only that she was trembling either with rage or terror, as her mother wrestled with her lips for something to say, coming up blank and letting her mouth flap open and closed. *Be off with you*, one of them had said. *And don't come back.* That might as well be what Brenda has said now.

She tries to say 'I'll be off then,' and 'I won't come back,' but what comes out is 'I'll be back,' which is somewhere between threatening and ridiculous. She scrunches up her face to keep the tears inside.

Edie doesn't turn back.

Asda cafe has a special meal deal on. Edie orders sausage and chips and a tea at the counter from a girl who can't be long out of nappies. It's busy, and she finds herself hovering with her tray waiting for a free table.

By the time she's seated, her chips have gone cold. She saws one of the sausages into little pieces and pops a bit in her mouth. She doesn't really feel like eating, but she's already wandered round the supermarket for an hour and still doesn't want to go home.

She sighs. Of course, Brenda and Carol are entitled to invite someone else – space in the car is as good a reason as any to bring in someone new – but why didn't they tell her?

And why Sue with the hair thing? Sue with the hydrangeas she could understand, but not Sue with the hair thing. There's that laugh for a start, and the way she talks about famous people but always gets their names wrong. Like Donny Jepp or Wonzel Deshington.

Edie prods at another piece of sausage. It had been her idea in the first place, the aqua aerobics. She'd seen it in the *Chronicle* and it had a lovely picture of someone who looked a bit like Hilda in a sunflower swimming hat. Of course it wasn't Hilda. You couldn't have paid Hilda enough to wriggle into a swimsuit. 'Do I look like a duck?' she asked the few times Edie suggested they take the boys to the swimming baths. But the woman in the picture had a smile a bit like Hilda's was if you could catch her unguarded. There was a list of classes at the end of the article and aqua aerobics for the over-sixties jumped out at Edie.

'We should go,' she had told her friends over their Tuesday afternoon cheese and crackers in Edie's garden.

They'd fretted about swimwear and finally gone to British Home Stores to try on costumes. Carol getting stuck in the too small halterneck: Brenda nearly falling out of the changing room.

They loved it. The actual class and the iced buns in the cafe afterwards. Until Edie won the lottery and moved to Darras Hall.

Edie glances at her watch. They'll be drying off and heading to the cafe now. She looks around the cafe, quieter now, just the clink of spoons stirring burnt coffee. The old man who smiled at her has his eyes closed, snoring gently. *I'm just like him. Old and alone.*

She pulls the bus timetables out of her bag to figure out her journey back, but it all seems too much, too complicated. She crumples up the papers and puts them on her tray. *I used to sometimes walk home from here.*

Maybe she wants to go for a little walk instead. Just for old times' sake, just to see if the old street has changed much since they left.

4

Before

Edie's never been on a date before. Well, not a real one. Last year, she went to Tim Jevon's Sea Cadet thing, but that was only because his mam had asked her if she'd go. It had been fine until he tried to hold her hand with his sticky one. She'd pretended to re-buckle her shoe so that he had to let go. They both kept their hands determinedly far from one another after that.

But this? This is a real date.

Edie is at Minchella's twenty minutes early, having finally succeeded in dispatching Patricia, who had insisted on tagging along for the bus ride.

'Ask him if he believes in ghosts,' said Patricia. 'Oh, and space. Find out whether he believes in space or not.'

'Who doesn't believe in space?'

'Have you been there?'

Actually, Edie was grateful for her inane chatter: it took her mind off her damp palms and thudding chest.

It's a bright, breezy day, and the air is sweet with vanilla and strawberry. *What should I order?* It's important that she doesn't get something too expensive – Jimmy is still an apprentice after all – but also, Patricia insisted 'Not too cheap either. It'll set a wotsit.'

Precedent, remembers Edie. She'll have to tell Pats later.

As the time ticks ever closer to two she peers in the window. *Should I wait inside or out?* She spots a neat little table with the chairs at a slight angle to one another. *That'd be good, not so face on.* Her feet stay rooted to the tiles by the door though. *Too embarrassing if he doesn't show. At least if I'm outside and he doesn't come, I can pretend I was just standing here to while away the time.*

She adjusts the waistband of her skirt. She's rolled it up to make it shorter like she's seen other girls do, but it feels a bit bulky around her middle. She smooths the blouse over the top in the hope that he won't notice this. Hopes he'll focus on the bright, pencil-shaped buttons she added herself to her mother's cast-offs.

'Eva!'

Edie cringes at the name. 'Hello there!' *Why, Edie? You stupid girl.* She can't quite believe that it slipped out when he asked. She panicked, wanted to sound a bit more glamorous than she is. And Eva? She doesn't even know an Eva except for Hitler's wife who people probably shouldn't talk about or try to name themselves after anyway. *I'll tell him my real name later.* After they've ordered.

He's looking smart, like he's really dressed up for a special occasion, but mildly uncomfortable: trousers that are a bit too short so his ankles peep out the bottom, a shirt that still has the folds in it from being packaged around a piece of stiff cardboard and pushed into a too-small bag, a tie that's slightly off-centre. But his shirt sleeves are rolled up and there's that throb of muscle in his forearm that makes Edie's stomach flip.

'After you.' Jimmy pulls the door open and folds himself into a funny little bow. 'Sorry. I'm not sure why I did that.' He blushes, and she falls slightly in love.

Edie's heels clack on the chequerboard tiles and she swings her hips a little, suddenly feeling very sophisticated. The ice cream parlour still bears all the Victorian charm of its origins: muted peach walls, marble counter, and framed prints of well-heeled visitors enjoying the seafront in its heyday. She's only been here once before for Patricia's mam's birthday a couple of years ago, and it is just as intoxicating as she remembers.

They take the nice table that she had spotted from outside. They're tucked into a cosy alcove at pie-quarters to one another. She is surprised at the length of his legs, feeling his knee knocking gently against hers under the table. She likes it.

Edie orders a Banana Split. Jimmy orders a Knickerbocker Glory. 'But we can try each other's if you like?' They order a pot of tea to share.

They chat while they wait for their ice creams, mostly about Hull. Edie had pictured elegant boulevards with chic, miniskirted women weaving confidently into designer boutiques. In her mind, Jimmy sat at an outside cafe table in the sun while said chic women sidled up to him.

'They talk funny there.' He pops a glacier of squirty cream into his mouth. 'And there's always a slight fishy smell. I fixed Joan Collins' car though.'

'What was she doing in Hull?'

'Searching for a hunky mechanic, I imagine.'

The hot thud of jealousy in the pit of her belly is unexpected, but not entirely unwelcome.

When he asks if she's listened to any good music lately, she's too embarrassed to tell him that the day after the Yella Welly, she went to Woolworths to buy 'Jimmy Mack' to play on Pats' phonograph.

An hour passes in a haze, Edie's insides turning to liquid every time he makes her laugh. And he makes her laugh *a lot*. He makes up a back story about the grumpy middle-aged couple behind them, glaring their way through a matching pair of cheerful sundaes.

'And when he retired from being a professional spy, he started spying on her, except he stopped when he realized that the most exciting thing she'd do in a day was unclog the bath!'

Edie barely recognizes her own laugh. It gurgles and releases itself freely, her head tilts back and her eyes screw so tightly shut, she fears she'll squeeze them deep into her skull.

He tells her about his dream to open his own auto garage, back up here in the North East. 'I'll call it McVey's Motors,' he tells her, flushing slightly.

'It has a lovely ring to it,' she says.

'Eva, I've got something I want to show you, if you'll do me the honour of coming outside with me.'

Ah, he still thinks I'm called Eva. She sighs. 'Listen, I . . .'

He waves his hands in front of his face. 'No! Nothing like that! I promise, I'm a respectable man.'

'Oh!' Edie laughs. 'I didn't think . . . I mean, I . . . yes. I would like to see the thing.'

He grins, stands and holds out his hand. Edie is delighted that it isn't sticky.

'Ta-da!'

When Jimmy takes his non-sticky hands from her eyes, Edie is standing in front of a smart, racing-green car.

'Is this yours?' He nods proudly. 'Crumbs! I don't know anyone who has a car.'

'Well, now you do!' He pulls a key from his pocket and unlocks the passenger door. It opens with a squeak. 'How would you like to be my first passenger?'

Edie smiles. 'I would like that very much.' Her mother wouldn't like it very much, but after a fleeting squint of guilt, Edie decides that she doesn't very much care what her mother would like at this moment. She hops in and smooths her skirt as he makes his way to the driver's side.

'What do you think?'

'Very nice.'

'I've been doing it up for months. Just finished it last weekend. I worked through the nights at the garage to have it ready for now. I wanted you to see it.'

Edie glows as he turns the key in the ignition. The car thrums beneath her and they pull away from the kerb. There's a little patch of denim where the fawny leather has been replaced and she runs her hands over the rough fabric, committing the memory of it into her palms.

They drive in silence for a while. Edie winds down her window and leans on the edge, a contented smile playing at the corners of her mouth. It's a gorgeous, breezy day, and the wind cools her warm cheeks. *I left the back window open!* Her mother will get cold or frightened, or maybe both, and she hasn't left a cardigan in reach for her. She's about to start panicking when Jimmy turns and grins that grin that makes the corner of his mouth crinkle like the cinema curtains, revealing slightly wonky but strong neat teeth, and in a heartbeat, she's forgotten what it was she was about to start worrying about. *Just for once, Edie, let yourself have this moment.*

They turn onto the coast road, where the salty sea breeze dances through her hair. Jimmy puts his foot down on the accelerator and Edie closes her eyes and lets the car carry her toward the clifftops, as though they're flying.

Jimmy finally turns the car into the driveway of Souter Lighthouse. He brings it to a stop a few metres shy of the cliff edge and the cloud-dappled sky fills the windscreen.

'Eva, I . . .'

'Oh Jimmy! There's something I need to tell you.'

He frowns. 'Who's Jimmy?'

'You are! You're Jimmy Mack.'

He laughs. 'I'm Ron. Where did you get Jimmy from?'

'I don't know. Patricia said you were called Jimmy McVey.'

'I'm not.'

'Right.'

'I'm Ron.'

'Right. Ron. Sorry Ron.' *Da Doo Ron Ron.* She shrugs. She still likes the 'Jimmy Mack' song, and she decides that it's still going to be *their* song. If he wants to see her again, that is.

Ron shakes his head. 'Now that we've got that cleared up, I have a surprise for you.'

'I thought this *was* the surprise.'

He's fizzing. 'No. *This* is the surprise.' He grins impishly and rolls up the sleeve of his shirt. An inky purple heart adorns his arm, and scrawled in the middle of it in shaky capitals is the name EVA. His eyes glimmer in the sun.

'Oh,' says Edie. She burns with a shame that floods from her head to her feet so buries her face in her hands. 'I'm so sorry, Ron. My name's not Eva. I'm Edie.' She keeps her hands on her face. Through the gaps in her fingers, the keyhole on the glove box mocks her with a sly grin and she scowls. *So stupid, Edie. You've ruined his arm with your German dictator wife lie.*

He slaps the steering wheel and she pulls her hands from her face. His face is screwed up like a raisin, laughing so hard that no sound is coming out, and there are tears rolling out of the sides of his eyes. She joins him, and soon they're clutching their bellies and each other, slapping the dashboard.

By the time their sides can barely hold them together, they dwindle to chuckles. Ron swipes the last few tears from the creases at his temple. 'Ah,' he says, 'well this is one to tell the grandkids.'

Edie thrills, her heart located somewhere between her throat and her mouth.

5

After

Edie raps lightly on the door. The doorbell is missing, its wiry guts spilling out of the brickwork. Over the road, Sue with the hydrangeas pokes her face around a curtain. Edie waves and Sue disappears.

'No!' The shout startles her and Edie turns to see an old man she doesn't recognize over the street, jabbing his finger at her. 'The millionaires have gone, so bugger off.'

He mutters something that might be *gold digger* at her and resumes his shuffle down the street.

It feels weird knocking on the door of her former home, odd not to have her keys with the little *I* ♥ *Mam* keyring dangling from them, but after being in the cafe, it was almost as if her body carried her here without her mind being involved at all. To her right, the Patels have replaced the old timber door with a bright red UPVC one. She imagines weird Albert cackling about frivolous doors, and feels sad for a moment that she wasn't a better neighbour to him.

'Yeah?' A young woman frowns from a crack in the door. She's dressed in black, a melon of a baby bump blooming beneath her

T-shirt. Edie's hands feel cold. Suddenly the woman shouts, 'I've told you before, you weirdo, piss off!'

Edie panics, but realizes that the woman is hollering at the man across the road. He folds his arms, harrumphs, but shuffles off towards the pub.

'Erm, hi I'm Edie, I . . .'

'Are you Tamara's grandma?' The woman shifts her weight and jams a fist into her hip. 'Has she sent you? Because I'm telling you now, if she sends one more of her trash family goons around here, I'll call the police.'

'I don't know any Tamara. I'm no one's grandma.'

The girl frowns. 'Who are you then?'

'I'm Edie.' Edie proffers her hand. 'I used to live here.' Edie retreats slightly as the woman folds her arms across her chest. 'Oh, god, I shouldn't have come.' She turns and strides back up the path feeling the woman's eyes bore into her. Her hand on the gate and the cold, slightly rusty iron under her fingers pauses her for a moment. Over the road, life carries on as though she was never there. The sum total of thirty years of existence in a place erased like it never really happened. *If there was something solid to hold onto . . .* 'Actually.' She turns back. 'Look, this is going to sound strange, but you've got this tree . . .'

'The apple tree in the garden?'

'Yes! I planted that and, well, I miss it. I wondered if I could maybe, if it isn't too much trouble, see it?'

The woman frowns again. 'You really don't know Tamara?'

'I don't know Tamara.'

'And Asif didn't send you?'

'No one sent me. I just wondered if I could see the tree. Is everything okay?'

'Yes.' She scowls for a moment then laughs. 'Bit stressed,

I s'pose.' She pokes her belly. 'Come in and look at your tree, Edie.'

In the weak but determined May sunlight, Edie's apple tree looks a bit sad. It's still bare, though the buds are beginning to fatten. A breeze shivers through it, dislodging a couple of hapless twigs and a loosening, a tumble of something in her belly.

'Asif was going to cut it down.' The woman is standing close, watching her carefully.

She looks older in the light than Edie first thought. She assumed her to be late teens from her clothing, but she can see now that she's probably in her mid-twenties. The thick eyeliner hoods her eyes and the heavy foundation stops abruptly around her jawline. Edie smiles tentatively then turns back to the tree.

'Do you want a cuppa?'

'Oh, that would be lovely. Thank you . . . erm, what's your name?'

The young woman is already making her way to the back door. 'Jade,' she flings over her shoulder. Edie watches her go then treads across the grass closer to the tree. She strokes the tips of her fingers across the scaly bark, glancing back to check that Jade isn't watching.

'Hello, lovey,' she whispers. 'I'm here. I'm sorry I couldn't take you with me. He wouldn't understand.' She leans her shoulder against the trunk. 'I think of you often. I'd love you to see the new place. Not my thing, but you'll love it.' She pauses. 'I wish you'd call.'

'Are you talking to the tree, Edie?'

Edie starts. 'I was . . .'

Jade laughs from the doorway, but not unkindly. 'Bit mental, are you?' She shakes her head. '"We're all mad here!" Tea's up.'

Edie follows her back inside the house.

Everything is different inside. For a start, there's no wallpaper, and slashes of paint in varying shades of purple streak the walls in the hallway and living room. The carpets have gone too, replaced by creaky laminate and thin rugs. Edie looks around for something familiar to grasp, but there are no remnants of their family, at least downstairs. The McVeys have been ripped out and replaced in only three months.

Jade puts two stout mugs on a cardboard box and plops onto the sofa. Edie joins her, folding her hands neatly in her lap.

'Well, it's looking different.'

Jade nods. 'Asif was meant to do the painting, but he buggered off with that slapper before we'd even decided between *Taut Mulberry* and *Berry Pleasure*.'

Edie nods as though she has any idea who Asif is.

'And of course, now I'm too knackered to finish it.' She sighs and digs two Wagon Wheels from a bag by the sofa. She proffers one to Edie who shakes her head. 'And his brother has gone all tyrant on me about the rent. I'm like "Man, I'm carrying your nephew, give me a break." And he's all "A lease is a lease, Jade."' She rolls her eyes. 'Bloody Asif. I could kill him!'

Jade unwraps her Wagon Wheel and stares at the hole where the fireplace used to be. Edie sips her tea.

'So, you're having a boy then? Due soon?'

Jade grins. 'Got another twelve weeks or so.'

'Boys are a delight. I didn't have a girl though, so I have nothing to compare it to.'

'You've got kids?'

'I have sons.'

'Right.'

They survey the room as though seeing it for the first time.

'I remember the day we moved in,' says Edie.

'Right,' says Jade, folding her arms across her belly. She's clearly not interested, but Edie can't seem to stop her mouth from galloping ahead.

'My husband carried the boys in. They were so wriggly, like little worms.' Jade lets out an audible sigh. 'You know, it was so dark and dingy, we thought we'd never get it sorted.'

'And did you?'

'Oh yeah. It was nice for a while. But then, well, money was tight, I was working all the time. It all got a bit much.'

Jade nods. 'Yeah, it was pretty grim when we moved in. I said, "Asif, I don't reckon anyone's ever cleaned it properly" and he was like "Yeah, know what you mean," so I proper cleaned it, but it's just rank, isn't it? I mean, you're old and stuff so you probably couldn't sort it properly, I get why it was so crappy now—'

Edie is embarrassed by the tears that spring into her eyes.

'Oh gawd, sorry.' Jade pats Edie on the arm. 'I didn't mean to offend you. I just meant I get it, why the house is so rank. That's all.'

Edie pokes a thumb in her eye, stemming the tears. 'It's okay,' she says. 'I tried my best. We just didn't have the money to make it as nice as I wanted. We tried and tried to make it perfect, but everything kept going wrong—'

'Maybe the house is cursed,' says Jade.

'Maybe.' They contemplate curses for a while. 'We had some happy times here though.' She sees the boys playing with cars in front of the fireplace, Sean running a toy truck over Hilda's feet and yelling 'Roadblock!' She sees Ron swinging them round while she panicked about them knocking things over. 'We've no valuables,' Ron had said cheerfully.

'Well, I should be going,' says Edie. There's no coffee table, so

Edie holds her mug out to Jade. 'It really has been very kind of you. Perhaps I could come back one day?'

'I'm going to be home pretty much all the time.' Jade barks a single laugh. 'Sure, come by again, Edie. Unless you decide to adopt a granddaughter and pick that Tamara woman.'

'I *promise* not to adopt Tamara. Nice to meet you, Jade.'

Edie lets herself out and has to lean on the door after she closes it. She suddenly can't breathe.

6

Before

Edie starts second-guessing the present on the bus.

'It isn't the most romantic thing you could have got him,' admits Patricia, checking her lipstick in the dirt-streaked window. 'I mean, if it was me, I'd have gone with something heart-shaped. Oooh! You could have got him one of those big chocolate hearts from Thorntons. They're nice. I've never had one, but their easter eggs are great.'

Edie hasn't bought Ron a chocolate heart from Thorntons. She's bought him a spanner.

The man in the tool shop said that all mechanics had their go-to favourite spanner, and she reasoned that if this became his go-to favourite spanner, he'd have to think about her every time he used it, which would be a lot. But now that she's actually got it here in hand, it feels a bit silly. She's wrapped it in brown paper and tied it with a red bow.

Nice spanner, her mother had said when she showed her, but that was really no mark of a good present. Not these days. Edie runs back through the checklist in her head, hoping that her mother will still be sleeping when she gets back.

'And will all of his brothers be there?' asks Patricia.

'I'd imagine so.'

'Good,' she grins. 'I want one.'

'Two of them are married,' says Edie.

'I'll have the other one then. Is he as tall and handsome as Ron?'

They're late to the Bamburgh Arms, because Patricia insisted that *fashionably late* is the only time to arrive at a party.

'It's not a party,' insists Edie. 'Just drinks at the pub.' But when they step through the door into the warm heart of the place, it certainly feels like a party. There are people wedged in every available space and partygoers are clinking glasses like a percussion section. It is immediately too hot for their coats.

'Wall-to-wall men, Edie!' shrieks Patricia, whipping hers off and throwing it over a coat hook. She adjusts her neckline so there's a generous crease of cleavage on view and pushes her chest out. 'Men!'

An old man with a paunch and a pink nose raises his glass to her. 'One right here,' he says.

Patricia wrinkles her nose. 'Where's Ron?'

Edie stands on her tiptoes trying to spot Ron's head sticking up from the crowd, but all of the men seem massive. 'Don't know,' she says. The paper around the spanner feels damp in her hand and she can't figure out how to get her coat off and wrangle her bag and the spanner at the same time.

'Edie!'

Edie spins, raising her arm to stop her handbag from falling off her shoulder, and in the process, hits someone with the wrapped present.

'Ow.'

'Oh, Ron! I'm so sorry.'

He is there in a blue paisley shirt and navy cords with his clean brown hair dipping towards his eyes.

'Hit the birthday boy in the face, why don't you?'

He's grinning, though there is a red splodge on the top of his left cheekbone, just under his eye.

'I'm so sorry,' she says. 'You got a new haircut.'

Ron touches his head self-consciously. 'It's a Beatle haircut,' he says. 'Harry said I should . . .'

'Harry said you should at least start trying to look like you're from this century if you want to bag a classy lady like that Edie you've been harping on about.' A face similar to Ron's grins from over his shoulder, his arms wrapped across Ron's chest in an easy manner. Ron's cheeks flush as scarlet as the splodge Edie has just inflicted under his eye. 'Hi,' says the face. 'Harry.'

Patricia immediately steps in front of Edie. 'Patricia,' she says breathily. 'But you can call me . . .' she flounders for something else. 'Well, Patricia, I suppose. Because that's my name.'

'And a very nice name it is too,' says Harry. 'Nice to meet you, Patricia. And you must be Edie?'

'I must,' says Edie. 'I mean, I am. Yes. I am Edie.' She goes as beetroot as Ron is and Harry laughs.

'Well, it seems that you two were made for each other.' He pats Ron on the back, who suddenly finds the sticky carpet fascinating. 'Is that a little birthday present for our Ronnie?'

'Oh,' says Edie, slipping the gift behind her back. 'It's . . . yes. A present, I suppose.'

Patricia tucks her arm through Harry's. 'You know, Harry, I'd go wild for a shandy right now.' She leads him away, winking at Edie with the subtlety of a pantomime villain.

Edie touches her neck, eyes glued to the carpet.

'You got me a present?'

'I did.'

'Maybe we could go outside and I could look at it there?'

It's cool outside and Edie is glad that she hadn't figured out how to get her coat off. They walk around to the back of the pub where a stiff sea breeze blows petulantly over the meadow between the cold North Sea and the civilization of Marsden, the frontier suburb of South Shields. They perch on a wall side by side facing the tall grasses and wildflowers that cover The Leas. Beyond, where the dark sky meets the horizon, the land falls away in a steep grey cliff and down to the cold lapping tongue of the North Sea. Sometimes when Edie looks across the water, she can't decide whether the waters are keeping her safe from something, or holding her back from seeing everything.

'Are you enjoying your party?' she asks.

Ron shrugs. 'It's a bit loud. It was just meant to be a party tea at home with the family then a couple of drinks with the lads, but Harry invited everyone this side of Newcastle.' He runs a hand across his head then pulls it away, as though he's surprised by what he finds there. 'Still getting used to this hair,' he murmurs.

'It's very fashionable,' she says, battling an image of beautiful Hull girls in mini-dresses swooning over his fashionable hair. *Maybe now he will only be interested in fashionable girls, not ones wearing their mother's old sailor blouse.* She shifts gear in case he's thinking the same thing. 'So, you're twenty-one. Do you feel different?'

'Not really. Should I?'

Edie shrugs. 'I didn't.'

'Oh! You're older than me. Sorry. I didn't realize.'

'Is that bad?' she asks.

'No,' he says. 'No, it's wonderful.' He stares at her for a long time, then looks out to sea. 'Did you have a party?'

'Oh no!' Edie shakes her head. 'No. I've never had a birthday party. Or any type of party. Or anything to indicate that my birthday was anything other than a normal day, actually.'

'What? Why?'

Edie stares at the sky looking for a pinprick star or something to anchor herself on. 'It doesn't matter.'

'I . . .' Ron looks at her upturned chin. 'My wish for you is that you celebrate all of the rest of your birthdays with people who care about you.' Her breath constricts. 'Seriously,' he says. He places a finger on her chin and gently guides her face so that she's looking right at him. 'You deserve to be loved and cherished and celebrated.'

Inside her body, everything has turned to liquefied light that is about to spill out if she moves an inch. She doesn't trust her voice not to crack, so she takes a deep breath, whispers, 'Thank you.'

The air around them grows still, the breeze slinks away, leaving them under a blank silence and a dark, starless sky.

'Twenty-one,' he says eventually. 'I'm officially a grown-up.'

'Exciting,' says Edie, taking hold of her breathing again. 'You could run for Prime Minister.'

He nods. 'I could. My first decree would be that you hand over that there present.'

'Oh,' says Edie. She coughs. 'It's not, well it sort of is, but in present terms, I suppose it's a bit . . .' Ron smiles. 'Sorry. I'm waffling. Here.'

Edie holds her breath while he unwraps it.

'A spanner!' he says. 'Lovely, Edie, thank you.'

'Turn it over.'

Ron squints at the spanner. 'McVey's Motors,' he reads. 'You got it engraved! You remembered!'

Edie is glad that under the greyish moonlight Ron won't be able to see how hot her face is.

'Oh, Edie, this is lovely.'

He takes her hand and holds it in his. The skin on his palms is warm and softer than a mechanic's should be, and that part in *Romeo and Juliet* about the palms in prayer being like a kiss starts looping and she gets flustered all over again.

'You know,' says Ron, 'I think that this is going to be my favourite spanner, and I'll use it all the time and whenever I touch it, I'll think of you.'

Edie breathes in the salt air and looks at the kiss of their palms and the lace of their fingers. She closes her eyes, just for a second, and wonders what it would actually be like to kiss him.

7

After

Ron finds her in the laundry tipping dirty knickers into the drum.

'Why don't you wait until we've got a new cleaner in?' he asks.

Edie notices a particularly sagging grey pair that have escaped, picks them up with her toe and shoves them in the machine.

'I'm perfectly capable of washing a few pairs of underwear, Ron. And it's embarrassing, having some stranger root through your foosty undies.' She slams the door and pulls open the detergent drawer. 'Besides,' she says, 'I need something to do.'

'Not this again.' Ron shakes his head and turns to go. Edie pours in the powder, twiddles the dials and follows him out into the hallway. 'You know, the world's our oyster now, and you're mooching about washing old knickers that frankly, you should have replaced before the cheque had finished clearing.' They're standing beneath the now reframed lottery ticket. Ron glances up at it, kisses his fingertips and presses them to the glass leaving a smear. *I'm going to have to clean that again now.* 'Why don't you do that today?' he asks. 'Go to Marksys, get some nice underwear.' He goes a strange shade of pink when he says it.

'I'd rather go somewhere with you,' she says.

He reaches for her shoulder, and she readies for a hug, or better still, a whisper that he'd like her to model some nice Marksys underwear, when he plucks something from her cardigan.

'You had a sock on your shoulder,' he says.

'Right.' She's annoyed again, annoyed that she thought she was getting some affection and wasn't, annoyed that there's now one rogue sock unwashed while the other laundry spins up a tempest in the machine.

'Best birthday present ever,' says Ron, gazing at the ticket again. He waggles his fingers in a wave and then he's gone.

'I'd rather go somewhere with you,' she repeats into the empty hallway.

She pulls a tissue from her pocket and wipes Ron's fingertips from the glass then puffs out a breath she didn't know she'd been holding.

She's never bought him a lottery ticket before, but when she and Carol had gone shopping for his birthday present, there'd been a Lambrini promotion in Kirkpatrick's pub, right opposite Burton's Menswear where she had been going to buy him a jumper.

'Lambrini!' said Carol. 'We've got to sample some Lambrini.'

So they'd sampled six different types, one of which tasted distinctly like cough medicine, and giggled their way through a plate of chips before a youngish man with a tray of shots said, 'You two remind me of my nan. Have a Sambuca.' They had the Sambuca and then Edie slid off her chair and Carol snorted so hard that she hit her head on a lamp. A barman had gently scooped them off the floor and said, 'I think it's time you two went home for a Horlicks, don't you?'

The shops were closed by the time they staggered out and Carol yawned, 'Just get him a lottery ticket or something.'

Edie shakes her head, picturing the two of them swaying into the newsagent by the bus station and Edie trying to pick out numbers. *Ron's birthday . . . my birthday . . . the boys' birthday . . . our house number . . . the boys' age . . .* Lost for ideas, she plucked a stone out of her handbag painted to look like a ladybird and counted his spots. *Eight.*

Ron had been less than enthused with the state of Edie *and* the lottery ticket, and also the fact that he had a drunk Carol in his living room when he just wanted to watch *Casualty* and eat pie and peas.

Ron reluctantly opened the ticket and Colin insisted on switching the show on. 'Good fella, that Nick Knowles,' said Colin approvingly when the presenter's face filled the screen.

'Would you like a shandy, Carol?' Edie had offered and Carol settled into the couch next to Colin and Ron.

'I think you two have had quite enough,' huffed Ron.

'Lad from my work won four thousand quid a few years ago,' said Colin. 'If we won that, maybe we could get a good TV instead of that thing.' He nodded at the boxy thing they still had, resting wonkily on the stand with a door hanging off and a pile of magazines where a missing leg should be. 'Here we go.'

Edie brought Carol's shandy and another one for Colin and settled herself next to them on the couch, idly plucking a pilled flap that got ripped about seven years before.

'Have you got your ticket there, Dad?' asked Colin.

Ron waved it in front of him and placed it on his knee. 'They're a bit close together, these numbers. You could have spread them out a bit.'

'I picked special numbers,' said Edie. 'Maybe we all could have conveniently had different birthdays.' She stuck her tongue out at the back of his head.

'Is that a six?'

On the screen, they'd drawn the first ball.

'No, it's a nine,' said Ron.

'Ooh, we've got that,' said Colin.

'Yay for my birthday,' said Edie. She stuck out her tongue again feeling weirdly vindicated.

'Have we got thirty-three?' asked Carol.

'Yes!' said Colin. 'Might be in for a tenner!'

'Eight!' said Ron. 'Get in! A tenner!'

Edie clapped. 'See,' she said. 'I got something right.'

'Oh my god!' Carol jabbed the screen. 'You've got twenty-six as well. How much do you get for four numbers?'

'I don't know,' Edie said, but her heart had thumped a bit and the corners of her mouth were twitching.

'Seventeen! Bloody hell,' Colin said. 'Sorry, Mam, but shit! Five numbers!'

Ron pressed his hand across his mouth and Carol dropped to her knees. Edie slid her legs from the couch and noticed that they were trembling almost as much as Colin's fingers holding the remote control.

'What is it we're waiting for?' Carol said.

'Five,' whispered Edie. 'Ron's birthday.'

A ball plopped from the machine and their collective heartbeat was a thudding percussion while the ball rotated, infuriatingly hiding the number from the camera, then it dropped down the chute and settled.

'Five!' they screamed in unison and they were on their feet in a jumping, pulsing, screeching scrum, the ticket pinched between Ron's shaking fingers at the centre of the maelstrom.

'We'll get a yacht,' said Ron. 'Sail the globe.'

'Or buy a tropical island.'

'How about a plane?'

Edie stopped and pressed her hand to her chest.

'Are you having a heart attack?' asked Carol.

'No,' said Edie. 'I'm just in shock.'

And she was quivering so hard she had to sit down. The others went right back to planning.

'I wonder how much a night with George Clooney costs,' says Carol.

'I mean, the big question is,' said Ron, 'is a Rolls-Royce too much?'

'What does James Bond drive?' asked Carol.

'An Aston Martin.'

'You should get one of those,' said Carol. 'Who plays James Bond again? I wouldn't mind a night with him either.'

Edie rose on trembling legs. 'I just need a spot of air,' she said, but nobody seemed to notice that she was talking or leaving the house. She stepped into the back garden, over the bin bag that had toppled over and made itself into a bird feeder for seagulls, over the corpses of rusty engines that had been there for decades and took a cold breath in. It was unfathomable how the others were able to think so clearly about what they wanted, while in her own head, everything was a technicolour blur.

She pressed her back into the bark of the apple tree, bare then after a brutal winter, and looked back towards the house. The kitchen window was open, and the shrieks from Ron, Colin and Carol carried loudly into the night air.

She has no idea how long she stood out in the cold garden watching the silhouettes of her loved ones dancing madly in the kitchen. When she returned, shivering, teeth chattering, she slipped up to bed, unnoticed.

She was excited at first, definitely. But there was also a

fluttering fear behind her ribs that she couldn't quite get a handle on. *What was she frightened of?*

Even now in their lovely house with a watertight roof and toilets that flush and carpets that you can lose your toes in, that fear stalks her around the corners, hides in their multitude of cupboards waiting to jump out and flatten her.

Everything was about to change.

8

Before

When they're walking side by side, Edie really notices how tall Ron is, how diminutive she is in comparison, and she likes it. There's something about the difference that makes her feel as though he's her protector, and she his precious charge. Like he's a knight and she's a damsel. Of course, she hates herself for thinking this way. It's not the way modern girls are meant to think. But sometimes she enjoys feeling like one of the fairy tale characters she used to read about, whose lives she wanted to escape into when she was a child.

Ron is telling her about his family and how they all got their names. They're walking towards the fair by Littlehaven beach, and the air is knitted with the salty, fishy cologne of the sea.

'My mam loves an "ld",' he says.

'A what?'

'An "ld". See, there's four of us, and our names all end in "ld": Gerald, Harold, Arnold and Ronald. I can only guess it's because she loves her own "ld".' He shrugs. 'Hi-ld-a. Ld.'

Edie laughs. She can't imagine what it must be like to have so many siblings, or a mother you can laugh about.

'Who were you named after?' Ron asks.

Edie grabs a strand of her hair that has caught on the wind and wraps it behind her ear. 'You know, I haven't the faintest idea.' She tries to keep her voice light.

They're nearing the funfair and Edie's pulse races.

'I've never been here before.'

'What?' Ron frowns. 'How? You could walk here in forty minutes from your part of town.'

'I've walked by it,' she says. 'Just . . . never actually been inside.'

He wraps his arm around her shoulder and she grows fifty feet taller. 'Well, Edie-Eves, you're going to love it. Of course, it's more fun at night, with all the lights and stuff, but . . .' He doesn't press it, the fact that she hasn't seen him at night since his birthday. 'But the day is great too!'

'I love it already,' she says, still glowing at the nickname she hopes will stick, and she really means it.

A metal-framed Ferris wheel painted blue stands like the Colossus of Rhodes gazing down on squealing children and harried parents. Right in the middle, a giant creamy shaded bandstand-like structure is filled with whirling cars promising *Spills and Thrills* for just a shilling. Stalls studded with red bulbs gleam like rubies. They're covered in signs that read *6s for 3 throws* and *Don't be SHY, come have a try* in apple-green paint. Striped awnings in post-box red and buttercup yellow top the stalls, protecting the giant teddy bears and fish that dart around plastic bags like confused pensioners.

It's the smells though that really set Edie's pulse racing. Something sweet, something toasty, and the meaty perfume of hot dogs and onions.

'It's incredible,' she says breathlessly. She doesn't add *Let's bring our children here*, because they've only been on four dates and he still has to go back to Hull tomorrow and *oh, god*, she doesn't want him to go.

Their Ferris wheel car is blue and creaks as it swings towards the clouds.

'Look at the view!' shouts Ron.

The sea spreads below them like a silver tea tray flecked with speckles of sugar. It's stupid, but Edie has never been able to picture quite how vast it is on her few short trips to the seaside.

With her mother, beach visits were always limited to a small patch of sand where Cynthia would draw a square and tell Edie that she was not to go beyond it. Once, as she collected seashells in a bucket, Edie had wandered out of the square and away from her sleeping mother. Folded in half like a peg, Edie had kept her eyes on the shells and followed a trail all the way to the lapping water. Pink, purple, white, the glint of the nacre in the sun, the tiny barnacles stuck to larger shells, the chink of shells hitting one another in the bucket. Then she'd straightened up and her mother was nowhere to be seen. Later, a neighbour spotted Edie and returned her home well after the sun had dipped below the horizon. Cynthia blinked from the half-open door, puzzled that the little girl clutching a bucket of shells wasn't sitting indoors reading a book. In the morning, Edie threw the shells into the street and crushed them with the scuffed heels of her school shoes.

Here, in the air where the gulls argue and the wind bites, Edie is such a long way from the scared little girl with the bucket of shells.

They stop just shy of the peak and rock back and forth in the breeze. Edie turns to point out a fishing boat.

'Oh!'

Ron has moved from his seat opposite hers to just beside her. He slides his arm around her waist and their lips find one another.

His mouth is soft, and Edie lets hers sink into it. Her pulse is hammering: *surely he can feel it moving through his own chest?* A throbbing warmth moves through Edie's body and her breath speeds up.

The wheel pushes into motion again and they come apart. Ron licks his lips.

'You taste lovely,' he says.

Edie can't stop the grin that spreads across her face. She could be a bit more nonchalant – she's going to seem very provincial compared to those worldly Hull girls – but she doesn't really care.

'You're a great kisser,' he tells her. 'Best kiss I've ever had.'

Edie looks away, a spark of jealousy flaring at the idea that Ron's lips have touched another girl's.

The fairground is coming up to meet them, or maybe they are going down, when Edie stumbles out her next words.

'That's the best kiss I've ever had too,' she says, still not looking at him. 'That's the only kiss I've ever had.' She's not sure why she's telling him this, and her neck feels warm as she does. When she looks back, his eyes are shining. 'You don't mind?' she asks. 'That I'm twenty-three and so inexperienced?'

Ron laughs. 'You never fail to surprise me, Edie-Eves.' He kisses her again. 'Well, there's your second,' he kisses her again, 'and your third. Let's see how high we can get that number, eh?'

This time, it is Edie who kisses him.

She hadn't meant to stay out until the darkness crept in and the fair lights twinkled like an observatory, but everything was so intoxicating that Edie started to lose track of time.

No. I chose to ignore time.

They're walking across the clifftops towards Ron's house so he can get the car and drop her off nearer home.

'I can get the bus,' she'd said, but he insisted.

Beneath their feet, the grass is scrubby, and if Edie turns her head to the sea, she could be in a Daphne du Maurier novel, all windswept and romantic and tragic.

'. . . couldn't you?'

'Hmm?' Edie tunes back to Ron.

'I said "You could still do something with gymnastics now, couldn't you?"'

'Ah,' she says. 'Not really. In gymnastic terms, twenty-three is ancient. I don't know. Maybe teaching or something like that would be fun.'

'But not right now?'

'Right now, bills must be paid and offices must be cleaned,' she says, matter-of-fact.

'But you could show me some gymnastics now?'

Edie glances up at him, fluttering her eyelashes like she's seen girls do in the films. 'Maybe if you asked me very nicely.'

He pulls her in and presses his hot breath to her ear. 'Please, beautiful Edie-Eves. Will you show me some gymnastics?'

His breath raises the fine hairs on her skin, sends a shiver all the way down her neck and into her back and legs.

'Since you asked so nicely . . .' she murmurs.

Then she pushes away from him, tucks her skirt into her knickers and runs. A cartwheel, then one, two, three perfect handsprings.

He's applauding, laughing, racing after her. She flips up into a neat handstand, feet pointing at the stars.

'This is brilliant,' says Ron. 'You're great.'

Upside down, Edie flushes. Then, her skirt falls over her head, and blind, she pictures herself like a plucked tulip. *Oh god, am I wearing terrible underwear?* She's about to come down when

Ron's hips are against her buttocks, his hands around the small of her back and he flips her upright into his arms, her legs around his waist and her arms wrapping together over his shoulders and he's holding her like they're two bits of the same person.

Edie's body is thrumming and she doesn't recognize herself in this confident woman gripping this beautiful man between her legs. She presses her lips to his and there's a ferocity this time, an urgency that is driving her closer and closer to him.

'Who are you?' he asks with breathless wonder. 'What have you done with my shy little Edie-Eves?'

'Maybe shyness hasn't really got me what I want,' she says.

'And what do you want?'

She hesitates. *No. I'm tired of holding back.* 'I want you,' she says. 'I want you. All of you.'

'Is this an invitation?' he asks.

'It is,' she says, kissing him again, and he sinks them both to the soft grass and clover, no holding back.

Part 2

Ball Number 8: Dots on a Ladybird

9

Before

'Eee, Ron. It's hotter than Hades' knickers in here!' Hilda McVey wafts the menu at a cleavage that stretches almost to her neck. 'Why have they got the heating up so high?'

Ron flashes Edie an encouraging smile. 'Well, I suppose it's quite cold outside.'

Hilda sighs. 'Maybe it's just my time, you know. The change.' She nods mournfully at Edie.

'What are you having?' asks a waitress. 'Specials are Irish stew or ham and mustard sandwiches.'

'Ooh, the stew,' says Ron. 'Edie?'

'Same please.'

'Mam?'

'Well, I don't know.' Hilda taps her chin with the menu, now soggy in the corner where it made contact with her sweltering bosoms. 'See, I had an Irish stew at Millie O'Rourke's the other night, and she's actually Irish, so I think I might be disappointed. Having said that, I'm not sure I fancy ham. Full of ham this week, because Jimmy Tidworth got rid of his pigs last weekend, so I'm still going on that.'

The waitress works hard to disguise a yawn.

'Let's see, let's see,' says Hilda, frowning at the menu. 'The ink's run on this thing, you know.'

'I can come back,' offers the waitress.

'No, no. I'll be right with you. Ah, what's your soup of the day?'

'Parsnip and leek.'

'Parsnip and leek? Who's putting parsnip and leek together? Like chalk and cheese they are.' She tuts. 'Right, well I'll get a small bowl of the Irish stew and the ham sandwich.' She hands the now floppy menu back to the waitress. 'I'm not that hungry anyway.'

The waitress trips away quickly.

'So Edith,' says Hilda. 'Tell me all about you.'

Edie takes a deep breath, but before she's opened her mouth, Hilda is talking again.

'I should warn you,' she says, 'that our Ron was pursued by none other than Joan Collins. Joan Collins! Lovely-looking lass, she is. And glamorous, just like our Ronnie. So, my standards are high for my baby, naturally.'

'Erm . . .'

'Are you living at home, still? Ron hasn't really said much about you.'

Ron mouths, *Not true*, at Edie.

'Well, I live with my mam.'

'And what's her name?'

'Cynthia.'

'Cynthia!' Hilda taps her front teeth with her fingernail. 'I've known two Cynthias in my time. From South Shields, is she?'

Edie nods. The bow on the neck of her blouse is digging into her throat and she regrets putting it on now. *Do I look all right?* she'd asked her mother before she left. *Lovely*, replied Cynthia, not taking her eyes off a pigeon limping across the pavement outside.

'Right, go on then. What's her last name?' Hilda's voice drags Edie back to the now.

'Laverick.'

'Laverick?'

Edie's breath tightens in her throat. 'Yes. Cynthia Laverick.'

'Never heard of her.'

Edie lets the breath out.

'Maiden name?' asks Hilda.

'Oh,' lies Edie. 'I'm not sure.'

'Not sure?'

'I don't know,' says Edie. 'We don't have any other family.'

'Well, you could ask her.' Hilda gives Ron a look that Edie can't read, but it involves some complicated eyebrow choreography. Ron ignores her, choosing instead to refold his napkin.

'And your dad,' says Hilda. 'Has he passed on?'

'I think so.'

'You think so?'

Once, when they were cleaning the cinema, she and Patricia watched *Treasure Island*, where Long John Silver's parrot Captain Flint repeated whatever he said. If she weren't so nervous, she'd probably laugh.

'I think so,' Edie says. 'I never knew him.'

Hilda's lip is pushed forward in a deep pout. It is the pressure of not tutting where she wants to at her answers.

'Could you excuse me, please?' asks Edie. 'I just want to wash my hands.'

She has scuttled away to the powder room before Ron has time to get to his feet.

'Well,' she hears Hilda say.

*

She's patting her face dry on a paper towel and surveying how blotchy her neck is. She's terrible at this. A splotched face that leaks out all of her private thoughts and nobody but Patricia to tell her when she's behaving oddly.

'Come on, Edie,' she tells her reflection.

Mirror Edie doesn't look all that motivated.

A toilet flushes and their waitress steps from inside the cubicle. She grins at Edie in the mirror then starts to wash her hands.

'My mother-in-law volunteered me onto a mercy ship bound for Sierra Leone,' she says. 'They're all terrible. And if you have boys, you'll be the same.' She pats Edie's arm. 'Want to borrow my powder puff?'

When Edie returns to the cafe floor, Ron and his mother are hunched together.

'Cindy Nicholson. I bet that's her. She even looks a bit like her,' says Hilda. Edie's heart sinks. 'Ooh! You never know. It might be hereditary.'

'What?'

'Hereditary. You know. Passed down.'

'Ah!' Ron jumps to his feet when he spots Edie, purple blobs appearing on each cheek. 'Hello,' he says. 'The tea is here.'

There's been a shift. It's on Hilda's breath and in the wafts of whatever that is coming off her. Is it disapproval? Pity? Either way, Edie doesn't want it. She'd hoped Hilda would look at her with admiration. *Ooh, she's lovely, Ron. I've a sparkling sapphire ring just lying around that would look great with her eyes.* Of course Hilda knows who Edie's mother is, most people around here do. Edie wants to yell, *It's not my fault, okay?* But if she was Hilda, she'd have reservations too.

'Edie's really good at gymnastics,' says Ron. Edie blushes, thinking about Ron's private gymnastic show up above Trow

Rocks. 'Back in the day, she got asked to join the Durham County team.'

'Did she indeed?'

'Yes,' says Edie. 'I was asked. But it was a long time ago now.' *I was asked but couldn't do it, because how could I have got the leotards or gone to the competitions?* Now she does handstands against the doorframe of the bedroom, closes her eyes and imagines a crowd cheering her name.

'That's nice,' says Hilda, 'I was never into sporting, meself. Too busy perfecting my embroidery. Now *that's* a useful skill, Edith.'

'Yes,' says Edie politely. *But not as useful as being able to hitch kick your menu into the sky and handspring off into the horizon before you've finished convincing Ron that I'm no good.* She arranges her face into something she hopes looks neutral. 'Well,' she says. 'I'm a cleaner. So I'm great at keeping things neat and clean.' She's searching for excellent wifely qualities to replace the images of a crazy woman cartwheeling through King Street that she's sure Hilda is picturing right now. 'And I'm pretty good with numbers, you know, adding and finances and whatnot.'

'Our Ron's hopeless at that stuff,' says Hilda. 'And with his Gerry an accountant, too! Shocking.'

Ron gives an exaggerated shrug. 'Well, I got the looks and Gerry got the brains. We can't win them all, eh, Mam?'

'Gerry's handsome too!'

'Gerry looks like a goat in a man costume, and you know it.'

Hilda addresses Edie. 'Gerry looks like his dad, god rest his soul. Nice bloke and all, but not a looker. Ron and the others take after me, you see.'

'You're lovely, Mam.' Ron kisses his mother on the cheek.

Edie's fingers are tingling. She kisses her mother, of course she does, but when her lips touch her mother's dry skin, it's as though she's the parent, that Cindy is the child. This is different. Hilda's eyes crinkle, making a junction around her eyes, taking delight in having raised a son who adores her. Edie burns with shame that when she's tending to her mother, she spends a lot of time sighing and looking out of the window wishing she was somewhere else. She bets that Cynthia has never felt adored by her daughter. Edie wants a son who worships her, who she can laugh with, whose future girlfriends will have to work hard to prove their worth to her.

'I'm a lucky woman,' says Hilda. 'I've got the best four sons a mother could ask for.' She strokes Ron's arm as though it's a cat. 'I don't half miss him when he's in Hull.'

'Aw, I miss you too, Mam. Especially your mince and dumplings.'

'I make a cracking mince and dumplings, Edith. You need one or two bobby dazzlers in your arsenal and you're a made woman.'

Their ease in one another's company is so alien to Edie, and this, more than anything that's come before, sets Edie's pulse racing.

'I want this,' she says, before she's had time to process whether it's appropriate or not.

'You want what, Edie?' asks Ron.

Mercifully, she's saved by the waitress balancing plates like she's the Scales of Justice.

'I want this Irish stew,' she says. 'Yum!'

10

After

When they won the lottery, they were assigned a winners' officer. The aptly named Lydia Ball has nostrils that flare like a Pamplona bull's, and a thing for jewellery with ducks on. On the seven occasions Edie has seen her in person, she has been wearing a different strain of duck regalia: necklaces, gem-studded brooches, earrings, and once, a gold cuff that wrapped around her wrist made entirely of tiny crystal mallards. Perhaps she is descended from some sort of famous duck breeding family, or maybe she wishes herself to be a semi-aquatic bird. Either way, she's an odd duck.

At first, she called twice a week, but lately it has been tailing off. Tempting as it is to watch *Homes Under the Hammer* and bury herself in another day of oblivion, Edie decides to take the duck by the beak and call her.

'Edith, sweetheart. How's it going?' Lydia Ball sounds like she has just woken up.

Edie jumps straight in. 'Did you hear back from *Bella*? I told you, I'm totally in for the *Dream Circus* thing.'

Two weeks ago, Lydia had floated the idea that she was being considered for a *Bella* feature: *Dream Circus 2008* where they'll dress up non-celebrities like her like ringmasters and strongmen. A full makeover and Dogtor Wagtail who came second in *Britain's Got Talent* were on the table, and Edie really wants it. It's not the promise of lunch at the Hard Rock Cafe and the photographer who did *The Apprentice* winner's wedding, nor the famous dog, but the *all publicity is good publicity* thing, and she wants to be as out there as she can.

'Ah yes,' says Lydia. 'Dream Circus. Great concept.'

The whole thing seems rather silly, actually, but Edie had her reasons for wanting them to be in the papers when they won, and they haven't changed.

'Look,' says Lydia, 'they're floating Pam St Clement as the ringmaster instead of you.'

'Oh,' says Edie, trying to picture Pam St Clement and coming up blank. 'That's a shame. Have you got anything else? A newspaper? A talk show? I'll go on whatever.'

'Tsk,' says Lydia before she hangs up. 'I'll see what I can do.'

Edie doesn't care that this woman is probably embarrassed for her. An ageing ingenue with zero talent suddenly thinking she has a chance to be something. *Let her think that.*

Edie wanders upstairs and opens her bedside drawer. There's her ladybird rock and her album of postcards that Patricia has sent over the years. Underneath is a scrapbook and she slides it out and puts it on the bed. Colin put it together for her and it's filled with all the publicity shots the lottery people did, as well as articles in the local and national newspapers. The first win of 2008 and the third biggest win in lottery history was always going to be a talking point. For a while, the McVeys were in the news.

'You know,' Lydia Ball had explained in that first meeting, 'you are fully within your rights to remain anonymous.'

Ron had looked at her then, given her a fathomless look that she couldn't begin to read. Then she thought of Sean and, pushing a wave of nausea and guilt down, said 'No. No, thanks. You can make all this public.'

Ron shook his head. 'If you're sure, Edie.'

Her head ran away with her then, dreaming things she hadn't let herself dream in fifteen years. 'Spread it far and wide,' she ordered.

She gazes across their back garden and remembers the view from the kitchen where she grew up, the one-bedroomed ground-floor flat with the yawning holes in the floorboards and the sink that kept coming away from the wall. The view was blinkered by the board they nailed over the broken window that didn't get fixed until Edie was nearly twenty. A shared concrete yard had a corner entirely dedicated to the broken debris of the people who came and went from the neighbouring flats: the skeleton of a wheel-less bike, a cracked toilet seat, a wet, mouldering rug slimed with moss. Young Edie stared over a garden whose wall was studded with shards of broken milk bottles to deter would-be thieves. Not that she and her mother had anything worth stealing, but it didn't stop the vandals who wanted to show their disdain for them by painting vile words onto the bricks.

Edie shakes the image away. Out of habit, rather than actual hope, she dials the phone number of the house in Jesmond and listens to the *This number is not in service* message.

11

Before

The Roberts radio that they keep on the kitchen bench is the most valuable item in Cynthia and Edie's flat. Edie saved for over a year, squirrelling away as much as she could spare from cleaning the cinema, then later, her full-time job. She'd bought it so that she could be like the other girls and know the words to popular songs, but after the anticipation, after the conviction that she'd morph into someone more like the shiny girls shopping for tights on the high street, it had spent most of its time tuned to the Overseas Service, which turned out to be the only radio sound Cynthia could tolerate.

Edie glances into the bedroom to check that her mother is asleep and then turns the dial, looking for Radio Caroline. Through the hiss of static, she finds a rhythmic beat and pulls her ear to the speaker. She puts the volume down low and sets the kettle on the stove top to make some tea. Today, she wants to get in the mood like everyone else who'll be at the park later, and she wants to try to start her day the way normal people do.

A song comes on that she half recognizes through the filter of Patricia's tuneless crooning, and she tries out dancing. *Bob bob*

bob. She catches sight of herself in the half-cracked mirror by the door and stops. *I look like a cork.*

She leaves the music playing quietly while she dresses. An A-line skirt from her mother's wardrobe that reaches halfway down her calves – blue chiffon with little white flowers – and a neat, white blouse that belongs to Patricia. A cream cardigan – just in case – and the really good leather sandals she found in the second-hand shop.

She doesn't look like the other women who'll be there today in their swingy dresses and bright sandals, but still, twirling in front of the dark glass panels in the door, she looks pretty nice. Maybe it's because she's now twenty-four that she's decided not to care about her lack of modern fashion sense, or maybe it's because Ron always says she looks beautiful, but whatever it is she's enjoying being different for the first time in her life.

There are ten minutes before Ron is due to pick her up outside Hunter the Butcher, so Edie dials back to the Overseas Service and checks the bedroom.

There's a small mound where her mother lies, the blankets rising softly up and down. A snuffle, like a little hedgehog's, makes the breath constrict in Edie's throat. On the bedside table, the pill she left for her mother is gone, the water glass drained. Edie lays her hand on top of the blankets, feels the rise and drop. *She's fine, she's fine, she's fine.* The mantra doesn't go far in quelling the churn in her belly, but she takes a big breath and tries to summon the musical beats back into her body.

Cynthia has been doing well for the past few weeks: no hallucinations, no manic behaviour, just the flat malaise she gets bouts of from time to time, but still Edie does all she can to make sure she'll be safe when she's out. She checks the back door:

locked, and the chain slipped across for extra security. She pushes one of the plastic kitchen chairs under the handle and wedges it tight. Edie slips the key into her handbag.

Outside, she locks the front door. First she deadbolts the bottom lock, then the second one she had installed just a few months ago, up near the top by the number.

With the keys zipped firmly in her bag and a quick glance at the windows to check they're all shut too, Edie allows herself a glimpse at the sky. Casting a grey light over the rusting shopping trolleys that lie in the gutters, and broken brown and green glass ready to puncture bicycle tyres or slash a fallen child's knee, a few wispy dark clouds and a limestone-hued wash seem to suggest that South Shields might well be in for an afternoon drenching. She briefly considers grabbing her umbrella, but the effort of unlocking the door again feels Herculean. She squares her shoulders and heads to Whiteleas Way where Ron will pick her up and the neighbours won't try to cause trouble.

There's a buzz travelling through the air the closer they get to the South Marine Park. It is alive and restless. Between them and the sea, the blue Ferris wheel stands sentry, preparing for a busy day, and Edie flushes at the memory of Ron's mouth on hers swinging high above the coastline.

Young men in well-cut trousers and women in swingy short dresses wave to one another and sing out greetings across the swelling volume of the crowd. The air is fizzy, and Edie laces her fingers into Ron's as they look for Patricia and her sisters.

Some of the assembled are singing the songs already, and Edie hums a faintly recognizable tune along with them.

'There's Pats,' says Edie, spotting her friend with two nicely dressed younger girls.

They have to jostle their way through the crowds to a cacophony of tuts and frowns. '*Sorry,*' they mutter. '*Sorry, our friends . . .*'

'Oh, Edie, can you believe it?' says one of Patricia's sisters, Judith. 'The Animals! Here!'

'No. It's very exciting,' she says, trying to sound like a normal person, and not one busy worrying about whether her mother is asleep or awake. Some of the buzz is starting to rub off on her though. She's never been to a music concert before, but she's starting to understand why girls in America might have been fainting and whatnot. Maybe it's not the music, or the people singing it, but this. This weird electric static that's rubbing all the hairs on her arms and the fibres on her dress and making everything stand on end.

Patricia has found a spot near the bandstand, and they watch men drag cables and speakers across a space usually dedicated to pipers and brass bands at the summer festivals.

'This is historic,' says Patricia. 'This park, this day. It's never going to happen again, and we're here, watching, listening, taking it all in.' She shakes her head, grins at Edie.

'I wonder where they are,' says the other twin, craning her neck around, standing on tiptoe.

The rolling, thunderous applause ripples from the front and out to the corners of the park. Beyond that even, diving through the fretwork of the Ferris wheel where Edie had her first kiss and skimming the surface of the vast, cold North Sea. Edie can feel it right through to the marrow. Ron grips her hand as the crowd surges forward, descending on the fence that is keeping the masses from getting too close to the bandstand. They're carried on the wave, finding themselves at the centre of this pulsing, throbbing throng.

From nowhere, five sharply suited men emerge, grinning at

the crowd. Piercing screams drown the applause, and Edie looks to Patricia to say *Look at all these crazy young things*, but Patricia is screaming wildly too.

Okay. Edie glances at the other women in the crowd. She is the only female in her eyeline not screaming; perhaps she should, just to fit in, but she's rigid, stiff with self-awareness so instead stands silently, a conspicuous buoy bobbing in this frantic ocean.

The band members wave, blow kisses into the crowd and settle behind their microphones and instruments.

'One, two, three, four.' The drummer clanks his sticks together and the band starts playing.

Oh, I know this one! It's really good!

All around, as though under a hypnotic spell, the crowd begins to dance as one.

Ron sings some of the lyrics in her ear. 'You know this one?'

'Yes!' she says. '"We Gotta Get Out of This Place"! I heard it on the radio.'

She's smiling now, and even her body is responding to the tune.

She's dancing and even singing a few of the choruses and she laughs and grips Ron's hand. *I'm part of this. I'm part of something magical!*

'This is a song for all of the lovers out there,' says the singer.

Ron wraps his arms around her from behind and she leans her body into his. He's so warm and safe and lovely, she closes her eyes and lets the music and his touch wash over her. If she could bottle this moment, she'd keep it forever, wear it like a perfume. Tears start welling, confusing and strange. *I didn't know that you could cry from happiness.*

The singer sings about waiting for someone to call him, and Edie understands his yearning in a way she couldn't have ever imagined a year ago. So in love, he has to write a tune about this woman. Lucky thing.

Ron turns her around to face him, and she opens her eyes as the crowds part and Ron dips to the floor.

'Have you dropped something?' she yells, but Ron settles onto his knee and grins up at her.

'I'm in love, Edie-Eves,' he shouts. 'Will you marry me?'

Like the park has been submerged in water, the roar of the crowd is suddenly muffled, water flooding her ears. The crowd is moving in slow motion, nodding, cheering. *I'm drowning, how can I be drowning?* She searches for a familiar face, or the surface, or something to grab onto.

'Yes!' shout the people around her.

Edie's heart thuds, breaking the surface of that strange, muted moment.

'Ah, looks like a proposal over there,' says the singer, and the whole park cheers.

Her hands are over her mouth and Ron is blinking up at her with hope or maybe fear. She wants to say yes. *Needs* to say yes, but the word won't come. Her head fills with her mother asleep under those blankets and one of the songs comes back to her: "We Gotta Get Out of This Place".

The band reaches the bridge and the singer says 'Well, did she say yes?'

She's still rooted to the spot, not speaking, and Ron is still just there looking at her, and so is everyone else.

Isn't this what you want, Edie? She clenches her fists. *What about Mam? He doesn't even know and he might change his mind. It's not that simple.*

'Sorry,' says Edie to Ron, the singer, the whole damn crowd. She doesn't need to elbow her way out because they part for her, this gasping, sobbing woman, drenched in tears while the singer is telling them how the woman in his song makes him want to jump.

Edie can't look back at Ron, because her heart will shatter into a thousand pieces and she'll be forced to walk through the shards forever.

Why didn't you just say yes, Edie? Get to the tricky stuff later.

Edie runs all the way across the road and up to the Lawe Top where she can look down on the happy crowd with one broken man in its midst, and out to sea where she wishes the current would scoop her up and deposit her on a foreign shore with no memory of who she is or the life she's just left behind.

The rain, when it comes, feels like a fitting end to the day.

The bedroom is dark save for a sliver of orangey light coming through the gap in the curtains. It falls across the bed in a stripe, slicing her tiny little sleeping mother in half. Edie moves like a shadow so as not to wake her, drying her damp hair with a towel and slipping out of clothes that are now three times their weight in fabric and sky tears and Edie tears.

After staring through the fug of rain at a churning grey sea until the sky turned dark, Edie had set off for home. Her feet, slick and slightly too small for the sandals, slid around, making the going hard, and as they slid, they rubbed on the top of her foot. Halfway home, about two miles into the nearly four-mile journey, she took them off and slung them in a park bin. Her skirt clung to her legs and an old man outside the Westoe pub yelled 'Ah can see ya knickers, hinny.'

And all the way, she couldn't stop seeing Ron's face. His frown. Those lovely eyes, looking up at her in hope, then confusion. She doesn't even want to think about how he looked after she left.

Rage fuelled her partway home – rage at herself, her mother, the world for offering her something she probably doesn't deserve – then despair carried her the rest of the way.

Edie sighs, pulls on a dry nightdress and tries to rub her arms warm. She lifts the cover and slides in beside her mother, hoping that the cold press of her flesh won't wake Cynthia. She waits until the warmth of the cover and the other body has thawed her somewhat before placing the flat of her palm on her mother's back. Through her hand, under the threadbare cotton of her nightdress, there's the thin flutter of a heartbeat. Edie's rage and despair are gone now, replaced by the sinking churn of miserable realization. *You've done it now, Edie.* She closes her eyes and tries to time her breathing to that of her mam.

'I caught a fishy once,' mutters Cynthia in her sleep. 'But I had to let him go.'

Edie pats her mother's back, rubs her hand in a slow circle until they are both tripping into the dreams of fish and rings which await them, Edie staring into the grey, flat expanse of the future she's just cast herself into.

12

After

'Ah, Edie!'

Jade answers the door with a scraper in her hand. Her hair is a mess and her black T-shirt is spattered with globs of yellow paint. 'Want to come look at your tree again?'

'That would be lovely. If it's not too much trouble.'

Edie couldn't wait to get out of the house this morning while the air was loud with Colin watching motorsports and Ron hollering down the phone to the cleaning agency. 'Two weeks!' he'd shouted. 'Ridiculous!'

She goes through the house and out of the back door to the tree and, once again, she checks to make sure Jade isn't watching.

'Hello, lovey. I came back.' She touches the bark, but today, she is oddly hollow. As though all of the words in her head have tumbled out and blown across the garden. She takes a deep breath and then walks around and around the tree, trailing her fingers across it. When she gets dizzy, she stops and stares at it.

She doesn't know what to do with her hands. Or her feet. She's swaying back and forth, pushing her weight from one foot to the other and she doesn't know why. She just feels a bit . . . agitated. Restless.

'Your dad,' she starts, but isn't sure what she was going to say. 'Colin . . . Carol, everyone. I'm just always . . . I'm alone.' She drops her voice to a whisper. 'I'm so alone.'

She picks at a stray ribbon of bark and sighs. A shift in the breeze, a breath of chill makes her pull her cardigan around her, so she heads back to the house.

Jade is standing in the sitting room with two mugs of tea in hand, grin semi-obscured by the rising steam. Edie smiles back, taking the hot tea from this virtual stranger who is waiting for her. She examines the cup that has a shiny gold crown on it and says 'Queen of Damn Near Everything'.

'Asif got me that for my birthday last year, when I was still his queen and Tamara some crap peasant.' Jade shakes her head. 'Bastard.'

On the box that is doubling up as a coffee table are a pile of envelopes ripped open leaving a confetti pile on the floor. They're all official-looking with those crinkly plastic windows that indicate a cold receptionist folding paper while her mind is elsewhere, rather than personally typed like they were in the old days, but Edie recognizes a demand notice when she sees one. Jade is staring into her mug looking as though she's forgotten how to drink and she looks so young and unguarded that Edie's heart hurts.

'Were you doing some decorating?'

'What?' Jade lights up. 'Yes! Getting the baby's room ready.'

'On your own?'

'Yeah well.' She shrugs. 'Mam's gone and my bro's in—' she whistles. Edie frowns. 'Jail. My brother's in jail.'

'Oh!'

'Yeah. He's an idiot.' She plucks a fleck of paper from her top. 'So, I'm decorating.'

'Would you . . . would you like some help?'

Jade snorts. 'From you? No offence, but what do you know about decorating? This place is a hole.'

'I have a lot of decorating experience.'

Jade raises an eyebrow. 'I *could* do with some help. But if you faint or break your hip, or fall off a ladder, I'm not taking you to hospital.'

Edie smiles. 'I promise that if I do myself a mischief, I'll get myself a taxi to the hospital.'

'Right. Well, how are you with stripping wallpaper?'

The boys' bedroom is exactly how she left it, save for an exposed patch of plaster where Jade has ripped off the paper. There are stripes of paint in varying shades of yellow in the gap.

It's a textured wallpaper with squashy circles on it, all in apple white. Edie liked it because it made the walls seem softer, and when Colin had moved back in after his divorce, it felt like anything she could do to make his world softer would be a good thing.

Jade hands her a scraper and immediately starts jabbing at the wall.

'What did you put this on with? Superglue?'

'Wait! You've got to get the paper wet. It'll come off much more easily.'

In the kitchen, Edie fills a dish with hot, soapy water trying to ignore the feeling of familiarity. Jade keeps things in odd places, but Edie feels her way around the room with the practised hand of a lifetime. She tries hard not to slop any water on the laminate as she makes her way back to the bedroom.

'See.'

She shows Jade how to soak the panels, and how the paper curls away easily once they've teased some of the adhesive from the wall. Jade goes back to work on the section near the window. Edie gets started on the panels around the door.

'You can't have been in your new place long. Have you finished decorating there yet?' Before Edie has time to answer, Jade laughs and says 'Well, wouldn't that be funny? If your place is half decorated and here you are doing mine?'

'No. It's done,' she says, too embarrassed to say that a man with a blue-tipped quiff did it for them. 'It's not really how I would have liked it, but it's done.'

'Where is it? Your new place?'

'Oh, over Newcastle way. North.' She hesitates. 'Darras Hall.'

Jade raises her eyebrows, whistles. 'Do you see any famous footballers around?'

'I wouldn't know one if I saw one,' says Edie. 'You don't really see anyone walking around. Not like here. Everyone drives everywhere in their fancy cars.'

Jade nods knowingly. 'That'll be the footballers. Love a stupid car, them lads.' Ron and Colin's fancy cars probably qualify them as stupid in Jade's world. Jade presses her hands into the small of her back. 'Oof. I feel massive.'

She runs a hand over her belly. 'Come feel. He's kicking now.' Jade grabs both of Edie's hands and rests them on the mound of her belly.

There's a quiver beneath Edie's palms, then something pushes into her hand. 'Oh!' A ripple moves under Jade's taut flesh. 'That's his head!' She looks at Jade, still gripping her wrists. The baby settles, slumbering in his safe, warm haven. They grin at each other for a moment, then Edie clears her throat and takes her hands away. She goes back to her scraping spot.

'Of course, bloody Asif hasn't felt his son kick. Too busy clubbing with sodding Tamara.' Jade stabs the scraper into the wallpaper viciously. 'You ever had your heart broken by a man, Edie?'

Edie has carried broken heart-shards in her chest for nearly sixteen years, but she doesn't tell Jade that. 'I put up this wallpaper for Colin when his wife cheated on him and he had to move back in with us. He was shattered into pieces.'

'But wallpaper heals a broken heart, right?'

Edie laughs. 'Glue it back together with a good strong paste.'

Jade pretends to dollop something on her chest with the scraper. 'There we go. Fixed!'

'Have you spoken to him?'

'No!' Jade pushes a hand roughly through her hair. 'Tamara is, like, his gatekeeper or something. I tried, after the last scan. Thought if he saw the picture, he might want to come back. Or, you know, at least be part of his son's life. But all I got was a load of abuse from her.' She closes her eyes, stroking her bump tenderly. She whispers, 'This little man deserves better.'

Edie wants to throw her arms around the girl and hug her. Wants to stroke her hair and rock her from side to side. Say *Shhh, there, there*, and tell her it's going to be all right. But instead, she dips her sponge into the hot water and presses it over a new patch of wallpaper. Weirdly, she's finding it quite relaxing. The last time she did any decorating, it was in this very room. They hired someone to do everything in the new house. Odd man, Delph was. All sharp angles and efficiency. Ron and Colin had nodded enthusiastically as he waxed lyrical about 'complementary semitones' while Edie perched awkwardly on the edge of the couch. Turned out that 'complementary semitones' meant 'grey'. Loads and loads of slightly different grey. Edie sighs. At least this little boy is going to have a nice sunny room to grow up in.

'Woah! Check this out!' Jade waggles her scraper at a hairy face poking through the paint. She scrubs a bit more from the wall, revealing a black hat on top of the face. 'What do you reckon that's meant to be? Looks like a rat in a hat!'

Edie closes her eyes. 'It's Paddington Bear,' she says quietly. And for a moment, she sees a brief flash of herself in an old shirt of Ron's dabbing paint on the walls. There's Hilda saying *He's looking a bit skinny, Edith! Could you make his face a bit more smiley?*

'Really?' says Jade. 'Haha, that'd give any kid nightmares!' She jabs at the spot a bit more. 'Shit! You painted this, didn't you? I'm sorry. It's not that crap. It was just a bit of a surprise.'

Edie swallows hard. 'It's okay. The boys liked it, and that's the main thing.'

'Of course!'

They had liked it. Until they hadn't, and then they'd harassed her for Basil Brush wallpaper or SuperTed or He-Man, but by then things were tight and they couldn't really afford to redo it. They'd had to make do with her poor man's Paddington, Colin all the way up until he'd moved in with Carly. They had just gradually put up more and more posters until the forlorn-looking bear standing outside a bright red telephone box had all but disappeared. After Colin's divorce, they'd finally papered over it, and Edie had shed a tear as she covered his face, trapping him and frozen particles of Edie's early motherhood days against the wall.

'I'm sorry,' says Jade again. 'My mouth runs away with me sometimes. Gives me brain a while to catch up, you know? Asif used to pull me up on it all the time.'

Edie realizes that Jade has stopped scraping.

'Are you okay?'

Jade sighs. 'Yeah. I just . . . you know, I vowed I wouldn't be like me mam, doing this alone. And yet here I am.'

'Your mother raised you alone?'

'Yes.'

'Mine too.' Edie puts her scraper down. 'And it's only as I got older that I realized how hard it must have been for her.

How lonely she must've felt.' Jade nods. 'But even if you're in a wonderful relationship, it can still feel pretty lonely at times.'

'Motherhood?'

'Life.'

Outside, seagulls squabble loudly. Jade nods, presses a paint-flecked forearm into her eyes.

'You don't have to feel lonely,' says Edie.

Jade turns away. 'Thanks.'

'You just need a purpose. You know, something to get up for in the morning.'

'True,' says Jade. 'This little one's my purpose now. What's yours?'

Edie hesitates. 'You know what? I don't know.'

Like peeling back the paper and seeing something you didn't know was there, Edie spots why she's been drifting around like a lost balloon. She has no purpose. *I need to do something.*

They work on, but Jade is humming now, a song Edie doesn't recognize. Edie's scraper slides neatly under the paper and she nips the corner between her finger and thumb. It's not particularly well adhered here. It's satisfying to pull the long strip away, the paper curling in its wake.

Edie gasps.

A long inky line, fading to grey. Short intersecting slashes. Letters scrawled in a shaky hand. Her head feels light. The room tilts. She sits on the floor, dropping her scraper on the way down. She brings her hands to her face, a tremor vibrating through them.

'Edie! Are you okay? Are you having a funny turn because of your age?'

Edie shakes her head. She wraps her fingers around one another to quell the shaking. Takes a shuddering breath. Is this what dying feels like?

'Oh look! A height line.' Jade bends to examine the markings. 'Is this from your boy?' She squints, tilting her head to one side. '"Colin". Is that him?'

Edie nods.

'And "Sean-o rules". Who's Sean-o?'

'My other son.'

She claps her hand to her mouth. 'Ah god. Did he pass away? Is that why you go talking to the tree?'

'What? No. He's alive and well.' Her eyes trace back up the line. At least she hopes he is. 'I just . . . I haven't seen him in a while.'

Edie sees them. Three, all the way through to fifteen. They take it in turns. They stand still, backs against the wall, holding their breath because everybody knows that makes you taller. Edie lays a hand flat across their heads. Pushing their hair down so as not to give an inaccurate reading. Carefully marking a line with a biro then handing the pen to each boy to write their name and age.

Then a line way up high when they had hit man height and been towering above her, even at fifteen.

'Come on Col. I swear I'm two inches taller than you.'

Edie laughing as her sons jostle one another. Why had they been measuring themselves that day? Was everything still normal then? How long was that before things changed?

'You've still got shoes on! Mam tell him!' Edie is tipping over and there's a plummeting sensation in her guts, like a heavy boulder dropped into water. It's all too much.

13

Before

Edie is tying the straps of her apron when Patricia flies into the storeroom.

'What the hell was that, Edie?'

It's been two days since The Animals and Edie has kept her head down and the front door locked since getting home drenched on Saturday night.

She tries to keep her voice level. 'What was what?'

'You know what!' Patricia stops talking when Maureen comes in to collect her mop and bucket. She smiles at the older woman and waits for her to leave. 'You know what,' she hisses. 'Ditching Ron in the middle of a proposal.'

'Oh,' says Edie. 'That.'

'Yes that. By the way, Eric Burdon thinks you're a crazy lady. What were you thinking?'

Edie examines the bristles of her broom, plucking away a clump of something resembling dog fur. 'I was thinking about my mam.'

'And?'

'And, I can't leave her. You know that.'

Patricia sits on the bench. 'There are places, Edie. Good places.'

'Yes, but not that I can afford.'

They contemplate the concrete floor in silence. She has telephoned a few homes, even got one to send the brochure, but despite promises from the kindly assistants, they are all well out of Edie's budget.

'Have you talked to him?'

Edie shakes her head. She is too ashamed to phone his house, probably to have his mother answer.

'Because he might help . . .' Patricia continues.

'No!' It comes out much louder and more forcefully than Edie anticipated. 'I can't ask that of him. It's too much.'

Patricia folds her arms. 'Are we about to fall out over this, Edie?'

'No!' Edie is surprised. 'Why would we?'

'Because you and I both know that Ron is a good man. Because you want a nice family and a bunch of children. And because I'd give my left bum cheek to have a man like him.'

Edie sits down beside her. 'Not going well with Alan, then?'

Patricia sighs. When she hit twenty-five and was still single, Patricia scoured the lonely-hearts columns – first locally, then she widened her net – for someone who would take her off her own hands. She found roofer Alan in the Stoke-on-Trent *Herald* and he comes for a visit at the end of every month.

'He's fine,' says Patricia. 'Just a bit . . . boring. Well, you've met him. You know.'

Edie does know. When they'd gone for lunch, he'd regaled them all with a convoluted story about slate tiles, pausing to deliver a punchline that he'd expected a raucous response to:

'Then we found out it was *slated* for demolition!'

The hesitation before Edie and Patricia's loud fake laughs was too long and painful to forget in a hurry.

'Besides,' says Patrica, 'he looks like a ferret in an overall.'

Edie snorts, and it's the first time she's smiled since she pushed her way out of the park.

'See. You've got a handsome man who loves you and wanted to do something devilishly romantic.' She pulls a face that looks like she's stuffed too many sherbet lemons in her mouth. 'He's kind and sweet and lovely and honest. And he'd pump you full of massive babies.'

Edie cradles her forehead in her hands. 'What have I done, Pats?'

Patricia stands, placing a hand on each of Edie's shoulders. 'Call his house, Edie. If you don't, I will.'

'I don't know what to say,' she says.

'You'll figure it out.'

Edie has never been to the Alkali pub. Actually, she's only been to two pubs in her entire life and one of them was for Ron's birthday, so it isn't terribly surprising that she hasn't been here. Both times, she felt conspicuous and naughty.

Patricia had advised neutral ground.

'Like Switzerland,' she said, nodding.

So Edie is standing outside a pub at 12:30 on a Saturday, with Patricia in tow to make sure she actually does what she needs to do.

'I can do this myself, you know,' says Edie. 'You didn't have to come.'

'I did,' says Patricia. 'I know you, Edie Laverick. Know what you're like when you get all shy and weird. You're like a turtle scuttling under your shell.'

'I don't think turtles scuttle under shells. I think they just pull their heads and feet in.'

'You've never seen a turtle,' says Patricia. 'How do you know whether or not they scuttle?'

'I called him, didn't I? That's not scuttling. That's being brave.'

She hadn't felt brave shivering in the phone box with a threepence gripped so tight it was giving off coppery blood smells like in the butcher's. She had pressed the receiver to her chest and stared at the wall for so long that an old man had hammered on the glass. *Stop ditherin', pet, and get on with it.*

For a fleeting second, she thought that it was Ron who answered, but it was Harry, who informed her that Ron was in Hull.

'Oh,' she'd said. 'Never mind.'

'He's back on Saturday,' Harry said. And she bit the bullet and told him where she wanted Ron to meet her. Harry gave a long sigh that she couldn't read. 'Okay, love. I'll make sure he gets the message.'

Edie had been scared to lean over ever since in case her insides came tumbling out. Harry would pass on the message, certainly, but would Ron actually turn up?

'Now, come here.' Patricia pulls down Edie's ponytail. 'You look like my Aunty Bibby in her casket, not a blooming potential bride in the prime of womanhood.'

'Better?'

Patricia steps back and surveys her, index finger to lip. 'Why didn't you borrow something of mine? Edie, lads don't want to see you looking like a pensioner.'

'Actually, I dig the pensioner look.'

Edie's pulse hammers at the sound of his voice. He's materialized from nowhere like a ghost and given Edie and Patricia as much of a fright as if he *had* been a ghost. He's not smiling though, face blank and pale as chalk. Despite the chill, Edie's cheeks burn.

'Ron. Thank you for coming,' says Edie and it sounds as mechanical as it feels.

'Thank you for inviting me,' he says with the formality of a statesman.

Edie wants to say more, but an army of stealthy thieves appear to have stolen her voice. A small croak emerges instead. She turns her attention to a dip in the pavement that has collected water and oil and now looks like a fairy's washing bowl.

'Shall we go inside?' asks Ron. His voice is still entirely neutral, which is more disconcerting than if he was angry.

Patricia steers Edie towards the door and the three of them head inside.

'Act nice,' growls Patricia while Ron is at the bar. Edie's fingers are trembling, she takes them off the table and pushes them under her thighs. 'And if he asks you again to marry him, I'll have a champers!'

Patricia takes a sherry from Ron with a nod then scurries away to a corner where she can keep an eye on proceedings while pretending to read *Valley of the Dolls*.

'I thought you might like a sweet sherry,' says Ron, passing Edie a glass.

Their fingers touch as she takes it from him and they both withdraw their hands quickly. Only two weeks have passed since the park and the music and the – Edie can hardly bear to think about it – *proposal*, but they've become strangers in one another's company. Edie sips the sherry and it is so sticky it makes her feel both grown up and like a child playing at adulthood all at once.

'I'd have come back last week but I decided to stay in Hull.'

'Oh,' says Edie, sick with images of him in swanky Hull pubs seeking solace for his heartache.

'Uncle Jim's birthday,' he confirms. 'Just wanted a bit of

company. Besides,' he says, 'I wouldn't even know where to find you, would I? You make me drop you off streets from your house and you don't have a phone number, so I was a bit stuck anyway.'

'You'd have come to find me? If you knew where?'

He frowns, but doesn't answer. Ron has a pint of something dark with a thick head across the top. When he sips, he swallows loudly and swipes at the milky moustache on his upper lip.

Edie wants Patricia to look at her, to give her some indication of how to act, but when she tries to catch her eye, Patricia, whose eyes haven't left her book, lets out a loud *Ha!* then nods approvingly at the page. There's a person-sized space between Ron and Edie, and their legs could be as unfamiliar as strangers' on a bus.

'So,' says Ron. 'You wanted to talk.'

'Yes,' she says.

Ron puts down his pint and swivels on the seat to face her. His big, long leg is bent up at a funny angle and Edie wants the touch of his knee against her leg like that first day at Minchella's. Her heart is a concrete ball in her chest.

Ron folds his arms. 'Well, you want to talk and I'm here and you're sitting silently staring at the chair. What is it, Edith?' She winces at the use of her full name. 'Do you want to talk or do you want to consider the merits of velvet on a pub seat?'

'I want to talk,' she says. 'It's just hard.'

'Hard? You know what's hard? Seeing the whole of the Marine Park look at you like you're a pillock. Seeing *The Animals* look at you with pity. Man! Alan Price gave me a thumbs down!' He shakes his head. 'Explaining to your mam and brothers who helped you pick out the ring that your girlfriend didn't answer and ran off instead. That's hard. So, if you've got something hard to say, how about you get on with it, so we don't both waste our afternoons.'

She has never seen Ron angry before, hardly recognizes the boxy jaw he's clenching. But although he's looking at her with flashing eyes and tight lips, his thighs are quivering.

'I'm sorry,' she whispers. 'I didn't want to hurt you.' She takes a glug of her sherry for courage. 'I wanted to say yes. Want to say yes.'

'Then why didn't you?'

Edie's shoulders are tucked around her ears. She lets them drop to the soundtrack of a sigh. This is it. Time to lay it out on the table if she wants to keep him. She glimpsed the flat wasteland of a future without him and she can't risk that being the path her life follows. She steels herself.

'It's probably easier if I take you to my flat,' she says. 'Will you come with me?'

They're halfway to Whiteleas before they realize that they've left Patricia in the pub.

When Ron turns his car into her street, she grips the door handle and views it through his eyes. Discarded sheets of newspaper dance across the road, heavy with chip grease from Howlett's Chippy. Three ground-floor windows are boarded up and a rusted gate hangs off its post. The houses have cracks running across their faces, doors that don't align with windows, paint that bubbles and flakes from the doors and ledges. The place is tired, sad and ready for pasture.

'You don't need to be embarrassed about where you live, Edie,' says Ron, though he's gripping the wheel tightly as they pass a huddle of young men with short, limp cigarettes hanging from their mouths surveying Ron's car with sneers.

If only this were the extent of it. She is embarrassed, and she hates herself for it, but the worst is still to come.

'Pull in by this lamppost,' she says.

She's painfully aware that she didn't manage to remove all of the paint last time. She thought she'd done it, but the ghost of the letters still remains across their front wall, C R A Z Y B I T C H still visible, along with the crude outline of a male appendage. Edie wishes she'd scrubbed harder, stayed out longer to get rid of all traces of the latest cohort of children who have listened to their parents' tales of the madwoman from number 46 dancing in the street in her underwear.

They get out of the car silently, and Edie notices that Ron locks the car then checks the handles twice. He looks down the street before shoving the key deep in his trouser pocket.

They pick their way over the cracked paving slabs with dandelions poking through, and Edie takes out her keys. She unlocks the first deadlock, then the second, then opens the door just a crack.

'Right,' she says. 'Are you ready to meet my mother?'

14

After

Edie can't stop twittering leading Jade around their Darras Hall house. Her face is hot, her fingers quivery and she keeps looking at Jade for a reaction, though she's not sure whether she's looking for approval or disgust. Jade just nods, lips tight, eyes alert.

When they first moved into the house, Ron had organized a minibus to bring some of their friends over for a housewarming party. Brenda had hovered stiffly in the corner of one of the sitting rooms for the whole night, Edie overheard her say that she 'wouldn't dare live somewhere like this'. Colin later heard her call it 'morgueish', while someone else said it would be like 'living inside a raincloud'.

It fell right into her lap, this solution. She recalled the crumpled message Ron left her on a torn envelope this morning, while she was staring at Jade's mattress on the floor, the emptied-out penny jar on the windowsill.

The cleaner meant to start on Wednesday cancelled, it said. *Absolutely bloody fuming! Does nobody want a job these days???*

'Jade, what was it you used to do for work?'

'Ah,' said Jade. 'I was a dinner lady. At the primary school.'
'And did you have to do any cleaning as part of it?'
'A bit. Why?'

Jade had taken a bit more convincing, but with the promise of a taxi and light duties, she'd surveyed the laminate for a while before relenting.

'Colin calls this the media room,' says Edie, 'but it's just another sitting room with a massive TV.'

'Oh, Edie. It's really nice. Smart, you know. Stylish.'

Edie glows. 'A bit more colour maybe . . .'

'Yeah,' says Jade. 'Or not. I'd love to live somewhere nice like this.'

Edie coughs, picturing Jade's upturned cardboard box table and the semi-painted walls. 'This TV is a magnet for dust,' she says. She panics, not wanting to sound ungrateful. 'So you're probably thinking *How do I get all this done in three hours?* Are you? But don't worry. I'll help out.'

'Oh, you don't need to help. I'll be okay.'

'I want to help,' says Edie. 'I've not got much to do.'

'Well,' says Jade, patting her bump, 'that'd be nice.' She looks around with a warmer look in her eyes. 'Shall we get started then?'

It's quick, light work and Jade has a good eye for dust and fluff. While they're working, Jade teaches Edie a song about 'apple bottom jeans'.

'So they look like an apple at the bottom?' Edie asks. Jade shrugs. *They sound comfy. I might get some.*

Jade shows her the dance where she bobs down low, and it's quite impressive until Jade says 'I can't get up!' Edie hooks her hands under Jade's armpits, rendering her a wriggling, giggling mess.

'Stop squirming,' giggles Edie, and the pair of them end up

in a heap on the rug clutching their sides. She's met by a sudden memory of her and Pats cleaning at the town hall back when they had the Mayor's office in there: Pats charging up and down with a wastepaper basket on her head, jabbing the mayoral robes with her broom. *I will never concede, good Sir Knight*, she had hollered, and Edie laughed so hard she fell over the desk. Then it's gone like a puff of air. *Where is Pats at the moment?* Last she'd heard, Patricia was in Singapore. They're long overdue a phone call.

In the gaps between conversations, Jade hums a quiet, cheerful tune.

'I read that babies like music,' she tells Edie, 'only, I used to listen to rock and metal before, so now I'm trying to think of gentle songs. What did you sing to your babies?'

Edie squints into the past for a moment. 'I don't remember singing them anything,' she says eventually. 'I don't think they were saying that then, about the singing.'

'They reckon it makes your baby cleverer.'

'Is that right?' What would have happened if she had sung to them? She's not sure Sean could have got too much cleverer. Her own mother used to sing, but that was no comfort to little Edie. Cynthia singing and swaying in the street, weird, mournful tunes without real words or meaning, just a haunted melody of grey and cloud and isolation. She blinks the image away.

'Mam, have you seen my driving gloves?' Colin strides into the kitchen. He's wearing a pink polo shirt and cream slacks. Edie has never seen Colin in such light-coloured clothing as she has the past few months. Now, he's got something new on every day and is starting to resemble a chalk drawing.

'They're on the microwave.' Edie puts her cloth down. 'Colin, this is Jade.'

He turns from the cupboard, a packet of crisps in each hand. 'Ah,' he says. 'Hi.' He surveys the mound of her belly. 'Baby, is it?'

'No,' says Jade in mock indignation, 'just too much chicken jalfrezi.'

Colin turns a disturbing shade of purple. 'Oh, I . . . I'm . . .'

'Nah, only messing,' says Jade and flicks his arm with her duster.

Colin snorts in relief. 'Christ! I nearly had a conniption!'

'Ha!' laughs Jade. 'I congratulated one of the other dinner ladies on my first day working at the school cafeteria. *Peritonitis*, someone whispered. Well, I was mortified!'

Colin laughs, and Edie realizes it has been a while since she saw him laughing, maybe even since before his divorce. He's smiled since the lottery win, grinned, but not that lovely hearty laugh he has.

Later, over a tea and a fondant fancy, Jade says 'Colin's nice.'

'I think he's lonely,' says Edie.

'Lonely? A lovely fella like him?'

Edie smiles. 'Why else would he be living with his mam and dad in his thirties? And he doesn't have all that many friends. He was always the shy one.'

'I was lonely before Asif,' says Jade, and she sounds very small and young. 'He got me out of a bad place and I thought that was it, you know?'

'Yes,' says Edie, 'I do.'

'I thought it would be easy to find someone to love you, but it's not, is it? So a few years ago I moved back in with my mam.' Jade sighs. 'Then I lost her too.'

'Oh, I'm sorry to hear that.' Edie puts her hand on Jade's. 'That must've been hard.'

Jade shrugs. 'Not really. She seems pretty happy. Besides, it means we can go on holiday to Faliraki whenever we like.'

'I've been a bit lonely lately,' says Edie, but then she stops. She's here in this house with a husband and son and here's poor pregnant Jade with a brother in jail and a mam in Faliraki wherever that is, and a partner who left her for someone else. *Stop wallowing.*

Ron is going to ask questions when he sees that she has found them a very pregnant cleaner, but she is starting to feel better. There's something very easy about Jade, and although Edie's old enough to be the woman's grandmother, she is thoroughly enjoying her company.

And it's this that she's missing. Company. Carol's one-liners and Brenda's dry wit. Putting the world to rights over tea and a biccy or a bottle of Blue Nun. How things would be so different if they ran the world. Synchronized, side-tearing laughter, causing mayhem at the back of aqua aerobics. Edie wants that back.

'Jade, you don't happen to like aqua aerobics, do you?'

15

Before

It's odd to have made it to twenty-five and to have never been in a church before, or not one that she remembers, anyway. There's a photograph on the mantelpiece of a baby in christening garb that says *Edith* on the back in blue ink that has blotched and fattened in time, so it would seem that she was at least taken to a church once.

The photograph is corseted with crease lines. Edie likes to think that it's because it was lovingly carried in a purse by someone, though, in darker moments, she suspects that someone crumpled it up. Maybe threw it on the ground. Still, at least it was important enough to be rescued. She hopes her mother did it, pressing out the creases between the pages of a thick book, stroking the surface until it was at least straight enough to prop up against the ceramic shepherdess statue filmed with dust.

On the morning of her wedding, the photograph lives in a suitcase with the other sad symbols of her existence. Apart from the mattress that she slept on last night, the rest of the furniture has been sold, the lease surrendered, the less wearable clothes of her mother's donated to the second-hand shop. The Lavender

Hill House people said she wouldn't need much, just comfy day wear and nice pyjamas.

Edie's only comfort in taking Cynthia to Lavender Hill was that her mother didn't really seem to understand what was going on.

It's a mental home, she'd told Patricia. *They just call it a care home to make it seem nicer.*

And the nurses or carers or whatever they were called did seem nice, but there was something so desolate about the powdery purple drawing room where she'd left her mother staring out of the window.

'I'll visit all the time, Mam,' she'd told her.

'I miss you when you go out,' was Cynthia's response.

Edie had sobbed in Ron's car for a solid hour before she was able to let him drive her home. 'When we get our own place . . .' he'd said, harking back to the day he had first met Cynthia. He'd charmed her that day, made such a fuss and she'd been delighted, then he'd stepped back quietly when Cynthia had cried, letting Edie comfort her. 'We'll look after her,' he'd said. 'I can help for now, then when we get our own place, we can bring her home.'

Today, Edie perches on the edge of the mattress while Patricia kneels, trying to make her look special with the help of Yardley's finest.

'Can you please let me pluck these eyebrows, Edie? You look like a merkin came to your face to die.'

While Patricia is removing hair and a considerable amount of skin from her face, Edie surveys the wedding dress she bought second-hand from the newspaper ad. Like most of her clothes, it's at least ten years out of date, but she's pleased with how it turned out after she hand-stitched some mother-of-pearl beads to the neckline and added a lace applique to the skirt.

'Ron's going to be wild when he sees you in that,' says Patricia. 'You'll look like Debbie Reynolds.'

'Really?'

'Yes. And he's going to be all handsome and you two are going to be gorgeous and me and my buck-toothed roofing ferret can be your ugly friends.'

'You're not ugly!'

'I know! But I'm ugly by default when I'm next to a stoat in a suit who gets excited by loft insulation.' She shakes her head. 'I'm so glad he's got an emergency drainpipe situation today. Maybe I'll get a little dance with Harry. When he sees my best moves, he'll fall wildly in love with me, I'm sure of it.' Edie giggles. 'Don't you be laughing at my dance moves, Mrs nearly McVey!'

They grin at one another.

'Are you nervous?' asks Patricia.

Edie smiles. 'About marrying Ron? No. About Mam being in the same room as Hilda McVey? Very.'

Patricia brushes a stray eyebrow strand off Edie's face. 'I promise, I'll take good care of her.'

'Thanks.' Edie nods as her friend cups her cheek. 'What?'

'Nothing, I just . . .' Patricia smiles lightly. 'If that Ron of yours ever breaks your heart, he'll have me to deal with, all right?' Edie swipes a rogue tear from the corner of her eye. 'Now don't you dare go crying this make-up off, Edie.'

'Thanks, Pats,' says Edie. 'You know you're my . . . well, I . . . you . . .'

'I know,' says Patricia, planting a kiss on the top of her head. 'I know.'

Harry has borrowed a shiny Ford from their uncle's garage in Hull to drive the girls and Cynthia to the wedding.

'Good luck, ladies,' he says, giving them a thumbs up. 'See you on the other side.'

'And you're still single, are you?' asks Patricia from the front seat.

'Pats!' Edie swipes her friend.

Harry beats a hasty retreat into the church.

'I'd trade Alan in for him any day,' she whispers, gazing longingly at him. 'Oh bugger!'

'What?'

Patricia pushes a foot from under her soft pink bridesmaid dress. It is housed in one of Edie's chunky green velvet house slippers. Edie giggles. If this is the only thing that goes wrong today, they're in for a fantastic wedding.

In the church lobby, while Pats practises walking down the aisle in slippers, Edie takes a deep breath. 'Are you ready, Mam?'

'Where's my bag?' asks Cynthia. Edie passes her the battered handbag she's had for as long as Edie can remember. Cynthia digs around throwing out used tissues, and a dried-out half slab of Kendal Mint Cake. 'I got this for you,' she says.

She holds out her palm to Edie. In it is a small stone, painted to look like a ladybird.

'Oh, Mam,' says Edie. She swallows hard. 'Those are my best memories, painting rocks and hiding them in the park with you.' She kisses her mother on the cheek, dampening her skin with a rogue tear. 'Thank you.'

Edie keeps her eyes on the altar at the front, on Ron's straight back and freshly snipped hair. She keeps her steps even and slow like she's seen brides in films do, followed by Patricia, whose slippers she can hear slapping on the flagstones of the church. And she keeps her hand tightly gripped around her mother's.

From the corner of her eye, she sees the powdery blue hat

borrowed from Patricia's mother topping her own mother's head and, from beneath it, Cynthia's eyes glaze over the pews on the right filled with Ron's extended family. Edie hopes that the medication keeps her calm for the whole day.

The left-hand side of the church is empty, save for Patricia's parents and her two sisters.

Pitiful, thinks Edie. *Those are all the friends I've managed to accrue in all my time on this earth.*

At last, Ron turns to look, and his mouth drops into a little O. He grins. *Beautiful,* he mouths. When she reaches his side, he pecks her on the cheek and takes her other hand.

For a moment, she is suspended between her two lives, holding the hands of both her mother and her almost-husband. She's in limbo between her past and her present: between Edith Laverick and Edie McVey. She swallows hard, then passes her mother's hand to Patricia.

'You're a very beautiful lady,' says her mother, so quietly Edie might have imagined it. Her heart beats so hard it threatens to burst from her chest. She is quivering, then Ron's fingers, warm, steady, around hers, gives them a squeeze and laces his fingers between hers. The heat of his palm travels through her hand, up her arm and gives her thudding heart a gentle stroke. She smiles up at him, and there's a film covering his eyes. *Don't cry, don't cry.* She turns her face to the priest about to tie them together till death do they part.

The vicar is a pointy man. Nose, ears, jaw, elbows. He's all acute angles and sharp lines. She doesn't hear a word he says, because she can hear someone sniffling continuously somewhere from Ron's side of the church. She hears the bit where he asks if anyone objects to this union and there's a honk, like someone has released a goose into the sanctum.

'Sorry,' says Hilda. 'Sinuses.'

It's a relief when the vicar says, 'I now pronounce you man and wife,' and Ron kisses her. Someone claps, and then they're out and enveloped in a blizzard of confetti, heading to the Alum House for vol-au-vents and beer.

'Well, you do make for a pretty bride.'

In the function room over the pub, Edie walks amongst these strangers, who insist on kissing her cheek and patting her arms, feeling like a stranger to herself.

'Thank you,' she says graciously, in a voice that doesn't sound much like hers. 'Thank you so much for coming.'

Ron's giant brothers take it in turns to pick her up and spin her around like she's a doll. At one point, she's hoisted onto their shoulders while they chant *'Another Mrs McVey, another Mrs McVey'* to the tune of *'The Farmer's in his Den'*.

'Oh dear,' she says, while Pats hops up and down hollering *'Yeeha!'*

There's a table piled with gifts and she gets itchy and unworthy every time she looks at it. There are more things there than are in her entire flat. Or were in her flat. She reminds herself that it's not hers any more. From tonight, she'll be living in Hilda's cosy coastal house, and she'll actually be allowed to wake up next to Ron for the first time ever. Pats said she should get up early to powder her pits and brush her teeth so as not to scare him off straight away.

'Wait until the first time you're ill to put him off you,' she said. 'It'll be too late by then.'

Edie stands on her toes and tries to look over the sea of Ron's ridiculously tall family, trying to find Patricia again, but she hasn't been seen since before the cake. She is too hot and dizzy, she just wants to hold something familiar.

'Smashing wedding, hinny,' says an old man who's at least the height of two Edies so must be related to Ron.

'Thanks for coming,' she mumbles.

'Ah!' Patricia is hovering by a stool in the corner, by the diminutive figure of Edie's mam.

'There you are, Mrs McVey,' says Pats. 'I was just looking for you.'

It takes Edie a moment to remember that she is Mrs McVey now, and has the dubious honour of sharing a name with the formidable Hilda.

Patricia pulls Edie onto a stool beside Cynthia and drops her voice. 'Listen, I think I should take your mam back. Harry said he'd drive us to Lavender Hill.'

'Okay,' says Edie. She leans over to her mother. 'Have you had a nice time, Mam?'

Cynthia nods, but her eyes are glazed over and her hair is tufting out like a dandelion clock. There's a button missing from the top of her dress and Edie reaches for the untethered threads poking out of the fabric. She gives them a gentle tug and they come away from the fabric easily.

'Did you take my button?' Cynthia asks. She looks down. 'Is this your dress?'

'No, Mam. It's yours. We got it for you, remember?' Edie takes her mother's hand in hers. 'It's going to be strange not sleeping beside you.'

'I like sleeping,' says Cynthia. 'I remember you sometimes when I'm asleep.'

Edie cracks a little like a splintered mirror.

'She's tired,' Pats says. 'It's been a big day.'

Edie kisses her mother on the head and walks her and Patricia to the door. She has to work hard not to think about Mam going back to Lavender Hill House and sleeping all alone, wrestling with the guilt every time she gets excited about the thought of getting into bed with Ron. She wants to grab Cynthia's hand, yell *Please don't go!* What they had, small and insignificant though it was, is about to leave her to fend for herself. *I'm not ready! There's still so much I need to learn.* She takes her mother's hand again, opens her mouth, though she doesn't really know what it is she wants to say.

'She'll be okay, Edie,' says Patricia, reading her face as always. 'Better even. Round-the-clock care. Harry's gone to get the car.' She spins Edie to face her. 'Now you keep your mind on the job at hand, okay? Give your man some sweet, quiet loving, and for the love of all things sexy, do not think of Hilda.'

Edie swallows, forces out a laugh, knowing now she'll be thinking of nothing but Hilda. 'We've done it before, Pats, as well you know.'

'Yeah, but not with the Hildabeest in the next room listening in!'

'Get out of here!'

Edie waves them off as the Ford carries her mother back to her new life. 'I love you so much, Mam,' she whispers to the back of the car. She sighs, and goes back inside to find her husband.

Husband. She thrills at the word.

'Lovely dress, Edith.'

'Did you throw the bouquet yet?'

'Have you got any vol-au-vents without egg in? Only eggs give me chronic wind, you see.'

Edie moves through the room smiling and nodding, but Ron is nowhere to be found. Nor is anyone familiar-looking now that everyone from her side of the church has left. She sees Hilda leaning against the bar with a half of stout; any face she recognizes will do right now.

'She's pretty, certainly,' Hilda is saying to a woman. Edie fluffs up at the compliment. 'You know our Ronnie could have had Joan Collins?' Edie's face burns and she's about to turn away when Hilda says 'But I've never seen Ron this happy. He lights up around her.'

A spring wells in Edie's eyes. *I light him up!*

'Yep, like a Christmas tree,' Hilda says. She takes a swig of her sherry. 'I wonder if people ever noticed Derek glowing up around me.'

The woman cackles. 'You set Derek alight all right! Set a furnace under his bum!'

They laugh uproariously.

'There you are, wife.'

Edie jumps when Ron wraps his arms around her and brings his chin to her shoulder. She blinks away the tears threatening to spill.

'I can't wait to consummate this marriage,' he whispers. 'Then wake up next to you every day for the rest of our lives.'

'You won't be saying that when you see me with my hair unbrushed and my make-up smudged.'

'You're lovely to me, whatever is happening with your hair and your face.'

'What about when I get old and wrinkly?'

'Then I'll be old and wrinkly with you,' he says, his breath tickling the shell of her ear. 'I think two sets of wrinkly faces cancel each other out, anyway.' He brushes his nose across her cheek. 'I'm not going anywhere, Edie-Eves. I'm yours for life.'

Edie, fizzing inside, turns and kisses her husband.

Part 3

Ball Number 17: Colliery Street, Boldon

16

Before

The lid of the serving dish is removed, spewing out the pungent scent of onion and copper. Edie's stomach contracts. She wishes she could push open the back window, let some of that delicious sea-salt air flood the room and take away the food smells.

'There you go.'

Hilda parks herself at the table, a satisfied grin on her face.

'Thanks, Mam. This smells great.' Ron nudges Edie. 'Doesn't it, Edie?'

Edie suppresses a shudder. 'Lovely, Mrs McVey.'

Hilda McVey narrows her eyes. 'Good food, this. A strapping lad like Ron needs his meat.' She smiles softly at her son, before training her beady eyes back on Edie. 'You could do with a bit of meat on your bones too. What was that mother of yours feeding you?'

Edie forces a tight smile onto her lips. 'We mostly ate sandwiches and soups.'

Hilda scoffs, shoving her sleeve up her arm. She plunges a ladle into the gloopy mess, dumping it on the mound of mashed potato cooling on Ron's plate. Edie is delighted to see her pink and orange scarf dip into the gravy, depositing a slug-trail smear of meat-grease across her white blouse. *Hah! Gravy boobs.*

The meal will be as painful as every other meal Edie has endured since moving into Ron's house after the wedding. Hilda serves up something rich and meaty, inevitably leading to overnight protracted and repeated bathroom trips. There was never much money for meat growing up, so dinners were often soup, a sandwich or whatever else she could cobble together that her mother would eat, and her body protests in the face of liver and sweetbreads. While they're eating, Hilda rattles through scandalized gossip about people Edie has never heard of. Ron's mother finally martyrizes every neighbourhood girl that Ron could have married while making overhand digs at Edie.

It's not right, Edith, married women going to work.

I mean, trim figures are nice and all, but they're no good for pushing out a strapping baby!

You couldn't stop a pig in a passage with those twiggy pegs of yours.

And Edie's personal favourite: *You should count yourself lucky. Our Ron could've married Joan Collins, you know.*

Hilda ploughs through her offaly stew, slurping and masticating loudly. Edie grimaces internally, hoping that her face isn't betraying her. She dips a hunk of bread in the gravy, avoiding a congealed lump of grease resting on the corner of her plate.

Ron's warm leg pushes against hers. She battles the grin she still feels every time he touches her. His rough fingertips trace a ribbon on her thigh. Edie shivers. His fingers stray towards the inside of her leg, and then he's caressing the tender flesh close to her groin. She nibbles the soaked bread, trying hard to keep her breathing steady. Her legs part and she pushes her body against his eager hand.

'And then Agnes Stoddart says she bets her piles are bigger than mine!'

They sigh in synch, Ron returning his hand to the table. Edie squeezes her legs together. She calculates how much they still need to save before they can buy the garage, start saving again for a deposit on a house, and frowns. They are stuck here for at least another two years. If Edie lasts that long.

She's not complaining, not really. It's lovely to be in a warm house with the sea at the back, where the carpets run all the way to the walls and there are paintings of meadows blooming with wildflowers. Hilda keeps the fireplace ready, and the lamps low and warm. At breakfast, they eat soft boiled eggs kept warm in a pretty ceramic hen, toast from a smart toast rack and tea brewed to perfection in a tea-cosied pot. Just over a mile from Edie's old neighbourhood but a world away from the dogs that barked and sirens that wailed all night. Here, the neighbours bring each other scones and gossip, not vandalism and thinly veiled warnings. There are no broken bottles threatening bicycle tyres on this street. No stench of urine and faeces overspilling from the communal toilet in the yard. Here, the pleasing scent of the lemon and vinegar Hilda uses to clean the windows.

But still, she can't wait for them to be on their own.

'Mind, no funny business while I'm at bingo.' Hilda jabs her spoon across the table at Edie, droplets of gravy splattering the tablecloth. 'It's only Wednesday. Save it for the weekend. You might be man and wife, but this is my house and you'll follow my rules.'

'Oh, Mam!' Ron circles the table to plant a kiss on his mum's head. He stands behind her, a dutiful hand on her shoulder. 'We're going to listen to *The Clitheroe Kid* and have a slice of that lovely Battenberg you made.'

Ron licks his lips suggestively at Edie. She bites her lip.

'Oh, you're a good boy, our Ronnie.' Hilda pats her son's hand, oblivious to the fact that he's now pointing at Edie and thrusting his hips. Edie giggles.

'Nothing to laugh about, my girl. You'd be lucky yourself to have a good son like Ron.'

I'd be lucky to have enough sex to get pregnant. With your indignant jowls quivering at me all the time, who needs the pill?!

Edie isn't on the pill, unlike most girls these days. Never has been, despite their flagrant disregard to consequences in the run-up to the wedding. She wants Ron to fill her belly with big fat babies that she can feed and love and call her own. Little chance with the ever-hovering Hilda and her frown of doom.

They go to the door to wave off her mother-in-law and the rest of her scuttlebutty coven, all stiff hairspray and twittering chatter.

'Bye, ladies. Enjoy.'

The door is barely shut when they slam their lips together. Edie's fingers work Ron's buttons in a flurry. Her cardigan is on the floor and her skirt hoisted around her waist, Ron's hands pressing her thighs. She pushes her hands through his hair. He grabs her face and they pause, breath shallow, chests thumping.

'I love you, Edie-Eves.'

She smiles, then kisses him hard.

They sink to the floor right there in the hallway. Edie pushes him onto his back and climbs on top.

'Oh yes!'

Edie unbuttons her blouse to the symphony of his moans. She grinds down on top of him and presses her lips to his ear.

'I've been wanting to do this all day.'

They kiss again, his fingers teasing at the elastic of her underwear.

'... I forgot my ... Oh my!'

Hilda's keys clatter to the linoleum.

'Oh god.' Edie buries her burning face in Ron's chest. Time stands agonizingly still.

'I told you to wait till the weekend!' Hilda looms over them. 'Now, that's no way to do it if you're trying to get her pregnant, Ronnie. Edith, you've got to let him tilt you underneath and let gravity do its thing.'

Edie prays for the scratchy rug to devour her.

17

After

Edie tells Jade to skip the upstairs this time because today is aqua aerobics day.

They pop off to separate bathrooms to don their swimsuits. Edie regards herself in the mirror. At the leisure centre, the class participants are all over sixty, so no one cares that it's a veritable sea of wrinkly flesh trooping from the changing rooms to the shallow end, but here, in her own bathroom, Edie can't stop staring at the papery folds around her knees and inner thighs. *At what point did I get old?*

She wraps a towel around herself and heads to the indoor heated pool at the back of the house.

Ron and Colin had almost lost their minds when they saw this. It was the only house they'd seen with an indoor pool, though as far as Edie was concerned, that was the only thing marking it out from the other six they'd viewed. All with unnecessarily large rooms that she couldn't imagine their sagging sofas and scratched tables lurking shyly in. It hadn't occurred to her that they'd get new furniture. 'I did like the one with the billiards room,' Colin said. 'What do we need a billiards room for?' Edie had asked. 'What even is billiards?'

If anyone had asked – and they hadn't – Edie might have mentioned that she would have liked a house near the beach, near where she and Ron lived with Hilda when they were first married. In fact, she'd had a sneaky look in the estate agents' windows just last week to see if anyone was selling a house just like Hilda's. They'd been happy there: truly happy. She places a hand across her chest, searching for what that felt like but comes up blank. She sighs. *Still, I'm looking forward to getting in the pool with Jade.*

Edie has only actually been in the pool twice since they moved in. Both times, she floundered around alone feeling as though she was being watched. The second time, she actually was being watched by a disapproving neighbourhood cat at the window. Under the moggy's glare, she had scuttled out of the pool and back into the kitchen to do something less ostentatious like eat toast and examine her fingernails.

Folding glass doors occupy a whole wall, offering views of the huge garden. *An aperture of horticultural delight*, was how the smarmy agent worded it. *When did 'nice garden view' become a dirty term?* Outside it's grey today, and the rain that fell earlier has streaked the glass, turning the landscape into a murky watercolour. She fumbles with the controls, trying to figure out which one works the light.

Jade comes in wearing bike shorts and a vest that says *Who's Your Daddy?* She blushes slightly, spotting Edie noticing. 'The only thing I can wrestle the watermelon into these days.'

Edie faces the wall to take off her towel, then scuttles down the steps into the water. It's nice and warm. Not bath warm, but warmer than the leisure centre pool water used to be. She grabs two bendy pool noodles from the side and waves them in Jade's general direction. 'I got these.'

'I hope you know all the moves, Edie. I've only been a couple of times.' Jade pulls out some strange little boxes and connects them all together with a complicated-looking junction of wires. She taps some buttons and Edie realizes that they are little speakers connected to a tiny contraption. 'Asif's iPod,' she says. 'Ha! Bastard's not getting it back. It's his iTunes. Hope that's all right.'

'I'm sure it'll be lovely.' She's heard of EyeTunes. *Are they English or European?*

Jade jumps straight in at the deep end and swims down to meet Edie where the water laps their chests. Edie hands her a pool noodle.

'So first we've got to . . .'

'I can't really hear you, Edie. Just do the moves and I'll copy.'

Edie nods, but her head goes blank. *Why can't I remember any moves?* Jade nods encouragingly.

Edie plants her feet apart, Jade following suit. She starts bending her knees in time to the music. She holds the pool noodle out in front of her and pushes it out and in through the water. She's pleased to realize that she can keep up with the relentless beat and starts to feel a loosening in her hips and knees.

She warms them up for the whole of the first song. Jade seems completely oblivious to the beat, and Edie smiles for a moment, thinking how much she's like the utterly uncoordinated Brenda when it comes to linking movement and music. For a moment, the injustice of her friends enjoying aqua aerobics with hair thing Sue instead of her steals her breath. But Jade's brow furrowed in almost painful concentration is incredibly sweet. She drags herself back to now.

By the end of the third song, Jade is starting to look a bit pink. In the silence between tracks, she puffs her cheeks out.

'Blimey, Edie! You've got forty-five years on me and you're moving like a professional!'

Edie ducks her head. 'Well, I was a gymnast, you know.'

'It shows!' wheezes Jade.

Edie smiles. It feels good to be active again.

'EDIE!'

Edie glances at the door. Ron's large frame is haloed by the hallway light. Edie stops marching on the spot and waves her noodle at him. Jade, oblivious to the new arrival, carries on marching and pumping.

'Why have we stopped?' she yells. Jade follows Edie's eyes. 'Ah.' She stops pumping her arms, but weirdly, keeps marching.

'Can you turn the music off?'

'What?' Jade keeps marching.

Edie puts her hands over her ears then makes a cutting gesture. 'What?'

'The music. Off.' She waves at the thumping speaker.

'I can't hear you, Edie! I'll turn the music off.' Jade rolls onto the side of the pool, staggers to her feet and switches off the music. For a moment, the only sound is the tiny plunk of droplets plopping from Jade's hair onto the tiles.

'Hello, Mr McVey.'

'Hi there . . .'

'Jade,' says Jade. 'I'm your new cleaner.'

'You're our new cleaner?' Edie can see Ron struggling against blatantly staring at Jade's belly, so he's pointedly staring at her nose instead.

'I'm your new cleaner,' Jade repeats. 'Do you want to do aqua aerobics? Edie's a really good teacher.'

'Is that right?' Ron's saggy jowls seem to have gone to war with his mouth. Edie isn't sure whether he's bemused or furious. 'Well, I'll leave you to it.'

'Bye, Mr McVey,' says Jade politely.

When he's gone, Edie's not sure why her belly is suggesting she's about to get into trouble, as though she's a schoolgirl again about to get yelled at for an overdue library book by a pointy librarian.

'Shall I put the music back on?'

'Yes, all right.'

Edie gets them to do the dog paddle hover, but can't get the opposite hand to leg coordinated, which in turn, makes Jade flail like she's drowning.

'Sorry,' she says to Jade. 'I'm doing it all wrong now. Look, shall we call it a day?'

Jade agrees, and as they stumble from the pool and Edie waves Jade off to the guest showers, she finds herself hot with failure. She did aqua for five years. *How can you not even get the dog paddle hover right?*

Later, when Edie is helping Jade into the taxi with her stuff, Jade pats her arm. 'Thanks, Edie. That was exactly what I needed.' She pulls her in for a loose hug.

It's been a good while since Edie had a hug and before she can stop herself she tightens her hold and squeezes Jade back. Jade lets her for a moment, then gently releases Edie, but with a kind smile. Perhaps that class wasn't such a failure after all.

Ron has made a pot of tea. He sits at the table tapping a teaspoon on the back of his hand.

Edie rubs her hair with a towel and joins him.

'You looked like you were having fun.'

'I was!'

'I . . . Edie, what are you doing?'

'Drying my hair.'

'No! That! In the pool. With the cleaner.'

'Aqua aerobics. You told me to do that.'

He pats her hand. 'I sort of meant do it with your friends, not with the cleaner.'

'Her name is Jade.'

'Jade the cleaner.' He takes her hand in his. 'Look, I don't know what's going on with you, sweetheart, but why don't you invite Carol and Brenda over?'

'Carol and Brenda don't want to come.'

'Well, then maybe you can find some new friends locally. There's that Russian woman about your age at that place with the fountain.'

'She's terrifying!'

'I'm sure she's lovely once you get to know her.'

'She made the checkout girl in the Co-op cry.' Edie goes out of her way to avoid walking past the scary Russian woman's house. 'What's wrong with Jade?'

'Nothing!' says Ron. 'She seems really . . .'

'Really what?'

'Round. Edie, when is that baby of hers due?'

'It's not a baby, she just had too much chicken jalfrezi,' says Edie, but Ron isn't smiling. 'Soon. Maybe ten weeks.'

'Why did you employ a pregnant cleaner who's only going to get more pregnant and then go on maternity leave?'

She hasn't told him how she met Jade, or their connection. She is worried he'll think that she's mad, constantly going to their old house, or pining, or some equally odd trait that he can't quite wrap his head around.

'Look,' he says gently. 'I'm so sorry, Edie-Eves. You're here and your friends are twenty miles away. I could drive you to aqua aerobics with Carol and Brenda.'

'I don't want to do aqua aerobics with Carol and Brenda. I want to do aqua aerobics with Jade.'

'Edie, she's a pregnant teenager that we're employing to clean our house.'

'She's twenty-three.'

'Okay, well she's a pregnant twenty-three-year-old that we're employing to clean our house.' Ron pours a tea for her. It's in a stupid little ceramic cup instead of her favourite mug that Carol got her for her sixtieth. 'Edie, I'm not sure what you're trying to achieve here.'

'Achieve?' She laughs, although it's not actually funny. *Has Ron really not noticed how lost I've been?* 'Well, maybe a healthy body and a nice new friendship. That would be a good achievement.'

'Sweetheart, I know what you're like.' He tilts his head, shrugs. 'One minute she's the cleaner, next, you're helping her out with the high cupboards, before you know it, you're cleaning full time again and she's on the couch watching *Countdown* and you're fetching her biscuits.'

That sounds lovely. She grins, hoping her face doesn't give away that she's halfway to doing that anyway. She sips her tea. 'Yuk! What's this?'

'It's oolong. The lady in Fenwick's said it was a gourmet tea.'

'It tastes like moss.'

'It's gourmet.'

'It's grim.' Edie pushes away from the table and puts on the kettle. She gets the Tetley out and finds her mug by the sink. She keeps her back to Ron while she waits for the water to boil.

'Edie, I want nice things for you now,' Ron sighs. 'You just seem a bit . . .'

'A bit what?'

'I don't know.' He screws his face up. 'Like you're trying a bit hard to be humble.'

'Trying a bit hard to be humble?' Edie tips the scalding water into her cup, slopping some on the counter as her hand trembles. '*Trying* a bit hard? To be *humble*?' She shakes her head. 'We're from Boldon Colliery, Newcastle's dirty little cousin. I *am* humble. Everyone in Boldon Colliery is humble. We're nothing special. All we've done is moved twenty miles north, not scaled the Alps. We won the stupid lottery, that's the only thing that makes us different! We're no better than everyone in Boldon Colliery. Or Jade. We're just normal people in a stupid house with ridiculous cars.' She slops the milk into her drink and fishes out the teabag with a spoon. She doesn't look at Ron as she slams the soggy bag in the bin, splashes of tea landing on the floor, and marches out of the kitchen.

Sod you, Ron.

In the hallway, Ron's latest *Top Gear* magazine sits on the table under the framed ticket. She tears the front cover off, folds Jeremy Clarkson and his Ferrari into a paper aeroplane and watches him sail into the front door where he crash-lands on the mat.

And sod you too, Clarkson.

18

Before

She almost misses the bus to Stoke-on-Trent but, thankfully, one of the passengers left his suitcase at the station, so the driver turned around to get it for him.

'Fate,' winks the old man, reunited with his luggage. Edie winks back.

She'd been visiting her mam at Lavender Hill House before getting the bus to see Patricia and time had escaped her. 'I'm doing so well, aren't I?' Cynthia had said as Edie was readying to leave. Cynthia had shrunk slightly since moving into the home, and slumped in that oversized armchair, she looked like a child. Edie had needed a few moments to pat her wet face down in the bathroom before returning for the goodbyes. 'You're doing just great, Mam,' she'd said and Cynthia had lit up like a fairground. 'Tell Patricia hi,' she whispered when Edie was almost out the door.

She needs this trip. Needs to get out from under Hilda and Ron's feet. It's not that she's unhappy. She isn't. Ron is wonderful, making her smile and laugh and waking up with his heavy arm across her waist is even better than she dreamed it would be. But she is tired. She's cleaning at the Bamburgh Arms now, as well as the town hall and Betty, the girl who replaced Patricia at the end of last month, is so slow, Edie ends up doing twice as much now anyway. She tips herself into bed yawning every night, sometimes before Ron is even home from the garage. And Hilda hasn't been nearly as bad as she imagined she would be, but Edie really wants a space to call her own now. Somewhere to make the cushion covers and throw blankets she's been snipping patterns for out of the newspaper.

For the next three days, she'll help Patricia get ready for her wedding, though Patricia readily admits that she's done everything already and just wants a natter with her pal for old times' sake. Pats has spent the last few weeks moving her stuff down there, but last week, they hugged goodbye at the bus station and cried on each other's shoulders. It already seems like a lifetime, and time stretches out in front of her like a flat, fogged mirror. When she calls, Pats says that it's like Newcastle, but with 'more pottery and less friendly'.

'Awful long way to Stoke-on-Trent,' says a woman with a basket of apples on her lap.

'Yes,' says Edie. 'Hours.'

'What you going to Stoke-on-Trent for?'

'A wedding.' Edie points out of the window, though she's not sure why. 'It's my friend. She's marrying a roofer.'

'A roofer!' says the woman. 'Does she love him?'

Is the woman amazed that anyone could love a roofer or something else entirely? Edie shrugs. 'I don't know,' she says. 'I expect she will in time.'

'Hmm,' says the woman, and promptly falls asleep.

When the bus pulls into Stoke-on-Trent, the sleeping woman wakes up long enough to yell: 'Tell her: if she doesn't love him – run.' She snorts and chews at something from her dreams.

Edie giggles, already looking forward to telling Pats the story.

Patricia greets her with a huge hug.

'So happy to see you, Edie. These Stoke-on-Trent lasses think they're better than Geordie girls.' She steps back and surveys Edie's neat waist. 'No bun in the oven yet, then?'

'It's been a week, Pats!' laughs Edie. Then, serious, 'It'll happen, won't it?'

'Of course! Now, I have to tell you right now about Alan's mother. Christ, Edie! You think Hilda's bad! This one's bought me a plot in the local graveyard. I think she's planning on doing away with me.'

They're staying in the boxroom of Alan's Aunt Peggy, who Patricia suspects to be entirely deaf but good at lip reading. It's a tight fit, two women, three suitcases and a wedding dress: made tighter still by the fact that the wardrobe is steepled with wedding gifts for the happy couple.

Patricia sighs and pokes her wedding dress which mushrooms out from amongst cheerfully wrapped boxes. Edie adds her own to the pile.

'It's not much,' she says. 'Money's a bit tight at the moment while we save for the garage.'

'Still got his heart set on that, has he?' says Patricia. 'Let me take you out for a cream bun and you can tell me all about work and if bloody Maureen is limping on her left or her right these days. I swear, Edie, it switched every twenty minutes. Arthritis, my foot!'

Half an hour later, squashed into a corner table by a fogged-up cafe window, Edie concludes that cream buns taste the same wherever you go, and there's something both reassuring and depressing about this.

'So, I've been reading about these young people,' says Pats over tea. 'They don't get married, they don't clean offices or eat Hilda's horrible cooking or save for deposits on dreary flats in Harton. They get on buses and cross the continent and go to India and Afghanistan and places like that.'

'Really?' Edie frowns. 'Why would they do that?'

'Adventure,' says Patricia. 'It's called the Hippie Trail. They travel for days and days at a time and see things and eat things and meet people.'

'Sounds a bit pointless,' says Edie. 'What do they do when they're finished?'

'Well, come home, I suppose.' Patricia shrugs. 'Or maybe not. I mean, who's to say who you'd meet doing such a thing?'

'Sounds crazy!'

'I suppose.' Patricia drops another sugar cube into her tea. 'Alan's Aunt Peggy won't let me have sugar or anything nice before the wedding. No butter on my "cob", no milk in my tea. She's a tyrant. Says I won't fit into my wedding dress.'

'Hilda's trying to do quite the opposite. She's trying to fatten me up for babies. I feel like the children in "Hansel and Gretel".'

'Swap you.'

'Are you excited? About the wedding?'

'No,' says Patricia. 'Anyway, tell me about the bus woman again?'

'She said, "If she doesn't love him, tell her to run."' Edie licks the last dollop of cream off her finger. 'I should have told her you never listen to anyone.'

Patricia smiles but looks away, watching a stray tear of condensation make an escape down the window. 'Too right.'

*

It's a light breeze that causes Edie to wake in the thin grey light of morning.

'Pats, what are you doing?' Edie rubs her eyes and sits up. Patricia is halfway out of the window with a bright yellow toaster under her arm.

'I'm doing it, Edie.'

'Doing what?'

Patricia's eyes glint out of the gloam. There's a wildness that Edie has never seen before. She kneels up and peers out of the window. Below the sill, a bag spitting out tea towels and tablecloths leans against the wall.

'I'm going to get on the bus.' She puts the toaster on top of the bag and clambers back into the room, then hauls her suitcase across the floor. 'Bugger, this is heavy.'

The room is littered with sheets of wrapping paper, bows and boxes. Picture frames and doilies and cushions lie like hurricane victims on the tallboy and floor.

'This is madness, Pats! What have you done?!'

Patricia jumps back onto the bed and takes her friend by the shoulders. 'No, Edie. What's madness is marrying someone I don't love. This is the Sixties. We don't have to turn into our mothers any more.'

'But, Pats . . .'

'No. You can't change my mind, Edie. I've been thinking about us, women, people. About my mam and how she wanted to learn Chinese and visit the East, instead of growing big and bored and lonely with a man who can't even take her to the beach on her birthday. I'm not having that. I'm going off to live and breathe and be.' She points to her suitcase. 'I'm taking some stuff to sell, getting a passport and getting on that bus.'

Edie can't decide whether to say *Patricia Lydon, unpack that suitcase at once!* Or to help her shove it out the window. It's one thing to move to Stoke-on-Trent, quite another to traverse the Khyber Pass with a bunch of strangers speaking in different languages and eating leaves or whatever it is they eat over there. If she does go, Patricia's mother will act shocked, but a tiny smile will creep across her face when she thinks no one's looking. Because, despite being a model mother and loyal wife, there's always been a little something – a tug, a twitch – of dissatisfaction about Mrs Lydon that finally makes sense.

Edie wants to say *Please don't leave me*, but her beautiful, fiery friend needs more than a boring shingle enthusiast and a pre-prepared burial mound. She hops out of bed and takes one end of the suitcase.

'You promise to send postcards?'

Patricia nods. 'I promise.'

They wrestle the suitcase through the frame, taking a fair bit of paint off in the process.

'What shall I tell everyone?' asks Edie.

'Tell them whatever you like,' says Pats, kissing her on the cheek. 'Look after yourself, Edie. I'll always be here for you.'

And then she's gone, dress billowing as she leaps out the window, leaving Edie staring into the empty yard, relieved that Aunt Peggy lives on the ground floor.

Edie lets out an enormous *whoop!*

Well done, Pats, she whispers to a judgemental red-brick wall. *Well done, girl.*

19

After

There's a good sun this morning and a blonde light washes everything into dazzling brightness. The glare bounces off the marble counter tops and Edie again wishes they'd got a farmhouse kitchen with wood and painted doorknobs. Not this sleek stuff. It reminds her of American films where glamorous women have penthouses and wear their clacking heels indoors and never cook but always seem to have an abundance of champagne and strawberries in their space-age silver fridges. Ron's voice in her head says, *Never happy, Edie*, and she shakes away the image of a ceramic pot with a lid the shape of a hen to keep the eggs warm like Hilda used to have. She has no idea where you'd even get such a thing these days.

Ron is frying sizzling strips of bacon while Colin fiddles with his fancy coffee machine.

'Would you like a coffee, Mam?'

'I don't like coffee.'

'But this is good stuff. Like in the cafes, and Paris.'

'Bon appetite!' says Ron, passing her a bacon sandwich, along with a stiff envelope. 'For you, Edie-Eves.'

She plucks a handful of tickets out of the envelope. Four little orange-edged rectangles announcing that two people will be travelling first class from Newcastle to London and back again in August. A further four tickets proudly declare that their owners will be attending a matinee performance of *Jersey Boys* and an evening show of *Blood Brothers*.

'A theatre trip?'

'West End, no less.' Ron sits back in his chair grinning. 'And there's a printout in there of the hotel. I asked them on the phone to do that. To send the printout. Look, it's a bit fancy! And I booked you this special massage and hair and nails package thing for the Sunday morning. They were fully booked so I had to pull a few strings. I splashed the cash a bit, told them how special you are and, suddenly, they agreed!' He shakes his head as though he has just this moment learned that people like to do things for money. 'You're going to be treated like royalty.'

The only musical the three of them have ever seen is *Cats* at the Tyne Theatre that time, and that unwanted Christmas gift still leaves a bitter taste in Edie's mouth. She sees them sifting through old clothes to find their fanciest things, tights with a hole in the toe, and her weeping inconsolably when the tattered old cat threw her memories all over a cold pavement.

'It won't be like *Cats*, Edie.'

'You nearly peed yourself, Dad, when that creepy cat fella stroked your arm.' Colin laughs loudly, and Edie marvels that he seems to have forgotten everything else about that Christmas.

Ron shudders. 'His leotard was really tight.'

Edie makes herself smile. 'That's lovely, Ron. Thank you.'

'My pleasure!' Ron gives her a chaste peck on the cheek. She pats his leg. 'And now, Colin. Your present.'

He tears at his envelope with the enthusiasm of a puppy with a sock. 'Ah, Dad! Really?' Ron nods proudly. 'But this sold out months ago! How did you . . .? Did you . . .?' He examines the paper in his hand. 'You did! Dad, these are full VIP!'

'What is it?' Edie cranes her neck, but can't see the details.

'The *Top Gear* Roadshow. At Birmingham NEC.'

'Wow! That's brilliant. Dream come true, eh, Col?'

Ron and Colin immediately begin babbling about who's going to be there and what cars they can expect to see. Edie's really, *really* not a fan of cars, but she's enjoyed watching them get excited about things again since the win and they seem closer than they have in years. She picks up the programme sent alongside the tickets. It's glossy and stiff: a picture of men with folded arms standing in front of a fast-looking car adorns the front cover.

'Great engine though.'

'This is on the ninth.'

'What?'

'The roadshow.' Edie stands. 'It's on the ninth.'

Ron's face suddenly falls. 'Edie, I'm sorry. I didn't realize that was the date—'

'So I'm going to be here all on my own?' Edie's voice is low and wobbly.

'Edes, I'm sorry, okay.' He sighs. 'Look, I had to pull some strings to get us these. It's a dream for Colin. And we can do something the next night.'

'The next night isn't relevant. My birthday is the ninth.' She fights back a sob. 'You said I'd never have a birthday alone. And I haven't and I love that . . . and what, without Sean . . .'

'Oh, love.' Ron winces. 'Edes, it's just this one time. This is the only date they had left and even they were a struggle. I'm so so sorry, love, I will make it up to you.'

'You said . . .' Edie dislikes the wobble in her voice. She tries to shift it. 'We've hardly spent any time together recently. I thought we could do something nice, go somewhere new now we can finally afford it.' Then quietly, 'I've been looking forward to doing something nice with you.'

'So what's the theatre trip then, if not us doing something nice together?'

'But that's after.' The tears are beginning to well now. 'And the phone . . .'

Ron and Colin side-eye one another. For the last fifteen years, Edie has received a silent phone call on her birthday. The speaker never says anything, just breathes quietly on the other end. She figured out that it was Sean calling a few years in and, since then, she talks into the empty silence, reassured at least that she is being heard.

Of course, Ron and Colin don't believe her. 'It could be anyone,' said Ron last time. 'You've got to stop doing this to yourself.' They're never home when he calls, give each other shifty looks when she tells them about it. But Edie knows that it's Sean.

And now that they've moved, he won't have their new number. She's made sure they are listed in the phone book though, and let local newspapers come and photograph the house with the number visible in the hope that he can look up the number and find them.

'Look.' Colin puts his hand on her arm. 'The main events are over by six anyway. We could leave at five. Be home around eight. How does that sound?'

She wants to say *Yes, please. Don't leave me alone in this big, strange house on my birthday*. Instead, she gives Colin a tight smile. 'It doesn't matter. Enjoy the roadshow.'

He looks at her for too long before turning back to his breakfast. Edie glares at the side of Ron's head and wonders if he ever even thinks about her any more. She sees swinging dark hair and a woman in tight jeans and shadows in an alleyway. Edie shakes her head to dislodge the memory, but it sits there, a stubborn cobweb that she can't quite reach.

20

Before

They're like butterflies, these babies. Just when you think you've caught one in the net, it flutters away, and the knotty strings of the net are just that – knotty strings: empty and tangled and useless.

Edie looks down at the ugly, mocking bloom in her underwear. She'll have to throw these knickers away: can't face Hilda's tuts, or worse, the pitying tilt of the head if she tries to wash them. Patricia's jaunty postcards from dusty-sounding bazaars in Cairo and Istanbul are written in code. *Did you manage to bake a ham yet?* they'll say. Or, *Have you been cooking lots of toad-in-the-hole?* She wishes she was here to wrap her in a hug, then make her snort with laughter. Wishes she could talk to someone about the broken shards of hope gathering at her feet.

This one's number six. She hasn't even told Ron about it, doesn't want to see the disappointment stamped on his lips again.

Who might you have been, little one? she asks softly. *Who would I have been?*

She slips the underwear off and balls it up, trying to avoid looking into the toilet bowl. She doesn't want to see her disappointment in clumps of flesh and blood. She shoves the offending underwear deep into her pocket.

Edie pulls the chain, dries her eyes on the back of her hand. *You should be used to this by now.* But she isn't and it stings her eyes and her skin and her poor empty belly.

There's a part of her – a nugget somewhere in the depths of her head – that says *Maybe it's for the best, Edie.* That the universe is trying to tell her something.

'Shhh,' she says to the voice, soothing it like she would a child. 'Shhh.'

She washes her hands with a new bar of Pears and heads downstairs to bury the underwear in the kitchen bin.

Hilda is elbow-deep in soapsuds singing 'Cushie Butterfield' in a key not designed for human voices to reach or ears to process. Though they've been living with Hilda for nearly two years now, it has only been in the last few months that Edie has come to a grudging respect for Ron's mother. Certainly, she's judgemental and loud, but there's a simplicity to her that Edie admires. Things are just things. Everything is exactly what it is in Hilda's world. She doesn't wallow around in her head like a disintegrating potato in soup. And since they finally got the deposit for the garage last year, Ron has been working and working to get that off the ground while they start saving for a house of their own.

'Ah, Edith. Not working today?'

Hilda's hands are covered in bubbles from the sink, like she's wearing fluffy evening gloves.

'The offices are closed. Burst pipes. Got some workmen in.'

Hilda looks at her consideringly for a moment then grins. 'Excellent! I'm in the mood for fish and chips. Would you like to join me?'

Edie wouldn't like to join her, but she *would* like fish and chips.

And besides, she can't come up with a decent enough reason why she shouldn't go. She pushes her hand into her pocket, suddenly worried that the underwear is glowing like a beacon from her skirt.

'Yes. That would be lovely. Thank you, Hilda.'

Hilda flicks the soap off her arms and back into the sink. It floats like snowflakes, and Edie is struck with an image of the three of them at the dinner table on another childless Christmas. She turns from Hilda, a lump in her throat that can't be swallowed down.

'I'm just going to fetch my cardigan,' she calls in a strangled voice.

They walk across the meadowy grasses of The Leas, sandwiched between the steep cliff drops that lead to the sea and the rest of Britain. Below the earth, the catacombs of smugglers' caves hide in the cliff sides with all their secrets and deceptions and heartaches huddling away from prying eyes. Hilda puffs from time to time, but otherwise, the only sound is the screech of coastal gulls battling for scraps of a discarded picnic over the smeared-mirror surface of the North Sea.

For a moment, Edie imagines that it is her own mother she is walking across The Leas with a gentle sea breeze blowing Cynthia's brittle spun-sugar hair out of her eyes.

She keeps her eyes on the ground, trying hard not to think about the baby dripping out of her like raindrops. She can't let her head rollercoaster again like it did the first time.

It had happened in the night, and Edie had walked out into the dark and the rain, grief-blind and broken. At the forefront of her memory are Ron's shifting eyebrows, the frown lines like a child's drawing of the sea etched across his forehead, gently guiding her back inside. It wasn't until the next day that Edie realized that Ron did for her what she had done for her mother in the past: guided her home like a child. The thought that she was turning into her mam had set her off into a panic. In the weeks that followed, she worked hard to smile again: at Ron, at the tip-a-wink grocer, at the other cleaners with their smoky breath and tinpot laughter. Then the taunt of her still-tender breasts, the grapefruit mould of her belly would bring it all back, winding her, stealing her air, rendering her powerless against the tide of battering emotions and a head that couldn't stay afloat.

Colman's is busy, but Hilda shoulder-barges a young man in a Concord-wing collared shirt for the little table by the window. He scowls, but correctly reads that Hilda is not a woman to be messed with and slopes away. Edie flashes him an apologetic shrug, but she only half means it. She's tired and sad and wants to sit in the comfy chair looking at people who are having ordinary days.

Hilda orders for them both: battered cod and chips with a pot of tea.

'On me,' she says.

Edie takes off her cardigan and drapes it over the back of the chair. The window is clouded with condensation, and for a moment, she has to work hard not to write the name she'd picked out for this one in the mist.

'Now,' says Hilda, resting her elbows on the table and clasping her hands together, bringing Edie's attention back from a name it was too early to have picked out anyway. 'I wanted to have a little word with you.'

Edie withers slightly. Hilda's 'little words' are often long and convoluted, sandwiched between so many layers of inconsequential detail, Edie gets lost and is never entirely sure which bit is supposed to be the 'little word'.

Hilda searches Edie's face. 'You work too hard,' she says softly and Edie's breath gets stuck in her chest somewhere. 'Course, in my day, women didn't work so we could concentrate a bit more on the baby side of things. You career girls have made a rod for your own backs, really.' She shakes her head ruefully. 'Anyway,' she continues, 'that's not what I wanted to talk about.'

She pauses to frown at the empty space on the table where their tea should be, then clears her throat.

'You and Ronald seem to be having some difficulties getting a baby in you.' She nods. 'Or at least getting one to stick. So I thought you might like a little bit of wisdom from someone who's been there.' Hilda waves away some imaginary objection Edie has put up. 'I know, I know. You look at me and you think, "What would she know? She's pushed four strapping lads out of her." But it isn't that simple, and I'm going to tell you something I've never told Ron.'

Edie's body has tensed of its own accord. She pictures the underwear, now stuffed between the mattress and the bed frame at home, and feels her ears heating up. Whatever is coming, Edie isn't ready for it. Whatever it is, there will be no going back.

'There were five more,' says Hilda after a pause. 'Five. Some as early days as yours have been, some late and big and so real. And one was eight weeks earthside, but little and sick and just not ready for the world.' She sticks a finger in the corner of her eye. 'The sad never goes away, Edith. Never. So I do understand.' Hilda picks up her fork and twiddles it in circles. 'But if you want it, you have to put that aside. Keep on trying. What do they call it? Perseverance, I think.' She shrugs. 'Anyway. Keep trying is what I'm saying.'

Edie wants to pat Hilda's beefy hand: to say, *I never would have guessed it*, but she's at once very rigid and at the same time too soft, like ice cream in a hot room.

'Ah,' says Hilda when the teapot is placed between them. 'About time. I'm parched!'

Hilda pours, then rolls up her sleeves. 'So,' she says. 'Down to the nitty gritty. If you want boys – and I'm telling you, you do, because they're a heck of a lot easier than girls – you've got to go at it at particular times. My mam used to say, "Saturday shenanigans sire sons," but I prefer the saying "Weekends warrant willies."'

Edie almost spits out her tea.

'So, you need to really get down to it on Saturdays. Worked for me. All my lads conceived on Saturdays, except Ron, but he was more likely the early hours of Sunday morning, cause his dad had been down the Grotto and it took till the morning for me to sober him up enough. Still, close though.'

Involuntarily, a grin spreads across Edie's face. She can't wait to tell Patricia about this conversation next time she calls, her voice all tinny and far away. She'll gag!

As Hilda launches into an animated monologue about the best angles for impregnation, complete with complicated hand gestures, Edie tries to let her mother-in-law's demonstrations of 'tilting' and 'pumping' fade into the bustle of the cafe. There's a glimmer of something, faint but present, there behind the noise and the ache. Maybe, just maybe, she's going to be okay after all.

21

After

A light breeze rustles the hawthorn at the end of their drive. Edie braved a three-quarter-length sleeve to try out the bakery she's been hassling Ron to go to with her, and the soft hairs by her wrist shiver as she squints up at the late-spring sunshine winning the battle against the clouds.

The curtains in Ron's bedroom at the front are firmly drawn. An odd jolt passes through her as she pictures him slumbering there alone. The body she has lain beside for more than forty years seems like a stranger's when imagined from the bottom of a gravel driveway flanked by spring elms.

She'd asked him to come to the bakery again yesterday, but he'd met her with a yawn and a 'Maybe. If I'm up.'

Across from their house, the scary Russian lady stands just outside her gates, a young man squatting by the gatepost at her feet.

'More quickly,' she yells in her heavy accent, as the young man tears weeds from the hairline of the brickwork. 'Fast, fast.'

The woman is wearing what looks like a safari hat that's too big for her. A creamy, rosebud-studded nightdress billows provocatively, her hands are encased in gardening gloves, and she is wielding a pair of secateurs.

Apart from the three of them, the long, wide road is empty. Almost eerily so. In Boldon, the street was always bustling with people going somewhere or doing something. Running a hyperactive toddler to the park, dropping in on someone or other, chatting loudly outside the convenience shop. Here, save for an occasional jogger or dog walker, the streets are oddly quiet. Edie pretends to be looking for something in her handbag as she turns into the street and starts walking.

'Hey, hey, lady.'

Edie contemplates ignoring her, or shouting *Please dear god don't talk to me*, but the ever-present polite English woman who's never said boo to a goose is left behind as the other two ideas beat a hasty retreat out of the realms of possibility.

She stops, waving limply as she turns.

'Come here.' But the woman is already marching across the street brandishing her garden weaponry. She stops about a foot in front of Edie and looks her up and down. The secateurs are between the two women, and Edie briefly wonders if she plans to stab her with them.

'Why you not being nice to your husband?' Her accent is fast and sharp.

Edie frowns. 'I'm sorry?'

'Yes,' yells the woman. 'You should be very sorry. Your husband is a nice man. My husband was a very bad man.'

'Right.'

'Ron is very nice.' She says his name as *Rrrrn* with a rolling R and a missing vowel, so it sounds like a purr.

Edie stares at her. The woman stares back. Edie clears her throat and steps around the woman.

'Where you going?' The secateurs are in Edie's face and the scary woman attached to them has somehow got back in front of her, blocking her way.

'I'm going to buy a cream bun.' Edie isn't sure why she has volunteered so much information, or why her voice has gone overly posh.

'No!' The woman points the secateurs back towards Edie's house. 'You go home and make nice. You not nice to your husband, some other lady will be.'

'Well, thank you for the advice,' says Edie. *Carry on walking! Ignore this crazy woman!* But her body has other ideas. Edie slowly turns away and retraces her steps back towards their stupid house with the stupid Greek statues and the five-year-old mock Georgian pillars. *This is a ridiculous place.* Over her shoulder, she sees the woman making a shooing gesture at her. *A stupid place full of crazy rich people.* Her heart is thumping. *You're a grown woman, for Pete's sake, why are you doing as you're told by a crazy neighbour?* Closing the gate, she observes the strangely dressed neighbour charging back to her own home like a jousting knight.

'Weed faster, boy,' she hollers at the poor sap who had stopped to watch two old ladies face off in the street.

Edie considers lurking behind the tree until she has gone back inside, but, judging by the resignation on the face of her employee, they're going to be out there for a while.

She sighs and heads indoors, wondering if Elton John fancies a house swap.

Later that morning, Edie writes 'VANCOUVER' across the last boxes and gives a satisfied nod. It's been a while since she has finished the *Woman's Weekly* crossword. She used to ask Ron for help if she got stuck on a clue, or, for anything vaguely popular culture-related, she'd ask Colin, but neither of them have been around much lately. A bunch of magazines languish around the house sporting unfinished crosswords, until she puts them by one of the toilets and, inevitably, the empty boxes get filled.

'I thought you'd gone out.'

Startled, she swishes a messy line across the page. She flings the magazine on the table, making a surprisingly loud slap for a cheap bundle of paper.

'I did, Ron. I was about to go to the bakery. But then I came back.'

'Tea?'

'No.' Edie does want a cup of tea, but is inexplicably irritated that Ron hasn't asked her why she came back. 'I met your Russian lady friend in the street.' She isn't looking at him, but Ron stops what he's doing. 'Had a nice chat, we did. About how horrible I am to you, apparently.'

She hears his sigh.

'Edie, I . . .'

'Oh no. It's fine. We all need someone to talk to, right? About our terrible spouses.'

He comes towards the table, hands upturned like a supplicating saint. 'It's not like that, Edie.'

'What is it like then?' Edie can hear how clipped her voice sounds.

'Verushka needed some help with her car.' When he says her name, he rolls the R, making Edie's fist clench. 'Absolute beauty, she is.'

'Who, Verrrrrushka?' Edie imitates the roll, lips curling.

'No! Her car. Really lovely Aston Martin. Slate grey, sleek as you like. Of course, she drives it like a hippo in Doc Martens. Stamp, stamp, stamp.' He shakes his head.

'Why didn't you tell me you'd fixed her car?'

'Are you jealous?' He's grinning.

'Well, I don't find it that funny, that's all,' says Edie. 'You're always out somewhere squirrelling away. You never spend any time with me any more.' Ron sits with a sigh and Edie fights a wave of indignation. 'Oh, I know, let's all get exasperated with silly old Edie, shall we? She wants this, she wants that, she's never happy. She's the luckiest woman out there and she still moans. Selfish, wicked Edie. And now I'm just rattling around this big house on my own thinking about how Sean—'

'Oh, Edie,' says Ron, waving an open palm to the room. 'Look at this place! Moving here was the fresh start we needed.' He nods approvingly to the room, as if seeing it for the first time. He takes one of her hands, drops his voice soft and low. 'I thought we could leave a bit of the past behind.'

'It's not the past!' says Edie. 'It's my all the time. My present. My future. I can't—'

'Edie,' says Ron, but then he stops with his mouth open. 'Look, Verushka asked if I thought you'd like to join her lady golf team. Someone's out with whiplash apparently.'

'Hmph,' grumbles Edie, her hackles lowering slightly. 'Probably from being a passenger in her car.'

They both smile, fleetingly, and Edie marvels that her handsome Jimmy Mack is still there in the grin, hiding behind this wrinkly thing she's stood by through all of this. She wants so badly for it all to be okay.

'Ron, I . . .'

'I wasn't moaning about you,' he says. 'Promise. I just said that you weren't very happy with me at the moment.'

'I'm not.'

He nods. 'Do you think you might be happy with me by the time we go to London?'

'Oh, I don't know. Do you think you might have changed the *Top Gear* Roadshow tickets for a day other than my birthday so I don't have to spend it alone without a single one of my boys?'

The air is thick as custard. Ron opens his mouth, reaches into his pocket for his mobile phone, then gives his head a barely perceptible shake.

'Edie, I . . .' He runs his hand through his hair, sighs again, then he's up and out. Four and a half minutes later, she hears the whisper of Ron's Jaguar on the gravel.

She hits one of the stupid grey cushions with a fist and it feels good. She does it again and again, until it's not enough any more. She needs to get up, do something. She stands.

Without giving herself time to think, she unbuttons her cardigan. Right there in the lounge, with the curtains wide open to the blank-eyed street that doesn't care, she takes off all her clothes leaving them scattered on the couch. She jogs through the house to the pool room, takes a running dive and swims and swims until her shoulders ache and her lungs are bursting and her head is clear.

22

Before

Edie likes it: she likes having a full ripe body, a far cry from her usual twiggish form. She likes the balloony mound of her belly that pushes her clothing out. She likes her cherry-tipped breasts and their swelling secret liquid gold that she is brewing up in there. But more than that, she likes the feel of the baby pulling and changing direction like a school of fish in a current.

She likes, too, the way her limbs are softening and opening, easing back into her gymnast's body. Her legs butterfly all the way to the sides when she pulls the soles of her feet together, and she can almost – almost – sit into a side split again. She just about has space to do this between the bed and the wardrobe in a room that is now cramped with a cot and an extra set of drawers for the baby's clothes.

'You look like a little pumpkin,' says Ron, kissing her head.

Ron's pregnancy glow is shining almost brighter than hers: business is booming and since they got far enough into another pregnancy to start believing that babies were coming, he's been walking on air. At Hilda's birthday party surrounded by his family, flushed with the success of the blossoming McVey's Motors, Ron could barely keep the tears from falling, patting Edie's belly, and saying 'This is everything I ever dreamed of.' Over egg salad sandwiches and sliced malt loaf, they'd toasted their bright future.

They are, of course, still living with Hilda, which was not in their life plan, but they are making the best of it. The garage is starting to make money now, but neither of them had anticipated some of the other start-up costs – signs, advertising, insurance – and their deposit pile dwindled. They've started again, but now, with the baby on the way, they've had to dip into it again to get all the baby things organized. Hilda says she *supposes* it is okay if they stay, but she's almost as glowy as Ron, and Edie suspects she's just as excited as they are about having a baby in the house.

She is around halfway through the pregnancy when a doctor mumbles something about two heartbeats.

'Mine?' she asks, and the doctor stares at her like she's just said, 'Jelly and ice cream,' instead of reaching a perfectly logical conclusion about a confusing statement.

'Three, if we include yours, Mrs McVey. Which we don't.'

'Twins! Crumbs.'

Ron goes an attractive shade of yellow and appears to have lost the use of his facial muscles.

At home, Hilda gives her the royal treatment. Edie doubts the Duchess of Kent was waited on this much.

'Twins,' Hilda says admiringly, eyeing Edie's growing belly. 'Never managed twins, myself, but I would have liked to. Well done.'

'There's two of them, Pats,' she squeals when her friend phones. 'Can you believe it?'

'So happy for you, Edie. Your dreams are coming true.'

'And your dreams?' she asks.

'Ah, I've no time for dreaming,' says Pats. 'Too busy loving. I'm telling you, Edie. The world is populated with foreign Rons!' She pauses. 'And the occasional foreign Alan, unfortunately.'

'That is unfortunate.'

'Well,' says Pats. 'They still need roofs in Morocco.'

'Oh, Pats,' she says. 'I'm so proud of you. Look at us, doing a better job of being happy than our parents.'

If it isn't Patricia calling from some dusty phone box in a cardamom-spiced piazza, it's Sandra or Beverley or Jean from Lavender Hill House. When they do, she immediately hits the cradle to disconnect the call. She keeps the receiver pressed to her ear and pretends to talk, smiling at Ron or Hilda if they pass. She isn't sure why she is pretending but she's suddenly terrified of sharing her pregnancy with her mother. It's stupid, but she's consumed with the idea that her mother's problems might somehow infect the babies. She hates herself for thinking that: knows deep down that if the babies are going to inherit Cynthia's problems, they're going to come directly through Edie anyway, but she just doesn't want them around her. *Mmhmm*, she'll say. *A tea dance! How wonderful. Yes, yes, of course. I'll be there Monday. Thanks for calling. Bye bye.*

'Is your mother doing well?' Hilda will ask.

'So well.'

She just can't face it right now, none of it. She just wants to concentrate on keeping the babies safe in her belly and getting them out fully intact, so she shoves the letters from Lavender Hill House into a drawer and once a month when Hilda is at bingo and Ron has a pint with his brothers, she burns them in a ceramic pot she keeps tucked behind the rhododendrons at the bottom of the garden.

*

More appointments, they tell Ron. More, because Edie is so small and twins take up a lot of room and also – the doctor clears his throat – because 'Mrs McVey is older.'

'It's not even a two-year difference,' says Ron. 'She's only a little bit older.'

The doctor frowns, then says, 'Not than you, Mr McVey. Being in her thirties, she's older than *normal* mothers having their first baby.'

Edie's pulse hammers in her neck. That's all she wants, to be a normal mother, doing normal mother things with her normal babies that she pushes out of her normal body.

Doctors in pinstriped suits push cold stethoscopes against her belly and murmur amongst themselves. They wrap tape measures around her thickest parts and speak in tongues. Occasionally, they ask Ron a question about whether Edie is feeling the babies move, or if she has developed haemorrhoids.

I'm right here, she wants to scream. *Ask me!*

But they frighten her, these men, with their crisp lines and clever foreheads.

When they return from an appointment where a snarly doctor muttered about the 'irresponsibility of a geriatric mother' when Ron was talking to a nurse, Hilda takes one look at Edie and bustles Ron out on a tartan paint errand. Over pear cake on the back steps under a cloudless Friday sky, Hilda says, 'The secret is to nod, smile and agree. When my boys were born, they left us to it. Just me, Vera Sellers the midwife and a bundle of clean towels.' Hilda licks her thumb and jabs it into the crumbs on her plate. 'That's the way it's always been, you know. Just women getting on with women's things. But then the lads decided they didn't like this magic stuff we could do without them and wanted to get in on it.' She pushes the crumb-thumb into her mouth, sucks it and frowns. 'I mean, what does a man know about what's happening in there!' She laughs. 'And not just the physical stuff. The bit where your heart and soul get knitted in with your baby and you're stitched together for life. How can they understand that?'

They're watching *The Two Ronnies* on TV when the contractions start. Ron immediately breaks into a panic and starts repacking the bag Edie has already carefully packed with things for the babies and things for herself that she doesn't really want Ron to see: a little painted rock and the ginormous post-birth knickers and the ugly, tea-stain-coloured nursing bras.

'It's time,' he says, waving her bra like a flag of surrender, 'it's time! Oh god, I'm not ready!'

'Not ready?' snorts Hilda. 'What've you got to be ready for? It'll be Edie doing all the work.'

'Stop it, Ron,' says Edie. 'It's fine.'

Hilda plucks the bra out of his hand and puts it back in the bag. 'If you want to make yourself useful, get the kettle on and make us a tea, why don't you.'

'The kettle!' says Ron, and runs upstairs.

Edie and Hilda's eyes meet and even as the wave of the next contraction starts, they both start smiling. There's a giggle bubbling up in Edie and she tries to suppress it, but it escapes, surprising them both. Hilda sniggers, and then the pair of them are laughing so hard that tears drip from the corners of their eyes. Edie is delighted by her own calmness, and Hilda gives her an approving nod. *Let him panic*, she mouths, and the two of them get on with laughing at the ridiculous trials of Henrietta Beckett and waiting for Ron to realize that the kettle isn't in the bedroom. She'll tell the twins this, when they're bigger. The funny story of their dad on the day they were born. Abruptly, she stops laughing, adrift in the fact that nobody has ever shared her birth story.

Ron runs back downstairs. 'The kettle isn't upstairs,' he shouts, and opens a cupboard. Edie and Hilda crack up once more.

Eventually, they have to tell him to sit down, and they leave for the hospital just as the sun is coming up the next morning.

23

After

Edie has one leg in her swimsuit when the doorbell goes.

'Jade,' she shouts from the shower room, 'are you ready yet?'

'Yep! I'll get it.'

Edie pulls the suit onto her other leg and hoists it up. She surveys herself in the accusatory mirror: she doesn't look too bad for an old woman with a saggy chest. Her breasts look like they're sort of in the right place with the help of that weird built-in crop top thing she'd been in two minds about. There's a dip where her waist used to be and she isn't anywhere near as flappy on the inner thighs as she thought she was. She bets Pats has an entire wardrobe of swimsuits wherever she is now. Hong Kong. Pats sent her a picture of the rooftop swimming pool where she's staying now.

'Edie!'

She wraps her towel around her and steps out.

'Oh!'

Ron's scary Russian friend is in her hallway wearing a buttercup-yellow swimming cap with pink flowers on. *What's her name again? Verushka with the rolling Rs.* Behind her, a short woman with long dark hair stares at the carpet. She's holding a bathrobe and has a towel folded over her arm.

'I have come to the aqua aerobic class.'

Edie blinks. 'Sorry?'

'For the class. She,' Verushka jerks her head at the woman behind her, 'said you teach class in water.'

The short woman flushes. Edie looks at Jade who shrugs.

'Well the thing is,' Edie starts. Verushka is glaring at her. Edie's pulse stutters in her throat. 'It's not really a class, as such. It's just me and Jade doing the moves in the pool with music.'

'Sounds very much like class to me.'

Jade taps Edie on the shoulder. 'I told Linda about it, you see. The other day.'

The dark-haired woman – Linda, presumably – nods.

Everyone is now looking at Edie. She tries really hard to find a reason why Verushka can't join in, but aside from *You're quite scary*, she can't really find anything.

'Well, I suppose we should go and get started then,' says Edie, raising her eyebrows at Jade. 'Pool's this way.'

They troop down the hall in silence, Edie a stranger in her own house. The silence follows them all the way to the pool, where it is then magnified by the tiles.

'Where you go to limber up?' asks Verushka.

'Um, just here, I suppose.' She points to a square tiled area beside the water.

'I always limber up,' says Verushka, unzipping her velour tracksuit to reveal a tiny fluorescent-pink triangle bikini top. The bottoms aren't much bigger. She's pulling it off though. She can't be a day under sixty-five, but looks like she's borrowed the body of a Barbie without the boobs.

'For an old lass, she's got a pretty good bod,' whispers Jade, except they all hear it because of the acoustics.

'I know,' says Verushka. 'I am hot fox.'

Edie has to bury her face in her towel to smother the laughter rising. She can't look at Jade; it'll be game over if she does.

Verushka throws her clothing to Linda, who catches, folds and piles it on the lounger. The bikini-clad pensioner then immediately starts doing deep pliés with her eyes closed and sighing out big breaths. Edie and Jade can barely keep their jaws from dropping. The woman is ridiculously agile.

'I'll get the speaker on,' says Jade, then, mouthing something at Edie that might be *Holy ball sacks!* she starts fiddling with the music.

'Erm, would you like to join us, Linda?' asks Edie.

Verushka's eyes flick open, though she's down in a deep lunge now. 'No. She is my cleaner. She is here to hold my towel.'

Linda immediately picks up Verushka's towel and holds it out. Verushka nods.

'Hang on a second,' says Jade. 'And I hope you don't mind me speaking up, Edie, but I'm Edie's cleaner and I join in. It's not very fair if Linda can't join in too. I only told her about it because she said she can't get to classes any more 'cause of work.'

Edie's heart thuds. Linda is a puce colour and Verushka has developed a judder in her jaw. She's still mid-squat.

'Besides,' Jade says. 'It's more fun with more people.'

Verushka straightens. 'You might be right,' she says. 'But she has no swimsuit.'

'I've got an old Jazzercise leotard,' pipes up Edie. 'She can wear that.'

Linda chances a look at Verushka, standing there like a centurion.

Verushka sighs, rolls her eyes. 'Very well. She may join.'

Edie's hands are shaky so she plunges them under the water. Her three pupils wait, chest-deep in the water, expectant looks on their faces.

The song is sunny, bouncy. She racks her brain for some fun warm-up moves and remembers Verushka's plié, so they start with some good bends. There's a percussive little drum roll and cymbal crash at the end of each bar, so she adds a wriggle and hip jut.

'Ah, yes. Sexy moves,' says Verushka approvingly.

It's oddly powerful, and as the tempo rises, something surges from way down in her feet all the way up through her head.

'Two, three, four,' she yells to their marching feet. 'Get those arms wide, ladies. Just like you're flying.'

She's still only got two pool noodles, so she has to get inventive with the noodle moves. They end up in pairs each holding the end of a noodle as Edie instructs them to lean out like they're dancing with Fred Astaire before they spin in.

'That's it. Now twirl the other way, Linda. Towards me, not away.'

They twirl in towards one another, meeting in the middle of the noodle.

'I've never heard her laugh before,' whispers Linda to Edie, nodding at Verushka.

After, when they're drying off, Edie finds herself inviting Verushka and Linda to stay for crisps and shandy.

'What is shandy?'

'You're going to love it, Vee,' says Jade. 'Used to work in a pub, me, before I was a dinner lady. I make a quality shandy.'

'I've got Skips or Quavers,' says Edie. 'What do you fancy?'

'I do not eat this food,' says Verushka. 'You have fish?'

'Fish?'

'For protein. After exercise.'

'I've got fish fingers,' says Edie. 'I can do you a fish finger sandwich.'

'Okay. I will eat this.'

It's quite surreal, eating crisps and fish finger sandwiches and drinking shandy with a bunch of people she didn't know until, well, today really. And oddly, she's about as comfortable as she used to be with Pats, or with Carol and Brenda after years of friendship.

'You like being rich now?' asks Verushka. 'After you so poor before?'

'I . . .' *Does she?* Today, sitting with new friends after splashing in her own pool, she likes being rich. But if someone had asked her when she was outside Brenda's house replaced by Sue with the hair thing, or almost begging Ron not to leave her on her birthday, she'd have said that she doesn't know how to feel. It's all so fast. That she sometimes wishes they were still ticking along in their crumble-down mining village surrounded by their friends. Not to mention still living in a house where Sean could find them. *Ungrateful. That's what she is.*

Everyone is looking at her and she realizes that she hasn't answered Verushka's question.

'Oh yes,' she says. 'It's very nice.'

Jade tips her head sideways. Verushka narrows her eyes.

'I was poor,' says Verushka. 'Yes. So poor. I left Leningrad with only my ballet shoes and fur coat I stole. I marry only rich men, so I not be poor any more.'

'Men, plural?' asks Jade.

'This man,' she waves a hand across the road towards her house. 'He was my fourth husband.' She taps Jade on the leg. 'So you still have time.'

Jade laughs. 'Fourth! Where do you find the energy?'

'I have lots of energy,' Verushka says. 'I make energy. I take lovers. One of my lovers was in the KGB.' A suggestive pout ghosts her lips, then it is gone. 'I will not die with regret for things I did not do or people I did not marry.'

Edie tips her head to the side. *Regret for things I did not do.* She has regrets for things she has done, but what things does she regret not doing?

'I have none,' says Verushka, 'but you are full of them, Edith. You wear them like a hat. What are you regretting?'

'I . . .' Edie opens her mouth, then closes it again. Where to start with everything she regrets? Before she has time to think, the words come tumbling out of her. 'I regret losing track of my son.'

Her confession hangs in the air. The other three women chew their sandwiches slowly, watching her carefully. Edie berates herself for her misinterpretation of her relationship with Sean – as though he's a hat she left in a cafe, as though there is nothing more to their estrangement than a simple case of forgetfulness – as though she wasn't responsible for the awful thing she did. She opens her mouth again, closes it, then blurts: 'No. We didn't lose track. Not really. I drove him away.'

Verushka chews the last piece of sandwich delicately, and dusts her fingers on the paper towel that Linda laid by her plate. 'You lose track, you find track. You drive away, you drive back,' says Verushka. 'No problem.'

Finding track? Could she? Verushka makes it sound so easy. Edie pictures Sean, a different version of the nearly-man she last saw. A man, like Colin, but with the gentle train of freckles that runs across his nose that always made him look slightly younger than his twin. Maybe he's married. A child perhaps that looks just like him. She imagines them laughing together in a cafe, talking, fixing things. Find track? Maybe she bloody well can.

24

Before

Nobody mentioned the smells.

Oh, they mentioned the *newborn* smell: heaven and candy floss and lightly scented talc. That's what they made it sound like. And it is, sometimes, when they're freshly towelled from the bath and popped into recently washed terry towelling sleepsuits. But the rest of the time, the sweet, pungent tang of a soiled nappy hangs like a thick cloud shrouding them all. It makes Edie gag. Somehow, Ron and Hilda can coo, *Did somebody do a little whoopsie?* while nuzzling their faces into the babies' necks. But the scent floats up and her stomach lurches, knowing that she has to once again get to the coalface and clean up the mess.

It's not just the babies though. It's her. Not only her unwashed hair, or stale clothes that she hasn't time to launder, but that curdled yoghurty smell that seems to waft from everywhere. Her milk is fresh daily, so why does she smell like she's left some to go off on a summer's day in a heatwave? And there's the stale blood that continues to fall. It smells of pennies gripped too long in sweaty little hands and it repulses her. So does the scent of old roast chicken that steams out of her armpits.

But more than that, beyond the smells, her babies terrify her.

It's their soft fontanelles, thin as dishwashing liquid bubbles that she's scared she'll pop at any moment. The throbbing of their pulses behind it makes her dizzy. And the birdish flutter of their hearts beyond the thin strands of rib-bones. They're too small, too fragile, and Edie is sure she's going to drop one and watch the pieces shatter all over the lino of Hilda's kitchen floor.

'The love is instant, isn't it, Edie?' says Hilda, her smile softer, squishier than a marshmallow.

'Instant,' says Edie, but her voice sounds far away, like a plane all the way up in the sky.

It's not that she doesn't love them: more like she's not sure how to. Hilda is so natural with them. When they cry, she pulls them to her meaty shoulder and they snuffle the tears away into her neck. Her hand rubs their backs in firm circles while she *Shhh, little man, shhhs* into their hair.

Edie watches, tries to do the same, but her movement is stiff, her voice clipped. Her hushes sound more like a mechanical snake hissing and makes the boys cry more.

She wishes she could ask her mam: to say *How did you manage all by yourself and being the way you are?* But she can't do that, so she has imaginary conversations in her head that usually end with her crying. When they do call from Lavender Hill, she keeps hanging up and regaling the silent receiver with happy news of her little boys. It's been over a year since she visited, and though she still talks to her mother on the phone occasionally, she doesn't know what to say to her any more. Before, she couldn't have imagined keeping something like this from her mother. When those first little cell clusters made piecrust promises to turn into people, she imagined sharing the joyful news with Cindy. Taking her out for tea and a scone and saying 'You're going to be a nanna!'

Had visions of Cindy erupting into an elated giggle and clapping her hands. 'Me, a grandmother!' But with each miscarriage, Edie grew a shell around herself. By the time she started to show, she had grown so accustomed to keeping it all inside that she just stopped visiting. When the carers call to ask when she'll next visit, she makes lame excuses about work and Ron, implies that she'll visit next week, at the weekend, just not right now. She feels the judgement in the silence between their dialogue, but the cheques from Ron keep clearing and so everyone keeps up the charade. Edie makes Hilda and Ron believe that she's visiting, when in fact, she nurses a hot chocolate in the 1A Cafe, trying to let the hot sweet liquid soothe the guilt before climbing on the bus back to Hilda's again.

And more than her shame at her own secrecy, when she thinks of her mother, she is filled with a hot, inexplicable rage. *Why didn't you prepare me better?* she wants to scream. *Why did you make such a mess of me that I don't know how to do this?* But it's a hollow rage that dissipates, leaving her empty like a punctured balloon.

'You know when you get those tiny little blackouts?' she says to Hilda one morning, 'where you lose, oh, I don't know, a fraction of a second?'

Hilda frowns. 'No.'

'Oh,' says Edie.

It's like she disappears from herself for a moment. As though time jumps forward without her and she's left blinking into a space she doesn't recognize. She decides not to mention it to the health visitor when she comes.

'The babies are thriving, Mrs McVey,' she says. 'And how is Mummy?'

The health visitor is a slip of a thing, a girl really without a wedding ring. Beside her, Edie is an old, round beldame.

'Great thanks,' says Edie too brightly. The health visitor stares for a fraction too long. 'I'll see you to the door.'

'Well, bye then,' says Edie on the step as the health visitor walks away. Then, she's on her bottom, legs stretched out in front of her, halfway down the path. 'Oh!' she says, and then she's laughing too hard, then sobbing. 'I don't know what happened.'

Hilda is on the doorstep with one of the twins in her arms. The health visitor races cartoonishly back to the door, scooping the crumpled Edie-heap into a neat ball. She speaks over Edie's head.

'Can we help get this mama some rest, please?' She gently steers Edie inside and pops her onto the couch, then instructs Hilda to make sure Edie takes better care of herself.

'Pft,' says Hilda when she's gone. 'What does she know? I'm telling you, Edie, spinsters like her are soft. Rest shmest. Welcome to motherhood.'

'I don't know,' says Ron, looking between his mother and his sagging wife. 'If the health visitor says . . .'

'That health visitor is twelve. She's never pushed a person out of her clacker, let alone two!' Ron reddens. 'This is normal. She'll be fine, won't you, Edie? You just need to buck up and knuckle down.'

Through the film of tears coating her eyeballs, Edie can't fathom which way to buck and which way to knuckle any more, but clinging hard to Hilda's declaration of *normal*, Edie nods.

At night, she shivers in just her half-slip between the babies, who are swaddled as tightly as pigs in blankets on a Christmas plate. She falls behind a thin veil of half-sleep, shattered every forty minutes or so by one of the babies needing to feed. A swift roll one way or the other, and her breast is in the correct baby's mouth, the stillness of night punctuated by the *suck suck* of him taking her milk.

You should be enjoying this, Edie, she curses, wincing at the ferocity of hard gums on tender flesh. *Isn't this what you wanted?*

She tries, but the nagging little voice that taunted her about the lost babies shouts *You aren't cut out for this, are you?*

Maybe I'm not. Maybe I can't.

But she goes through the motions, picks them up when they cry, sings the lullabies she learns from Ron and Hilda, pats their tiny little rumps to sleep and hopes, pray god, that nobody notices. When she scavenges five minutes alone in the bathroom, she swipes at her swollen red eyes, sandpaper-rough, desperate for sleep, and stares at the stranger in the mirror. *Haven't your dreams come true?* She jabs the mirror. 'No more dreams for you,' she hisses. She combs rough fingers through the knots in her hair, tugs out strands desperate to leave her head.

You don't deserve this life, Edie. You are not enough.

25

After

'I need to talk to you, Ron.'

Ron's shirt front is peppered with toast crumbs and it is a hard fight not to dust them into her palm and throw them in the bin. He points to his mouth and chews hard.

'What've you got on your toast?' Edie asks. She sits down, waits while he swallows.

'Guevara jelly and Chantilly cream,' he says eventually.

'Guevara jelly? Like Che Guevara?'

Ron frowns. 'Che Guevara? Did he play for Man U?'

'The Cuban Marxist, Ron.' She shakes her head. *And people think I'm the crazy one.*

Ron nudges the jar towards her and she reads the label. 'It's artisan,' he says. 'Got it from Bamburgh Castle gift shop.'

'It's guava jelly, not Guevara jelly. When did you go to Bamburgh Castle? I'd love to go to a castle. Why didn't you ask me?'

'Edes.' He takes the jar back off her and examines the label. 'It wasn't planned. I just went for a drive then my bladder said, "Get rid of this, Ronnie!" So I stopped off. Had a little look in the gift shop.'

'You hate a gift shop.'

'I don't!' he says. 'I hate the overpriced tat you get in a gift shop.'

'But you like it now you can afford it?'

He grins. 'Don't be mad, Edie-Eves. Let's go on Thursday. Or . . . actually, I'm busy Thursday. Wednesday?' He nudges her shin with his toe. 'I'll give you a fiver for the gift shop.'

'Why can't we go on Thursday? Where are you going?'

'I'm just doing a thing.'

'A thing.'

He nods. 'A car thing. I don't think you'd like it.'

'You could have asked.'

'Wednesday,' he cups her cheek. 'Just you and me, anywhere you choose.'

She'd like to say yes, but his mysterious disappearing act is really starting to grate. She moves back, just slightly, so that his hand drops from her face.

'Where is the box of stuff I used to keep in the bottom of the wardrobe?'

'What box?'

'The box. A boot box.'

'You could get new boots now of course,' says Ron. 'Fenwick's boots if you like.'

'I don't want boots, Ron,' she snaps, standing, slapping her hand on the table. Ron gives a little jump. 'You don't listen to me any more. I want to find the boot box. I haven't seen it since we moved.'

Ron drops his eyes to the table. 'I do listen,' he says quietly. He licks his thumb and pokes it into the crumbs. 'I asked the removalists to put our old tat in the garage.' Edie bristles at the word *tat*. Nothing in that box is tat. 'There's a big cupboard at the back. It might be in there.'

'Thank you.' Her hand smarts where she slapped it on the table.

'You can't get into it right now though. I've got the Jag parked right up in front of it.'

'If you could move it before you go off on your next mystery errand, that would be helpful,' she says and heads for the pool to swim another angry lap.

She waits until Ron and Colin have taken both cars to some fancy motoring club dinner thing before beginning her search for the box. The first major hurdle is that she can't find the light switch for the garage. Being hermetically sealed from the elements and startlingly well built, the garage is a study in darkness. Save for the pale rectangle of light from the hallway which, being cased in a dark grey shade, is pretty dim, illuminates only a small area of the concrete, she still can't really see anything. As a non-driver, non-car-loving walker, she really has no reason to be in the garage, hasn't been in there much, and she certainly can't picture a cupboard. What she does remember though, is that the garage is the size of a small aircraft hangar. 'Perfect for if we get a few more cars,' Colin had said when they viewed it.

She starts by edging slowly along the door wall, running her hands across the plaster, but finds nothing resembling a light switch. *This place is ginormous.* She runs her hands up the wall as she walks. It would be just her luck that the control was perfectly placed for her tall husband and son and not her. When her fingers reach the corner, she starts to trace the perpendicular wall.

'Ow!' Her shin smacks into something hard. She rubs the

bone and shakes her head. *Surely it must be on that first wall?* She retraces her way back along it, fingers working all the way, but finds nothing. She slips through the door returning to the main body of the house.

I'll get a torch.

In their old house, they kept a torch in the top kitchen drawer next to the cutlery. Hilda used to do the same, which is why they adopted it as a home for a torch too. But there's no torch in the top drawer, just the fancy Christofle cutlery and a lone birthday candle. *Could I light that?* She shakes her head. On what? Their weird magnetic cooktop? Her burning shin?

She stands in the middle of the kitchen, hands on hips, surveying a room she doesn't know and a house where she doesn't know where anything is, and sighs.

Plan B then.

Verushka answers the door in a pair of yellow leggings and a black leotard.

'I'm sorry,' says Edie. 'Were you doing a workout?'

'Ballet is not a workout,' says Verushka. 'It is life.'

Edie grins. 'Of course. I'm sorry to interrupt.'

'No, no,' says Verushka. 'I finish my fouetté practice for the day. I can still do sixteen. On the left.' She nods vigorously. 'Most twenty-year-old professionals cannot do sixteen fouetté on the left.'

'Well done,' says Edie. She clears her throat. 'Erm, I wanted to ask you something.'

Verushka drags Edie over the threshold and into an entrance hall with a wide, sweeping staircase running up the middle. Each newel post is topped with a bronze statuette of a ballerina wearing just a flimsy scrap of material. Edie can't stop staring.

'I know,' says Verushka. 'They are me. Kiki Smith made them. Commissioned by my fourth husband, may he burn in hell.'

'Wow.'

'Yes wow. I am impressive woman.' Verushka blows a kiss at the sculptures then turns back to Edie. 'You come in here and fix this thing, then I answer question.'

The *thing* in question is a remote control, and it isn't broken, it just has one battery. By the time Edie finds her one and pops it in, Verushka has settled onto the couch in one of her many sitting rooms with her legs folded under her like a pretzel, shoes lying on the rug. Edie hands her the remote control.

'I want to watch *Casualty*,' says Verushka.

'Right.'

'You know who makes my shoes?' asks Verushka.

'Erm, a shoemaker?' guesses Edie.

'No. An artist,' says Verushka. Edie examines the tiny fawn leather things crossed over with an abundance of straps. 'I will only have artist make my shoes. When I was a child, I had no shoes of my own. I have to borrow my brother's shoes in the winter. I will only have good shoes.'

Edie tucks one foot behind the other, trying to mask her nice Marks & Spencer's plimsolls, though she can't imagine how hard Ron would laugh if she said she was getting shoes made by an artist.

'Sit,' barks Verushka.

Edie laughs, less afraid of a woman who can't replace a lost battery than she was of the secateur-wielding lunatic in the street, but sits anyway.

'What you want to ask?'

Edie licks her lips. 'You said the other day about getting back on track.'

'Yes. I am wise.'

'Indeed,' Edie agrees. 'But I'm wondering, how would *you* go about getting back on track? If you were me, I mean.'

'You want to find someone, correct?' Edie nods. 'I have an ex-lover.' Edie blushes at the casual use of the term and Verushka lets out a saucy *mmmm*. 'He was KGB. No question. You give me the name and last known address. He will find.'

Edie grins. 'I was hoping you might say that.' She reaches into her pocket then pauses. 'And he wouldn't hurt him, would he? I mean . . . KGB. They do have a bit of a reputation.'

'He not KGB any more. This is small favour.'

'Right,' says Edie, and finds herself unfolding the piece of paper where she has written Sean's name and date of birth, fingers electrified by the thrill running through her body.

26

Before

Edie has lost count of how many times she has switched sides tonight. The babies are insatiable, sometimes both feeding at once, which means that she has to sit up and cradle them in an arm each. Sean has a nappy rash, red and tender and so raw, Edie can feel his pain through her fingertips when she rubs the ointment in. And poor Colin keeps spitting up an acidic bile that causes him to flail immediately after, spattering everything around.

Edie glances at the clock on the teasmade. It's just after three, and she's had around twenty-six minutes of sleep since going to bed with the boys at nine. The saying 'I could sleep on a clothesline' was definitely uttered by a new mother. She could sleep on a clothesline, train line, landmine, any of the above.

She'd gently suggested to Ron that some people were using formula these days. *That way the dads can help out. Right*, he nodded but said nothing more. The next morning, Hilda had launched into a speech about lazy mothers and the poison of formula milk and short-changing the babies. *Besides*, she'd said, *someone has to have had enough sleep to earn the bread,* and Ron had stared guiltily into his cornflakes while Edie tried to prop her eyes open wide enough to glare at the side of his head.

She hooks her little finger into the corner of Colin's mouth, and he detaches from her with a little *pop*. She lays him down on her left, watches as he snuffles and rolls onto his side. To her right, Sean's belly is moving up and down, a snore fluttering across his lips. She gives his tummy a gentle pat and slides down to the foot of the bed.

There's a crumpled smock on the floor – an ugly brown thing Hilda gave her – and she slips it over her head. At the door, she looks back at the boys, wondering how long it will be before they're crying out for her again.

She pauses at the foot of the stairs, like an intruder in her own home. She just wants a quick snack and a drink then she'll be back up to the boys before the sheets have fully cooled from her body heat.

On the couch, Ron is folded like a paper crane. He's too large for the springy velour seating with the hard, unwieldy wooden arms, but it's better, he says, than working with machinery when he's tired. He heads up to bed with Edie and the boys, reads the comics in the paper until he hears Hilda's tread on the stairs, then pops back down with a blanket and pillow.

Edie pauses at the fridge, plucks Patricia's latest postcard from under a magnet. Kabul, it says on the front. Edie doesn't even know what country that is.

Edie! Hope mammy life is as wonderful as you hoped, it says at the top. Edie sighs, pushes open the fridge and searches for the hunk of cheese she saw Hilda put in there after dinner. It's turning hard, but Edie takes a huge bite anyway.

I'm here in Kabul stuffing myself with quabili palau and admiring the views (men)! (Hi Hilda!) Yesterday, I girded my loins to travel by horse to a two-thousand-year-old Buddha statue with a guide called Ikram (yum!). It's amazing how far a yellow toaster can get you!

She signs off with *kisses for your gorgeous boys (and you too Hilda!) xxx*

Edie has never felt older or saggier. She looks at the chunk of cheese in hand. *Or hungrier.* She takes another bite, followed by another, and another, and two more, until there is nothing left of the cheese. 'Damn,' she says, but couldn't have stopped if she'd wanted to.

She turns her attention then to the pantry. A box of Carr's water crackers is ripped open, the dry biscuits shoved in her mouth without ceremony. Edie looks down at the crumbs gathering in her swollen cleavage. *God, I'm disgusting.* But she can't stop now that she's started.

The crackers are dust-dry, so she turns on the tap and puts her mouth against the spout. *So thirsty.* She leaves the tap running, in case she needs some more.

Two, three more crackers, shovelled in like she's a starving woman, then she's tipping the box upside down to catch the last dust motes of biscuit.

The box falls to the floor, and so does Edie.

She clutches her stomach. Stuffed like a Christmas goose and she's disgustingly ashamed.

A quick walk. That'll help. A little voice deep, deep in her centre says *A quick walk away and never turn back.* She slaps her forehead, dulling the voice.

Ron's boots are by the door, his thick socks stuffed inside. She sniffs the damp wool and smells something faintly vinegary. *What are you doing, Edie?* She pulls on the socks, jams her feet into shoes that reduce her feet to the size of children's, and heads into the night.

Just a walk. Just to walk off this food. I'll be back before anyone notices.

All along Moor Street, people have been getting ready for Christmas. Wreaths hang expectantly on doors, waiting for carol singers and visitors to come knocking. Through open-curtained windows, there are glimmers of tinsel adorning trees and mantelpieces. Just a few more weeks and she'll get to wrap up presents that the boys are too small to open.

She could, at a moment like this, allow her mind to wander back over her own empty-promised childhood Christmases, but the night is crisp, the velvet blanket of sky dotted with pinprick stars, so she concentrates instead on shuffling along the frost-laced pavement trying to keep Ron's boots on.

Her walking rhythm is oddly soothing and percussive. She chants '*Go go go go*' in time with her steps and for a few minutes wonders how long it would take her to walk to Kabul before her proper brain catches up with the weird intruder in there. 'Stop it!' she says, then looks around the deserted street to see if anyone heard. 'Stop it.'

The pain in her stomach is starting to subside, leaving in its wake the gnawing hunger she can't sate. Just another thing nobody told her about motherhood. Was her own mother hungry all the time? She sees her mother taking birdish little nibbles out of everything Edie put in front of her, thinks of her ever-diminishing frame and can't picture her full and ripe and ravenous. Edie shakes her head. *No point dwelling on that.*

She's starting to puff for breath now, and she's surprised to see that she has walked to the abandoned lime kilns that look out over the sea. She stops, pushes her hands into her hips and bends forward to take in some more air.

Edie used to be able to walk for miles. Run, skip, cartwheel. These days, a half-hour trot destroys her.

She hopes the boys haven't woken up yet, stretching their

mouths for Mammy's milk. How old was she the first time she woke up to find her mother wasn't there? She'd been so frightened. Five? Six? She woke shivering, the blankets a heap on the floor. 'Mam?' she'd said, and she'd blinked until she could make out the faint outline of the bedroom. '*Mam?*' she'd said again, and a cold breeze had snaked through the bedroom, alerting her to the open door, a symphony of cat yowls and a tin can clattering across the street. It was a chilly night: a bite in a crisp, autumn, star-toothed sky. Under the weak wash of a dying streetlight, Cynthia danced. The light and shadow of the street made her look like some sort of ethereal being, like one of the fairies in the illustrated Perrault book from school. Her mother's eyes were closed, arms weaving above her head, hips swaying side to side. She was singing too, something low and mournful. The curtains in the neighbouring flats had started to twitch. Lights came on, bleeding through too-thin curtains. 'Come on in, Mam,' she'd said, voice shaking. 'My insides are falling out,' said Cynthia. 'I have to dance to keep them in.'

Edie blinks quickly. She can't be like that, not with her boys. She pictures them, their rosebud mouths forming little Os, and she smiles. *They are lovely*. But then she sees those mouths gaping into screams and that shrill, piercing siren that says they need her again and the thought exhausts her. Her feet are aching now. She slips off Ron's boots and wonders how far away daybreak is.

'Jesus, Edie! We've been frantic!'

Ron pulls her into a tight embrace at the front door, and she breathes in the petrol and grease smell that seeps from his pores, no matter how much he washes.

Behind him, in curlers and slippers, Hilda holds one of the babies to her chest.

'Well, she's home safe and sound, Mr McVey,' says the gruff-but-gentle policeman who collected her from the kilns. Then quietly, he adds, 'Might be a good idea to call in a doctor tomorrow.'

'Thanks so much, officer.'

The policeman hesitates. 'Erm, we can talk about it later, but you know that I have to make a report. 'Cause of the Children's Act.' He catches Ron's alarmed expression. 'Oh, no, nothing to worry about. Just, you know, a formality. Nothing to worry about.'

'Okay,' says Ron, clearly worrying. He waves the policeman off, adjusts the blanket that the man left behind that Edie is now wearing like a cape then pulls her into the house.

'I'm sorry,' says Edie.

'Sorry? Edie, we were worried sick! You left the front door open, the tap running, a biscuit crime scene in the pantry and then you weren't there!' He plants his hands on the sides of his face. 'We thought you might have . . . well, we thought . . .'

Hilda says, 'I'll take Sean up to bed. Colin's sleeping soundly.' Her steps are snow soft.

'I just needed a walk,' says Edie. 'I wasn't going to be long.'

'Hours, Edie. We've been looking for hours.' Ron sits heavily on the sofa. 'Edie, do you need help?'

'What?' she laughs. 'No, I'm doing very well, thank you.' She laughs again, and it does sound a little crazy. Too high-pitched, too tinkly, like a grocer's bell. She plops down beside him. 'I'm exhausted, Ron,' she whispers. 'And I'm not really sure I know who I am any more. Or if I ever really did. You know, I'm just—'

Ron sighs. She swallows down the rest of the words. The *I'm not sure how to be a mother*. The *I'm such a failure*. The *Maybe you'd all be better off without me*. 'I'm okay.'

'If you're sure . . .' says Ron, dubiously. He examines her face for a moment, taps his fingers on her thigh. 'Well, I've got a big day tomorrow. I'm glad you're home safe.' He kisses the top of her head. 'You and the boys are my world, Edie-Eves. I just want you to be happy.'

'I am,' she says. Her voice sounds far away from this room.

Dr Farley doesn't ask all that many questions, but his eyes search her face every time she speaks, and they keep searching after she's finished talking. He prescribes a little pill that she takes each evening over supper. He writes down a formula brand for Hilda to buy at the shops.

'Am I insane?' asks Edie.

'We're all mad here!' says the doctor laughing. Edie frowns. 'Mad Hatter? *Alice in Wonderland*? Never mind.' He shuffles his papers.

'The policeman did a report,' she says. 'Is that bad? Am I in trouble?'

'Oh,' says the doctor standing. 'I wouldn't know about that sort of thing.'

'I've failed,' says Edie.

'You'll fail if you are too tired to succeed. This should help.'

The boys are to be placed in their cot, bellies full of thick formula. Edie is to get eight hours' rest each and every night and – doctor's orders – Ron and Hilda are to assist with the feeding.

Bone broth stew, thick, hearty meals three to five times a day. And lots and lots of tea.

'It takes a village, they say,' says the doctor. 'Let's put your village to work.'

In three days, the little blackouts stop. In a week, she starts to feel stronger. In two, she does a headstand in the bathroom and giggles. *Much better!* And she's ready to be a good mother to her boys.

She's coming down the stairs after laying the twins down for a nap when she hears Hilda's voice over the clanging of the soup ladle in the kitchen.

'If keeping her right involves drugs, then so be it.' The kettle whistles and cups chink against one another. 'It wasn't like that in my day. Lasses just got on with it. But these days everyone's so sensitive.'

Edie allows herself a little smile. Hilda would never let anyone describe her as sensitive. She'd have them clipped round the ear before they'd got to the end of the word.

'Still, you won't be having any more, so you'll not have to worry about her going through this again,' says Hilda.

Edie frowns.

'Don't, Mam.'

'I can't say I'm not disappointed, But maybe it's for the best, love.'

'You know why I said it. When they asked me.'

When they asked him what?

Ron's voice floats into the hall again. 'She didn't know what *tubes tied* meant. I saw it on her face. I would have asked her, but they needed a decision and, you know how she was.'

It's blurry, the birth: the edges bleeding somewhere into the recesses of night, going from the calm woman gently labouring in front of *The Two Ronnies* to being certain she was dying. The surges, when they came, were lightning bolts ripping through her body, threatening to tear her seam to seam. She was barely aware of the screams, but her throat was gripped in a squeezing fist and she couldn't breathe. 'She's haemorrhaging,' people kept yelling and everything was red and grey and loud and fuzzy. Then nothing until she woke up on a cold slab in the operating theatre, the lights like car headlights, startling, too bright. 'Should we tie her tubes, Mr McVey? Like we said.'

She pictured her insides laid out like an explosion at a ribbon factory; then the surgeon tying the ends up in neat bows before stuffing them back inside.

Ron had closed his eyes, ran a hand across his face. Then he nodded slowly.

'Thank you,' said Edie, even though no one had asked her anything. *Who wants to leave their innards all messy and tangled?*

Hesitating on the bottom stair, hearing this again, her stomach plunges. *Is that really what it means?*

She backs away, but trips over Ron's boot which is lying on the rug. She lands on the floor, wincing as a sharp pain shoots through her coccyx.

'Ow!'

They're looking down on her, heads tilted.

'Did you have a little accident, Edith? Come on, Ron, help her up.'

'I tripped over your shoe,' she says, shaking him off when he takes her arm. She climbs to her feet herself, shaking, furious. 'I'm not crazy,' she says. Then louder: 'I'm not crazy.' She turns her back on their watchful eyes, and heads back up the stairs. *I'm not.*

27

After

The following Thursday, they're joined by a woman called Jean, who plays on Verushka's lady golf team, and her cleaner Nicky.

'I live at the house with the orangery,' she says proudly.

'An orangery?' asks Jade.

'Yes, an orangery,' says Jean. 'I'd just got back from Seville and you know how they've got that orangery at the cathedral?' Verushka is the only one who nods. 'Well, I thought, *I've got to have an orangery!*'

'Jean need to work on arms for backswing,' says Verushka, wobbling the skin under Jean's arm. 'Lots of arm work today. Jean is very bad at follow-through.'

'I am,' nods Jean, who Edie guesses to be eighty if she's a day.

Edie imagines Jean getting yelled at on a golfing green by Verushka and immediately feels some sympathy for her.

They're also joined by a pointy woman in her late sixties called Sarah Moss who introduces herself with a limp handshake and an air kiss to both of Edie's cheeks. Her cleaner is Jess, who confesses that she can't swim so can she *please stay in the shallow end?*

To distract herself from images of Sean being bundled into the back of a white van by a beefy Russian, Edie's spent the last week watching aerobics videos on YouTube that Colin found for her on his computer. Some of it is rubbish, but it has inspired her to think up some new moves of her own. Moves like *Clackers*. That's what Jade called them one day, so they're officially calling them *Clackers* now. They swing one leg out to the side then bring it in to the other and switch, like those executive toys with the balls that sit on the desks of pinstriped men and clack back and forth. Edie can feel her hip joints loosening and strengthening at the same time.

'That's it, Jean. Keep it steady. Listen to the music, Jade. Three, four. Well done everyone.'

Edie applauds at Jean's sterling clackers, glows as the pensioner puffs up under Edie's praise. When she's lying in bed at night, a little voice tries to taunt her. *All these wasted years.* Whether it is tutting about her newfound profession or how long it has taken her to finally start finding her boy isn't clear. But she shoos it away and gets on with thinking about new moves and the silly names she comes up with for them, like *the Arctic Roll* where they jump up high and turn around, or *the Cheesy Wotsit* where she gets them to bend backwards, curved until their hair hits the water.

And today, it is not just the rush she's getting from teaching that is making her heart pump a bit faster. Verushka said she had news from her KGB friend, and so the cool-down is a little warmer than she'd usually do, but she's keen to get to the crisp-and-shandy chatting afterwards.

'Brilliant class, Edie,' says Jean as they settle at the kitchen table for snacks. 'I'm really feeling it in my wings. My backswing is going to be so much stronger. Your husband doesn't mind you having loads of ladies splashing around in his pool?'

'Well, firstly, it's not his pool. It's *our* pool.' Edie sips her shandy, resisting the urge to pump Verushka for information before they've nibbled their first Quavers. 'And also, he's never been in it, despite insisting that we got a house with a pool. He can't swim, you see.'

'Good to know,' says Verushka cryptically. 'Important to know their weak point.'

'Right,' says Edie. Perhaps she should lock Ron's door whenever Verushka comes over . . .

Of course, Ron doesn't know there's a bunch of women in their pool doing aqua aerobics. He was so weird about her doing aqua aerobics with Jade, he might have some form of mini-fit about a couple of rich pensioners, some middle-aged women and a very pregnant lady who could give birth at any moment flapping their wrinkles and dimples about in his pool water.

Besides, she can't remember the last time he was home on a Thursday morning. When she looked in the pocket diary she bought him with his name in gold letters on the front, she had noticed only a scribbled blue circle next to ten a.m. on Thursdays for the next couple of months. She flipped back and saw that the circles only started a couple of weeks ago. Perhaps Verushka's KGB friend might be able to track down her husband next.

But Edie is enjoying this. She loves that here's a millionaire ex-ballerina laughing along with a woman who can't afford a coffee table, and Edie is the beating heart of the group.

'So, Edie,' says Verushka, stretching out both of the 'e's. 'I have an update.'

Edie's heart is tapping out a strange military rhythm in her chest.

'Victor is in the hospital,' Verushka continues. 'We may be delayed.'

'Who's Victor?' asks Jess.

'Verushka's ex-lover in the KGB,' Jade says.

'Edie has enlisted him to find her long-lost son,' Verushka nods. 'But he cannot search with a punctured kidney, so we wait.'

Edie's belly sinks. For the last few nights since she handed the scrap of paper to Verushka, she has been a tangled circuit of loose wires, sparking and fizzing any time anyone speaks to her. She pushes herself up, opens the fridge door and pretends to search for the artisan tartare sauce she bought for the fish finger sandwiches. The steel door gives her something to hide behind, and while the women chat on, Edie focuses on the limp curtain of a lettuce leaf while she gets her breathing back under control.

'Ah,' says Jean as Edie returns to the table, a bright smile fixed on her face. 'A mystery. I love a mystery. I've read every Agatha Christie twice!'

'Poirot is my favourite,' says Sarah Moss. 'I could watch them all day. I love figuring out who dunnit.'

'Well, maybe you can help the search,' says Jade. 'We all can. Just until Victor is well.'

Nicky says, 'My sister works for the Post Office. I bet she could get some addresses.'

And they all start piping up with their relevant search skills.

Edie bites back a tear at these women she barely knows, wanting to help her. She slowly nibbles a crisp so she doesn't crumble completely.

Misreading her mind, Jade whispers, 'Nothing beats your mother's instinct, eh?' and Edie stings with shame. *Would they be so keen to help her if they knew what she'd done?*

28

Before

Her mother is sitting stiffly on her bed staring at the wall when Edie arrives.

Though she's been living here now for years, Cindy still looks like a fish out of water against the flocked wallpaper and brown carpets of Lavender Hill House. There's a part of Edie that wants to scoop her mother up and carry her home to Hilda's place. And another that baulks when she pictures Hilda and Cindy under the same roof.

'*Will you pass the carrots please, Cynthia?*'

'*I know what the seagulls are saying about you, Hilda.*'

Edie shudders.

They need their own three-bedroomed place so they can bring Cynthia home. But every time they start to make headway, something rears up and bites a hole in the bottom of their savings. There's Cindy's care of course that takes a significant chunk of Ron's salary. The loan repayments for the garage. There's the fact that Ron paid half for his mam's new cooker because 'well, we live here too,' which is fair enough. But there's also the fact that Ron is a shade too generous with his brothers. He paid for Harry's wedding breakfast a few years back which almost wiped them out entirely when he revealed he was having it at the Grand Hotel in Tynemouth. Not to mention the chunk he gave his older brother Gerry to help when some of the slate came off his roof, or the removal van he hired to help his other brother Arnold move to Scunthorpe.

Well, it's not like we'll need the third bedroom for more babies.

She once asked him if he thought they would ever be able to afford a four-bedroomed place. 'A room for Mam and another for more babies.' He'd tipped his head at her, concerned, then hugged her tight. 'One thing at a time, Edie-Eves.'

'How are you, Mam?' Edie asks now.

Cindy stares straight ahead.

In total, there was almost a year between when Edie's baby bump started showing and when the twins were finally big enough to leave with Hilda so she could come and visit. In that time, her mother shrunk, in height and width, but more so in presence, in the space she took up in the world. Not that she'd ever been big, but in Edie's absence, she'd folded in on herself like an origami crane.

Edie's visits have picked up again, but though she leaves the house every week under Hilda's cheerful 'Send my best to your mam,' she only actually comes about once a month, and she's on first-name terms with the waitresses from the 1A Cafe.

'Mam?' she tries again. 'Are you all right?'

Cindy turns her head slowly, looking straight at Edie with an arctic clarity in her eyes. 'You had a baby,' she says accusingly.

'I . . . what?'

'You had a baby,' repeats Cindy. 'You had a baby and you didn't tell me.'

Edie's shoulders slump, her bag dropping to the floor. 'How did you know?'

'Susie said.' Cindy points vaguely at the wall. 'Susie said "I saw your grandbaby." And I said I haven't got a grandbaby. I forget stuff, but I wouldn't forget a thing like that.'

Edie looks anywhere but at her mother.

'It's not nice!' says Cindy suddenly. 'It makes me feel sad.'

Edie sinks to her knees, slumping her head into her mother's lap. 'I'm so sorry,' she says and then she's crying, hot wet tears into her mother's skirt. 'I wanted to tell you, you know. Wanted you to be part of it all. But I'm so ashamed. I thought I'd be good at this. But I'm not. I'm awful. I wanted to show you how well I could do, but it's hard. It's so hard being a mam and I'm bad at it. I haven't brought them to see you because I don't know what to do any more. And I'm ashamed of how I felt about you and it wasn't okay. You were doing it alone, and oh, god, I so want you to sit by me and tell me I'm doing all right. I am, aren't I, Mam? I am doing all right, aren't I?'

Her mother's hand comes to rest on top of her head, a holy benediction, a blessing. Edie sobs and sobs, losing all sense of time under her mother's gentle palm. A tug of something from the past, a shout, a man's voice, angry and incomprehensible, her mother's hand stroking her hair, is there, but it dissolves under that same soothing motion. Time stops, and Edie is safe again.

Eventually, she dries her eyes and sits up. Her mother's cheeks are wet and Edie dabs her face with her sleeve.

'I'm sorry, Mam.'

'You will bring the baby, won't you?'

Edie bites her lip. *How do I tell you that there are two of them? And that your grandbabies are nearly three?*

*

There's never time to dwell, because the twins take up all her energy.

'Imagine you were doing this *and* running a house,' says Hilda. Edie prickles.

'I like that you don't dress the boys the same,' says an old lady who lives down Hilda's street. 'Twins always get lumped together. I am one. I know.'

Edie smiles and takes the compliment, stops short of saying that you really have no choice but to dress them differently when you get all of their clothes from charity shops and they're unlikely to have two identical outfits in the Oxfam on Westoe Road.

She made the mistake of buying a *Scooby-Doo* hat last time she was in a second-hand shop. It wasn't for one of them in particular, she thought they could share it.

'You can't just buy one *Scooby-Doo* hat, Edie!' said Ron as the boys wrestled for it on the living room carpet.

'I like to dress them differently,' she said, happy to have the old woman's comment at her disposal. 'They're individuals, Ron.'

'Yes,' he said. 'But they don't know that.'

It does amaze Edie just how different they are. *How? You shared a womb, digested the same amount of protein and love. And then we all shared a bed and milk and germs. I kissed you both the same amount, dabbed the same amount of powder on your little bottoms, spooned you the same pureed apple and banana. How are you so different?*

Sean, with his freckles and snubby little nose, is more physical, more angry and combative. He can't just leave the potato on his plate if he doesn't want it: he has to fling it across the room from a furious arm. He runs, he jumps, he pushes, he pulls. Edie finds him exhausting.

Colin is softer, quieter. His brow furrows while he tries to figure out what she's thinking, which isn't too hard with her stupidly open face. He holds out his chubby arms for Ron, strokes Edie's knee when she looks fraught, offers Sean a toy when he's kicking the furniture.

But for all of their differences, there's a thread that connects them that scares Edie. *You'll exclude me one day. You'll knot each other up in secrets and I won't have a clue.* They can have a conversation without a sound passing either of their lips. They move sometimes in perfect unison. Sean wakes before Colin's nightmare takes hold and reaches his hand for him.

They're growing up and with every passing moment she can feel them slipping away from her. Every new word they utter is another that will carry them forward without her. Every new skill, every new facial expression is a stamp in the passport of who they're going to become, and even this young, she can feel their need for her growing frailer and frailer.

She missed out on so many of their early needs because she was so wrapped up in herself, and now, she's not the only one who can provide for them, and this makes her unbearably sad.

'I want time to stand still,' she says to Ron, 'so we can take our time getting it right.'

'No time for that,' says Ron, pecking her on the head. 'Just got to get on with the time we've got.'

But Edie would trade a foot for a time machine.

29

After

When Jade doesn't turn up on Thursday, Edie calls and calls, but to no avail.

'The lad knocked,' says the taxi company woman when Edie calls, 'but no answer.'

'Jade, please call,' she says into the dull *fssh* of the voicemail service of Jade's phone.

She sends messages, calls hydrangea Sue from over the road to see if she can drop in, calls and calls and calls, but nothing.

'I tried, Edie,' says hydrangea Sue, 'but no response.'

In the end, she has no choice but to go herself. She's pulling the bus timetables out of the drawer, when she thinks *Sod it, I'm a millionaire* and calls Blue Line taxis.

When she finally answers the door, a blue hoodie, too long in the arms, covers Jade from the top of her head to her knees. 'Hot enough to make the devil blush' it says across the chest with a sexy pouting female devil where a chest pocket would be. It is straining over her belly, but other than that, Edie would say that the jumper belongs to someone considerably taller and wider. Jade's dark eyes blink from the cavernous depths of the hood.

'I'm heading out,' says Jade. 'I'm trying to be cognito. Or is it incognito?'

Jade agrees to the Asda cafe. Edie is just relieved that she is still alive.

Over tea, Jade twiddles a strand of hair around her finger. She's taken the hood down, and Edie can see the red rims, the clumpy mascara around her eyes.

'Jade, what's going on? There's nothing so bad we can't try to fix it.'

Jade scrunches up her face and reaches into the pocket of her hoodie, withdrawing a crumpled envelope. She slides it across the table keeping her eyes on the floor as Edie reads.

Eviction notice. Edie skims the text for detail, but there's so much legal jargon she can't wrap her head around it.

'There must be something we can do,' says Edie. 'Call the landlord, speak to the council. Something.'

Jade shrugs. 'At the Citizens Advice Bureau, they said I didn't have a leg to stand on because I breached the contract not paying the rent.'

'Oh, Jade.' Edie runs through solutions in her head. Jade could stay with them. Edie could pay off the overdue rent. Edie could—

'Don't you be thinking you're going to pay stuff for me,' says Jade, reading her mind. 'I am not a charity case.'

'Jade . . .'

'No, no, we'll be all right. We'll go to a hostel or something if Mam can't have us.'

'You'll do no such thing, Jade Kelly!'

Edie wants to cry. Instead, she thinks furiously.

'I know a lawyer,' she says, eventually. 'My friend, well sort of friend, ex-friend maybe, Carol her name is, her daughter Gemma might be able to help. She's a lawyer. Does something to do with house contracts.'

Jade frowns, her eyebrows tilting toward one another like planes careening into a dogfight. 'I can't afford a lawyer to get un-evicted,' she says.

An idea slides into Edie's mind, only semi-formed, but it makes her head throb. Gemma would know how to do it. *Oh god!* She has a flutter of panic when she imagines running it by Ron. He'd say no. That's a given.

Between booking the roadshow and all the time he's spending out of the house, she just doesn't feel that she can talk to him at all. The circles on Thursdays, the trips out, the random visits to castles. Not that her current slate is squeaky clean. She's giving secret aqua aerobics classes in their pool, she's blasted open their big family shame and invited some strangers in to help look for Sean, and she's paying a wage and taxis for a cleaner who isn't a cleaner and isn't doing all that much of the cleaning. But there's a defiance forming in her gut. She just wants to do the right thing, be a good person and in her heart she wants to help Jade and her little boy. She's struggled. She knows what it's like to have an uncertain future stretched out in front of you. Besides, she's been inert so many times when she needed to take action and she's ashamed. Maybe if she can do one thing right, one thing really well for someone else, maybe the rest of her tilted universe might dip back into balance.

'No!' Jade leaps from her seat, startling Edie so much that she drops her cup with a clatter, slopping tea everywhere. Before she can blink, Jade is tearing across the cafe. 'Get back here, you man-thieving bitch!'

Edie abandons the tea-soaked table and launches herself after her. 'Jade, wait!'

She dodges a fallen chair felled by Jade's fury, hurdles a crouching toddler and makes some good ground in catching her. Shoppers scatter by the exit and Jade and Edie spill into the car park at the same time. Edie catches a glimpse of a copper-curled woman leaping into a Kermit-green Ford Ka, then careening out of the car park with a screech of tyres.

Jade is doubled over, her breath left behind somewhere near the checkouts.

'What was that?' asks Edie.

'That bitch . . . Tamara.' Jade straightens and her face is beet red, streaming with tears. 'I can't, Edie. The hate, the sadness . . . I just.'

Then she's marching at speed again and Edie has to jog to keep up.

'She was just there with her fucking shopping bag of meringues and strawberries and sex food and cava. Just getting on with her life while mine's falling apart. And she's got him and clothes that fit and a flat that she owns and a proper job and a mother who doesn't piss off on eight-month holidays and I'm just here growing fat and stupid and homeless and ugly with an old woman I hardly know as my only friend. I'm a pathetic loser.' They're outside the off-licence on North Road now. Jade pushes open the door.

'Jade, what are you doing?'

But Jade is inside.

'Coo-ee, Edith,' says a voice. Edie closes her eyes. Hair thing Sue is weaving across the road with that bloody awful thing on her head moving independently from her like an animated weasel. 'Have you been going to The Ritz with Craig Ravel Holewood?'

'I can't talk now, Sue.'

Clocking that Edie is outside an off-licence, Sue says, 'Ooh, are you buying some champers for a bit of afternoon living lavish?'

'Bye, Sue,' Edie says and pushes into the shop, cursing herself for wasting time with Sue.

At the counter, Jade is zipping up her purse and taking a bottle of red wine from the counter.

'Jade, stop! What are you doing?'

'Leave me alone,' says Jade. 'I'm sad, okay?'

'You should be ashamed of yourself,' Edie says to the cashier. 'Selling wine to a distressed pregnant lady.'

He shrugs and goes back to his magazine. Jade barges her way past Sue in the doorway.

'What's happening, Edith?' asks Sue.

Jade stops outside the shop, unscrews the lid and takes a giant swig. 'Ugh,' she says then goes in for a second.

'Jade, stop it! Your boy!'

'Eee, Edith! It's like that Winey Amehouse documentary,' says Sue.

'Shut it, Sue.' Edie tries to wrestle the bottle from Jade, but her grip is surprisingly strong. Pedestrians gather in murmuring clumps around the scene. 'Give me the bottle, Jade. Now.'

Jade tries to pull it closer to her chest, glaring at Edie, but Edie grabs her. 'Do you want your son to be taken off you, Jade? Do you? Because then you really will have nothing.'

Jade loosens her grip for a moment. Edie takes advantage, swiping the bottle from her hands and dropping it on the pavement. It shatters, shards of green glass drowned by the ooze of cheap, red liquid.

Jade's mouth drops. 'Oh, Edie. What have I done?'

Edie gathers her into her arms. 'It's going to be okay, Jade.' She turns her head to the assembled lurkers. 'Show's over, people.

Off you go. Yes, you too, Sue. Do be sure to embellish the details when you tell everyone, won't you.'

Somebody tuts – probably Sue – but they do as they're told and move on.

'Let's get you home.'

Jade lets Edie tuck her into bed, and she is compliant as a tired child, addled with remorse.

'What about my baby, Edie?' she whispers. 'What if I've hurt him?'

'Sometimes, all that stress and grief makes us do stupid things,' Edie tells her. 'And anyway, it was just one sip, love. Not enough to do any harm.'

Jade nods miserably. 'But it's not real grief if he's still alive, is it? I thought grief was for dead people.'

'Of course it's grief. Losing someone is hard, whether they're dead or they've left you or whatever.'

'I wish Asif had died instead of leaving me. Because at least I'd know that he still loved me.' She fiddles with her earring. 'If you know someone loves you, it's okay to be sad that they've gone. But if they just leave you for friggin' Tamara . . .' She chokes on her love-rival's name. 'I feel stupid, Edie. For still loving him.'

'Oh, Jade,' she says, her heart contracting hard.

'How do you live with it, eh? The idea that you weren't enough for someone? Or worse, that you were such a terrible person, they couldn't be around you?'

There's a gentle sting of a tear forming in Edie's eye.

'I mean, it's the questions that keep you awake at night. The *What did I do wrongs?* Do you know what I mean?'

'I do know what you mean,' says Edie. She glances around

Jade's room that used to be hers, the walls silent witnesses to conversations just like this. 'But sometimes it's not the *What did I do wrongs*, but the *How can I make up for the wrongs I did?* that keep you awake.'

30

Before

'It's marvellous, isn't it?' says Hilda. 'They didn't have this sort of thing when my boys were growing up. We're going to have a nation of little geniuses!'

The boys are sitting cross-legged on the carpet watching *Rainbow*, all mesmerized and lost to the room.

'Yes,' says Edie, though she's not sure about the educational merit of a bear settling an argument between a pink hippo and whatever it is that Zippy is supposed to be. Besides, she's still fuming with Ron.

'Look what Daddy's got!' he'd sung from the front door before he'd even got his boots off. The boys had been in raptures at the new colour TV he brandished.

'We can't afford this!' said Edie. 'We're saving for a house, or had you forgotten?'

He'd kissed her cheek. 'Live a little, Edes, why don't we? When did you get so stuffy and uptight?' She wanted to argue, but he was already building the boys into a frenzy about all the wonderful things they were going to see now.

Ron's been strange since they were finally granted a business loan for him to expand the garage into the old sewing machine repair shop next door. Spending in a way he never had before.

'How?' Edie had asked. 'We're miles off target.'

'Great rates,' he said, presenting her with a bright pink cardigan.

Edie sifts through the post, hoping for a postcard from Patricia. *Where was it she said she was going next?* She can barely keep up with her friend's travels: in the last couple of years she's received postcards from Paris, Istanbul, Tehran, Kandahar, Lahore and Varanasi. She can't decide whether the sensation she gets when holding the postcard in her hands is envy or terror. Her pulse rises and if she closes her eyes, she can almost hear the sounds of chatter in loud, foreign tongues, smell spices and herbs, and feel her skin pricking with the heat of a relentless dry sun.

There is no postcard today, but there is a letter for Edie, addressed in her maiden name.

She lays the rest of the letters on the hall table and takes the envelope through to the kitchen.

While she waits for the water to boil, Edie opens it.

Fuggle Rummery, it says across the top. *Solicitor and Legal Representative.*

There's something in the officialness of the document and the crisp paper that tells her this is something major. She tucks it into the waistband of her skirt and makes tea for her and Hilda, milk and Jammie Dodgers for the boys.

The boys dive in like seagulls. 'One each boys. And make sure you give some to Nanna.'

'Oh no,' says Hilda. 'They're like prefab walls superglued together with strawberry evil.' She winks at Edie. 'You boys can have my share.'

It confounds her how soft Hilda is with her grandsons. She

catches glimpses of the mother she must have been to her four boys, even during a war. *I get why Ron turned out well.*

'I'll be back in a minute,' Edie says. 'Save me a biccy, boys.'

But the boys have switched their focus back to Zippy pretending to be a motor car in a traffic jam.

She perches on the back doorstep to read the letter, the neat, angled corners framed by the scrubby grasses of The Leas and the vast North Sea beyond. It's a perfect spring day and the loose tang of salt cleans Edie's lungs as a bath would her body.

> Dear Miss Laverick,
> I write on behalf of the estate of your deceased father Mr Sidney Laverick.

She reads the name a few times. It's alien and weird and wrong, this name next to the word *father*. There's something so intimate about *father* and here is a stranger's name printed beside it and the words dance around on the page.

Your deceased father.

Her. Edie. Her father.

There's something, like a gentle tug on the corner of her dress, a tickle, a breeze that won't go away.

Oh, Siddy. Her mother's voice? Edie blinks hard and long, then forces her eyes back to the page.

As the sole heir to his estate, it reads, *I would be grateful if you could telephone or visit my office to further discuss the inheritance.*

Inheritance sounds like something Jane Austen would write about, not something a former cleaner at South Shields town hall would need to worry about. She's light-headed: a stiff wind could carry her off to Scotland. She puts the letter down on the step beside her, wraps her arms around her knees and thinks about disappearing into the leafy fabric of her skirt.

She doesn't tell Ron about the letter: she folds it up and hides it in last year's diary tucked between doctor's appointments for the boys and inane details of bill due dates. He's so preoccupied with the garage these days that she doesn't want him to worry about how she might be taking the news of an errant father that she could have known but didn't. Besides, when he's home he's glued to the television watching this thing or other so much that she wonders if he's forgotten that he even has a wife.

A neon sign for the outside. That's what he's going on about this week, because he saw one on TV all bright and gleaming. 'For the winter, Edie,' he says. 'So people can see it through the dark and the fog.' When Edie pointed out that the garage is just behind the Queen's Head which is lit up like Bonfire Night all of the time, Ron shook his head and said 'Garages, Edie, are a thing I understand. We need a neon sign.'

She doesn't tell Hilda either, pretending instead she has a doctor's appointment when asking if Hilda could mind the boys.

'I'll take them to the park to feed the ducks,' Hilda said.

Edie helped bundle them into their jackets and hats this morning, stuffing their pockets with the heel of a stale loaf and some biscuit crumbs.

'Be good for Nanna,' she told them.

Only when she thought they were long out of sight did she go and put on her neatest tweed skirt that makes her look like she should be at the helm of a skiff crossing a Scottish loch.

The phone rings as she's about to leave. She pauses in the hallway, blood feeling cold and still in her veins. She counts, *five, six, seven, eight* rings before the silence chokes the hallway once more. She squeezes her eyes tight shut. She's been avoiding phone calls from Lavender Hill House again. She still hasn't taken the boys to meet Cynthia. Besides, this outing is about the father she knows nothing about, and that is not somewhere she is willing to go with her mother. Not now. Not today.

Edie's a little out of breath when she gets to the address on Edward Fuggle Rummery's letter. He has an office in Beach Road on the top floor of what would have once been a lovely big house.

When she telephoned, the secretary sounded just like her, and Edie imagined herself in a job like that instead of cleaning offices for bored councillors and middle managers like she and most of the other girls from school had done. Perhaps she should talk to Ron about going back to work when the boys start school. Maybe she could do a job where she answers phones and writes appointments in books and sends letters instead of scrubbing toilets.

'Hello,' smiles an efficient-looking woman when Edie reaches the top floor. 'You must be the former Miss Edith Laverick, now Mrs McVey. Please take a seat and I'll let Mr Fuggle Rummery know that you have arrived. Do you take coffee or tea?'

That's how you get a job like that. Looking efficient and then actually being it.

'Tea, please,' says Edie, her voice suddenly croaky.

'Excellent.' The woman has a file tucked under her arm and a pen in hand. She disappears through a door.

'Ah, Mrs McVey.'

Mr Fuggle Rummery not only has a name freshly peeled from the pages of a Dickens, but he looks like a caricature of Mr Pumblechook, and there's a general air of dust and medicine about the man.

'Come on in,' he says, striding back through the door he just came through. 'Well, sit down then.'

Edie does as she's told, crossing her legs and balancing her handbag on her knee. *I look like a spinster aunt.* But she doesn't want to move now that she's in that position for fear of looking antsy.

'Your father,' Mr Fuggle Rummery peers over his glasses at a piece of paper on his desk. 'Here it is. Blah blah blah, Sidney Laverick, blah blah Edith Laverick, only daughter. Yes, this is it. This is you and he.' He reads silently, his lips running over the words. 'Yes, right. He's left you his home.'

'What?'

'His home. His house. His abode. A property in Boldon Colliery.'

'Really?'

'Yes.' Fuggle Rummery waves the sheet of paper. 'Oh, don't get too excited. It's just a little miner's cottage. Nothing fancy. Let's see. Two bedrooms.' He blows a puff of air. 'Right by the colliery, I'm afraid, so there'll be soot-streaked men traipsing past your window day and night. Ghastly! And the dust! Oh!'

Edie's brain is whirring to make sense of what this giant man is saying. She has so many questions, but forming them is quite out of her grasp.

'So if you decide to sell, we can help you with this too.'

He folds his arms across his chest waiting for a reaction.

'Erm, did you know him?'

'No. Never met the chap in my life.'

There seems to be a lot of blood collecting in Edie's ears, throbbing and pulsing like a shifting tide. She forces some air into her throat. 'Did he . . . did he die recently?'

'End of last year,' he says. 'Aged fifty-nine.'

'Oh.'

'Yes. Miners don't seem to last long, unfortunately.'

*

Edie takes the long way home, down past the fair and the amusements with their penny cascade machines. Perhaps her father might have brought her here, if things had been different. Her small hand in his large, calloused one. Maybe dirt under his nails from a day down the mine. Or maybe he would have scrubbed himself raw with a bar of Wright's in the bath before taking his little girl out for the afternoon.

Of course, it's possible that he was just a horrible man and she's actually had a lucky escape not knowing him. After all, he – or at least someone he knew – was aware of her existence, to name her in his will. *What kind of man doesn't bother finding out about his child?* All the same, it's hard for her not to imagine the something that could have been.

While she walks, shadows of little Edie and Sidney walk just behind. Dad and Edie throwing chips for the seagulls at Littlehaven. Dad and Edie rowing across the boating lake in the South Marine Park. Dad buying Edie an ice cream topped with monkey's blood from Minchella's. Dad picking up Edie and swinging her high in the air like Ron does to the boys that has them shrieking and the glorious sound of a child's laughter ringing on the breezes.

Why didn't that happen?

And there he was, all her life just there in Boldon. Just down the road. And she's missed her chance now to ask him.

A boy on a scooter darts around her and she presses her hand to her mouth to stop whatever it is that's churning and boiling inside from coming out.

31

After

'The eagle has left the nest,' says Jade into the phone, watching Ron's Jag glide across the gravel. Across the road, Verushka's curtains twitch, then, bizarrely, a flashing red light pulses once, twice, three times from a window.

Cars draw into the drive. Sarah Moss emerges from a hedge and women stream like ants through Edie's front door.

'Crumbs, Jade. We appear to have gathered a few more.'

Edie loses count at twelve, finding it hard to concentrate with all these female voices bouncing off her tiles. It's not just that stealing her attention today though. She has an appointment later, and her dossier of helpful information for the KGB agent stuffed into an envelope by the front door.

'I hope we do *Arctic Roll* today.'

'I did some stretching this morning.'

'Here, Ethel, how does this nose clip thingummy work?'

Edie is keeping a careful watch on Jade. She seems brighter, but still, there's a gnawing worry whenever Edie pictures them tussling over that wine bottle. Where did that decisive version of herself come from? Where has she been hiding all these years?

As if reading her mind, Jade smiles over at her. 'I'm okay, Edie. Honest.' She touches Edie's arm and says, 'I'm watching you too.'

After the class, Verushka offers to drive her into Newcastle.

'Are you going to do a spot of shopping, Edie?' asks Sarah Moss. 'Only there's a sale on at Fenwick's.'

'Edith has an appointment,' says Verushka. 'Victor is out of hospital now. His liver fixed.'

'I thought you said it was a kidney?' says Jade.

'Kidney, liver. KGB get stabbed everywhere.'

Edie has no idea what to wear for a meeting with an ex KGB agent. While the other women chatter in her kitchen, she ducks up to her bedroom to try things on. A skirt suit? To show how serious she is? Or perhaps something stealthy, in case they need to run away from someone. She settles for a neat but motion-friendly black skirt and a matching turtleneck. *Perfect.*

Victor is late, which doesn't help Edie's erratic heartbeat to calm or her breathing to come any more easily. Nor did Verushka's driving, which was very much like riding a dodgem at the fair or being pummelled by a rhino. *Stop, start, stop, start, brake, brake, brake.*

Edie runs her finger across the envelope in her hand. She wasn't sure what Victor would need from her, so she's brought a couple of photos, including one of Sean in his school uniform looking neat and shiny, and there's the clipping from the newspaper with the boys who got top exam results in 1990. There's also a postcard he sent Colin from Val d'Isère, the handwriting faded to little more than a grey watermark. When Edie sifted through her photos, looking at that cheeky grin, those glittering eyes, made her feel quite dizzy.

'Edith?'

She jumps up too fast and her envelope slides to the floor. 'Hello!' she says.

Victor has already bent to retrieve it for her before she has time to see his face. The Tyneside Cinema Cafe is busy, but not so busy that she won't be able to hear him over the noise. He stands, and she's confronted with a smallish man with an enormous wiry moustache. Everything behind it is pink and a bit doughy. Edie expected him to be grey and sharp-lined. He's wearing a dark coat and a bulky jumper with a collar and tie underneath, and she gives him a quick once-over for a gun. *Silly Edie. He wouldn't have it somewhere obvious.* She shivers at the thought, pictures a bullet bouncing off the mirrors and chandeliers.

He hands her the envelope without smiling and they sit.

'Thank you for coming,' Edie says, hushed. 'I appreciate that you just got out of hospital and all. Is it better? The kidney? Or liver?'

He flicks his eyes from side to side.

'Sorry!' she says. 'I shouldn't say too much, should I?' She shakes her head. 'I ordered a pot of tea for two. So as not to look suspicious.'

He clears his throat just as the waitress brings over a tray of tea and biscuits and so Edie sits back as though she is just a normal person meeting a friend for tea in a cafe. She smiles, too big, too bright, and rests the envelope on the seat beside her.

When the waitress leaves, Edie leans forward again. 'I have a message from Verushka,' she says. Victor's eyes light up. 'She says "The daffodils are melting."' He chuckles and stares into his empty tea cup. She doesn't want to dwell too long on what the missive might mean or whether she's just passed on something dreadful, so she swallows and presses on. 'I didn't know what you needed, so I put everything I could think of in here.' She tips her head to the envelope. 'Shall I slide it across the table, or will I leave it on the chair and you can pick it up before you go?'

Victor clears his throat again. 'Listen,' he says, then he pulls his mouth into a grim line. 'I cannot help you.' His words are clipped and strange, accent unfathomable.

'Oh,' says Edie, trying and failing not to let the disappointment show on her face. 'Verushka said . . .'

He nods, runs a hand across his mouth, mussing up the moustache. 'Yes. But I cannot.'

Edie sags. She's been building up to this ever since Verushka mentioned it. A swift investigation, an address scrawled on an old receipt, then perhaps a train ride, a dramatic reunion and a fat happy ever after. She curses herself for that fleeting dash of hope.

'I understand,' she says. 'You're probably risking your life even being here.'

He laughs then, softly, covering his eyes with his fingers. 'I'm not what she thinks I am,' he says.

'Well, no,' says Edie. 'You have to go undercover and things. She understands that you have to have some secrets.'

'It's worse than some secrets,' he says. 'How well do you know Verushka?'

'I just met her really,' says Edie. 'She's my neighbour.'

'Edith, can *you* keep a secret?'

Edie giggles most of the way home. It's helping with the disappointment, laughing about what Victor just told her.

He didn't just recover from a kidney or liver puncture from a stab wound. He was having a haemorrhoidectomy at the RVI because rather than having been stabbed, he actually suffers from an aversion to high-fibre foods. And he hasn't been stabbed, ever, because he's not in the KGB.

'What, never have been?' Edie had asked.

'Never,' he said.

Victor isn't even Russian – he's from Stockton-on-Tees and has never been further than Marbella. He worked for KP, the snack manufacturer, until he retired last June, driving around, trying to get hotels and health clubs and pubs to stock their snacks instead of competitors'. He'd listed some of the snacks he used to sell and Edie found herself more impressed than if he had been in the KGB.

'Did you get free crisps?' she asked.

'Yes,' said Victor. 'And nuts.'

Verushka, as it turned out, overheard him having a business meeting in a hotel in Hebden Bridge. *Remember*, he'd said to the manager, *I'm with KPP.*

'KP Products,' he said. 'KPP. That's what my division was called.'

He hadn't understood why a small pointy woman had dropped a beermat into his lap with *Meet me in the bathroom* scrawled across it, but, recently divorced and convinced his romance days were over, he'd jumped at the chance.

'And I did not regret it,' he said, flushing at the memory. Edie hadn't known where to look. 'Then she whispered "I come pre-approved by Vladimir Kruchkyov," and I thought, "Uh-, she's got the wrong end of some sort of stick," but it seemed easier to be a man of few words with a fake accent than risk losing that little whirlwind forever.'

In the taxi, Edie squirms, embarrassed for Victor, though even she can understand how Verushka might intimidate a person into pretending to be something else.

'Besides,' said Victor. 'It was exciting being someone else. Someone mysterious, not just the salted peanuts guy. I grew this especially.' He stroked the moustache with pride. 'You won't tell her, will you?'

It was a waste of an afternoon really, except it wasn't, because she finally feels as though she is doing something. And maybe now that she's done something, she's ready to do something else. Time to go dig out that box.

32

Before

The red bricks give the overall appearance of grey. The house looks as though it has just walked through a blizzard of ash and slumped to the pavement hoping the two houses on either side will prop it up. Hard to believe that they are only five miles from Hilda's house and the fresh sea breeze. Harder still that it's only four miles from the flat she grew up in with just her mother.

'Look at it with rose-tinted specs on, Edie,' Patricia said when she called from Varanasi. 'Imagine it as the dream palace it could be.'

Patricia does spout some hippy guff these days, but she might be right on this one, because if Edie keeps on looking at it with her Edie-eyes, she might cry.

She barely has the key in the front door when the one beside it swings open, making her jump.

'Hello.'

The man has a face all squashed up as though made out of bread dough. So squashed that his eyes have disappeared and gives the impression of an uncooked biscuit with a pipe stuck in the front.

'Hello.'

'You must be Sid's kid?'

It takes Edie a moment to realize that he means her. 'I suppose I must.' *Sid's kid.* What would it have been like growing up referred to as *Sid's kid*? 'Did you know him?'

'Oh, aye,' says the doughy man. 'Down pit together, me and Sid.'

She could ask him now: ask him what Sid was like. Ask him if he ever talked about the little girl he left behind with her mother, or if he missed her, or if he was a good man. But instead she examines a brick that seems to be trying to break free of its front wall battalion.

'Well, I'd best get on,' she says, waving her key.

He chortles. 'Oh yes, you'll have work to do.' He plucks the pipe from his mouth and uses it to draw a circle in the air around the house. 'Sid was a right dirty bugger. You'll be cleaning for weeks.'

'Right.' She pushes the key into the lock. 'Well, nice to meet you.'

'I'm Albert,' he says. 'With the marrows.'

'Excellent.' Edie doesn't know what a marrow is or whether she's supposed to know about Albert and his marrows. Maybe it's a miners thing.

It's dark inside. Edie leans against the door and blinks until her eyes adjust to the gloom. She's in a small, square hallway, untouched by the light from any window. A flight of narrow stairs stretches deeper up into the dark. She finds a light switch and flicks it. There's a hiss, but nothing happens. She flicks it back off and the hissing stops. Edie doesn't know much about electrical things, but if an electrical thing hisses at you, it's probably bad. She'll have to get Ron to look at that, when she gets round to telling him that she's inherited a house just around the corner from his garage that belonged to a father she didn't know she had.

Edie puts her hand on the first doorknob which comes off in her palm.

'Bugger,' she says, shouldering the door.

She trips into a living room, and though the curtains are drawn, there's just enough grey light to make out clusters of boxes and dust crammed into the corners. Her nostrils are filled with nicotine and coal dust and old food and stale beer. A dampness clings to the air. Edie coughs.

Stepping over boxes and piles of material, she makes her way to the window and opens the curtains. One side of the curtain pole topples as she tugs, a shower of dust raining into her hair.

She should have left the curtain up. Left it up, locked the door and walked away. She could have thrown the key in the bin and pretended that she'd never met with Mr Fuggle Rummery in his squashy office. She need never tell Ron about the house and it could just fester along here nicely until the rats ate the furniture and termites devoured the walls.

But no. Now that she's ripped off the curtains and let a little bit of weak daylight in, she's under some sort of spell and is stuck with the place.

She puts her hands on her hips and surveys it with her cleaner-eyes, the one she used to use when brushing crumbs off the Mayor's desk, or emptying the bins in the basement where old files and creepy clerks were kept. Only this is a much bigger job.

Albert was right: Sid was a right dirty bugger.

A lone armchair sags, a deep bowl pressed into the seat where her father's bottom sat hour after hour. She shudders, has to look away. The only other item of furniture is a glass-topped side table, identical to the one she had at home growing up. Maybe her parents bought them as a pair, then took one each when they split up. The idea depresses her more than the alternative: that they both happened to like exactly the same coffee table. And no one would ever know that, apart from their one daughter. The glass is smeared, and without touching it, Edie can tell that there are substances there that she will have to chisel away.

Beneath her feet, the carpet is thin and cheap. It's hard to tell what colour it is. Brown, maybe? Towards the edges of the room, curls of weave have come away from the rest of the carpet. Sections of the wallpaper peel away in ribbons, the wooden frames around the windows are splintered and crumbling. A sad, bare lightbulb hangs from the ceiling. Piles of clothes and some half-filled boxes are dumped across the floor. A poker lies beside a dead fire in the grate.

The room is desolate. How could the prospect of staying with her and her mother have been worse than this? *Were her problems worse after Sidney left, or did he leave because she was the way she was?* She plucks a piece of paper from one of the boxes.

Wanted, it reads. *A living wage.*

There's a picture of a stern-looking miner on the front. It's a generic picture, but Edie can't help thinking, *Dad*, as she looks at it.

There aren't any photos, or at least not in this room. No pictures on the wall. Just a United Dairies calendar hanging from a nail still turned to November 1976. Edie flicks back through it, searching for even a scribble in his handwriting, but it is empty.

The rest of the house is no improvement.

There's a cracked window in the kitchen, a hole in the

floorboard in one of the slope-ceilinged bedrooms and the toilet is leaking, which has left a giant bubble in the kitchen ceiling which Edie is scared will pop on her head.

She puts her head in her hands.

She needs Ron.

Through Ron's rose-tinted lens, it looks better.

From the moment he carried the wriggling twins over the threshold – one over each shoulder – the dank, tiny rooms started to morph into something that could, at a deep squint, look like a semi-liveable family home.

'Oh Edie!' he says, kissing her. 'Our dream has come true.'

She listens to his talk of stripping walls, of putting in a flower bed against the back fence. And the boys are on board with helping him rip down curtains and stamp down cardboard boxes. 'You always see the good amongst the rubble,' she says. *Maybe that's why you love me.*

Edie rolls her sleeves up and puts her cleaner head on. *Really, it shouldn't be that hard.* If she could make those beer-soaked carpets at the Bamburgh Arms come up good, she can surely do the same here. And once Hilda gets on board, they're unstoppable.

It's weeks of scrubbing and sanding and painting, both women and the twins emerging at the end of each day covered in dust and grime, falling into chairs at Ron's garage just before closing time demanding tea and biscuits.

'Daddy, we smashed a thing and Mammy and Nanna said it was okay.'

It's the light that changes first. They scrub the windows with white vinegar, excoriate the old dark paint and replace it with white. Then the walls are scrubbed clean and splashed through with a toothpaste-white wash. They rip up the carpets, sand down the floors and replace the surround on the fireplace with some old tiles Hilda's neighbour was getting rid of.

Edie manages to get an old sofa from an advert in the newspaper and re-covers it with some fabric she found at the Red Cross Shop; there's enough left over for curtains and suddenly the living room starts looking comfortable and inviting. It's one room, but it's enough to give them hope.

She's delighted, and it's such a far cry from how she grew up. When Edie was a child, she was scraping limescale from taps. Rats lived in their pantry, cockroaches held her hostage at the back door.

Ron, jovial all the time, calls it their 'little castle' and gets the boys to trumpet his arrival home.

'And it's only five minutes' walk from the garage,' he likes to tell people. 'It's like fate or something.'

Whenever he says this, Edie gets a little choke of sadness. She could have passed Siddy on the street when she was helping set up the garage. Ron may have had a cheeky lunchtime pint with her dad and never have known it. She scans her memories for something – a face, a feeling – those times she was right there near the mine and the pub and the garage, but comes up blank.

A month in and they've got a cosy living room and kitchen. Two and the bathroom is clean and functional. Just under three months after she inherited it, she takes to the final room with her paintbrushes.

Ron's brother Harry and his wife have taken the boys out today so Edie and Hilda can get everything finished and ready for moving in. Edie takes the crumpled picture that she cut out of the newspaper and smooths it on her lap. She's not confident, but thinks that if she can make a general outline in pencil she can make it work from there.

'I'm not sure, Edith. You can't go wrong with a nice wallpaper.'

'Wallpaper's expensive,' she says, and sketches out a big Paddington bear holding a bloom of balloons in his paw. 'Besides, I think they'll like it.'

'Well, when it's painted, I suppose it might be quite nice,' says Hilda grudgingly, but as Edie adds colours, she suddenly becomes John Berger and critiques Edie's work like she's scribbling on the *Mona Lisa.*

'All I'm getting from the bear is sadness,' she says. 'Maybe he needs some brighter balloons?'

The paint dry, twin beds installed and a bright green rug splayed on the floor, Edie spins in the centre of the room and laughs. *I've done it! I've got a house and a room for my boys.* She plops onto the rug and grins at Paddington. 'See,' she tells him. 'This is how to do it.' She gives him a wink, imagines him nodding his approval.

When the house is finally ready, Edie thought Hilda might put up a fight, a battle to keep her youngest son and grandsons in the house, because Ron's brothers who live in Scotland and Birmingham and York now have all had girls, so the twins alone will be carrying on the McVey name as Hilda likes to remind them. But no. She's quite happy to help them pack up and even moves the van forward a day when she hears there is an earlier slot.

'What's the rush, Mam?' Ron asks.

'There's only so much *Mr Benn* I can watch,' she says, settling into her armchair in front of the TV before they've even got the last box into the van.

It's nice to experience life as a family of four for the first time. All together under their own roof.

'Of course, one day we'll upgrade to a three-bedroomed place,' says Edie.

Ron wrinkles his nose. 'Why would we do that? Oh, maybe when the boys get bigger, I suppose.'

Edie stares at him. 'I meant for Mam,' she says eventually. 'So she can come and live with us finally.'

'Oh right,' says Ron, his cheeks flaming.

At the weekend, Hilda brings them a shoot from her apple tree and they plant it ceremoniously in the back garden.

'For good health and happiness,' says Hilda, and they toast the tree with glasses of apple juice.

'Is that a thing?' says Edie. She just remembers the Adam and Eve story about snakes and temptation and reckons that's probably a rubbish omen, but then again, that garden was paradise and theirs looks over a soot-blanketed coal shed so she reckons they're probably quite safe from temptation.

They settle into life in the village. Ron walks to work, and some days, when the boys have got up early, they'll all go to the garage together. Edie realizes that she can cut across the fields to the pond in the centre of neighbouring village Cleadon and she bundles the boys into scarfs and mittens that run through their coats with string and takes them to feed the ducks. Sometimes, they collect little stones and paint them at home, then leave them scattered around the village like breadcrumbs, like Edie used to do with her mother on the days when she was functioning and bright.

As they emptied the house of rubbish, Edie looked for traces of Siddy in boxes and in the drawers and wardrobes, and found nothing. For some reason, this makes her sadder than if she'd found something shocking, like a long-lost sibling or a criminal record. But no. Siddy Laverick was an empty shell.

Maybe I didn't miss out on anything. But sometimes, she worries that he was an empty vessel because he didn't have his family there with him.

She tries to talk to weird Albert.

'Kept himself to himself, did Siddy,' he says, squinting. 'Never one to talk about himself. Or his past.'

Just once, he mentions 'trouble with this woman' and Edie's ears perk up, until she realizes that he's talking about a dispute Sid once had with the woman in the house opposite about feeding cats.

Edie washes laundry in the tin bathtub in the garden like women did when Hilda and her mother were young. One day they'll get a washing machine, Ron says, and then things will be really easy. Sometimes, when she can push her mother's sad face out of her mind, she pretends to believe that he's right.

33

After

She's doing it, and no one's going to talk her out of it.

Edie has covered all of the grey couches and the table that's shaped like a plectrum in old sheets and has a collection of paint colours and disposable foil baking trays by her feet. In her hand is an A3 page with a picture of The Leas on it. She probably didn't need a photograph: the view from the back garden of Hilda's house is imprinted in her memory and eyes and heart. It is a photo she'd taken on a perfect day with Harry's Yashica. A perfect, breezy spring afternoon where the light was just starting to dip behind the houses and tentacles of sunlight reached through the gaps and onto the grasslands that separated them from the cliffs. The sky is a gentle blue and the clouds are tufted with pink, like fairground candy floss. Even in the old picture, the sea and sky look alive, as though Edie could stretch out her arm and feel the gentle scratch of salt on her skin. The girl at Boots asked if she wanted it blown up big and she'd nodded, marvelling at the things they could do now with a grainy old print.

She got two copies. One, she plans to put in a frame and hang on her bedroom wall, next to the spot where she wants to dissect her scrapbook and put all of Patricia's postcards from across the globe. On the second copy that she has in her hand, she's drawn a grid, and on the wall in front of her, the one facing their front window, she's marked a matching grid in pencil.

'Here goes nothing,' she says to the light grey wall.

The woman in the fancy paint shop had been right: foil trays do make excellent mixing palettes. She swirls a dark green in with a light green to try to match the exact same colour as the tufty grass between the house and the cliff edge. She starts at the bottom left, trying to get the swish of the rushes that used to tickle her ankles when she ran through it.

When the boys were small, before they moved to Boldon Colliery, they used to run along The Leas, stamping paths through the longer grasses, plucking dandelion clocks and blowing them. There was that time Colin had just licked his lips and Sean blew a dandelion in his face, and all the tiny little ghost parachuters had stuck around his mouth.

'I a hairy baby,' Colin had cried and it took all Edie had not to burst out laughing. She'd caught Sean's eye and he was smirking, and they'd had to look away from one another.

'See,' she says to her paintbrush. 'We were close.'

That's what she wants to capture here. Not just the beauty of the rugged North East coastline, not just the cliffs that whisper secrets of shipwrecks and smugglers and kittiwake migrations in their limestone crevices, but the joy that she used to get when she looked out over this little enclave from Hilda's warm kitchen. Little tender moments, her and Ron, her and the twins, trapped in the fibres of the landscape.

Edie paints all morning, and only when she is finished does she let herself step back and look at her work.

It's a tiny bit wonky. She realizes now that the picture was on a slight angle, so the sea doesn't quite run parallel to the skirting board, but still, maybe she's captured some of the mood of The Leas. *She'll* recognize it anyway, and that's the important thing. It's a five-metre-by-two-metre version of her happy place and she now can't wait to sit and admire it with a cup of tea and a Garibaldi.

She pulls the sheets off the chairs and the plectrum table and drags one of the grey velvet monstrosities to the centre of the room. She turns it, so that it faces her mini-Leas, and has a little sit. *Yes. This will do nicely.*

It doesn't feel quite finished though.

'These stupid grey cushions,' she says to the couch. 'Who puts grey cushions on a grey chair? Who wants to play hide and seek with cushions?'

In the afternoon, she gets a taxi to Whitley Bay, where Jade assures her the charity shops are 'amazeballs'. She only wants a few cushions, just to brighten the place up a bit, and doesn't like the idea of generic cushions the same as everyone else has. Besides, she likes a charity shop and it's been a while since she's had a rummage.

'Why do I need to justify myself?' she asks her handbag and the taxi driver sniggers.

In the first charity shop, she picks up a cushion with lemons printed all over it.

'Yellow goes nice with grey,' she says to the cushion. She'd said the exact same thing to Sean when they'd been to buy his Dame Allan's uniform and he'd complained about the tie he was going to have to wear. She also finds a green one printed with terriers wearing crowns which makes her giggle. *Jade might like that.* She then finds a stack of Catherine Cookson books that she hasn't read. 'Might as well,' she says. She can't remember when she last bought a book, or in fact, when she stopped having time to read, despite the endless stretches of empty time she finds herself faced with since the win and giving up her job.

She hits four charity shops and her fingers are aching with bags by the time she flags down another taxi. All up, she now has five brightly coloured cushions, two lace doilies, nine books and an orangey rust-coloured throw blanket which could have come from a bazaar in Morocco and makes her think of Patricia.

But the jewel in the crown here is the ceramic hen to keep eggs warm, identical to the one Hilda used to have in her kitchen. 'I've always wanted one of you,' she whispers to the hen.

In the little sitting room, Edie arranges the bright cushions and the throw on the chairs. She takes the metal sculpture that looks like a broken tractor off the shelf and tosses it in the bin, then arranges her books along it, leaving a few on the plectrum table that she's put by the chair and topped with a lace doily.

'Perfect.'

She's settled into the chair with her tea and a biscuit when she hears Ron and Colin get back from wherever it is they've been. Their conversation, muffled through the closed door, halts.

'Edie, what the hell . . .?'

The door swings open and Ron and Colin stare at her with the sort of horror you might see in a film. *A bit melodramatic for a bit of paint and a couple of doilies.*

'What have you . . . why have you . . . what's that?'

Ron gestures at the wall.

'It's a mural, Ron. That's what they call it these days. A mural. Of The Leas.'

'What? Why?'

Edie grins. 'I like it.'

'Did you do it yourself, Mam?'

'I did.'

Ron and Colin exchange a look. 'And you painted on the door.'

Edie nods. *Edie's Reading Room* is painted on the door in big swirly purple letters.

'Edie, we paid Delph a lot of money to decorate this place.'

'And you didn't have to pay me a penny to improve it. Imagine that!' Edie takes a sip of her tea and leans back in the chair. 'Now, if you don't mind, I'd like to get back to *The Rag Nymph* here.' She picks up her book and reads until they retreat, whispering something. A minute later, Colin pops his head back round the door.

'It's not bad, Mam. Well done.'

He disappears again and she smiles, then lets out a contented little sigh. They will be trying to figure out if she is in fact going mad, and perhaps she is, but now that she's carved out a proper space for herself in the house, she's ready to start tackling some of the other things she needs to deal with.

Of course, she could always say to Ron and Colin *Let's do this together! Let's find our Seany.*

But this feels like something Edie needs to do for herself.

34

Before

A group of women stand around the edges of the playground. They're in small clusters and twitter confidently to one another, some with prams, others with small children running around their ankles. Edie hitches herself to the outskirts of the group, a space between her and the others.

How do they all look so relaxed? *She* hasn't managed to get a thing done today: the laundry basket is foaming over with dirty socks and grubby shorts, the dishes are a teetering pile in the sink and she hasn't even thought about what they're going to have for tea. It would be easy to blame the mess on first-day nerves about the boys starting school, but despite only being in Sid's old house for a year, and despite all their hard work, it took less than six months for everything to start to slide. Maybe it's the dust from the pit or the Sisyphean task of tidying toys. Perhaps it's the relentless energy she ploughs into raising two rowdy five-year-olds, or all the years of cleaning other people's spaces that makes her exhausted at the thought of scouring her own house, but Edie can't remember when she last felt in control. She sighs and knots her fingers together.

'First kid?'

A woman appears at her side with a jam-spotted child under her armpit, a second attached to her calf. Her hair is looped into a messy knot on the top of her head and she wears baggy dungarees. Her face is dominated by a lopsided grin.

'Don't worry. It gets easier.' She nods towards the school. 'One starting today and another in class three. Just got to get these two in and I'm a free woman!' She pumps a fist in the air like an athlete.

Edie gives a half-smile. She adjusts the waistband on her tailored skirt, suddenly aware of how very formal she looks next to this woman. In fact, glancing at the other women in the yard, she is dressed more formally than them all. *Trying too hard, Edie. Why can't you just be normal?*

'Here they come.'

A door is pushed open by a rotund woman Pied Piping a gaggle of children behind her. She grips a small boy in green trousers by the hand. As she leads them towards the gathered mums, Edie realizes with a start that the boy in the green trousers is Colin.

'He was wearing his uniform,' she murmurs to no one in particular.

The wobbly line of children explodes like a firework, as youngsters scatter to greet their parents. Shrieks and excited gabble accompany the thump of small-people feet, the occasional cry penetrating the chatter. Mams sweep their children into hugs, younger siblings gaze with wonder at the intrepid adventurers who have survived their first day at school.

The woman gripping Colin's hand makes a steady beeline for Edie, greeting her with a tight smile and a tilt of the head.

'I'm afraid Colin had a little accident,' she winces, proffering a plastic bag that Edie hadn't noticed before.

'Oh.' Edie takes the bag.

'It's okay.' The woman pats Colin on the head. 'But if you can work on the toilet training at home, that would be helpful.' She passes Colin's hand to Edie like a baton.

Colin stares at the gritty grey surface of the playground. His cheeks are red. Several of the other mams and their dirty-kneed offspring have stopped to listen.

'I'm sorry. He does. I mean, we did. He's usually good, it's just . . .' She trails off. The woman nods primly and turns to leave.

'Oh!' She turns back to Edie. 'I meant to say, Sean was wonderful. A total delight!'

Edie stares at her retreating back as the woman waddles back towards the building.

'It didn't work, Mammy,' says Colin.

'What didn't work?'

He holds out a sweaty palm, a rock painted to look like a ladybird in the centre. 'It didn't work. You said . . .'

That morning, Edie had knelt on the ground by a sniffing Colin who didn't want to go with the loud children into the squat brick building.

'I want to stay with you, Mammy,' he whispered.

Edie had wanted him to stay with her too, but this was what had to happen, wasn't it? Children have to go to school and leave their anxious mothers in a broken pile on a threadbare carpet. Those are the rules and normal people follow them.

'Sorry, Col,' she said, more firmly than she intended. Her voice was sharp and bright. 'You can't. You have to go to school.'

His bottom lip had trembled in that way that broke her every time and she pulled him in for a quick, tight hug.

'Look,' she'd said, fishing around in her bag for the rock she always carried in her bag. 'Ah, here you go. A ladybird.' Colin turned it over in his hand. 'My mammy gave me this,' she said, 'to make me feel brave when I was nervous once. If you get worried, you can hold it, think of Mammy, and everything will be all right.'

'Will it?' he'd said dubiously.

Now, Edie takes the rock from his hand and shoves it back into her bag, trying as she always does when she looks at it to push her own mother out of her mind. The thought that Cindy might have experienced this same anxiety when Edie started school sets the prickling guilt into motion all over again, and she vows that soon, *very soon*, she will take the boys to meet her, even if Cindy hasn't mentioned them since Edie cried all over her.

'Can't stand Miss Tilsley.' It's the dungareed woman. 'Our Steven had trouble with her. Called him a hooligan!'

Edie scans the yard for Sean. She spots a flash of him chasing another small boy across a hopscotch grid.

The dungareed woman plants the jammy child on the ground and kneels by Colin. 'Are you okay, little man?' He nods bravely, but his damp eyelashes blink too fast. 'Don't worry. I weed myself two weeks ago on a hen night. No big deal.' She shrugs. 'If you ask me, Miss Tilsley could do with weeing herself a bit more often. Maybe she could wee some of her sourness out.'

A giggle and a bubble of snot erupt out of Colin. He swipes his sleeve across his nose and smiles. The woman puts out her hand to shake.

'Pleasure to meet you, sir. I'm Carol.' Colin shakes it, then grins at his mother. Carol stands. 'Looks like Gary's found a new friend.' She nods over to the two small boys hitting each other with twigs.

'That's my Sean.'

'Twins! Nice.' The woman takes the two children she brought with her by the hand, briefly checking to make sure they are both hers. 'We live just over there.' She waves a hand vaguely in the opposite direction to Edie's house. 'Why don't you come for a cuppa and the boys can play?' She jerks her head towards the other mams. 'I'll tell you which of these arseholes to avoid. Gary! Bring your friend. They're coming for tea.' The woman charges towards the boys. 'Meet you at the gate.'

Edie frowns. A couple of the other mothers are ogling her unashamedly. Colin tugs her skirt.

'Mam. Can we go?'

Edie takes him by the hand and starts walking. She hears the whispers.

'My Nicola was toilet trained by two. No accidents.'

'Two! Our Janet was twenty months.'

Carol turns back to her, points at the mothers one-upping each other and mouths *Arseholes*.

Edie gives a feeble half-smile. The one-upping mothers glance down their noses as she passes and her cheeks burn, heart thudding hard and high in her throat. Might the teacher report it to someone?

'We have to make a report,' said the policeman, bringing her home that night in the cold. She presses through the group fighting tears and heads to the gate, where Carol is rearranging the jumper of an older boy.

'Holy crap! You look like you need more than a tea!' Carol links her arm through Edie's. 'I'll do the kids some sausages and we can have a natter over a nice vermouth.'

Edie and the boys settle quickly into the rhythms of the school week. On Mondays, she packs them both off with their little bank bags filled with carefully counted change and a scrap of paper with their names on so they can eat shepherd's pie and jam sponge off aeroplane trays in the school hall.

On Tuesdays and Thursdays, she makes sure they're both

wearing neat vests and underpants, makes sure they've got their plimsolls in their bags for PE, and on Fridays, she checks they've got their spelling lists and their reading books before they go home.

But Friday teas with Carol and her tribe have become the part of the school week that they all look forward to the most. The sweet release of the ringing bell at three forty-five signals the end of lonely days at home thinking up tasks to fill the empty hours between nine and three. Edie looks forward to two formless days with her boys without the misery of not knowing if they're safe or happy or well.

Edie and Ron have their first proper money argument on a Tuesday.

She'd been flicking through the magazines with Carol two Fridays previously and they'd spotted an ad for Jazzercise. A picture of a woman in shiny tights and a leotard declared that Jazzercise™ wanted instructors, and to call the number below for more information.

'You'd be great,' said Carol, holding out the receiver to her. 'Didn't you do gymnastics?'

The helpful woman on the line had taken her details, sent an information pack and, before she knew it, Edie had ordered the leotard. It's really nice. A bit higher in the bum than she would have liked, maybe, but she can always put some tights underneath.

'Looking good, Edie-Eves,' she says, twisting to see her full reflection in the bedroom mirror. Maybe Ron'll touch her bum and whisper 'After the boys have gone to bed, you're mine.' She gives her reflection a saucy wink.

Ron and the boys are watching *The Wacky Races*.

'Turn that down for a sec,' calls Edie from the door. 'I want to show you something.' She waits at the door until Muttley's laugh is smothered. 'Ta-da!' She steps in front of her tiny audience and strikes a pose. 'What do you think?'

'Are you going swimming, Mam?' asks Sean.

'No,' says Edie. 'I'm doing Jazzercise!'

Last week, there was a woman on TV showing some of the moves. Edie followed along, delighted that she could do them all, and could do some of them better than the instructor. *Made for this!*

She does some now. She starts with the knee bounces, clicking her fingers and nodding her head. Her hair is bouncing like the woman on TV. Then she keeps bouncing, but goes side to side, clapping her hands as she goes.

Sean jumps off the sofa and starts doing the movements with her. She does the wiggly hip move and Sean almost falls over trying to do it too. Colin hops up, jumping up and down and clapping his hands, and then the three of them are laughing and bouncing and clapping hands.

Look! I'm a fun mammy!

She glances at Ron, who has his arms folded, and his face has gone a weird pinky colour. Edie stops.

'What's wrong, Ron?'

'Just stop it, Edie.' His voice is quiet. 'What are you doing?'

She laughs and flops onto the sofa beside him. The twins keep on dancing. 'Jazzercise. They're doing it on TV.'

'And you need this suit to do it, do you? With your bum hanging out? Can't just do it in your normal clothes?'

'Well, not if I want to teach it.'

'Teach it?'

'Yes. There's a teacher training course in the Masonic Hall starting in January. I've filled in the application form. I just need to pay the fee then I can teach the classes.'

'The fee? You have to pay to be a teacher? That's ridiculous, Edie.'

The boys have stopped jumping.

'Of course. You pay to do the course then you're qualified. Then you can teach the classes.'

'Right. So you pay to do the course, you pay for the leotard, what then? Do you have to pay to hire a hall?'

'I think so.' Edie's face is hot. 'I thought you'd like this. You always said I should use my gymnastics again. That's what this is, Ron, and before you know it people will be paying *me* to come to the classes.'

'Paying to come and watch your arse bopping around, you mean.' Ron's jaw is a hard line. 'This is stupid, Edie.'

'What?'

'I said this is stupid.' He stands up. 'You're not doing it. I forbid it.'

'You forbid it?'

'Yes. Forbid.' He walks to the door and opens it. 'I'm slaving my guts off for this family and you're frittering money on a dance class and a leotard.'

She could mention the TV, or the fact that she saved them money by inheriting a house, or the fact that he keeps lending their savings to his brothers but never chases them to pay it back, but she doesn't. How can he be that generous with his brothers but deny her this one little thing? The Ron who thinks she's fantastic and kisses her on Ferris wheels?

Colin has placed his hand on her knee. Edie slides hers over the top of it.

'This is not a job,' Ron snaps from the doorway. 'It's a scam. And I can't believe you'd fall for something so pathetic.' He slams it behind him, hard.

Pathetic. The word stings like a slap.

Part 4

Ball Number 9: Edie's Birthday

35

Before

Lavender Hill House could easily win a competition for the least aptly named building in Britain. Vomited up from the hangover of an architect's shattered dreams, the bile-coloured bricks and squat institutional stature shout *incarceration* rather than *loving repose*. Some window boxes make a brave attempt at cheer, but whoever is in charge of horticultural arrangements is either dead or too depressed by the architecture to take their work seriously.

Still, it will have to do until Ron and Edie can afford a bigger house so she can come to live with them.

It's a dreary Monday afternoon when she finally brings the boys for the first time, and Ron's accusation of her being *pathetic* still smarts. Edie's nerves are frayed, but she really doesn't want to go home and sit in the stilted silence that has hung in the air since the fight. The twins have whined since she collected them from school, bundled them onto the bus, then walked them here in a drizzle.

'Mam, it smells.' Colin tugs at her sleeve.

'Stop it,' she snaps, then feels bad. 'Why don't you go play with your brother?'

Sean has found an old *Bunty* annual on the bookshelf and it covers his face, his thin legs sticking out from the bottom. Colin trots over to join him, then in a few moments, they are sniggering behind the book.

Edie isn't sure why she's nervous. It's not about her mother, not really. Although this will be the first time she's met the boys, it's unlikely that she'll grasp the concept of who they are and how they are related to her. Not these days. The deep, genetic link connecting her mother and the boys is little more than a cold whisper in a hot room.

No. What she's worried about is judgement from the boys. That at five, she is presenting them to a woman they've never met and hoping for a glimmer of a connection that transcends familiarity and might not happen. That they will look at this small, birdish stranger with disgust or fear or worse: pity, and that they will tar Edie accordingly. Sometimes she pictures a trace of what she did when they were babies imprinted into their souls, like a tattoo of her failure.

'Here she is,' says a singsong voice from the door. A woman in faded pink scrubs leads Cynthia into the dayroom.

Edie's mother is swamped in a purple cardigan that is definitely not hers and her hair is unkempt. The woman notices her looking.

'She wouldn't sit still long enough for me to brush her hair,' says the carer defensively.

Edie smiles as though it doesn't matter, but it does. She never used to let her mother leave the house looking anything other than neat, and there's a tug of guilt just south of her belly button.

'Sit down, Mam,' says Edie, aiming for lightness, but her voice comes out tight and high. 'I've brought some people for you to meet.'

'Is this an appointment?' asks Cynthia.

Edie stands, taking her mother's arm and guiding her to a mossy velvet armchair that's seen better days. She glances at the boys who are engrossed in the *Bunty* and clears her throat.

'Sean, Colin. Come over here and meet Nanna Cynthia.'

Colin peeps from behind the book, but Sean keeps on reading. Edie waves her arm to Colin. 'Come on,' she says. He stands, puts his head down and walks over slowly. 'Sean,' says Edie, a bit louder. 'Come here.'

By the time Colin reaches the chairs, Cynthia is staring at him, lower jaw hanging loose.

'Who's this?' she asks.

'This is Colin,' says Edie. 'Colin is my boy.'

'Did he steal the laundry, Edith?'

Edie laughs lightly. 'No, Mam. No. Colin didn't steal any laundry.'

'Someone stole my laundry,' Cynthia tells Colin. 'All my dresses.'

'You should tell the police,' says Colin solemnly.

'*You* should tell the police,' says Cynthia. She turns to Edie. 'He should tell the police.'

Behind the *Bunty*, Sean sniggers. Whether at something in the book or the strange interaction taking place, Edie isn't sure, but she flickers with fury.

'Sean. Come here.'

He sighs, takes his time tucking the book on the shelf, then shambles over with his hands in his pockets looking everywhere but at Cynthia and his mother.

'Who's this?'

'Mam, this is Sean, my other boy.'

'It's George,' says Cynthia. 'My Georgie!'

Edie doesn't know any George, let alone a little Georgie that Cynthia might know. She's never mentioned a George before.

'I'm not George. I'm Sean,' says Sean.

'My Georgie, my Georgie came back,' says Cynthia, and grabs Sean by either cheek.

'Get off me!' roars Sean. 'Get off me or I'll scream.'

Cynthia is trying to pull him in closer.

'It's okay, Sean,' says Edie. 'She's just a bit confused.'

'It's not okay,' says Sean. 'Mam, she's hurting my face and she smells.'

It's like a snap travelling through her body, propelling her hands to grab Sean by the shoulder. For a moment, he looks relieved that he's being rescued, but it's fleeting.

'How dare you speak to your nanna like that,' she yells, shaking his arm, tightening her grip. 'How dare you! I didn't raise you to be rude and obnoxious.' She wants to go on, tell him the trouble he'll be in when he gets home but his eyes are wide with terror. *Oh god. Why is it always Sean who gets the brunt of my frustration?* Releasing his arm, she notices that her hands are shaking. 'Oh, Seany, I'm sorry. I scared you, didn't I? God, I'm so sorry!'

He takes a step back, eyes brimming. He clamps his jaw shut to stop the tears from falling, then he's off and running. He's out of the room before Edie has taken stock.

'Colin, please can you sit here with Nanna Cynthia while Mammy goes to find Sean?' He shoots his new grandmother a sideways glance, then nods dubiously. 'I won't be long,' she says, patting his arm.

But by the time Edie reaches reception, he's disappeared. 'He was too quick,' the desk woman says, wringing her hands. 'I was letting someone in when the lad darted past me and out into the street.'

'Which way did he go?' asks Edie, trying to keep a lid on her terror.

The woman shrugs helplessly. 'Dunno. Just out.'

'Well help me!' Edie wails. 'He's only five.'

Edie barges past a confused couple and out into the street. Left, right, she can't see him either way. She puts a hand across her heart to quell the thump, but it doesn't do any good. She is stock-still and incompetent and her baby is loose in streets too big for him and she doesn't know where to start.

'Oh my god oh my god oh my god,' she mutters, tapping out the rhythm on her chest with her hand. 'Where are you, Seany?' She wants to run but her feet are rooted to the pavement and even if they'd move, she doesn't know which way to go, certain that if she chooses the wrong direction she'll have lost him forever.

She turns in rapid circles on the spot, eyes scanning frantically up and down the street, but, save for a couple of errant shoppers and two men chatting on the steps of the pub, the street is quiet.

'Hey, missus,' shouts one of the pub men. 'Are you looking for the kid what ran off?' She nods, not trusting her voice to work. 'He ran that way.' He waves a half-smoked cigarette across the pub car park where a small alley leads out to the town hall and a busy intersection.

Edie nods and takes off at a run.

The concrete beneath her feet is uneven and she stumbles, but keeps her balance. Darting between the parked cars, trying to suck in enough oxygen to propel her to Sean, she concentrates on the rhythm of her feet on the ground – *one two one two* – instead of the insistent little voice saying *What have you done?*

There's a lurch in her belly. Where was that gut instinct? That roaring, primal desire to keep her offspring safe?

She rushes down the alley that pops her out into the bustle of the intersection. Cars, buses, pedestrians jostle to be the loudest thing on the street and harried office workers step around her. An old woman with a shopping bag knocks into her arm and a drunk man salutes her.

'Sean!' she hollers, loud, raw. 'Sean!'

There's a thick, pulsing fog gathering at her brow and temples. *Where is that tie? Where is that eternal, invisible umbilical cord that's supposed to tie us together for life? Why don't I have a clue where my baby might have gone?*

'Sean!' she tries again, but the breath has gone out of her lungs. It's half-hearted, weak. *Just like me.*

'Are you all right, pet?' asks a middle-aged woman with a green hat on.

'I've lost my boy,' she says, and saying it out loud makes her cry: hard, raggy tears.

'And you don't know which way he went?'

'No.' She crumples, the woman catching her before she hits the pavement. She has failed.

The woman smells like her mother. 'Well, maybe you should head down to the police station.'

The policewoman brings her a watery tea and a biscuit.

'I've called Lavender Hill and your husband. Someone's bringing your other boy here then you can wait until your husband picks you up. In the meantime, PC Dobson is out in the car having a look for him, and we've got a bunch on foot looking around too. He can't have got too far.'

'Will they find him?' There are pins and needles stinging her fingers and toes, and she's at once so light and heavy that if she tries to stand she's not sure whether she'll fall to the floor or float off through the window.

The policewoman smiles. 'I'm sure they will. Kids run off, Mrs McVey. It happens from time to time.'

Colin has been crying when he arrives. 'The cabbage lady went away and I was all alone.'

She pats his head, pulls him in for a distracted hug, but her head is racing across scenarios where Sean is dead. She gulps fusty air mixed with bile that keeps rising from her gut. *I'll give you anything*, she pleads with the universe, *just bring my boy back to me.*

'Edie!'

Ron bursts through the door towards her. He pulls her into an embrace that's too hot and she can't breathe. She pushes him away, raking her fingers through her hair.

'What happened?' He takes hold of her elbows, frowns. And she sees it. It's just a flash, nuzzling quietly beneath his concern, but it's there. Blame. Blame, and something else, but Edie can't read what it is. There then gone, replaced with worry again.

She steps away from him and covers her face. She lets out a groan, frightening herself with the noise. It sounds like an injured animal, guttural and raw.

'Edie! We'll find him.' Ron clears his throat. 'We'll find him.'

He's been gone more than two hours before a uniformed officer leads a stricken little boy into the room. Dried snot has crusted above his top lip like frozen sea foam, his eyes are red and puffy, his legs covered in scratches.

'Oh, Seany!' Edie is on her knees kissing his grime-streaked cheek, pulling him tight to her chest. Beneath his ribs, the flutter of his heartbeat is both reassuring and terrifying and she holds her heart over his until their rhythms match. Only then can she pull back and look at his face.

There's misery written all over it, but his eyes scare Edie the most: a flinty, icy something rests in them when he looks at her.

'I'm so sorry,' she whispers. Then the flint is gone and, perhaps she imagined it.

'I was scared, Mam,' he says. Scared to be lost and away from her, or was he actually afraid of her?

It is a silent car ride back home.

For three days, she doesn't let Sean out of reach, sleeping on the floor between the boys' beds with a hand on his foot, keeping him home from school.

'Too much, Edie,' says Ron softly on the third evening, steering her to their bedroom as tenderly as she or Patricia used to with her mother.

On the fourth day, Edie relents and lets him go back to school. 'We're doing the pommel horse,' he complained when Edie had said no. 'Please?'

She's folding sheets and fretting when there's a knock.

'Good morning,' says a rotund man in a blue checked shirt resembling pages in a maths notebook. 'I'm Nick Hughes. Can I come in?'

It doesn't occur to Edie to say no or to ask who he is. She leads him through the hallway and into the living room where the laundry is piled across the couch and the armchair.

'I'll just move these sheets,' she says, but she's already caught him taking in the room: the crumpled clothes-mountains, the toast crumbs on the floor, three half-drunk cups of tea left to grow cold on the coffee table, and the blossom of green mould on the wall by the window.

'Excuse the mess.'

She lifts an armful of pillowcases from the chair and indicates to him to sit down. He brushes something off the seat before easing down.

'I'm the social worker who has been assigned to Sean.'

'What?'

'Social worker,' he repeats slowly as though his diction was the issue. 'The incident on Monday with the police put Sean in a position of great danger and it is our duty to ensure that your children are safe in your care.'

'What?' she says again. 'Of course they are. They're my boys.'

'Even so . . .' says Nick but leaves it there.

Edie takes a deep breath and realizes that her hands are shaking. She sits down, wedging her hands under her thighs.

'My boys are my world,' she says. 'I love them more than anything.' Her cheeks are hot and clammy at the same time and she shakes her head to take some of the heat off them.

Nick leans forward onto his elbows. 'Mrs McVey, this isn't the first time your ability to care for your children has been in question, is it?'

'Yes!' she says, then, 'Oh.' Of course: that first winter, her feet rolling around in Ron's boots and the biting cold through that nightdress and the ache in her belly and her boys lying in bed without her and a policeman returning her home. 'That was different,' she says, forcing a shaky smile onto her lips, aiming for breezy, then worrying that might appear flippant. She pushes them into a neutral straight line.

Nick gives her a long look. 'I'm not here to make trouble for you, Mrs McVey. But we have a duty to ensure all children are safe.'

'They are safe!'

There had been news articles about the updates to the Children's Act a year ago, maybe two. *Well that's good*, she'd said when Hilda read out a section from the *Shields Gazette*, thinking that maybe she could have done with a Children's Act when she was growing up. *Nanny state*, Hilda had said. *Mark my words, they'll find any excuse to interfere.*

'Well, the policeman was concerned about the bruises on his arm and shoulders.'

'That could have been from anything,' she says, but knows that Nick will see that she's lying. Her stomach somersaults. *What if he's right? What if I am a danger to my kids?*

Nick Hughes walks around their house, looking at the fingerprint-smeared windows, at the sagging mattresses in the boys' room, noting things in a book. She's ashamed of the ammonia stink in the bathroom where Colin keeps hitting the rug and not the bowl when he pees.

'I was just about to wash that rug,' she says, and he gives her that look that says *Stop lying*.

When he's gone, she falls to the couch amid scattered underpants and tatty knickers and sobs.

We'll be keeping an eye on you, he'd said as he left.

Edie puts her hands over her face like a child. *If I can't see you, maybe you won't be able to see me.*

36

After

At their last class, Edie had vaguely mentioned her birthday, then the roadshow and, before she knew it, some plans had developed into an aqua social that happens to coincide with Edie's birthday and the *Top Gear* Roadshow. The women were collectively annoyed about Colin and Ron leaving her today.

'Especially because of the phone thing,' said Sarah Moss.

'You know, you can keep the same phone number when you move house,' said Jess.

'What?'

'Yeah, I did when I moved to Heaton.'

Edie wishes someone had told her.

A few suggested The Baltic. Nicky, Jess and Jade were pushing for a Wetherspoons. But Edie was insistent: they would be spending her birthday lunch at the Redhouse right on Newcastle's quayside for an infamous pie.

'What is pie?' asks Verushka, perusing the menu.

'It's traditional English food,' says Linda. 'It'll put a bit of meat on your bones.'

'I want nothing on my bones but skin,' says Verushka, but

orders a steak and brown ale pie with mash, peas and gravy anyway.

It's not that Edie is a massive fan of pie, but a few days ago, Colin showed her the *Chronicle* website on his computer which has an archive feature showing nights out from years gone by. He'd spotted Carol's Gary in a picture, he said, and thought she might like to see what a spanner he looked with his tongue poking out all drunk and sideways.

'And this is a thing?' she asked.

'Yeah. They had photographers out all over Newcastle in the nineties, taking photos of all the lads and lasses getting mortal all over town.'

She stayed on and clicked through the pictures after Colin had gone out and long into the afternoon, until she'd spotted someone familiar in the corner of a photo.

She'd squinted at it, leaned in close to the monitor to check she was right, but it was definitely him. Her insides went to liquid. Sean.

Not only was he in the photograph, but he was behind the bar, suggesting that he worked there. She checked the caption: *The Redhouse – 1993*.

Now in the pub, they're taking up the whole of the front bar, wedged into three booths under the window, enjoying the warmth of the August sun.

'So where did you say your friend is now, Edie?' asks Jean.

'Hong Kong at last check. She used to manage hotels. Top ones, you know, with cocktail menus and rooftop bars and stuff. Since she retired, she can just go and stay at any of them, whenever she likes! So now she just moves around them, staying as long as she likes! What a life, eh?'

'You should go to Hong Kong to see her,' says Jean. 'I was there before the handover.'

'Is it good?'

'So good,' says Jean. 'The food, Edie!'

'Maybe I'll ask Ron.'

'Why you ask Ron?' asks Verushka.

'Well, I just . . .'

Verushka throws down her knife and fork. 'Edith, if you want to go somewhere, go. You not need Ron's permission. You are a free, independent woman with means and needs. You go Hong Kong. No more fight. Okay?'

The rest of their table has gone quiet.

'She's right, Edie,' says Jean. 'Life's too short.'

'You think I should go? To Hong Kong?'

'Hong Kong, Azerbaijan, Turkey. Go wherever the hell you like, Edie. I swear, if I could afford it, my feet would never touch the ground.' Linda grins. 'Live, Edie.'

'Maybe I will.'

They're on to their second or maybe third drinks when Edie braves a trip to the bar to ask about Sean. It is a long shot, she knows, but a manager or somebody might have been here for a while. The barmaid is an appley woman with a bright smile and lovely teeth. She doesn't look much older than early twenties though.

'Have you been working here long?' asks Edie.

'About a year,' nods the woman. 'Ages.'

'I don't suppose there's anyone who worked here in the early nineties, is there?' The girl frowns. 'Only I'm looking for somebody, see. Someone who worked here in 1993.'

'Jonesy might have been here then, but his memory's not that great.' She leans over the bar. 'Between you and me, I think he might have a drinking problem.'

'Right,' says Edie. 'Still, if he's here, I'd love to talk to him.'

The barmaid nods. 'I'll see if he's in the cellar.' She disappears through a doorway and Edie looks around the bar, trying to picture Sean here, using his floppy hair and cheeky smile to charm the customers. He must have been working here during his university holidays, to supplement his grant. She has a pang of misery, knowing that he was just here, less than ten miles from a family trying to plug the holes his absence left in their lives.

As though she's conjured him from the recesses of her mind, she sees him. He's in profile, about ten metres away, ordering something further up the bar.

'Sean,' she whispers.

He looks just like he did that last time, only with thumbs of grey at his temples, a thin stubble on his chin. So like Colin, just slimmer, more angular.

'Sean,' she whispers again, then pushes past Linda and Sarah Moss making their way to the bar. Her elbow catches a half-filled wine glass and a cider bottle waiting to be disposed of, smashing them to the floor.

'Edie!'

Sean is turning away, a drink in each hand, giving no indication that he's seen or heard her. 'Sean,' she says, louder.

He has dipped out of sight and Edie follows.

'Sean!' louder now.

A voice at her back says, 'Edie, what are you doing?'

She has lost sight of his head, but he can't be far away. The interior of the Redhouse is labyrinthine. Alcoves, nooks, passageways winding and twisting in all directions. She dips into a space, interrupting two strangers staring meaningfully into one another's eyes. 'Sorry,' she says, and moves around their table.

It's darker the further inside she goes. 'Sean?'

And behind her, Jade's voice, 'Edie?'

Edie turns into an inglenook, complete with a soot-dusted fire grate. It's a dead end. She's alone, and obviously in the wrong place. She turns to go.

'Edie, what are you doing?'

Jade has followed her into the nook.

'I saw Sean,' she says.

'Sean?'

'Yes. Sean. Did you see where he went? We have to go find him.'

'The man you were following is Sean?'

'Yes! Jade, why are you being so weird? This is what we've all been looking for! He used to work here and boom! Here he is!' She laughs, a high, shrill laugh.

'The man you were following is Colin's twin?'

Edie wants to shake her. 'Jade! We've talked about this. Yes! They are twins.'

Edie shoulders her way out of the nook.

'Edie, the man you were following is Asian. I'd say Korean at a guess.'

'What?'

'Korean, Edie. Are you trying to tell me that Colin has a Korean twin?'

Edie laughs again. 'No.' Then she stops. *Is it possible that Jade is right?*

'Come on,' says Jade. 'I'll show you.'

Jade takes her hand and leads her into a small courtyard dotted with tables at the back of the pub. The only occupied table holds the man she just followed. Same shirt, same hair, but *god*! How could she have thought that was Sean? He's around sixty, and is very clearly Asian.

'What's wrong with me, Jade?' she whispers. She's suddenly

tired with a blistering headache popping at the corners of her temples. 'Am I mad? I just wanted to tell him that I'm sorry.'

'Oh, Edie.' Jade pulls her into a hug as a lone tear snakes down Edie's cheek. 'I'll take you home.'

As Jade gently ushers her towards the exit, Edie's stomach rolls and she burns with the shame of her own stupidity. *Jesus Edie! You can't even trust your own eyes.*

Back home, after being safely deposited by Jade who promised to call in the morning, Edie gulps down three glasses of water, then gives in to the soft welcome of her armchair in her reading room. *Why can't I just be normal?*

She's letting Catherine Cookson transport her down to Jarrow Docks when it hits her that she ran off before speaking to the old barman.

I'll have to go back tomorrow.

37

Before

Hilda comes for tea every Thursday, like she's been doing since they moved in. Well, since they got the heating fixed, anyway. Edie and the boys go to meet her at the bus stop, and she has usually filled their mouths with aniseed balls and pear drops before they even get back to the house. Edie's given up protesting about the sweets-before-dinner thing.

Usually, Ron finishes up early, locks up the garage and arrives home around the same time. Every week, Hilda does a variation on 'How's that for timing, my little Ronnie?' and the boys squeal and Ron tries to kiss everyone without getting grease on them. There's a metallic sting to his skin and a hot, sour odour under his arms. But for the past few weeks, he's still in the garage long after the boys have eaten and been deposited in the bath while Hilda huffs on the sofa and watches *Crossroads*.

'Just busy,' he says whenever she asks. The flow is unsteady for general maintenance trade, so he's buying bits and pieces and scraps and used cars to fix up and sell on. He's good at it too, but it's slow and long and hard going. 'It can take a while to see the profit,' he says. At home, he floats around with unfocused eyes. Even the boys can't always roughhouse him out of it.

'It's pretty normal,' says Carol whenever Edie mentions it. 'Everyone can feel a bit low after a big high like the centenary.'

During the mine's three-day centenary celebrations, Edie had started to feel like a proper part of the community. Their dingy little street had been festooned in flags and bunting, and the whole neighbourhood had come together to make the village look as lovely as possible in preparation for the street party, as though royalty itself was planning on dropping in. Carol had given Edie leftovers of a tin of paint and she'd been able to make the front door and the window frames sparkle. At the party, the colliery band had played into the night and Ron had danced with Edie like he never had before, much to the delight of the boys. *I love you, Edie-Eves*, he'd said as the boys waved sparklers under a chandelier of fireworks. Edie could have frozen time, the vibration of Vera Lynn's "We'll Meet Again" in the mouths of heavy brass thrumming through her bones and Ron's fingers trailing lazy eights across her lower back.

Ron had come down fast and hard after that, straight back into being distracted and absent. In the bedroom, she wraps her body around his when the lights are down, only to be met with the stiff rise and fall of his shoulders. One night, Edie slinked across the room in the silk nightie Carol insisted she buy from Binns. That at least garnered a reaction.

'What's that?'

'A nightie.'

'Made from?'

'Silk.'

'What am I? The king of Siam now?'

Edie sagged, wrapped her arms across the cold silk, shivering suddenly under a square of indifferent moonlight through the window.

'You don't think he could be having an affair, do you?' she asks Carol when she tells the nightie story.

Carol shrugs. 'Who knows what blokes do.'

Tonight, Hilda has sighed her way through Edie's clumsy shepherd's pie and a half-successful treacle pudding with custard, and is waiting on the couch for Ron to get home. Edie keeps checking the time, and the boys are restless.

'Think I will have that second cuppa, Edie,' Hilda says at last. 'Eeh, I can't believe she's having an affair with him, can you?'

'Who is?'

'Jill,' says Hilda. 'Her.' She flaps a hand at a woman on TV. *Crossroads* is on, and Hilda laps it up like it's real life. 'And with her stepbrother and all. Rotten.'

'What's a naff air?' asks Colin.

'It's when you kiss people you're not meant to,' says Sean.

'Hilda, do you think you can watch the boys for a bit? I'm going to pop to the garage and see if Ron's nearly done.'

Ron's garage is tucked into the alley that runs down the side of the pub. From the corner entrance to the Queen's Head, she sees that the garage shutters are down, the neon light off. Edie is about to turn and go, when there's movement there through the fog of her breath. Just a flicker of a shadow, but there's someone there. She's not sure why, but there's a lurch in her guts. She could just call out, but instead, she finds herself scootching along the alley and ducking into the open yard behind the pub. From the yard, she can observe McVey's Motors without being seen.

The light from the pub spills all the way across the cobbles and illuminates the otherwise unlit alley. Ron's outline is tall and imposing. She's always felt so safe being with him in the dark, little and protected by this towering figure. He leans against the wall and straightens his hair with the palm of his hand. He sighs, and she flushes, an intruder in this quiet moment when he thinks he's alone.

She steps backwards as quietly as she can, intending to go back home, to pretend that she saw the garage locked up from across the road and turned around again. If she goes through the yard she can pop out at the other side of the pub and head back without him seeing her. She's taking her second step, when Ron is joined by someone else.

It's a woman, around Edie's height, but, even as a darkened figure in an unlit back lane, there's a confidence to her movement, a swagger. Her long, straight hair swings below her waist and from the shape of her legs and bum, she seems to be wearing tight jeans.

'Bye, Ron,' says the woman's voice through the dark. 'See you next Thursday.'

Edie races the distance back to their house, heart beating out an uneven percussion in her chest.

He can't be, she tells herself. *She's just a customer, a late-night tyre puncture needing to be rescued in the night.* After dropping her keys twice, she's talked herself round, and by the time she sits next to Hilda on the couch, she's certain that he'll come in and regale them with a tale of an annoying customer just as he was closing up. *Clueless!* he'll laugh and shake his head.

But he does no such thing.

'Quiet day,' he says before even sipping his tea. 'Just need a bath. I'm filthy.'

Later, clean and in fresh pyjamas, he snakes his hand across Edie's waist.

'You haven't touched me since the centenary,' says Edie.

'I'm sorry, Edie-Eves,' he plants a feather-soft kiss on her throat. 'You know how it is. Work, the boys.' He slides his hand under the neckline of her nightdress. 'Can I make it up to you?'

'Do you think I should get some jeans?' she asks Carol a few days later.

'Jeans? You? No, Edie. You're too classic for jeans.'

'Classic? You mean old-fashioned?'

'No,' Carol smiles. 'Edie, you've got this wonderful style of your own. Why would you go changing?'

'I don't know. Move with the times.' She gives Carol a squinty side eye. 'Be sexy.'

'You'd look like a convict in jeans,' says Carol. 'Leave the jeans to the mucky mammies like me and Brenda Buggins.'

At the weekend, there's Smartie tubes for the boys and a bunch of roses for Edie.

'So it's better now,' she tells Carol in a voice that's pitched a little higher than it should be.

'Right,' says Carol.

Still, when the next Thursday swings around, she's ready with an excuse for Hilda so she can pop out. Edie ducks behind some bottle crates piled in the pub yard, feeling stupid and guilty. She imagines Ron walking past and spotting her hiding between empties. Part of her wants to go home, push herself up from this ridiculous position, go and hug her boys, but she can't seem to move.

The garage door swings open and a white rectangle of lights spills onto the cobbles. Edie waits with her heart in her mouth.

'I'll be back in two weeks, Ron,' says a woman's voice, and her shadow materializes in the light. Edie can't tell from the shadow if it is the same woman as last week, but she guesses that it is. Then the woman steps into the street, hair swinging, and climbs into a car. The door slam is like a bomb detonating, though the pub revelry continues without pause. Edie is trembling and her legs can barely hold her.

The car drives away and Edie is torn by the absurd notion of chasing her down, and racing into the garage to confront Ron. She does neither of these things, remaining in a squat like a lunatic, perfumed in the stench of stale beer.

A few moments later, Ron steps into the street. He's whistling something, and Edie can't remember ever hearing him whistle. He checks the padlock on the garage and sets off for home.

A customer, Edie tells herself again. *Just a customer. He couldn't. He wouldn't.* The way he held her last week and the furious lovemaking that was over almost before it had started. *He couldn't do that if there was someone else, surely?* But she is shaking: a deep tremor that throbs and pulses all of the way from her feet to her hair. *Or maybe that's exactly what he'd do because there's someone else.*

Her breath is raggy and loose, like her lungs have been punctured and they're trying frantically to keep all the air from leaking out.

She walks to the colliery gates and the reassuring symphony of the rattling train and the steel-on-steel grind of machinery that knows no circadian rhythms. Under the soundtrack of local industry, she sags against the wall and lets her shuddering breath drown in a sea of noise.

'I need to talk to you, Pats,' she says when her friend calls from Istanbul.

'I need to talk to you too. You first.'

'I mean, are you absolutely sure?' asks Pats after Edie's spilled her heart down the line. 'Because I just can't believe for a second that Ron would do something like that. She has to be a customer.'

'Well, if she's a customer, why hasn't he mentioned her?'

'Does he tell you about every customer? Every gasket, every

headlight, every . . . nah, that's all the car words I know. But does he?'

'No.'

'There you go then. Why would he mention her?'

Pats' logic makes her feel a bit better. 'What about the roses?'

'What about the roses? I'd love someone to buy me roses.'

'He hasn't got me roses before.'

'He probably couldn't afford it before!' says Pats. 'Look, Edie: you've got a house, two lovely boys and a husband who brings you roses.' Her voice has hardened and Edie isn't sure she likes it. 'What more could you want?'

When Edie doesn't answer, Pats says, 'You're it, Edie, you and Ron. You're that couple: the benchmark for everyone else.' Her voice is softer now. 'Look, you didn't actually see him doing anything wrong, did you?'

'No.'

'So trust him.'

'Thanks,' she says, though she isn't so sure.

'So anyway.' Pats puffs out a great gust of air. 'I should have said something earlier, but . . .'

'Maaaaam! Colin's burnt his finger!'

'Coming!' she yells. 'I've got to go.'

Later when she is tucking the boys in, Edie realizes that Pats didn't tell her whatever news she had.

She adds *bad friend* to *suspicious wife* on her mental list of failings as a human.

38

After

Jonesy has a face that could do with a good iron. The other barmaid was right when she suggested that he might have a problem with alcohol: he smells like he laundered his clothes in Newkie Brown. He agrees to chat to her for five minutes, though after clocking eyes on him, Edie isn't all that optimistic about his memory.

He tilts his head at the picture that she printed off from the *Chronicle* website.

'Aye,' he says. 'I remember him. Posh lad innit? From Jezza.'

'Jezza?'

'Jesmond.' He plucks a cigarette from behind his ear, pops it in his mouth. 'Aye. A uni kid. Just worked his holidays.' The cigarette bobs up and down while he speaks.

'And do you remember which university he was at?'

Sean had accepted a place at York University. That was the plan when he finished his A levels, to go there to study English. But her investigations at the time had come up blank. She had phoned first, then when none of the halls of residence had heard of a student called Sean McVey, she had turned up and knocked on all of the doors. Finally, under a dwindling March sunset, a kind administrator had checked the database.

'There was a Sean McVey enrolled,' she'd said. 'But he withdrew a few days before Freshers' Week.'

'Durham. I remember because the bar girls were always going gaga about how clever he was,' says Jonesy, plucking the cigarette out of his mouth and tapping it on the table. For a crumpled man with a drinking problem, he has a fairly decent grasp on the past. He shoots her a sidelong glance. 'Police, are you? Has he done something wrong?'

'No! I'm his mother.'

Jonesy raises his eyebrows. 'His mother sometimes used to come in. Used to sit at the bar chatting to him. And she wasn't you.'

Edie fights a surge of bile. 'What did she look like?'

'Fit,' he says, pushing the cigarette back behind his ear. 'Well fit. Told him an' all. He hit me.' He chuckles, as though people hitting him are amongst his most treasured memories. 'Only reason I remember him, to be fair.'

She can't imagine her clever, sophisticated boy hitting someone. And over that woman too. Edie shudders.

So they were still in touch after Sean went to uni. And spending cosy time together during his holidays, by the sound of things.

Time to go to Jesmond.

Edie thought she would recognize the house when she saw it, but either her memory is terrible, or the street has changed so much. Nothing feels familiar about the place, as though she is intruding on somebody else's memories.

She's glad that she found a torch under the sink in the laundry last night, glad she'd gone back into the garage and found the light switch and dug her boot box out of the cupboard.

On her bed, she'd lifted off the lid. First, her fingers found the sandwich bag, two tiny teeth clinking gently against one another. Then a piece of card, yellowing with age, on which two locks of hair have been stuck with now crunchy Sellotape. She lifted the muslin wraps – one navy, one sky blue – to her nose and inhaled. There was dust and the faintest hint of a discontinued laundry soap that forced her eyes closed for a second. *Don't get distracted, Edie*, she thought. Under the trinkets of her babies' early days, she found the letter, the last one she sent that got returned.

She barely recognized her spidery writing. It looked like the scrawl of the unhinged. No wonder it got sent back.

Sean McVey, it said, *c/o Mr and Dr Pike-Oberon*, with a Jesmond address barely legible underneath.

She shuddered at the sight of their name. Edie turned the envelope over.

Return to sender. No longer at this address, it read. A little further down it said *Sorry Edie. B x*

But standing here on this street that should be throwing bad memory after bad memory at her, she's got nothing. Perhaps she imagined them. Maybe the Pike-Oberons don't actually exist, or perhaps they only did in the worst of her dreams. She thought that back then too. Kept thinking *Surely this can't be real? Surely they can't be real?*

She checks the address again. Number 49, that's definitely it. The gate at the end of the front garden is hanging open and the front lawn which was always so neatly trimmed is browning and overgrown. The house itself is still imposing though, and that more than anything starts to stir something: the feeling that this stately, smart old girl of a building was judging her before she even stepped foot inside.

Edie walks up the path slowly, suddenly conscious of her baggy jumper and stretchy-waisted skirt. *Silly how smartly I used to dress when I had nothing. And look at me now! A multi-millionaire in a tattered jumper!*

She hasn't planned what she wants to say and that makes her pulse thud. And she doesn't know which of them she's hoping to see more, but a vision of all the Pike-Oberons makes her feel sick to her core.

The beautiful Victorian front door is in need of a lick of paint, and she finds herself feeling a bit sorry for it. *I could paint you up nice, door.* It is when she presses the brass doorbell that it all comes back. That dread, that fear. Her mind goes fuzzy around the edges and she has to grab the stonework by the door to hold her up. Her head is hot, and she presses it into the wall, appreciating the coolness.

'Can I help you?'

Edie looks up at a girl she doesn't recognize. She's around seventeen or eighteen with long blonde hair gathered in a bun high on her head.

'I said "Can I help you?"'

Edie takes a deep breath and stands up straight. 'I'm looking for David or Bianca,' she says. The names feel heavy in her mouth.

The girl turns and yells into the house. 'David! Someone here for you.' There's a rumble within the house, like someone running downstairs, and the girl vanishes, leaving Edie peering through the crack in the door.

There's music coming from upstairs: that rappish type that Colin sometimes has on the radio when he's driving her somewhere. 'I like the music from the Sixties,' she tells him whenever something comes on that makes her ears hurt. 'I know, Mam. But this is great driving music,' is his go-to response.

Edie can't see from here how much the house has changed, but there's something a little worn about the entryway.

'Hello?'

When the door swings open, a young, slightly confused-looking man appears in the hallway.

'Hello?' repeats Edie.

'You were looking for David?'

'Yes. Is he here?'

The man grins. 'I am David.'

'Oh. There's no other David? A grandfather David? An Uncle David?'

'I'm the only David who lives here.'

'Are you sure?'

He laughs. 'Is everything okay?'

Edie looks back down at the envelope. 'This is the right house?' she says, waving it at the man.

'It is,' he says, examining the paper. 'But I don't know those people. It's a student house, see? We rent it from the university.'

'Ah,' she says, deflating.

'I'm sorry.'

She turns to leave. It hadn't occurred to her that they might move. People in Edie's world don't really move, unless of course they win the lottery. She's halfway down the path when there's a yell.

'Wait!' says young David. 'Hang on a sec.' He darts back into the house and returns with a small rectangle of card in hand. 'The owner's son did drop by once. Left this card. To forward on any mail.'

He pushes the card into her hand.

Nathaniel Pike-Oberon. 23 Old Elvet, Durham.

Edie shivers, pulls herself together, then kisses David on the cheek. 'Thank you.'

39

Before

Just before he walks into the exam, Edie slips the little ladybird rock into Sean's pocket. He doesn't seem to notice, and he is clutching his pencil case at his chest with both hands.

It's stupid. A rock won't make her clever son less nervous, or squeeze knowledge into his brain that isn't there to begin with, but it makes her feel better at least. She and the other waiting parents settle into stiff-backed chairs and no one, it seems, is willing to make eye contact with anyone else.

Edie counted nine boys trailing into the exam. Nine boys plucked from primary schools all over the North East to decide which two could secure a full scholarship to see them through five years of top-notch education.

He wants it. Already, at ten, Sean wants to use his brain and be challenged and succeed. Edie saw hunger grow from the moment Mrs Adams called them into the office to offer them the scholarship exam.

And now he's here and will be either one of two triumphant, or seven disappointed. Two who will have their minds filled with wonderfully clever things, be surrounded by wonderfully clever people and get to do wonderfully clever activities. Seven will have to live with the could-have-been junctions through the rest of their lives.

'The opportunities for a boy like Sean are second to none,' said Mrs Adams.

Edie asked about Colin, but Mrs Adams pressed a smirk into a flat line.

'This is for the sharpest minds,' she said. 'Colin, while wonderfully good at practical subjects, is not quite the cognitive all-rounder that Sean is.'

Ron had said no when she first mentioned it. 'Why?' he asked. 'What's wrong with sending him to the comprehensive?'

'It's about opportunity, Ron,' she said. 'Giving him a better chance than we had.'

'We did just fine,' said Ron. 'And besides, it's not fair on Colin.'

'Why should Sean be held back because of Colin?' she asks.

'You just want to argue with me,' said Ron. 'Everything I do or say is wrong these days, isn't it?'

'No,' she said, but really, she has been picking fault in just about everything. He'd laughed in her face when she asked him outright if he was having an affair. 'There's only ever been you, Edie-Eves,' he'd reassured her. And when she'd hidden between the crates again and again, there had been no sign of the woman, not after she'd talked to him. Perhaps she'd scared him into ending the affair. That's what she's chosen to believe, to keep herself sane. But still, in moments when he's staring into space, she can't help but let her imagination convince her that he's thinking of that other woman, that he's learned to be more careful.

'Oh, Pats,' she said when her friend called from Tbilisi. 'He's got the chance to really make something of himself.'

'That's great, Edie,' said Pats. 'But listen, there's something—'
'Oh sorry, Pats. Hilda's just arrived with half a chicken. Got to run. Miss you!'

When she describes the school later she'll say that it was *lovely*, but truthfully, Edie's aware of how shabby and unpolished she is here, a rough stone. The buildings are imposing redbrick infused with history and cleverness, the halls echoing with the successes of boys gone by. She dressed Sean in his nice stuff that Hilda bought for the boys last Christmas – long trousers, collared shirt – but his haircut is all wrong, his shoelaces tattered. They were greeted on arrival by sharp, confident boys in pressed blazers and straight ties.

'Welcome,' they said, shaking hands with both Edie and Sean. 'Come this way.'

Edie's shoes scuffed along the parquet floor, and they were flanked on their route by walls of wooden shields with the achievements of boys gone by etched in gold script. There was a hush and Edie wondered what sort of intelligent things were being thought and taught behind those closed doors.

'Take him for the exam,' Ron had conceded wearily. 'But don't come complaining to me if Colin gets all resentful and angry later.'

'Colin's not like that,' she'd said, more confidently than she felt, but it was niggling, tugging at the corner of her brain.

'What did you read at university?' a jacketed boy asked her.

'I didn't go,' she said. 'But I like Catherine Cookson books.'

The boy had bitten his lip, disguising a smirk. Another boy said, 'Regional literature, how charming.'

Edie flushed, and, to her disappointment, so did Sean.

When the letter comes, her fingers are shaking. She wants to open it alone in case she has to prepare Sean for the let down.

'Regardless of the outcome,' said the school headmaster after the exam, 'all of the boys here will be accepted on enrolment, even without the scholarship.'

Edie doesn't want to have to explain to Sean that if he doesn't get the scholarship it'll be his parents' poverty standing in the way of his glimmering future, not his brains.

To the parents or guardians of Mr Sean Christopher McVey,

It is with great pleasure that we would like to offer Sean a full five-year scholarship (conditions apply) to study at Dame Allan's School from this September.

Edie can hardly breathe.

'Oh my god,' she whispers. 'My god!'

Her hands shake more than they did before she opened the letter and she has to sit down, hands to her mouth in case her heart escapes and leaps off the table.

'Oh my god.'

She isn't sure whether the flutter in her chest is elation or pure, blind terror.

40

After

There's a note taped to the phone. *Gone out*, it says. *Won't be back until dinner. Ron.*

No kisses, she notes. *Where the heck is it that Ron goes all the time?* There's a familiar churn in her belly that she recognizes from crouching behind beer crates and sniffing his shirts on laundry days. That sensation where her pulse threatens to leap out of her throat.

She taps out Verushka's number, who answers with a breathy purr.

'Fancy a drive to Durham?' asks Edie.

'You want get your passport, yes?'

Edie had clean forgot about the aqua ladies encouraging her to go to Hong Kong. 'Oh, I could do, I suppose.' She lets herself imagine a future where she's introducing Sean to Patricia with the sun setting over the Hong Kong skyline. 'Can we pick up Jade on the way?'

'Yes,' says Verushka. 'I will call her as soon as I finish my barre work.' She pauses. 'Nureyev said that my barre work was second to none.'

Colin is on the couch watching *Escape to the Country*.

'Hey, Mam, check out this place in Hertfordshire. It's got a vineyard! Would you have considered a vineyard in Hertfordshire?'

'I'm not even sure where Hertfordshire is,' says Edie.

'Me either.' He goes back to the show, taking gentle sips on his coffee. 'Where's Dad?'

'I came to ask you the same question.'

On screen, a middle-aged couple are sipping wine and talking about the merits of owning a vineyard. 'It seems like a lot of work,' says the woman. The presenter nods vigorously. 'Yes, but isn't that what your escape is all about? Seizing opportunities?'

She could be more ambitious with her seizing and opportunities, she supposes, but she can't even keep track of her husband, so vineyards and the likes are probably way beyond her capabilities.

'Is he okay?' asks Edie. 'He's never here.'

'Well, he joined that motoring supper club thing, so he's off doing that a lot. And of course, taking the Jag for cruises.' Colin nods as though this is an acceptable use of a man's time. 'I have an idea though: if you want to know what each other is doing, talk to each other.'

In the show, the couple are now looking around a cavernous barn. 'Listen to that echo,' laughs the presenter, and Edie stomps to the TV and presses it off.

'Hey,' Colin protests, but stops when he clocks her stony face.

'Col,' she says. 'Do you know where Sean is now?' Colin sighs but she continues. 'I know that you have this mobile phone now and all this technology and Facelog and all of these things, so you could probably find him if you wanted.'

'I don't know where he is. I could maybe find him if I wanted,' Colin says quietly. 'But perhaps I don't want to.'

But he's your twin! she wants to scream. *Why?* She's interrupted by a knock at the door. Colin lets out an audible breath and gets up to switch the television back on.

'You spoke to him after the funeral,' she says. 'How did you find him? Did you know that he didn't go to York University?'

Colin's eyes widen. 'How do you know that?'

She waves a hand. 'So how did you find him?'

'I didn't,' he says, finger poised over the power button. 'He called me.' He presses the TV on. 'And that was the last time I spoke to him.' He pushes the switch and the couple are poking grapes and laughing about something.

Colin wouldn't lie to her: he doesn't know where his brother is now. She imagines Sean finding out about the win. *Hey,* a colleague, or a girlfriend or an in-law might have said, *these lottery winners are called McVey too!*

Ron had worried back then about what the imbalance would do to the boys' relationship. Worried that Colin might get resentful or that the privileges heaped on Sean would throw the pair off kilter. Colin always said he didn't mind, but everyone else seemed to think otherwise. Perhaps this, like everything else that seemed to go wrong with this family, was her fault. Perhaps her ambitions for Sean ripped some of that connective tissue tying them together from Colin.

She glances at the lottery ticket on the way to answer the door. *What if Sean comes back because he wants some money?* Could she deal with having him back in her life on superficial terms? And what would that do to Colin? Is there a little part of her that wants Sean to see Colin thriving? To see him being the successful brother for once?

She takes a breath, pushing the questions down. *One thing at a time, Edie.*

One thing at a time.

They pick up Jade, who, it would appear, Verushka didn't actually call and is surprised to see a pair of pensioners in an Aston Martin picking her up.

'Put on shoes,' instructs Verushka. 'We have mission.'

'Mission?'

'Visiting someone.'

'Visiting someone?'

'Stop with the echo,' says Verushka. 'Yes. Edie has found Bike-Oblong boy.'

'Bike-Oblong?'

'Pike-Oberon,' says Edie. 'I've found Nathaniel Pike-Oberon. In Durham.'

'Ooooh!' says Jade, clapping her hands.

'Why are we going this way, Vee?' says Jade while the Aston Martin winds its way down the back roads.

'Scenic,' says Verushka. She huffs, 'And also they not like to see me drive.'

'Who?'

'The licence man,' she says.

Edie catches Jade's look of abject terror in the rear-view mirror. They're both clinging onto their seats working hard not to let their heads dislocate from their bodies.

Edie smiles at the back of Jade's head, watches nails covered in cracked purple varnish like spider socks stroke the mound of her belly. If Ron can keep secrets from her, she can keep this one from him until it's too late for him to do anything about it. Edie spoke to Carol's Gemma yesterday, and things had looked like they were heading in the right direction with the house, but then again, Gemma had used a lot of words Edie didn't understand. Still, this is the point of hiring an expert.

The house on Old Elvet is a terrace with a royal-blue door with a fresh stuccoed surround and well-maintained sash windows.

'You want me to knock?' asks Verushka.

'No, thanks,' says Edie. 'I should probably do this myself.'

She's seeing his neat hair and his unscuffed shoes and that confident posture that all of the boys at Dame Allan's seemed to have back then and is annoyed that she's letting herself feel cowed by the image of a child from years ago.

A wiry man in navy-blue trousers and an expensive-looking cream cable knit jumper answers the door.

'Can I help you?'

'Nathaniel!' she says, only it comes out as *Nafyl* because she's shaking.

'Who's asking?' he says with a frown.

She pauses, clears her throat. 'Edie. Edie McVey. Sean's mam.' It's been years since she described herself as that, and it chokes her a little. 'I'm trying to find him.'

He looks at the ground. 'Oh,' he says. 'Is that right?'

Edie nods.

'Well, Mrs McVey,' he says, a tang of bitterness in his voice. 'Sean and I have lost touch, somewhat.'

'Really? You were so close.'

He gives a humourless smirk. 'Well,' he says. 'Things change, as well you know.'

Nathaniel starts to close the door.

'Wait!' she says. Nathaniel pauses. 'Maybe you know somebody who might know where he is?'

He is so thin, this man. Thin and pointy and sharp, though his shoulders are hunched. His hairline is high, hair tufty and thinning at the temples. Where is that bright-eyed boy who was polite but ever so sly?

'I'm not sure if my *mother* is still in touch with him. I wouldn't know. Bit of a sticking point in our family, you see.'

Edie frowns. 'And your mother is . . .?'

'In Devon.'

'Right.' She takes a deep breath. 'Do you have an address or a number I could get?'

He shakes his head. 'You've got some nerve. You and your family ruined mine, so if you will, kindly, please leave and get on with your miserable little existence somewhere else.'

'No,' she says, stamping her foot, and it comes out louder than she meant it to. She raises a shaking hand, though she's not sure what she intended to do with it.

He looks at the hand and smiles, though it doesn't reach his eyes. 'What are you going to do? Push me?' He smirks again as her stomach drops. 'Go on. Run along now.' He flicks his fingers at her as though she's an annoying fly.

Edie turns, blinking away the threat of tears. *All these years and they're still making me feel small.* She's reaching for the car door handle when Nathaniel shouts: 'If he wanted to find you, he would have done it by now.'

Verushka and Jade are leaning against the car doors, glaring at Nathaniel. Edie turns back, her heart thudding.

'Disappointing when you strip the gilding off a lily,' she says, 'and realize that it was a weed all along.'

Nathaniel glowers, shakes his head then slams the door. Jade and Verushka nod approvingly.

'I have no idea what you just said,' says Jade, 'but it pissed him off.'

'Good.' Edie nods, her heart rate returning to something closer to normal. 'He always was an arrogant little thing. But at least his awful mother shouldn't be too hard to find now.' She heads back to the car. 'Shall we go somewhere for cake?'

She could do with some sugar to stabilize her, and not for the first time, she worries that something is wrong with her. Or perhaps it's just the heady rush of grasping back the reins.

41

Before

'Don't hang up this time,' the voice insists.

It's Margaret or Maureen or something from Lavender Hill House, the woman says. Something about having only been the manager for a few weeks and sorry for not having met Edie yet. Edie is not sure why she hasn't hung up yet. Her visits dwindled since the Sean incident – once a month, once every two months, until eventually it was just two or three times a year and never again with the boys. When they phone, she can't bear to hear how much worse her mother is getting, how much less she understands with each passing day. 'Hiking!' said the carer last time. 'Said she wanted to go hiking! Can you believe it?'

Edie's preparing her excuses as to why she can't visit or when she might be able to make it again when she hears the word *condolences*.

'Can you say that again please?' asks Edie. 'I didn't hear you.'

The woman explains that Cynthia passed away about half an hour ago. That she's very sorry for Edie's loss and will be happy to assist with funeral arrangements.

'Funeral?' says Edie, and the sound gets switched down on the TV.

Ron does all of the arrangements, though there isn't too much to do. Cynthia didn't really know anyone, but one of the assistants from the home offers to come 'to represent Lavender Hill House'. Edie tells her not to bother. In her spartan will with nothing to leave behind, Cynthia's only request was 'to be next to my Georgie again'. Edie doesn't know who Georgie is, and there's no more than a wisp of the name somewhere in the back of her memory. But with nobody else to ask, she's at a loss.

'Just another way that I've let her down,' she says to Ron.

They wait at the double doors to the crematorium for the car to arrive with Cynthia's crumbled body. Sean is throwing little rocks at a dandelion that pokes up from a crack in the concrete.

'Stop that, Sean,' says Ron quietly. He pulls Colin to his side and smooths down a lick of hair that, like the boys, clearly wants to be somewhere else.

Ron tugs at the collar of his shirt. He's not comfortable in formal wear, but Edie also suspects that the discomfort extends to not really knowing how to behave in the circumstances. He barely knew Cynthia: he himself had only been to the home three times with Edie, but mostly he found reasons not to come, limited to a chipper 'How was she?' on her return.

Edie worried in the run-up to the funeral about exposing her boys to death. *What is the right way to do it?*

'I've got some sad news,' she said. 'Nanna Cynthia has died.'

'Who?' asked Colin.

'The lady in the cabbage house,' said Sean.

'Do you remember anything else about her?' Edie asked, surprised that the presiding memory of their one visit was the smell, and not the fact that Sean got lost and could have been taken from her. They shook their heads, and there was a breath of relief that came from thinking maybe he hadn't been traumatised by the whole thing.

'Right,' said Colin.

'She was my mammy,' said Edie.

Both boys frowned at the idea that Mammy might have a mammy.

'Good job it wasn't proper Nanna what died,' said Colin and turned back to the TV.

Cynthia's coffin is small, so small it could be housing a child and not a woman in her sixties. All those times Edie tucked her into bed, as though she were the mother and Cynthia her baby. The last night she did it, just before the wedding, just before Cynthia went to Lavender Hill House, she'd pressed a gentle kiss to her mother's head. 'I feel safe when you do that,' Cynthia had said and Edie had to leave the room, to sob in the bathroom. Maybe that's what death felt like for her mother. Like being gently wrapped and kissed by the only person who loved her.

There's just seven of them there making up the congregation: the McVeys, Hilda, Carol and the vicar. Pats had asked if she wanted her to come from Kos, but Edie insisted that she stay where she was.

'Honestly, Edie. I don't mind. I want to be there for you.'

'Oh, please don't,' said Edie. 'It'll only make me feel more wretched, dragging you from your travels.'

'If you insist . . .'

Ron keeps looking sideways at her throughout the ceremony while the vicar recites generic platitudes about life interspersed with the few facts anyone knows about Cynthia. He asks Edie if she wants to say anything. She opens her mouth, closes it, then cries 'I don't have the right words.'

'There are no right words,' whispers Hilda. 'Just the words in your heart and mouth.'

She stands, wobbling at the knees, and makes her way slowly to the front of the room.

She can't look at the faces of anyone, nor can she see the coffin without wanting to lie down inside it next to her mam. Instead, she looks at the ceiling, fixing on a thick cobweb that waves like a curtain when the breeze hits.

'You tried,' she whispers. 'You tried so hard. I'm sorry. I'm so, so sorry.' She gulps, struggling to get enough air into her lungs. 'I'm sorry, I'm sorry,' she says again.

Ron stands, takes her by the hand and tries to lead her back to the pew, but her feet stay where they are.

'I didn't get her a cardigan,' she says to Ron. 'What if she gets cold?'

Ron looks to the ceiling then back at his mother. 'Edie . . .' he says, but the vicar steps forward.

'Thank you, Edith,' he says kindly, then gently pushes her back to her seat.

A worker comes forward and lifts a sad bouquet from Lavender Hill House and a bunch of flowers from Pats that are on top of the coffin. Then the curtains start to close. The music plays and everyone stands and watches the curtains and listens to the mechanism of the rollers carrying her away. Ella Fitzgerald sings something about loving and Edie says 'Is that it? Is that all she gets?'

Her eyes are dry, but inside, her organs feel flooded, like she's drowning. It's the questions, swilling around that are choking her. She takes a deep shuddery breath and Ron pulls her close and she buries her face into the thick fabric of his jacket.

They head outside into a cloudless, flat day and Sean whispers to Colin 'I don't get why she's upset.'

'I need a minute,' she says to Ron, and on unsteady legs heads for a bench amongst the memorials of lovers, mothers and grandfathers. Perhaps Sid – *Dad* – has a memorial somewhere here. Perhaps they'll forgive each other in the afterlife so that they don't have to be lonely any more.

She sits on a bench. An orphan.

A memory comes back to her then: way back, when Edie was little. Six maybe. Six or seven. They were reading the comic strip *Orphan Annie*, Cynthia on her back with legs up the wall, Edie resting her head on her mother's belly. 'I think, Edith,' she'd said. 'Think I'd have preferred to be an orphan than have my bastard dad.' Edie had said 'You'd make a lovely orphan,' and Cynthia had laughed. 'You too!'

Edie doesn't feel much like a lovely orphan. More like a tyre with a slow puncture. By the time she gets to Cynthia's age, she'll have deflated entirely.

She picks at a flake of wood peeling away from the armrest of the bench. She read once about all the different stages of grief, but at no point does she remember the part that said *You have failed this other person miserably and now you have to live with what a horrible person you are.* She peels away another shard, and another, then she stabs herself in the finger with one of the strips. She pulls it back and it snaps, leaving an angry spelk between the pad and the nail. She watches it a moment, then it starts to throb. *Good. That's what you deserve.* She does it again and again and again until there are four stiff splinters fencing her finger and all she can feel is the hard pulsing in the skin.

Edie stares at her finger, reddening already, and lets the tears come. She cries for her finger, for the visits she didn't make to Lavender Hill, for the small, birdish woman they just packed up in a coffin. She cries for Cynthia's laugh, for the singing voice that sounded like Anne Shelton when she was having a good day. She cries for the lost woman walking the streets in her underwear, for the crying woman begging them not to take the garbage bin away, for the stigmata-wristed woman strapped to a stretcher and hauled into an ambulance.

She cries for her mother, for herself, for everything they could have been if things had been *different* somehow. If they'd changed her medication, or if she'd somehow managed to dodge the illness that plagued her mind that made rough boys paint awful words onto their house.

She's lost track of how long she has been gone. On the walk back to the car, she examines the spikes of wood beneath her nail, thinking now how stupid it was to push them in there. She'll have to get Ron to take them out, while she sits like a child on the arm of the sofa and watches.

The boys are already in the car when she heads back, keen to get out of this place and play football in the back garden. The doors stand open like elephant ears.

'Edith,' says Hilda. 'Look, I know it's no comfort now, but at least you'll be able to get up off the breadline again.'

'Mam!' hisses Ron, and she's wrapped in arms, face pressed into the jacket and breathing in the comforting smell of his body coming through the laundry detergent. 'My Edie-Eves.'

She's got Patricia's latest postcard in her handbag when she makes her way to Lavender Hill for the last time. On the bus, she keeps pulling it out and examining the images in squares: a sweeping beach with an impossibly blue sea, a fisherman mending a net, bougainvillaea climbing the side of a shuttered white house, some proud but crumbling ruins of a something-or-other.

Edie sighs. She told her not to come, but she'd give anything to be sharing a slice of cake with Patricia right now. She pictures them on the beach from the postcard sipping lemon juice and sitting neatly on folded towels.

'It'll be okay,' dream Patricia says.

At Lavender Hill, her mother's things are waiting for her in a beach bag with the word *Babycham* and a cavorting deer skipping across it, and a small shoe box.

'Sorry, we didn't have a better bag,' says the woman on the desk who Edie doesn't recognize. 'And would you like the refund in cash or by cheque?'

'Refund?'

'Yes. You were two months in advance. So you get those two months returned. It was all in the contract. So, cash or cheque?'

Edie wanders down Beach Road with her hand clasped over her bag. She's never had this much money on her before. *Would it be really bad if I bought an ice cream?* It might be, because it is Ron's money after all, but now that she's thought it, she wants nothing more than a soft whip from down by the fair.

It's breezy but not cold, and Edie doesn't want to go home to her empty house and absent husband. The boys are off to Carol's for tea anyway to try out their new computer. 'We went for an Acorn,' said Carol. So Edie is going to be all alone anyway while her sons play with technology that sounds like a squirrel's breakfast.

She hasn't looked in the bag of her mother's things yet, but she suspects that they'll make her feel unbearably sad. Small clothes with the scent of overcooked vegetables woven permanently through them. Tatty underwear, maybe the comb and mirror set Edie bought her for Christmas. She doesn't really want to see this life laid out in a collection of stuff she couldn't even pay a charity shop to take off her hands.

There's the guilt too. That she could have done better somehow: not put her mother in a home while she chased her own dreams of a family. Maybe she could have talked Ron into letting her stay with them. They could have put a little bed in the living room.

Edie crests the hill that will carry her down to the funfair, still closed and shuttered against the lingering trails of winter. The air carries the whispers of yesterday's children and sadness settles heavy on her shoulders.

She's about to cross the road to the ice cream kiosk that stays open come hell or high water, when she spots a familiar, tall shape peering up at the Ferris wheel inside the fairground. His back is to her, but that back is as familiar to her as the rest of him.

Ron isn't wearing the overalls he went to work in this morning. He's in a collared shirt she's never seen before and jeans that finish a tiny bit before his shoes, leaving an inch of ankle poking out the bottom. She blinks for a minute, thinking that she might have imagined him.

Then he turns and grins her that grin and her Jimmy Mack is right there.

She crosses the road and he wraps his arms around her. She's at once tiny and insubstantial, in his big strong arms. How much she's always loved having this towering man enveloping her in a safe embrace. She just wants to feel safe again.

'What are you doing here?' she asks into the fabric of his shirt. There's a smell there that she doesn't recognize, clean and slightly spicy.

He kisses the top of her head. 'Mam called. Said you were going to Lavender Hill to pick up the things.'

'How did you know I'd come here?'

'Maybe I just know you better than you know yourself,' he says.

'You took time off work? For me?'

'Of course,' he mumbles into her hair.

He's still holding her, she can still feel the warmth of the day's engines on his fingers, hear the thud of his heart through her collarbone. He never takes time off.

'But you always say if you're not there, we're losing money?'

Ron hesitates for a millisecond and then shrugs. 'What could be more important than you, right now?'

She leans back, looks up at him. 'Really? So why are you all dressed up? Why do you smell like that?'

'Smell like what?'

'Like the fragrance department in Binns.'

'I had a wash.' He pauses again. 'I had an appointment in town.'

An appointment with a swingy-haired woman in jeans? He isn't looking at her face, but surveying the sky over her shoulder instead.

'Ah,' she says.

'Ah what?'

Edie stares down at the concrete. There are dollops of worn-down gum on the pavement like islands on a grey sea and she has a desperate longing to leap into the pavement like the children leaping into the chalk drawings in the *Mary Poppins* film. Maybe she could land on Patricia's island though, not a carousel horse race.

He drops his hands to his sides with a huff. 'I just came to meet you, okay. I wanted to check you were all right. Not too sad.'

I'm a burden. A crumbling ruin like the buildings on Patricia's postcard. *My husband doesn't even trust me to get home with a bag of old clothes.*

The money is burning a hole in her handbag. She can see the woman with the jeans and the long hair standing here next to Ron instead of her. Someone worth having a good wash for. *Maybe that's the type of woman Ron should be with. Someone who can look after herself. One with a womb full of functioning tubes.* Maybe the boys too would be better off with a mother who isn't sad all the time, or wasting money on leotards, or hiding behind crates in the pub yard.

Maybe I can make life easier for everyone.

Maybe I can disappear.

42

After

'You should get a mobile phone,' said Ron when he came home with a box from the Carphone Warehouse. 'Went in for a phone for the car, came out with a phone I can take anywhere!'

Edie can hear it now, ringing somewhere. She vaguely recognizes the song. Something about someone begging for mercy, and catchy though it is, she can't understand what's wrong with the sound of an actual phone ringing.

She follows the sound into the laundry and then narrows it down further to the basket of dirty pants and socks she brought down this morning. After a little rummage, she plucks it out of a trouser pocket and carries it as though it is a rodent she has just retrieved and not a tiny phone flashing blue with alien urgency.

'I'd have washed you,' she says to it, 'if I hadn't heard you ring.'

She isn't planning to look at it, but then she does. The Edie who is trying organize clothes for their big theatre trip this weekend wants to ignore it, but the Edie who crouched behind the beer crates, the Edie who checked his pockets for rogue receipts and sniffed his jackets for foreign scents takes over her fingers and she sees a little icon on the screen heralding the arrival of a message. She flips it open, feeling as though she's about to get a missive from a spy to tell her to pick up a briefcase from under a park bench at 15:00 hours.

She squints, dropping the phone when she sees the name.
Sean.
She picks the phone back up again and reads the message.
You still on for next week, Dad?
She puts the phone face down on the table, and her hand trembles as she does. In fact, she's trembling all over and she brings a hand to her face so that she doesn't tremble her heart right out of her mouth.

'Oh god,' she whispers. 'Oh god, oh god, oh god.'

How long have they been in touch?

She presses a hand against the wall to steady herself, touches the pulse in her neck and it hammers against her palm.

She jumps when she hears the toilet flush, picks the phone back up, shoves it in her cardigan pocket and scurries into the kitchen. In a moment, she's let herself out of the patio doors and she's hightailing down the garden, weaving between Hercules and Amphitrite, ducking behind the neatly trimmed bushes, no idea where it is that she is heading, just away, away from her husband who has been speaking to the son she thought they'd lost contact with fifteen years ago.

Well, the exhaustive internet searching for Dr Pike-Oberon in Devon was a waste of time.

She's full of questions. So many questions and they're unspooling out of her so quickly that she can hardly grasp them. The edge of her vision is blurring and there are pulsing colours vying for space in her vision.

At the end of the garden, she clambers onto the stepladder that the gardener uses for pruning. She hooks her armpits over the head-high wall that separates them from some grassy parkland beyond and jimmies herself up. She swings a leg over then slides down, dropping to the grass. She takes off at a run. *Why are you running, Edie? Where do you think you're going?*

She looks ridiculous, she can tell. She slows as she passes a terrier chasing a stick followed behind by a puffing owner. 'I can't keep up,' says the dog owner, pink-cheeked and joyful. He glances down at Edie's bare feet and scurries on.

Edie turns for a row of low-hanging trees that line the perimeter of the park. In a moment, she has ducked under one and has her back pressed against the bark.

So this is what he's been hiding. If Ron can hide this from her, what else has he been hiding?

The phone is still in her pocket and she draws it out. Her thumbs are quivering as she opens it once more. She presses the message button and is met with a list of names. Sean is the most recent, but below, there are messages from Colin, Harry, and then another from Sean.

She finds the arrow button and presses it down until it highlights the next message from Sean. She hesitates, thumb hovering over the button. What if it is something she really can't bear to know? What if they've been in touch all these years and Ron has watched her trying to glue her splintered heart back together and said nothing? How will she be able to move forward from that?

She shakes her head. If that is the case, she will deal with it. Now, she has to know.

The message is from last week. Saturday, in fact, when Ron was at the roadshow and she was chasing a ghost in a twisty old pub where Sean used to work.

Renata says you did well this week. She's suggesting another joint one in about a month?

Renata?

She flicks back to the message menu and scrolls down some more. There's another! It's from last month.

I'm not ready yet. Give me time.

Edie doesn't know how to see the message that he is replying to. She goes back and forward, but nothing shows up. Nothing to tell her what he needed more time for.

There is only one more message from Sean. It is from back in May, nearly three months ago.

Thank you for that, Dad. That was quite cathartic. I'm glad you've agreed to keep seeing Renata. We'll take it from there.

She has more questions than she had before. She presses the heels of her hands deep into her eye sockets, but the words still float around and she can still see them, even in the black crevasse she's created behind her hands.

Before she's had time to think herself out of it, she returns to the most recent message.

You still on for next week, Dad?

She pushes reply, types, **yes of course**. She waits a moment, then adds **Can we meet for a coffee first?**

It's almost ten breastbone-crunching minutes before the reply comes through.

No.

Then another. Not yet.

Edie arrives back in the garden in time to see Ron's car pulling out of the drive. Without his phone. She'll place it on the bench in the laundry and let him rediscover it himself at some point. She'd deleted the replies from Sean, just leaving the first one there — perhaps Ron will believe that he forgot that he opened it.

Verushka will help. Maybe Jade will come too. They can follow Ron next week. Figure out where he's going. They could borrow Jess' car — he'd recognize Verushka's. Jess has a Micra Ron wouldn't look twice at.

There's a postcard on the front doormat when she gets home, the faint tread of a shoeprint on top of the familiar handwriting.

My dearest Edie,

it says.

How are you? Decided to swap Hong Kong for Bali for a few weeks so I can have a proper relax. Not that I do much else! The hotel I used to manage here is lovely. It has an infinity pool and a spa. Most days, I have two massages! They have of course put me in one of the best suites with a stunning view over the cliffs and down to the sea. This is the life, eh? Anyway, enough about me! How's my Edie? How's your life of luxury? How's Ron and Colin?
Miss you, as always.
Love Pats. xxx

The picture on the front of the postcard shows a lovely hotel room, the covers of the bed scattered with petals. Beyond the doors, there's a pool right there and a fathomless blue sky spanning the horizon.

Verushka's voice floats into her head. *You not need Ron's permission.*

She examines the postcard, squinting at the detail printed in the corner.

'Kin-ta-mani Uluwatu,' she says. Then again. 'Kintamani Uluwatu.' It's so deliciously foreign and exotic and beautiful that she says it again. Then she goes to the study to see if she can find it on the internet. She types slowly with one finger, trying to get the spelling exactly right, and an image pops up that is almost identical to the one on Patricia's postcard. She clicks it, and then it takes her to a place called Booking.com. Ten minutes later, Edie has booked herself a Sky Suite for a seven-night stay for the last weekend in September.

'Hah!' she laughs. It's so much easier than when she went to Greece that time. Now all she needs to do is get a flight, especially since she got her passport in Durham the other day.

She's writing the details in her diary when the phone rings.

'Pats!'

The sob that bursts from her mouth surprises them both, a deep, guttural howl of despair, and everything comes tumbling out. The loneliness, Carol and Brenda's shunning, Ron and Colin missing her birthday, the phone number Sean doesn't have, Victor, the Asian man, the confused students in the Pike-Oberons' house. Nathaniel Pike-Oberon and, worst of all, Ron's message from Sean. She unleashes it all down the receiver in her big, sad, empty hallway in her big, sad, empty house.

'Oh, Edie,' says Pats. 'I wish I was there to give you a giant hug.'

Edie laughs, a soggy, pathetic laugh. 'Well, there's the one spark of good news!' She reads her booking information to Patricia. She is met by a crackling phone silence. 'Pats?'

Pats sighs. 'Edie, we need to talk.'

43

Before

Being on a plane isn't how Edie imagined it would be. She thought it would be more glamorous, but the flight from Newcastle to Rhodes is just like being on the bus from Boldon to Shields. Kind of busy, too cold and the air smoky as Bonfire Night. She tries to be polite when she coughs, but they've put her too close to the smoking area, so she's coughing every couple of minutes and probably will for the whole four-hour-and-ten-minute flight.

The woman at Lunn Poly was a bit taken aback by a woman wanting to travel alone to a Greek island at short notice.

'Are you sure I can't book you onto this singles trip to Alicante instead?' she said. 'You're going to have to get from the airport to the port and then get a ferry across to Kos. Bit of a faff, if you ask me. And Spain is lovely this time of year.'

The request for a one-way ticket was met with an open mouth. 'We don't really do them,' the agent said. 'I can only sell you a return on this route.' She fussed with some papers. 'Look, I'll book you in for a week, yeah? You look like you could do with a bit of sunshine.'

Handing over the cash from the Lavender Hill refund, Edie's fingers shook, her pulse hammering high in her throat. *Is this the stupidest thing I've ever done?* Perhaps. *But I've never felt this lost.*

She had taken her passport form to Liverpool and managed to get back the same day before anyone noticed she'd gone. She could barely tear open the envelope when it came back in the post.

She takes out Patricia's postcard again. It had arrived just before she went to pick her mother's things up, the day she realized that she was mostly a burden to her family. It spoke of cheer and good health, and felt like a lifeline, beckoning her back to the one person who'd always accepted her for what she was, warts and all. She herself is far from cheer and good health; without Edie holding them back, maybe her family will properly thrive. Maybe one day, she'll find cheer and good health buried under the mounds of silt and misery. She hopes the island isn't too big.

'Oh, I move around a lot,' Pats had said when Edie wanted to send her some photos of the boys. 'If I phone you all the time, you never need to worry about crossing me out a million times in your address book.'

'Excuse me, do you have the time, please?'

The air hostess smiles. 'Quarter past one,' she says.

Edie doesn't know whether she means quarter past one where they've been or where they're going, but she doesn't want to ask, so just smiles her thanks instead. Either way, Sean and Colin will have finished their lunches at their respective new schools: Colin tucking into some form of dysfunctional marriage of meat and potato from a plastic plate scratched with the disgruntled knife slashes of hungry kids gone by; Sean sampling a Moroccan chicken and rice salad, or one of the other plates of nutritional-and-slightly-exotic offerings outlined in the brochure.

The state schools went back earlier, so Sean went with her to drop Colin off for his first day last week, while he got to stay home for another few days. Colin, clean and trimmed in his new trousers, jumper and shoes, elbowed Gary in the ribs to point out one of the other lads from primary, and then they were gone, charging across the playground to greet old friends starting this new adventure together before she could give him one last squeeze. Sean, standing at the side of the road watching his brother gallop headlong into new memories with old friends, seemed so small for a moment. She'd tried to pop a kiss onto his cheek, but he'd shaken her off with a scowl.

This morning, she'd taken the bus with Sean in the too-big blazer that they've bought to last, the neat tie, his polished shoes that will undoubtedly pinch by the end of the week. 'I'm not sure I want to go any more, Mam,' he'd said when they sat side by side on the bus. 'Maybe I can just go to school with Col.' But he'd walked away without a backwards glance as soon as the gates were in view. She watched him dragging his satchel onto his still-narrow little boy shoulders trying to imprint every precious tuft of hair, every dip of that shuffly gait with the slightly out-turned feet into her mind. When she sees him next, perhaps they'll be the shoulders of a man, all wide and square like Ron's. She had taken such great, gulping breaths that a woman walking a chihuahua asked if she needed an ambulance. By the time she boarded the bus for the airport, her face and sleeves were drenched.

Now, only hours later, here she is, sitting on a plane far away from everyone she loves. *The Mad, the Sad and the Guilty*. Sean'll be standing in a sea of strangers now: strangers with privileged upbringings delivered to school in nice cars with tinted windows by parents with long names and unfathomable jobs.

And Ron? She can't. She can't even think about him because her heart will snap. *They'll all be better off without me.*

Finding Mandraki harbour is easy. Edie only has a small bag: just a few changes of clothes, underwear, a toothbrush and some photos. There's nothing else she thought she'd need, not really. Her clothes are sad and old, they don't own anything valuable and all of the useful things in the house, Ron and the boys are going to need. She couldn't live without a couple of shots of the boys larking around in the garden though. A formal photo of Edie and Ron on their wedding day, a jolly Hilda on one side and a blur of her mother on the other – she'd moved just as Ron's brother took the photo, but it's the only picture of Cynthia that Edie owns apart from the ones they took at Lavender Hill House where she looks so sad and lost. Well, those and the faded picture she'd found in her mother's belongings. A photo she had never seen before, two children, side by side, a boy and a girl. The image of one another. On the back, a faint scratch in graphite. *George and Cynthia, 1923.* Well, that explains the twins in the family. *My Georgie.* His absence weighs as heavily on her as if she had known him. However long he lived, he was gone by the time she was born.

She also had the foresight to bring a photo of Patricia too in case she needs to show people on her hunt for Pats. *Small island,* she'd said. Shouldn't be too hard to find her. Edie can't wait to see the surprise on her face.

Pats will understand why Edie had to leave – she ran out on her own wedding after all. And Pats implied that she wished her own mother would do something brave like running off from someone who doesn't appreciate her. It's not the same, of course, but Pats always knows what to do. They can figure it out together, like old times. Maybe Edie can get a job in the bar. Maybe cleaning.

On the ferry, she stands at the back, letting the breeze comb her hair, feeling the soft unknotting of her shoulders. The sea is as blue as the postcard. Her poor mother would never have seen a sea so blue or a sky so cloudless and big.

It is only when the ferry draws closer to land that Edie's stomach tightens. The harbour of Kos Town yawns across the whole of the horizon. At her back, the sun is dipping into the silk-ruffle water and lights from the buildings lining the marina twinkle in the bay.

When Pats said it was a small island, Edie pictured somewhere like Holy Island, but just this port alone has more buildings than the little place they went to on a day trip once. Even if she doesn't leave the harbour, it'll take her hours to visit all of these places.

I'm managing this beautiful bar by the water, said Patricia. *Went in for a casual bar job, ended up running the place!*

'Do you know this woman?'

A shake, a *no*, an óchi, a laugh. Some take the photo from her and peer at it, others give it barely a glance.

'She runs a bar,' she says. 'A nice one.'

Edie visits the eight bars within sight of the harbour on the first day. She spends her money carefully on a hat and bottled water, almost crying when the water runs out before midday. *Who knew that Kos would have more bars than Newcastle?*

On the second day, she ventures to the old town. It is as though she has wandered into a postcard and she can't stop turning in circles, wondering if this is really her here in this pretty place.

Stone buildings nestle between newer ones dappled by light squeezing through the leafy trees that line the street. Her nostrils twitch at the garlic and oil and lemon wafting from the cafes. Old men sip impossibly small coffees while wild-haired women weave between tables with plates of food: rolled-up leaves, colourful salads. She wanders past the plane tree of Hippocrates, the place the travel agent told her she 'must see'. She admires it for a moment, briefly forgetting her mission. The beauty of the cerise bougainvillea climbing the whitewashed walls almost takes her breath away. But when she plucks a flower from the vine and the petals tear like paper, the sadness twines itself back around her limbs, as steadfast as the climbing tendrils, reminding her why she is here.

In cafes, she points blindly at the menu, asks 'Do you know this woman?' in a halting voice pushing the picture of Patricia across the table.

Every interaction she has ends the same way. She tramps the streets by day, crawls, hot and dusty and despondent, into her bed under a lethargic fan and cries by night. There are other towns, she learns. Other resorts, other bars and she hasn't the time or the money or the energy to search them. When she's visited the last taverna lining the water at Psalidi beach, she gazes at the blank silver face of the moon refracting over the water, broke, alone, desperate, and drops to the sand. *That's it. I give up.*

On her last day before the return flight the agent insisted on booking, she doesn't even bother trying. She finds a book in the hotel lobby that is written in English, walks to Lambi beach and sits by the water letting the sea lick her toes. While she tries to concentrate on her novel, images of the boys keep elbowing their way in. She misses them, misses them badly. She has spent money they can't afford, left her boys alone, missed out on hearing about their first days at their new schools, and for what? To have eaten moussaka while crying on her own in a bar to an audience of pitying Greeks and embarrassed tourists.

She's a fool. A selfish, horrid fool.

When she imagines herself walking back into their house, she pictures being met by sad accusing eyes. A house that hasn't been cleaned and boys that haven't been fed and an apple tree that hasn't been watered in the dry September warmth.

She wraps her arms around her legs, pushing her eye sockets into her knees. It's painful, but no more painful than she deserves. She takes a deep breath and suddenly there's nowhere more she'd rather be than at home with her boys. *You can do this.* She can turn a blind eye to whatever it is Ron has been up to if he'll forgive her for running off.

Tomorrow, she will go home. Tomorrow, she will shuffle into the house, tail between her legs, and beg her boys for forgiveness.

44

After

It's a taxi ride from the train to get to the high street in Marske-by-the-Sea.

'Are you sure this is it?' Edie asks the taxi driver as he idles in front of a nondescript terrace next to a shoe repair shop.

'Yes,' he says. 'Now hurry up. I'm on double yellas.'

The first thing that strikes her is the smell. It's that salted tang, at once familiar, that suggests the sea is just a short breath away. She sucks in a puff of air, closes her eyes and once again pictures early morning cups of tea at Hilda's back doorstep.

She waits for too long on the pavement before approaching the house. Fear. Whatever waits behind the innocuous door with the pot of gerberas by the step will only disappoint. Besides, there are too many questions now and she fears that she'll burst with the pressure of them all. She straightens her hair, dabs her lip with her finger to see if there's any lipstick left on it and tucks her bag under her arm. A quick glance down tells her that she is wildly overdressed for whatever this is.

She doesn't need to knock. The door is opened by an old

woman with unnaturally copper hair. It takes Edie a moment to recognize her old friend.

'I know, I know,' says Pats. 'The hair. It went a bit wrong. Now I've got to wait until it grows out.'

They examine one another's faces for a moment, seeking signs of their old friend, of their old selves reflected in the other's eyes.

'I suppose I have a lot of explaining to do, don't I?'

Edie glances at the plain little terrace, the frizzy copper hair and the gently blurring edges of Patricia in a soft pink jumper. She nods and follows her friend inside.

The house is plain but homely with chintzy curtains and soft velvet lamps. Slightly dusty pots of dried flowers sit on shelves and table tops and a cascade of magazines spill from a wooden magazine rack in the middle of the room. Two straight-backed chairs huddle round a small table, and there's a pack of playing cards in the middle. It's an old person room, and Edie is suddenly sad that vibrant, pulsating Patricia got old.

'What do you think? Living the old woman dream, eh?' Patricia chuckles softly. 'I always said that I wasn't going to turn into my mother, yet here I am in a little terraced house in a small seaside town. Hah!'

'So this is your place?'

'It is.' Patricia stretches out her arms. 'All paid off too, finally!'

'You mean, you've been here a while?' Edie can't decide if she is delighted that Patricia is just a few hours down the road, or so hurt she can barely look at her.

'This is going to need a pot of tea. Or a gin. Do you fancy a gin?'

It was easy to get rid of the toaster and the other assorted wedding guff she'd managed to shove in her bag. Turns out yellow toasters were in high demand in Stoke-on-Trent in the late Sixties. Patricia headed to London with her freshly minted passport and the Penny Lane coat she'd swapped her bridal shoes for. Ticket in hand, she boarded the bus.

Morocco, Israel, Turkey, Iran, Afghanistan all passed by in a blur of incredible food and beautiful men who'd seduced her with their charm and flashing eyes. In Qatar, she'd paused for a while to fall in love with an engineer.

'Remember, I told you about him?'

He was the one who noticed the first lump.

'I thought I'd best get it checked. Thought I could go back once I'd got an all-clear. Stupid, I was.'

By '78, she was back in England and on a ward in Basingstoke.

'Cancer, they said. Well, they were pioneering new stuff then. I was one of the lucky ones. I was weak though, Edie. So weak and broken. But I got through it.'

'And you didn't go back? To your travels?'

'I didn't go back.'

'But why . . .?'

'I fell in love, Edie,' she grins. 'Oh, not that breathless, sweep-you-off-your-feet-Jimmy-Mack-got-a-tattoo-after-the-first-date sort of love. But nice. Gentle.' She walks to the windowsill and plucks a framed picture from the shelf. 'Here,' she says, handing it to Edie. 'This is James. Jim. Funny story: I got my own actual Jimmy Mack! Jim McCaffrey.'

In the picture, Patricia wears a demure baby blue trouser suit and a grin. Jim stares at the side of her face with adoration. Patricia must've been in her late thirties in the picture, but the man in the photo already has grey hair and middle-aged spread. Either side of them are two gangly teenagers.

'The children are . . .?'

'Jim's,' says Patricia. 'His children, Peter and Beth.' Patricia swallows. 'I met his wife when we were both in hospital. Christine. Lovely woman. She really helped me when I was having rough days.' She nods at another picture on the windowsill of a small black-haired woman. 'She asked if I'd keep an eye on Jim and the kids after she was gone.' She pokes the corner of her eye, then brightens suddenly. 'So you see, I couldn't go back after that.'

'And is he still . . .?'

'Alive! Very much so,' laughs Patricia. 'He's on a fishing trip with his friends today. We're hoping for a holiday too, maybe next year. We keep active.' She shrugs. 'I'm afraid the reality is so much duller than you could have possibly imagined.'

'You're happy?'

Patricia closes her eyes. 'I'm happy,' she says, a gentle smile across her lips.

'And . . . are you . . . well?'

'The cancer? Gone, for good I hope.' She pats at a space on her jumper that would have housed another breast. 'It came back, early nineties. You should have seen me, Edie! I looked like a shaved puffin! But I've been cancer free since '93!'

'But what about . . .?' Edie wants to say *What about me?* But doesn't really want to make it all about her. 'What about your parents, your sisters?'

'Funny story,' she says. 'Mam left my dad not long after I went. Moved to Hong Kong. She travels a lot. She's the one who sends the postcards to you!'

'What?'

'Yeah. She's still around, growing old in the tropics. Living my dream for me while I stepped into her old life.' Patricia shrugs. 'My sisters are off elsewhere too. Judith's in Germany, and Rita went to America. Dad's gone, so I had no need to come back to the North East.'

'I didn't qualify as something to come back for?' It comes out more bitter and hurt than she intended it to. Then she whispers, 'All that time.'

'I tried,' says Patricia half-heartedly.

They sip their gin and tea in silence.

If Edie is honest, she should have known something was up. Those times Pats had tried to tell her something, but she'd been busy, or wrapped up in herself, or wasn't sure that she could deal with her brave strong friend being anything other than fearless. When she was stressing about whether Ron was being faithful or not, Patricia was facing her own mortality alone in a ward in Basingstoke. 'Why didn't you tell me?'

'Shame,' she says. 'Shame that I wasn't living the life you thought I was living. You were always so proud of me, and I thought that I was giving you hope, giving you adventure. I suppose that was a little arrogant of me.'

'No,' says Edie. 'But you know that I'm proud of you no matter what, don't you? You didn't have to lie to impress me.'

'I know,' she says. 'But I wanted to make you proud. And it was fun, you know? Pretending. The more I did it, the more, for just a few minutes, I could believe it was true. Sad, isn't it?'

'So the pictures that you sent . . .?'

'Well, the shots of "me" from the back are actually pictures of Mam, can you believe! And Thomas Cook on the high street has an ever-changing display of places on a big window outside. Just had to stand in front of it and take a picture.'

For the first time today, Edie laughs. 'Patricia Lydon, you are incorrigible.'

'True,' Patricia says. 'Only it's Patricia McCaffrey now.'

Patricia stares down at her hands. They are thin and papery – an ageing woman's hands. Hands that have held her through the ups and downs: pulling her through the crowd at the Yella Welly, tenderly combing Cynthia's hair when Edie was too wrung out to do any more, putting Edie's wedding make-up on with gentle strokes. Those hands have lived an entire life without her and she reaches for them, squeezes them between her own. They feel both strange and at the same time so recognizable that the air leaves her lungs for a moment.

'I'm so sorry, Edie. Do you forgive me?'

'I'm so happy to see you, I'd forgive you for stealing the sun,' says Edie. 'As long as you promise not to lie to me again,' she says.

'I promise.'

45

Before

'We thought you weren't coming back, Mam,' weeps Colin.

The minute she walked through the door from the airport, both boys launched themselves on her, wrapping their arms around her waist, sobbing inconsolably. The three of them are still huddled on the hallway floor, Edie's own tears flowing as freely as her sons'.

Ron appears in the doorway, arms folded across his chest. There are damp patches at the armpits of his shirt and his hair looks like he put it on sideways. She's looking everywhere but his face, because the guilt took an even bigger bite on the plane home and she had four hours to stew in the misery of the cold, horrible fact that she had abandoned her family on a selfish escapade. 'Go to your room, boys,' he says. 'I'm sure you've homework to do.'

The boys look between their parents, then slink upstairs. Ron turns towards the kitchen and Edie follows that poker-straight back. It's messy, and the scent of burnt toast has woven itself into the furniture.

'I got your note,' he says. He's staring out of the window, voice far away and soft.

'I'm sorry,' she says weakly.

'You're sorry,' he says. 'Well, I suppose that's fine then, isn't it?' His voice is sharp and flinty now. 'As long as you're sorry, we can all just go back to normal, right? Forget that you didn't decide to leave your husband and abandon your children.'

'I thought . . .' she says, voice cracking like dried old paint.

'No, Edie,' he says, reeling to face her. His cheeks are pink, his eyes blazing. 'No, you didn't think, did you? You *assumed*. And as always, you jumped to the wrong conclusion and got all in your head and did something stupid.'

She smarts at *stupid*, not because he's wrong, but because it confirms exactly what she thinks about herself.

'I thought you'd be better off without me,' she whispers.

'Well, you thought wrong,' he says. She clings to that, grasps at his words, stuffs them into her pocket. 'The boys were devastated, Edie. They thought they'd never see you again.' He pushes his fingers through his hair and they're shaking. He notices them and folds his arms tightly across his chest, takes a shuddery breath. 'I didn't get your note until well after seven. By that time, Sean had been waiting for you to pick him up for three hours.' He shakes his head. 'It was his first day, Edie. He didn't have a clue what bus to get, or how to get home.'

Something grips her throat. 'What happened?' Her voice is small in the hot kitchen.

'What happened is that he went back inside the school. What happened is the phone rang for nearly an hour. What happened is that the school called the hospitals and then the police to see if anything had happened to you.'

'Why didn't they call the garage?'

'They did!' Ron snaps his head to the side. 'But I had to go out, okay? Had some parts to buy, all right? This isn't about where I was. This is about where *you* were.'

Edie looks at the floor. She's afraid that if she looks back up she'll see this last little connection between them snapping like a frayed thread.

'You'll be happy to know,' continues Ron, 'that we had another visit from the lovely Nick Hughes. Remember him, Edie? The social worker assigned to check that you are a fit parent?'

Her belly plummets.

'I . . .' she starts, but swallows her words.

Tears are falling down Ron's cheeks now. It is the first time she's seen him cry like this. There've been tears, a little drip in the corner of the eye, but nothing like this, raw and exposed. 'Edie, I . . .' He swipes them roughly with the back of his hand. 'You left us, Edie. You left me. I meant it when I said forever.'

'So did I,' she wraps her mouth around the words but no sound comes out. 'So do I!' she says, louder this time.

She so desperately wants to reach for him, but he shakes his head, pushes open the door. Edie waits until he's gone, counts to five, slaps herself hard across the face.

Nick Hughes is plumper than he was when she last saw him.

'We meet again,' he says, and Edie has the bizarre thought that maybe if she kissed him, he'd go away. *Not very professional*, notes Edie, as if she's going to be asked for her opinion on the customer service of a man who wants to take her children away.

'Can I come in?'

'No,' she says. 'I don't want you to.'

He nods, as though she has just confirmed what he already thought. 'I see.'

'I don't want you coming in with your judgy little eyes and your notebook, writing stuff down when you don't know anything about me or my family.'

Nick smiles indulgently. 'Fine,' he says loudly. 'Let's do this here.'

A couple of people in the street stop to look. Weird Albert pokes his head out the door. Edie spots Carol heading her way.

'Carol!' she calls. 'Thank god you're here.'

'Edie! I came to see if you're all right.'

Edie looks at Nick. 'You can come in. But she's coming too.'

His fake smile falters.

'What's the matter?' asks Carol. 'Scared of being alone with two women?'

Nick Hughes looks less comfortable with Carol in the room.

'It's not like she took her kids and left them on the battlefield in the Falklands, was it? I mean, they were at school and their dad was home.'

'He wasn't.'

'No, but he wasn't missing. He was at work.'

'He wasn't.'

Carol turns to Edie. 'Where was he then?'

'That is not the issue,' says Nick.

'I think it is,' says Carol. 'How come Edie's getting all the blame here? Have you spoken to Ron? Asked him why he wasn't where he was supposed to be?'

When Edie comes down from the bathroom after Nick has gone, she's pale and clammy. 'I don't know what I'm doing any more, Carol.'

Edie wishes that she could go back to Lavender Hill and pick up her mother's things all over again. She'd go straight home on the bus, have a bath, look through the stuff, maybe cry a bit, then wipe her face and put on her Good Mammy pants and look after her children properly.

'You know,' says Carol. 'It's not a crime to go on a bloody holiday. Jesus, Edie! Your mam's just died. Why shouldn't you go and see your friend?'

'I wasn't going to come back,' whispers Edie.

'Oh,' says Carol. They examine Edie's rug, starting to go threadbare where multiple feet have trampled parts of it flat. 'I almost left Ken once,' she says eventually. 'I squirrelled money away for nearly a year, then eventually, I realized that I didn't hate him. Just something had gone.' She clears her throat. 'It was a while ago now, mind. Things are good now. Hey, Jenny from the hairdressers is getting a divorce, you know.'

'They'd make the kids live with Ron, wouldn't they?'

'Who? Jenny's kids? Why would they have to live with Ron?'

'No. Mine. If we got a divorce.'

'Oh, Edie. It's not that bad, is it?'

'It's worse.'

'I've messed up so badly,' she says when Patricia calls the night after Nick's visit. 'I left them. I left Ron, I left my boys. I left them and I was there in Kos.'

'Oh, Edie,' she says. 'What did you do that for?'

'Because I thought they'd be better off without me.'

'What? Why would you think that?'

'Because they probably would be,' she says quietly. 'But I couldn't even do that right.'

'Oh, Edie,' says Pats. 'How did you . . .? Whereabouts did you go?'

'Kos Town. The main bit. I thought that's where you'd be.'

'Ah,' says Patricia. 'Ah. Well, the bit I'm in is more . . . not near there. More south, really. Also, when did you say you were here? I might have been away. I went to the other island. The one across . . . you might not have seen it actually. Kisseros. It's pretty small.'

'I didn't even see that on the map,' says Edie.

'No. I don't imagine you did.'

'Do you think they'll ever forgive me, Pats?' she asks. But her reply is the hollow fizz of a call disconnected.

Edie replaces the receiver as quietly as she can then stares around the dark, tattered hallway, where she needs to straighten the pictures, vacuum the carpet and see if she can fix the cracks she has whittled into her family.

Part 5

Ball Number 26: The Twins' Birthday

46

Before

At home, Sean carries his exercise books with great importance, comparing what he is studying with Colin's comprehensive curriculum.

'We've started Pythagoras,' he'll say. Or 'You're still on long division? It was just expected that we'd already know that stuff.'

His vocabulary is expanding too. He says things like *plethora* and *tumultuous* without stumbling, and it always sounds like he's using them correctly. Even his accent is starting to slide away, his *mam*s replaced with *mum*s, his *tea* replaced with *dinner*. The books he brings home are well preserved by a zealous librarian, and Edie sometimes reads them when she's alone. She used to love reading, isn't really sure why she stopped, but she finds herself leafing through *Martin Chuzzlewit* or *Lord of the Flies*, surprised when she sees that half the day is gone and the laundry still isn't folded and her stomach is growling.

'Sean,' she says casually. 'Did you know that *Animal Farm* is an allegory for the Russian Revolution?'

'Of course I do,' says Sean, rolling his eyes. 'Literally the first thing the teacher said.'

At Boldon Comprehensive, Colin isn't sure what they're meant to be reading and when he does bring books home, their spines are broken, pages missing, *Dean loves Claire* scrawled across the text. He still hangs around with Gary and Gareth Maw, while at Dame Allan's Sean is cultivating himself a whole new garden of friends: Alexes, Sebastians and even one Tarquin who they call 'TQ'. They've got double-barrelled names and holiday homes and parents who air kiss them on drop-off. One of his classmates' dads has a helicopter and another is related to the Duke of Northumberland. Meanwhile Edie darns frayed underpants and peers through holes in tea towels to decide whether they're ready to be put out to pasture.

It's great. Opportunity. Potential. But with every term, every exam, every debate club night, Sean is slipping further and further away.

Colin, she is sure, is feeling it as keenly as she is, but she doesn't want to talk to him about it, in case, by speaking it, she makes it real. He trips around with a half-moon smile and a nod and a 'Thanks, Mam,' when she pops his dinner on the table, a polite head tilt when Sean talks about fencing or Latin verbs. At times she can't help wondering if she is boiling Colin up with a simmering resentment. He doesn't say anything, but while Sean's school gets a visit from Princess Diana, Colin's school fails in a bid to bring in a Mr T lookalike for a talk on bullying.

'I think he might feel a bit left behind,' she says to Ron.

'Well, you wanted Sean to go there,' says Ron on the rare occasion she can pin him down to a conversation about it. 'You should have realized it would change things.'

He gives her strange, unreadable looks, like he's certain she's going to run off again at any moment. She's doing her best to act normal and to keep her promise to herself: stay loyal and dedicated to her family. No boat-rocking, no asking difficult questions about why Ron didn't get home until after nine the other day or why she couldn't get any money out from the cash machine last Thursday.

But when the late nights become a habit again, she starts unravelling from the edges again.

'Hilda,' she asks one teatime. 'Did Mr McVey ever . . .?'

'Hit me? Oh no. I'd have rolled him off the top of the cliffs in the nuddy.'

'No, I meant did he ever . . .' she looks for the most polite way of saying it but she's embarrassed '. . . play away?'

'Dip the quill into another ink pot?' asks Hilda. 'He wouldn't have dared. He was being a bit too friendly with Agnes Jackson this one night and I told him I'd chop it off.' She chortles at the memory. 'Hah! Should have seen his face! Priceless!'

'So he . . .'

'You don't think our Ronnie . . .?' Hilda shakes her head. 'Impossible. There's not a better lad in this world. And don't you forget it.'

Sean has been at the school two terms when he starts asking for things: a new Bernard Hinault bike, a golf set because Nathaniel Pike-Oberon wants to play against Sean, sailing lessons *because loads of the boys are sailing this summer.*

'We should have known this would happen,' says Ron.

Edie tries to placate him: *We'll get your dad to fix up Uncle Harry's old bike, can you borrow golf clubs? Would the swan boats at the Marine Park do?*

The harder she tries, the angrier he gets. 'You don't understand,' becomes his refrain.

In the encroaching warmth that suggests summer might be

on its way, she gets a phone call from some David Pike-Oberon about taking Sean to the south of France for a couple of weeks.

'We've got a beautiful place down near Eze, Mrs McVey. Beautiful,' he waxes. 'And Nathaniel and Sean have hit it off beautifully.'

Presumably, everything in David Pike-Oberon's life is *beautiful*.

'Well, it sounds lovely,' she finds herself saying, 'only we can't afford it.'

She wishes it back in her mouth the second it starts floating down the phone cord. Dame Allan's is great about not declaring which students are paying and which got scholarships, and she fears she may have just outed Sean as the poor relation.

'They'll have figured it out anyway,' says Ron when she tells him later. 'These people always do.'

'On us, Mrs McVey,' says David Pike-Oberon without a pause. 'We'll just need his passport details.'

She'll have to see if Hilda will be able to get Sean a passport as an early birthday present.

'On the one hand,' she says to Hilda, 'I feel bad because Colin can't go. I mean, when are we going to be able to afford a holiday for Colin?' Hilda folds her arms every time she brings it up. 'On the other, when are we ever going to be able to afford a holiday for Sean? I mean, an opportunity is an opportunity, right?'

'Well, you seem to have made your decision.'

Edie shakes her head. 'Not sure I could handle the rage and disappointment if I said no.'

'You're the parent, Edith.'

'Exactly,' she says, but she's not sure what she means by it and if she thinks too much about the whole thing it gives her a headache.

On Fridays, Carol feeds her kids and Colin Pot Noodles while Carol and Edie wonder about the subtle nuances of *Dallas* over a bottle of cheap fizz and nibbles. Some weeks, Edie and Carol take her tribe and Colin to discos at the miners' hall that the school lollipop man organizes. They lean against a wall sipping IPA remarking on which kid's shell suit looks the most flammable or which kid's dancing is the most psychotic.

'You should come,' she says to Ron. 'We could even have a little dance.'

'Too much work at the garage,' he mumbles. 'Got to get that Fiat Panda finished by Friday.' Or 'I'm tired, Edie. I'm working bloody hard, you know.' But he does start popping back for sandwiches at lunchtime sometimes instead of the cheeky pint he used to enjoy at the Queen's Head. Maybe Hilda has had a little word.

'We're all right, Edie,' he says sometimes when he's looking at her like she's made of glass. It's been a slow circling dance to get them to this point. For months, she was frightened to touch him in case he cracked, and he wasn't touching her either. But Ron contracting a stomach bug gave her permission to press the back of her hand to his hot forehead, graduating to a gentle back rub, then stroking his arm while he drifted into a fitful sleep. *Baby steps,* they call it, but it has felt more like a tortoise shuffle, and she has taken her penance with soul crushing silence. Finally, he's gone back to wrapping her in those hugs that make her feel as though she's the only thing that matters. 'We're all right.' She loves having his big arms twined around her and wants to slide right inside them and stay there forever, but in her darker moments, the doubts come creeping back in, especially when he comes home late or tells her there isn't any money for the microwave she'd still like to get.

Sean doesn't come anywhere with them any more: he's got *very important things* to do on weekends, like go to the theatre with Nathaniel's parents who get free tickets to everything because they donate so much to the Theatre Royal every year.

It's good. The boys are getting some independence and growing their distinct personalities. But she misses them tussling over the remote control or the silly wrestling games they used to play on the couch.

In Boldon Colliery, it's been three years since the pit closed and there's a general air of desolation about the street. It was exciting for a while, all the lads out there picketing. Edie would make them cups of tea and a plate of biscuits and send the boys out with them. But since they've gone, half the miners' cottages are inhabited by unemployed, bitter men and wives who can't get a bloody thing done with the men hanging around the house and kids who want a Scalextric for Christmas but will be getting a handful of nuts if they're lucky. Most of the houses have now sagged and limped into a state of disrepair, theirs included. Obviously, they're not in a position like the mining families, whose livelihoods were ripped from under their feet like that cheap tablecloth trick. But all the mining lads in the area who used to have cars have sold them or let them rust away to nothing in the street, so Ron's customers have trickled away.

The whole street looks sad and grey. There's a burnt-out Renault in front of the pub, seven houses have at least one broken window and another three have holes in the roof. Gates hang loose, weeds sprout and everything looks cold and damp.

Inside, Edie's slowly losing control of theirs. She can scrub and clean all day, but there's no shifting the mould that blossoms around the kitchen doorframe. When she gets up to do the laundry or put things away, she finds herself getting distracted. A book, a magazine, something on TV. Some days, she'll flick *Pebble Mill* on and then the next thing she knows, the boys are home, there are no clean socks and she hasn't even thought about what they're going to have for tea.

Carol's house on the other hand is cosy, insulated and bright. Her husband Ken's doing okay at work and she's got a SodaStream and a microwave now. The Fulcher kids are all wearing nice coats and trainers with air bubbles in the heels, while she scours the Salvation Army shops for stuff that doesn't smell too much like a miner's armpit for her boys.

They're shivering towards December when Moira next door mentions the cleaning job at the Queen's Head.

Ron isn't against the idea, which surprises her.

'The boys are getting older, Edie. Don't need you like they did when they were small.'

Hilda thinks it's an appalling idea and so does Sean. They gang up over Sunday lunch to dissuade her.

'It's not right, Edie. Being a career girl at this stage.'

Sean snorts. 'Cleaning a pub is hardly a career, Nanna. It's embarrassing, Mum. The lads'll take the mickey if they find out at school.'

Her assertion that they might actually be able to afford the shin pads like Peter Beardsley has or be able to send him on the annual ski trip seems less important than the unholy awfulness that Sean thinks he'll have to bear if his peers with university lecturer or hedge fund manager parents find out that his mother scrubs toilets and wears Marigolds for a living. If he knew how much she was trying to keep everything together, to save money so that he could do these trips, maybe he'd view her as something a little more worthy of his time than he does now. Well, than all of them do, actually.

None of them seem to have noticed that she's started making her own butter skimmed from the tops of milk bottles, or that their casseroles are made with vegetables from Albert's garden as a thanks for cleaning his kitchen once a week. Or that she lies awake night after night calculating just how much she will have to do to get them by on so little.

She hasn't the heart to spell out to Sean that if he wants to do his A levels at Dame Allan's, someone is going to have to sell an organ.

But Carol's in favour.

'Maybe you could squirrel a bit away, you know. For a rainy day. Or even better, a sunny one.'

She starts in January, and it's lovely not to have to sit in the cold kitchen trying to defrost her hands before cutting vegetables for soups that will keep them warm for only an hour or two. The rhythm of her days starts to make sense again and she loves having somewhere to go and be and something to do. *Pride*. That's what this is. Like she matters somewhere. If she wasn't there, the place would never be able to function. The patrons would bugger off somewhere else and the landlord would be selling the furniture within weeks. While she puts order back into the pub, she finds that she can arrange some of the splintered offshoots of her head at the same time.

47

After

'Who's Renata?'

They're rocking side to side in the first-class carriage of the East Coast mainline bound for their West End theatre weekend.

'I . . .' Ron tilts his head. 'Renata?'

'She called,' lies Edie.

'She called the house?' Edie nods. 'Did she leave a message?'

Edie takes her time pouring Sprite from a can into a cup. 'She did not,' she says. 'Who is she?'

'Renata?' He taps his teeth and if Edie wasn't so desperate to know who she is, she'd laugh at his badly acted charade. 'Ah, Renata. Yes. She's from the car valeting company. Yes, that's her name. I'd forgotten it for a minute there.'

'Right,' she says. Her belly is churning again, but that's partly the thrill of the fact that they're going to follow him next week and finally put some pieces of this ridiculous puzzle together. Jess said she'll drive them because there was no way on the planet that she'd ever let Verushka drive her car.

In London they dump their bags in the hotel, have a quick look at the palace, and head to the *Jersey Boys* matinee. It's quite good, but Edie's struggling to focus on Frankie Valli's escapades. She keeps shooting side eyes at Ron, looking for some hint of why he's lying to her. When they sing a stirring rendition of 'Big Girls Don't Cry', she finds herself nodding along. She's going to be a big girl and stop crying about things. She's just going to get on with doing them instead.

That evening, they make their way to the Phoenix. On the way, Edie says, 'I remember! That Renata woman said something about Thursday.'

'Ah, right,' he says. 'I suppose she wants me to take the car in on Thursday.'

'Don't you already have something else on Thursday?'

He furrows his brow. 'No. I don't think so.'

'My mistake,' she says.

In the pit, the orchestra plays a churchy-sounding dramatic overture, all trumpety and lonely. Edie's skin goes bumpy. A woman sings something haunted and a cold spotlight rises on a man in a jacket and tie.

'Did you hear the story of the Johnstone twins?' he asks. 'As alike as two new pins.'

'Twins,' Edie hisses. 'Did you know it's about twins?'

'No, Edie! I swear I didn't.'

'Shhhhhh!'

Tension creeps into Edie's stomach, gripping and twisting before winding up her spine like a vine, wrapping itself around her bones, reaching little shoots into her heart and lungs. Then it snakes down her arms and into her fingers and she's gripping the balcony in front of her.

They're only a few scenes in and Mrs Johnstone is agreeing to give one of her babies to Mrs Lyons for a life of privilege.

'I can't . . .' she says, jumping to her feet.

'Sit down,' hisses someone.

Ron's hand is on her back, the near silent whisper of 'Edes, come on,' but she's pushing past Ron, treading on toes, gasping now, dragging reluctant air into her lungs. She trips up the steps, bursts out the door and into the overbright foyer.

Two barmaids in striped waistcoats stop what they are doing, glasses in hand, cloths dangling from fingers, to stare at the woman wheezing against their freshly wiped mahogany bar.

'Are you all right?' asks one, but then Ron is by her side putting his hands on her face. Edie bats his hands away.

'It's too much,' she hisses. 'Did you do this on purpose?'

'I'm sorry,' says Ron. 'I just . . . it had five stars.'

'Five stars from sadists.' She pushes herself fully upright. 'Why can't you just be honest with me?'

'Edie, you can't really be having a go at me because you're not enjoying the show, are you?'

From inside the auditorium comes a rumble of applause. Edie folds her arms across her chest to stop the trembling in her fingers.

'The secrets,' she starts. *Am I about to open this can of worms right here in a theatre foyer that smells of roasted peanuts and wine?*

Ron jumps, plucks his phone from his trouser pocket. He frowns at the display. 'Hello.'

Edie watches his skin blanch to the colour of uncooked pizza dough.

He takes a shuddering breath. 'On our way,' he says.

'Turn right onto The Strand,' says a weirdly chirpy American woman. Ron navigates carefully through the streaking lights of weekend West End traffic. Edie watches him checking and rechecking his mirrors, twisting around before easing into gaps.

Usually when he's driving, she admires his casually shelved arm, the soft contours of his face. She likes the way he seems to have a sixth sense on the road, like he's gliding along from instinct. *Like a homing pigeon. But more elegant.* But tonight, Ron's knuckles bulge around the steering wheel, his eyes are restless and the line of his jaw is set in a hard square. Edie can even see a little pulse hammering in the corner of his mouth and she knows there's a matching beat inside her own chest that stamps out a panicked rhythm.

London passes by in a blur. She's seen it in films of course, but leaving the city in an Astra at 9:30 p.m. on a Friday night has stripped the glamour from the capital: a bundle of sleeping bag and cardboard presses close to a doorway; a young man stomps down a street, face illuminated by the bluish glow of a phone screen; a thin cat leaps onto a wall studded with broken glass, elegantly sidestepping the weaponry. People are just people, places just places. Londoners put out their wheelie bins just like people from Boldon or Darras Hall.

Neither Ron nor Edie speaks again until they're out of the city and on the M1.

Edie tries to piece together what's happening in her head. While they were teetering on the brink of an argument in the theatre foyer, Ron's phone had rung. Ron blanched, and in that moment, Edie knew that something terrible had happened.

'We have to go,' Ron had said. 'I'll explain when we're on the road.'

It was Carol phoning Ron, having got a call from Gary who got a message from Colin's ex-wife who is apparently still listed as Colin's next of kin. The chain of events doesn't make sense and Edie tries to picture them all in a line playing that kids' game of Chinese Whispers. It will be wrong, of course, the message that

Ron and Edie are currently scrunching up their faces to decipher. Wrong, but with a nugget of truth.

Colin has been in an accident in his car.

'He's okay, right?' says Edie once they hit the motorway, her voice cracking in a dry throat. 'That's what Carol said. Colin is okay.'

Ron closes his eyes briefly. 'He's . . . Carol said he's in a coma, Edie.'

'A coma?' Edie's heart stutters in her chest. 'Jesus, Ron. Nobody said *coma*.' She presses her hand to her mouth, pressing back a scream, pushing it into her throat.

'I didn't want to worry you,' Ron says, reaching for her hand.

'We have to get to him now!' She hits the dashboard, making Ron jump. His empty hand grasps the wheel again. 'A coma, Ron. A coma!' Her heart stops around behind her ribs. 'Can't we go a bit faster?'

I missed the ripping of my heart strings when my boy needed me.

Edie looks at the estimated arrival time on the car computer map: 2:46 a.m. She drums an anxious rhythm on her leg, suddenly wondering how two tense people are going to fill five hours of straight motorway travel without screaming.

'Tell me again what the hospital said,' she says as they pass Luton.

'They said he'd been pulled from a crushed Mustang on the A19.'

'What's the A19?'

'That big road near the tunnel. Know which one I mean?'

'No.'

'Well, it's big, all right? They reckon he must've lost control and hit the concrete pillars of the overpass. They can't tell for certain.'

'But he'll be okay, right?'

Ron puffs his cheeks and blows out a fat gale of air. 'A coma, Edie. He's in intensive care. A coma and intensive care are serious.'

'Yes, but people wake up from comas all the time.'

'They do,' says Ron. 'Except when they don't.'

'But he will. He has to.'

Ron slams the heel of his hand on the wheel. 'Edie, you can't get through this with blind denial as usual. Let's be realistic for once, shall we? Actually face up to things. Colin is seriously hurt. He may or may not recover. There. I've said it.'

Edie stares at her knees, clad in a neat tartan skirt. It's not the McVey tartan: she had planned to buy that but found the squares too little, the colours too bright. She isn't sure what this tartan is. Probably some murderous clan that pushed their rivals off mountains and sliced off their servants' limbs in draughty castles in days of yore. Maybe the modern equivalent is slapping a husband across the face in a Vauxhall Astra.

'This is not denial,' she says quietly, 'this is hope.'

They stop at a service station filled with truckers and local insomniacs. Dead-eyed teenagers wipe tables while tired drivers in a uniform of ill-fitting jeans and motorbike logo T-shirts stretched across bellies tuck into cheese toasties and sausages that have been sitting under a heat lamp for so long they look plastic. A thin woman with streaked mascara and a shaggy coat stares into the bottom of a Coca-Cola cup under the too-bright neon of strip lights.

In the toilets, they've tried to make the lighting a bit kinder, but no amount of 40 watters can hide the fact that Edie looks haggard. Like the horrible old witch in a fairy tale.

When she comes out, she finds Ron resting his cheek on top

of a Formica table. His features are all squashed together like a bulldog's. He sits up as she approaches, blinks a few times, rubs his eyes in heavy circles.

'There you are,' he says, but his voice is flat and dull. He pushes to his feet, puffing with the effort.

'Are you okay?'

'Yeah,' he says, 'just tired.'

She wants to hug him but the gulf feels too huge. She pats his arm instead and he reaches for her hand.

Ron nudges her awake. A faint pewter strip in the sky suggests that morning is on its way, and a couple of forlorn-looking trees stretch and groan in waking.

'Where are we?'

'Hospital car park.'

Edie's neck creaks when she rights it, and there's a greasy blob on the window that she used as a cold, unwelcoming pillow. A few cars are dotted around, but they are empty of life.

They step out of the hire car in subdued unison, slamming the doors, walking across the asphalt to the muted rhythms of mundanity.

'Ward eighteen, he's in,' says Ron. 'Critical care unit.'

The blue signs are too cheerful for the message they declare, and the hospital foyer too bright after the cocoon of a night in an Astra and the delicious ignorance of not having seen their son in a coma yet. Everything inside Edie's body is too stiff, joints, muscles and a well of churning misery frozen solid mid-seethe.

'Are we early?' asks Edie, 'I mean, what are the visiting hours?'

'Anytime,' says Ron.

Anytime in case your loved one inconveniently carks it outside appointed hours.

In the foyer, Carol rushes at them, wrapping Edie in a damp, crumpled hug.

'Oh, Edie,' she says.

Edie pulls back from Carol's arms and shakes her hand. She can't be there in empathetic arms, because somehow, it might thaw something that she's not ready to release yet. 'Thank you for coming,' she whispers, and she can't stop waggling Carol's hand up and down like a politician.

Ron cups her elbow in his palm, removes her hand from Carol's.

'Thanks, Carol. We'll go in now.'

Edie couldn't have prepared for the sight of her boy all taped up, tubes and wires connecting him to ominous-noised machines that beep and blip and click to keep her baby alive.

'Fuck,' says Ron. Edie has never heard him use that word before, and something in the crack of the *ck* splinters her apart. She squeezes shut her eyes, blind and fogged.

'I can't,' she says, backing into a trolley. 'I can't I can't I can't.'

48

Before

'Bugger!'

Edie clocks the time on the wall. If she misses this bus, she'll have to wait forty minutes for the next one and will definitely be late. She bundles up her tabard and shoves it in her bag, the accusatory pointed finger of a rubber glove sticking out the top.

If that toilet hadn't been blocked, if whatsherface with the tooth thing hadn't gone home sick it would have been fine. She could have made it home, had a quick wash and got changed into something a bit more presentable. As is, she's got a damp sleeve and dirty hair pushed off her face with a scarf. It's not even really a scarf, just the scrap of an old T-shirt that she cut into a strip to keep her hair out of her eyes at work.

It'll have to do. Better to be late than not there at all. She casts a lemony glance at the garage, where Ron will either be elbow-deep in engine grease or . . . she doesn't let herself finish the thought.

She shoulders the door and runs the two blocks to the bus stop, just in time to see its backside disappearing round the corner.

'No!'

She could head back to the garage, ask Ron to drive her over, but the traffic would be awful.

'Are you sure you don't want to come?' Edie had asked him the night before. 'We could go early, maybe grab a sandwich somewhere.'

'I've got so many jobs on this week,' he'd said. 'So many. Remember, Edie. I *am* my business. If I'm not there, the business is losing money.'

She leans into the printed timetable blurred behind melted plastic. *There's got to be another way than the two buses Sean gets in the morning.*

Edie traces her finger across the timetable. *If I get that one down to Shields, then the 56, then I might be able to get the other one that links from there.* Worth a try.

An hour later, she is not where she'd hoped to be. The heating is on full blast and Edie has to take off her coat and fold it into a damp ball on her lap. She checks her watch again. It starts in twenty minutes and there's no way she will get there in time for the start. She fishes the letter out of her handbag, scanning for the finish time, hoping at least that she can get to speak to some of Sean's teachers.

'You don't have to come,' said Sean.

'Of course I'm going to come.'

'Well, don't be late then,' he said. Then, 'And don't be weird.'

She bristles. She couldn't have imagined talking to an adult like that when she was fifteen, let alone a parent. Kids are just so much more confident these days. They're more like little adults. Or maybe that's just Sean.

On the connecting bus, she empties coins into the tray by the driver. 'You're fifteen pee short, lass,' he says.

'I'm sure I've got some more,' she says, fishing through her handbag, but in a bag mostly populated by old tissues and her cleaning tabard, the coins are conspicuously absent. 'I must have,' she mutters, knowing full well she's exhausted the pockets of her bag and there's nowhere left to look.

'I've got a schedule to keep,' says the driver, shrugging his apology.

'Please!' Edie takes a deep breath and turns to the passengers on the half-full bus. Some pointedly turn away, others watch her with curiosity. 'I'm late for my son's parents' evening and I don't want to let him down.' A woman counts three five pees and presses them into Edie's hand. 'I'm a mother too,' she says, then ducks back to her seat.

The bus inches through traffic all the way through the city. *Crawl hour, not rush hour.* She checks her watch again. Sean's teachers have only forty more minutes to sit and talk to parents about their darling wonderful sons and how marvellously they are all excelling at everything. She bets they're counting down the minutes. Listening politely as Miles or Tarquin or Quentin's mother asks an inane question about future university places or pretends to know something insightful about John Donne. She bets they are picturing a cool crisp glass of rosé on their kitchen counter in their neat houses in Gosforth or North Shields. Maybe they're looking forward to taking a bath in a double-glazed bathroom and dropping some Dewberry bath pearls into the steaming water.

The rain has just started and streetlights flicker on, giving the lamps ethereal ginger haloes.

Sean is going to be so upset with me. 'I'm so sorry, Sean,' she practises, but it sounds lame and overused. *He didn't really want me there in the first place*, she says to herself. *Will he be that upset?*

It's bucketing down by the time the bus draws to a stop near the school, and there's only fifteen minutes left of the parents' evening. Getting off the bus, she hears someone say 'Her kid's at Dame Allan and she's fifteen pee short of a bus fare. This is why I hate posh people.' She sprints towards the gates.

A sign near the entrance says *5th Year Parents' Evening: West Hall (first floor)*.

She darts past adults congratulating their smartly clad offspring and families deciding where to go for dinner and heads into the building. She is panting by the time she reaches the stone staircase and stops for a moment to catch her breath. Only then does she realize that she's left her coat on the bus.

'Bugger!' she says loudly, and is greeted by a glare from a woman in a pencil skirt.

Seats are arranged outside the West Hall, but they are empty, save for Sean in the middle of a stiff-backed sofa reading a book.

'Seany,' she says, and her voice bounces off the stone. 'Seany, I'm so sorry.'

His face is thunderous. It shifts to horror as he takes in her wet hair, the dirty shirt. 'You shouldn't have bothered,' he hisses. 'It's nearly over anyway.'

He stands, grabs her by the wrist and pulls her towards the wall as though he might be about to push her through one of those secret panelled doors these old buildings always have.

'You look a state. And did you wear that to deliberately embarrass me?'

Edie glances down at her shirt, one of the freebies from work. It's white with an image of a big square nail on the front. *Copperhead*, it says. *It takes some beating*. The rain has rendered it all but translucent, and the tattered lace around the top of her bra is on view. The dampness hasn't done anything to hide the sticky stains dotted across the surface where it has soaked up a fallen puddle of beer or a splash of port.

'I had to come straight from work,' she says.

He snorts at the word *work*. 'Well, I've got my report already so we might as well just go home. Maybe you can pretend to Dad that you didn't show up late and try to humiliate me by being dressed like a pikey.'

She's suddenly angry. 'You can't talk to me like that, Sean. It's not nice.'

'Not nice? What's not nice is you looking like an escaped mental patient and potentially messing up my future.'

'Sean, listen . . .'

'No, you listen.' His eyes are blazing. 'I have friends and a brain and a real stab at doing well here and you show up like a full crazy trying to make me look stupid. I'm not having it. This is my school, my place. You look like a weirdo here. You're not welcome.'

He turns, hauls his school bag onto his shoulder and heads for the stairs.

'Pet!' she yells. It's the wrong thing to say, and Sean kicks the leg of a chair.

A neat family exiting the hall look at her with a mixture of disgust and pity. Some older boys in blazers snigger and a man with a bushy beard tilts a sympathetic ear her way. She's seen those same looks on the people at the Post Office when her mother got kicked out or the time she begged at the grocery shop for a discount on a loaf of bread. *Shameful.*

She catches up to him at the top of the stairs. 'Sean . . .'

He reels to face her, red, furious. 'You are an embarrassment! I wish someone else was my mother!'

Edie splinters into a million pieces.

49

After

The nurse that seems to do most of Colin's care is called Rebecca. She's a redhead with a no-nonsense attitude that might be erring on the side of rudeness.

'Efficient,' nods Ron when the door closes after she's done her checks.

After Edie had run off, Carol found her sobbing over a bathroom sink. She'd got her breathing back to a steady pace and given her a long lingering hug.

'I'm here for you, Edie,' she'd said. 'I haven't been, and I'm sorry. I . . .'

It is good to be back in the familiar arms of a friend. 'I understand,' she said.

'He needs you, Edie.'

Back in the room, she found Ron folded at a weird angle like a portable tripod, knees at angles on a too-small chair, head resting on the bed by Colin's inert arm. Edie hovered in the corner of the room watching her pale, sick boy and exhausted husband and felt a scream vibrating deep in her guts. She pushed it down. *Be normal, Edie*, she thought. *Be normal enough to be there for Colin.*

Rebecca said they should talk to him, but she's self-conscious with Ron there. A bit like she would be if he overheard her talking to the apple tree. She does it anyway, in a halting voice that's a bit too high and bright for the flat grey of the room. It feels as though her voice is being pushed through someone else's throat.

She tells Colin about the hotel in London and how she couldn't remember whether the Buckingham Palace flag meant that the Queen was there or not, but either way, they hadn't got a look at her. She talks about *Jersey Boys* and how they had links with the mob.

'Of course,' she says. 'He did some good music, that Frankie Valli.'

'Why don't you sing some of their songs?' says Ron. 'I don't think he'll know any.'

'You sing something,' says Edie. 'You've hardly said anything. I'm doing all the talking.'

'I just feel a bit . . .' Ron slumps in the plastic chair. 'A bit weird, you know.'

'No,' Edie lies, 'I don't know. He's your boy, Ron. Talk to him like you usually do.'

Edie squeezes Colin's hand, taking care not to knock the IV tube sending vital things into his blood.

'Go on,' she urges.

Ron sighs, stands and walks to the window, hands pushed deep into his pockets. 'Right.' He clears his throat. 'So,' he says, 'they gave us an Astra to drive back in.'

'Cars!' Edie says, making Ron jump. 'How's that a good idea? Don't you think that's a bit insensitive, all things considered?'

'What do you want me to say, Edie?' His voice is clipped and low. He turns to stare at her, a huge shadow silhouetted against the whitewash of light at the window. 'That everything's going to be all right? That just thinking it will be is enough? What is it you want me to say? That bad stuff doesn't happen to nice boys from Boldon Colliery?'

She turns away.

'It's okay, Colin,' she says, filmy tears forming on her eyeballs.

'It is not okay,' Ron shouts. 'It is not okay! He might die, Edie.'

'Don't say that!' Edie jumps to her feet. 'Don't ever say that!' Her voice rises to match his. 'It's not okay. None of this is okay. If we hadn't won the stupid lottery, he wouldn't have even had that idiotic car. If you hadn't encouraged him to get it, to go on stupid fast drives, this wouldn't have happened.'

'So it's my fault, is it?'

'Yes!' she yells. 'No! Not completely, but partly.'

'You blame me?'

'No.' She sucks in a breath. She doesn't blame him. Not for this. But the anger is pulsing and throbbing through her now, and the only way is out. 'So tell me, Ron. Have you told Sean yet? Or maybe you're waiting until next time you meet up to bitch about horrible Mammy.'

The air in the room thickens: choking, cloying, too hot. There it is, out in the air like a toxic virus. Edie brings her hand to her mouth, afraid she might vomit. Ron is trembling from head to foot, and the beeping of the machines is too loud in the wake of their shouting.

'Ah,' he says. He leans his head back against the window. 'Ah,' he says again. He casts a glance at Colin on the bed. 'How did you . . .? Look, it's not how it looks, Edie.'

'No? Then how is it?'

'It's . . . well . . . we just.' He sits down and it's like the air whooshing out of a balloon. He temples his fingers, puts his elbows on the bed by Colin's legs. 'He invited me. His therapist suggested it and he asked me along.'

Her pulse is hammering in the side of her neck.

'We had a session. It was weird. Hard. He said a lot of things that were difficult to hear.'

'Like what?'

'Like . . . stuff about what happened.'

'And he didn't want me to go to the therapy with him?' She shakes her head, and the blood inside her brain sloshes about, blurring her vision. 'He's talking to you, but he's never even given me the chance to apologize? I tried. I tried so hard to find him.' She's shaking all over now. 'All I've ever done is try. Try to make your life better, try to make their lives better. I wasn't the one always at the garage doing who-knows-what. I was the one trying to hold it all together. It's not my fault we were poor. It's not my fault we didn't live up to his expectations. Why is it always just me that gets the blame? How come you're off the hook?'

'I didn't do anything wrong,' he says.

'Didn't you?'

They sit inside a stilted silence, breathing, trembling.

'What about the woman with the jeans?' she says. *It's all or nothing, now.* 'Or you making decisions about my body without my consent?'

He winces as though she's jabbed him with a needle.

'I made some choices to save our family,' he says. 'I did things to stop us McVeys from crumbling down to our foundations.'

'I—' she says, but whatever was going to come out floats out of her mind and dies with the word.

'You want to talk about blame, Edie. Let's start with you leaving us, shall we? Then move on to the way you drove Sean to the Pike-Oberons.' She screws up her eyes and shakes her head.

'I've been defending you for years,' he says. 'And I'm not sure I should have done.'

Ron's face closes down: shuttered like the roller doors holding back the empty heart of McVey's Motors. It's been demolished now, the garage, and in an electric, pulsing critical care ward, they're demolishing the last forty years of Ron and Edie.

And then the doors are swinging shut on his straight back, his stiff body.

50

Before

The missing him is vicious.

It starts when she gets up in the morning and has the delicious liberty of forgetting he's not there. Everywhere hugs a shadow of Sean: there he is on the bottom stair tying his boots, there he is poring over textbooks at the kitchen table next, there he is slamming the bedroom door, flushed and wild.

'It's only for a little while,' said Bianca Pike-Oberon when she came to pick him up in her shiny BMW. 'Just so he can focus on his exams.'

Sean wouldn't look at Edie and Colin was crying – properly sobbing – and Ron was gruff and polite.

'Thank you,' he said stiffly, blocking the front door with his frame. 'We, I . . . we're very grateful.'

'Seany, I . . .' But Edie didn't know what it was she wanted to say, and his stone-face would have stopped her anyway.

He took all of his meagre possessions when he left, so the only physical reminders are the pictures over the fireplace. She spends her time polishing the frames so she can look at the frozen imprints of his face. There's only one picture of the four of them all together from back in the late Seventies sometime when the boys were about four, and it stands in a cheap gilt frame on the mantelpiece. They were all wearing a lot of brown in those days, so the picture has a muddy quality. The boys are grinning, one on each of Edie and Ron's laps. Ron is pink-cheeked and wearing the heavy lids he gets after a couple of drinks. Edie is smiling, but if she examines her face closely enough, she looks like she's in the midst of some sort of crisis, cheeks tight, eyes wild.

She stares too long at Sean, and that face that she wiped and cleaned and kissed starts to blur. A face she looked at every day takes on the features of a stranger and she has to close her eyes.

If she's completely honest with herself, she can see that he was already becoming a stranger to her before the parents' evening, and though she recognizes the smiling boy in the early photos, the teenage Sean conceals secrets in smiles that he was never going to share with his mother.

The night before he left, Edie hovered outside their bedroom door, holding her breath to still her heartbeat.

'I'll still see you,' Sean said in a low, soft voice betraying a tenderness she hadn't heard from him in years. 'It's not so far.' His words were punctuated by Colin's sniffles, the occasional nose blow. 'It's okay, Col. It's going to be okay. I love you bro, okay. That's not going to change.'

She thought that her heart would shatter, pierce her skin with the splintered shards and let her bleed out.

'Watch her,' Sean had warned his brother. 'Watch her carefully.'

She shook her head at the injustice of it. *Like I'm some sort of danger instead of a confused and upset mother.* She'd backed away, thrust her face under her pillow and wondered if she were to die of a broken heart in the night whether he'd stay. Maybe that would be the best option for everyone.

After the conspicuous BMW pulled out of their little street, Colin had crawled under Sean's *Danger Mouse* blanket and wrapped himself into a cocoon, a terrifying weeping muffled by cotton and polyester. She'd watched from the door, impotent and still.

Sometimes she wanders around the house looking for solid traces of Sean. There's a bag of his old shirts in the top of her wardrobe, but other than that, he's left nothing concrete of himself behind, as though maybe he was never here at all.

Their house is so tiny that there wasn't an option to keep their childhood relics. Outgrown bikes were passed on to smaller kids in the street, clothes taken in bags to the charity shop for a third go around, old school books tossed in the bin after blank pages had been torn out for drawing on, or for Ron to cover in grease and use as receipts at the garage.

Nothing much.

When she gets home from work in the afternoon and Ron is still at the garage, Colin still at school, the silence yawns at her from the moment she swings open the door until one of them returns home.

'I'm sorry,' Bianca or David or Nathaniel will say when she calls, 'he's not here at the moment.' Or 'The boys are still at rugby practice.' Or 'Give him time, Mrs McVey.'

'Sean says he's sorry he missed you,' Ron says some days, as though he's called deliberately when he knows she'll not be home.

'Don't be silly, Edie,' she says into the empty house, heart thudding while she calls, only to be met with the tinny ring that stretches on and on or Nathaniel Pike-Oberon's stiff responses.

'Have a pleasant day, Mrs McVey.' He signs off with a flat poem of dismissal that leaves her bereft.

She starts chatting to the tree that she planted with the boys when they first moved in as though it is Sean. 'Hello, lovely,' she'll whisper when no one's home. 'Mammy's missing you.' A few times, she catches weird Albert watching her from the back bedroom window and she scuttles indoors, face flaming. 'Stupid woman,' she says to her reflection. *Stupid and mad.*

'Buck up, Edie,' says Hilda when she calls over on a fake errand. 'All boys leave home eventually. If they don't, you've mothered them too much.'

Yes, but most boys aren't taken away in a shiny BMW at fifteen because living with their mother is deemed the worst thing in the world for him by people who have no idea what his heart really sounds like.

Months after Sean's gone to stay with the Pike-Oberons, David Pike-Oberon calls to say that 'Bianca is willing to facilitate some time.'

They sit stiffly in the Eldon Square food court, Bianca Pike-Oberon looking as out of place as a lotus flower in a row of turnips in her crisp blouse and navy skirt. The boys order pizza slices and chips, while Ron sips a tea from a paper cup and Edie fights to keep her breakfast down. Sean won't look at her at first, then, while Ron is making small talk with Bianca and Colin is telling him a story about Gareth Maw falling off his stool in chemistry, he catches her eye, holds it for a second, then looks back to his chips.

'I can give you a recommendation,' says Bianca, looking at Edie.

'A recommendation for what?'

'A psychiatrist,' says Bianca. 'Not me, of course. As I'm treating Sean that would be a conflict of interests. But I can refer you to someone who would give you an excellent discount.'

'Thanks,' says Ron.

'I don't need a psychiatrist,' shrieks Edie. Other diners stare over. She drops her voice. 'I don't need a psychiatrist, and neither does Sean.' Sean stares at the table and looks like he's about to cry. 'We just need each other,' she whispers. 'We just need each other.'

'I appreciate that this is hard,' says Bianca. 'But trust me, Mrs McVey. I'm a professional.'

Later, when they are about to leave, Ron says 'Honestly, Mrs Pike-Oberon, do you really think you need to be here with us?'

'It's Dr Pike-Oberon,' she says. The woman looks at Sean, who is elbowing Colin and laughing at a passing woman with her skirt tucked into her tights. 'I'll talk to him,' she says. 'Ron, this is a delicate age. We need to tread softly.'

The following week, David Pike-Oberon calls to say they will *allow* the McVeys to take Sean out for a few hours *unsupervised*.

'Oh, thank you so much,' gushes Ron, and Edie wants to kick him in the shin, wants to kick Bianca and David Pike-Oberon in the shins. It's only meant to be a temporary thing, just so Sean can concentrate on his exams, but Edie is furious that they've taken it upon themselves to make up the rules and demand that everyone goes along with them.

'We need to do it, Edie. It's what Sean wants and we can't risk pushing him further away,' warns Ron. 'At least for the time being.'

It is more relaxed without Bianca glaring at them from under her big eyelashes. They go to the food court again and the boys have fish and chips.

'We don't have fish and chips at David and Bianca's,' says Sean. 'We have fish, but it's sort of grilled and has bones and they do it with tomatoes and green bits.'

'Is that right?' says Ron.

Edie doesn't say much, but she does listen. He's learning guitar, his French teacher says he's top five in the year, they went to an art gallery to hear a talk by some woman called Tracey, which Edie doesn't think sounds like a very artsy name.

'And get this,' he says, a pocket of batter hanging over his lip, 'David and Bianca have said I can stay with them if I get a sixth-form scholarship.'

'They didn't ask us!' says Edie, panicked.

Sean's jaw ticks. 'Right. And what's the alternative?' Edie stares at her hands for the rest of the lunch.

The realization that he doesn't miss her at all stings.

'How do you deal with your boys growing away from you?' she asks Hilda later.

'You don't,' says her mother-in-law with a lopsided grimace.

51

After

Edie strokes the hair back from Colin's temple. It's thinning with a confetti dusting of grey throughout. It is receding too, and she finds herself wondering what Sean's hair looks like now. *Ron could probably tell me.*

She's been by his side since they arrived this morning, except for an occasional comfort break, and now the day is tipping into a grey-brown dusk.

'Come on, baby. You can pull through. I know you can.'

His complexion has a floury tone and texture, like he's been in an ingredient fight at a bakery. Hilda tried to bake scones with the twins once and they were covered in flour which turned to paste in their chipped bath. Edie runs a finger down Colin's cheek, half expecting to see a white tip when she withdraws it.

Ron doesn't look at her when he comes back in. He sits by the other side of the bed and takes Colin's limp fingers in his.

'Ron, I . . .' Edie starts.

'Hey, Col,' he says softly. 'I picked up a *Top Gear* mag from the kiosk downstairs. Would you like me to read it to you? They're reviewing that Lexus we saw at the roadshow. Apparently, they're going to have built-in moisturiser in the air conditioning. Imagine that!'

There's a tiny tremor in his voice and he looks as though it is taking everything he has to keep his eyes on Colin.

'Ron...'

'Did you know that they employ paint inspectors? That's someone's job, Col. And they take exams four times a year! Heart surgeons don't even do that many exams.'

There's a clutch at the edge of her memory, little her, doing gymnastics for her mother. 'Look, Mammy! I'm a clown!' The blank, hard stare that couldn't be penetrated. Ron's wearing that face now. 'Mammy, Mammy, why won't you look at me?' And then later as she bracketed her mother's thin cheeks in her palms. 'Now listen, Mam. You don't open the door. Are you listening, Mam? This is important.'

'Please,' she says, and she's crying now. 'Ron, please don't ignore me.'

'And they only use leather from cows that haven't been near barbed wire. I mean, there's special and then there's barking. Or mooing.'

Edie gets up from her chair and walks to the swinging door. She pauses, hoping Ron will ask where she's going, but he carries on with his monologue about cars and cows. She blows her nose and there, just for a moment, he glances at her. It is fear that is printed all over his face. She's seen him scared and she's seen him angry before, but not like this, like he is about to split apart. Edie turns away and heads out past the almost empty nurses' station.

'Taking a break, are you, Mrs McVey?' Rebecca has her standard glare on, and it feels like some sort of accusation.

'Yes. That's all right, isn't it?'

Rebecca frowns. 'Of course it is. I wanted to come in earlier to tell you to have a moment to yourself, but I thought I'd wait until your man was back.'

'Right,' says Edie, wondering briefly if he is still her man. 'Well. Thank you.' She wraps her arms inside the folds of her cardigan and heads for the door control panel that will release her back into the beige corridors of the rest of the hospital: out there, where people are suffering from normal, fixable problems.

'They do a smashing sausage roll in the canteen, if you're hungry.' Rebecca is now leafing through a pile of paper so Edie isn't sure whether she's talking to her or the paper. Since there's no one else around, and piles of paper don't tend to indulge in pastry products, she assumes it is directed at her.

'Lovely,' she says.

Outside the sliding doors of the foyer, cars pull in and drop off visitors, most of whom are armed with an array of gifts: foil balloons, flowers poking out of cellophane, teddy bears in pink and blue hats. The sky is just starting to darken to a gunmetal grey and the first streetlamps cast faint, tangerine glows on the pavements. Edie guesses it must be evening visiting hours on the normal wards.

She takes a deep breath and struggles to push the air all the way down into her belly. The aqua aerobics instructor at the leisure centre, Judy, said that breathing right into your stomach was much better for you than normal breathing, but tonight, Edie's breath is sort of lodged in her gullet.

She leans against a wall, suddenly frightened of tipping into the slow-moving traffic that's vying for space at the drop-off point. She's pulled back a familiar curtain only to discover an alternative version of her life on the other side. *Was this always here?* she might ask, *just behind the normal curtain?* Maybe there's another reality perhaps where Ron married Joan Collins or the jeans woman and Sean and Colin had a normal upbringing with a nice normal mother instead. *Who's that strange pale woman watching us?* they might say over a home-cooked Sunday roast in a kitchen with terracotta tiles and a faithful labrador waiting for scraps.

'No!' yells a woman from the back seat of a taxi. The door gapes open, a mouth caught mid-scream. The driver leaps from the cab, runs to the passenger side and slips his arm under a rotund woman.

'Come on, pet. Let's get you in.' He pulls her from the car and deposits her on the concrete right in front of Edie. 'No charge, don't worry about it.' He hauls a holdall from the back seat.

'Uuuggghhh!' yells the woman, doubling over.

'Are you okay, pet?' Edie asks.

The woman turns her head. 'Edie. Go with me on this one.'

'Jade!' She wraps an arm around her shoulder and bends to join her. 'Are you okay? Are you in labour?'

'Ssshhh,' says Jade. 'I'm pretending so I get a free cab ride.'

'Ah.' Edie rights herself and shakes the cabby's hand. 'Thanks so much. I'll take it from here.'

'Good luck!' he says to Jade. To Edie he says, 'Too sad, isn't it?'

Edie nods. 'Too sad,' but she has no idea what she's agreeing with.

When the taxi has pulled away, Jade stands up straight.

'Thanks, Edie. I couldn't afford the fare.' She grins. 'Told him Daddy is missing in action in Buckmenistan.'

'Is that even a place?'

'No idea.' Jade winces. 'I wish Asif was missing in Buckmenistan. Especially if it doesn't exist.'

'Right. But why are you here if you're not in labour?'

Jade grins. 'I came to see you of course! And Colin, if they let fat pregnant lasses in. Wanted to put my acting skills to use and get here while I was still compos mentis. Have you had the sausage rolls from the canteen, Edie? They're to die for!'

Edie wants to lie down on the pavement and cry. A hideous premonition of Jade's baby being born and Colin dying at the same moment springs unbidden into her head and she stumbles back to the wall.

'Steady on, Edie!' Jade sets her right. 'I was worried. I hope you don't mind. Verushka called the other aqua girls. Look, I know I don't know Colin all that well, it's just . . . well, you. You've been my rock these last few months. Saved me from myself. I thought I could return the favour. I can't give much but . . .'

Jade hasn't finished her sentence before Edie has her pulled tight into an embrace. This woman she barely knows is here, offering unconditional love and support. It's almost too much for the fragile shell holding an emotional flood back. Edie lets the tears fall, and the two women stand together locked in an uncomfortable embrace at the front of an overbright hospital. Pedestrians step around them, and Edie doesn't care, because she couldn't stop if she tried.

Jade's hand moves in soft, soothing circles on Edie's back. 'I know, Edie. As mothers . . .' She gulps down a sob. 'As women . . .' She steps back, pulls a tissue from her pocket and dabs Edie's wet face.

Around them, patients and visitors, nurses and orderlies go about their own lives, finding strength in another coffee hit before a shift, or treatment promises or assurances that loved ones are getting better. At the eye of a whirling cyclone of human experience condensed and magnified in ways that only a hospital can, Edie takes a deep breath, gathering strength from this strange and glorious friendship, and readies herself to pick up the jagged fragments of her life to see what she can salvage.

52

Before

It's a polite dinner, but Edie has never felt more adrift. Ron pokes at unfamiliar vegetables and clears his throat each time he goes to speak. Bianca twitters and refills their wine glasses so often Edie starts to wonder if she and David are in fact alcoholics.

'Are you a Toon Army supporter, Ron?' asks David. His pronunciation is too clipped, his vowels too round to pull off the casual man-of-the-people air he's aiming for.

'Not really,' says Ron. 'I like motorsports, you know. Grand Prix and the likes.'

'Oh,' says David.

When Sean, Colin and Nathaniel have been dispatched upstairs, Bianca leans her elbows on the table.

'Now, Ron, Edie. There's something we need to discuss.'

Edie is nervous anyway. The setting, the journey, the company: they've all conspired to make her feel like a clumsy actor in a bad play. She's too hot, her dress is hanging weirdly around the neckline and there's a sprig of hair that refuses to stay in place.

'Tell me, Edie, did you ever get an appointment with Dr Telford?'

Edie shakes her head. Bianca probably knows full well that she made it as far as calling his office and finding out that his special discounted price for a recommendation from Bianca Pike-Oberon was £130 per session.

Bianca shoots an *I tried!* shrug to David and sends hope floating away. She'd hoped this dinner would be an end to it. A full stop on the last seven months so they can move forward and be a proper family again.

'Now,' says Bianca. 'As you know, Sean has been offered a two-year extension on his scholarship so that he can take his A levels at Dame Allan's.' Edie nods. She realizes that Ron is staring at the table and both Bianca and David are looking at her. 'We've discussed it, and everyone is on board to let Sean stay here for the next two years.'

'Everyone?' asks Edie. 'You've asked Sean about this?'

'Of course!'

'You asked our son to make a decision without speaking to his parents first?'

'Edie,' says David, 'Sean is almost sixteen. Practically a man. He is an autonomous being; a young man who is entitled to be listened to and have his views respected.' He smirks lightly. 'At sixteen, he doesn't need your permission to do much, except perhaps get a *tattoo*.' He curls his lips over the word 'tattoo' and Edie notices Ron checking his bicep to see if his is in view.

'But you still didn't think he should talk to his parents about it first, eh?'

'Edie . . .' mumbles Ron.

'You knew,' she says and it is not a question. 'You've been part of this *discussion* already?'

'Edie . . .' he says again, placing a hand on her arm.

'I've been holding out for this,' says Edie, turning to Bianca.

'Bringing him home. You said . . .' but she doesn't get to finish what Bianca said, because this kitchen, these competent, wealthy players with their fancy coffee machine and expensive furniture are dissolving into a piece of hideous abstract art before her eyes. 'How could you? You're a mother too.'

'Edith,' says Bianca, 'I'm also a psychiatrist, and I understand minds and healing. Sean needs time and space. He's a gifted boy . . .'

'He's *my* gifted boy.'

Bianca tilts her head and smiles. 'Of course he is. He'll always be your boy. But what we're suggesting is really not much different to boarding school. We're just offering a calm and focused environment where he can thrive.'

It's all Edie can do not to throw her knife across the room, to sweep the glasses to the floor and watch them shatter.

'Excuse me,' she says and steps out into the dark street to scream.

53

After

The women come.

On Colin's second day in hospital, a steady stream of aqua aerobics ladies drift up to the ward door from morning to afternoon and harass Rebecca until she fetches Edie and they press gifts into her hands.

Food, flowers, even a giant fruit hamper with tiny cards and words of love.

For Edie, says one. *No matter how bad it gets, we're here for you.* Their generosity wedges a lump in her throat that feels like trying to swallow dry porridge oats.

'I got our Liam to make you a *positive thinking* mix,' says Jean, handing her a strange contraption shaped like a lipstick case with headphones coming out of it. 'He enjoyed making it so much, he's going to trial it at Cafe del Mar next month!'

Sarah Moss pulls a thin computer from her bag. 'I made you this video on my computer,' she says. 'I'm not sure how to send it to you though. I hope you like Barry Manilow.'

Verushka brings a pair of tiny brass shoes.

'It will help with luck,' she says. 'They got me through four wars.'

They fit snugly into Edie's palm and the cold metal in her hot hand feels right.

'Thank you, Verushka.'

'Shoes, Edith,' says Verushka. 'Never forget about the shoes.'

Edie's brow furrows, until she recalls young Verushka not having any and feels tears pricking at her eyes. *Have faith that things will get better.*

Brenda comes too. 'I'm so sorry about everything, Edie. I've been a bitch.' She presses a jar into Edie's hands and she turns it over, trying to fathom what it is. There's a picture of a fish on there and possibly a Velcro roller. *Must've made this with her grandson*, thinks Edie. 'I've taken up glass painting. I'm not very good yet.'

Edie hugs the vase to her chest. 'Thanks, Brenda. I love it.'

The women bring her comfort in the face of the fact that Ron won't be in the same room as her.

When she enters, he stands, knees and hips popping like bubble wrap, and shambles straight out of the room. When she leaves for a break, he's there, lurking at the nurses' station, or on the squeaky vinyl seats outside the critical care unit doors staring emptily at the walls.

'Talk to me, Ron,' she says as they pass one evening, her voice cracking like shards of glass.

He's the same Ron that vacated his body leaving behind just a shell in the wake of Hilda's death. It's the same face he put on when he started his first day at Kwik Fit after he lost the garage.

Both times she panicked that she'd lost him. Both times she loved him back to his old self. But that Ron – the absent, hollow-eyed Ron – is the Ron that floats in and out of Colin's hospital room now and Edie isn't sure that she has the strength to warm him back up this time. Or if he even wants her to.

54

Before

Ron's been working on the cars for months now. Two Ford Fiestas in varying states of undress have perched self-consciously on jacks since April. When he first showed them to her, she'd frowned. One was navy-blue, missing a passenger door and spewing something wiry from under the bonnet. The other, a pleasingly bright post-box red, had no wheels and only a lonely driver's seat inside.

They're still only seeing Sean once every couple of weeks, meeting somewhere neutral and bland and exchanging strained pleasantries over tea and biscuits. Sometimes he cancels on them, citing study and *weekend prep* and *enrichment*. Sometimes Colin gets the Metro up to Newcastle and they kick a ball around the Town Moor.

But when Ron covers her eyes and with oily hands brings her into the garage, he's more animated than he's been since Sean went to live with the Pike-Oberons.

'Ta-da!' he says, taking his hands away. 'What do you think?' Now, one of the cars is a smart racing green, the other a handsome royal blue. They're like proper cars with all their doors and seats and windows intact.

'Oh Ron. They're amazing!'

'They've even got tape players so they can play their music.' He's grinning from ear to ear.

'Where did you find the time?'

He shrugs. 'Just think of their faces! How many of their friends have got cars of their own, eh? Well, I don't know about Sean. But none! None of Colin's friends have cars.' He's glowing. 'And how many boys at universities will have their own cars? Can't imagine many would.'

She sighs. 'Eighteen, Ron. Adults.'

Adults, and old enough not to live with controlling psychiatrists and smug lawyers. Ron's face has a determined hope to it, eyes shiny but with something hard and resolute in the jaw. Maybe he's also thinking that his relationship with one of his sons might be about to improve. Through her pain, she's neglected to worry about how Sean's absence is impacting Ron. She assumed that because he supported the move, he was okay with it, but the lines over his brow have got deeper, and narrow trenches have formed between his mouth and his cheeks.

But this! He is lighter and springier than she's seen him for months, years even.

'Our sons are lucky to have you, Ron.' She kisses his cheek. He blushes and scratches his head.

Edie listens to his grand plan of wrapping Colin's up in a bow and parking it outside and getting Carol to knock on the door nice and early before they've got out of bed, and how he and Edie will stay in bed while Colin trudges bleary-eyed downstairs and how he'll whoop and then jump around in circles and hug Edie and Ron and they'll go in two cars to the Pike-Oberons and put another bow on and they'll ring the bell and Sean will come out and see the car and he and Colin will shriek and scream and there'll be more hugs and maybe some tears, then they'll all go for a nice drive, maybe to the coast, and it's going to be absolute magic.

She can see it, clear as day.

The Pike-Oberons ruin everything, of course.

Bianca calls to say that, because Nathaniel had his English Language exam on his birthday, they are taking both the boys away for the weekend of Sean's birthday.

'New Lloyd Webber. *Miss Saigon* in London,' says Bianca as if Edie is supposed to know who any of those people are. 'You must come to the little soiree we're having the following weekend though.'

Colin is pleased with his car, but without his twin to share the excitement with, he has to settle instead for taking his parents for a drive to Penshaw Monument where they eat rapidly cooling pasties and talk about everything but Sean.

On Sean's party evening, they dress carefully and head out to the cars. Ron is driving Sean's over with the giant bow attached to the front and Hilda in the passenger seat. Edie, with a helium *Birthday Boy* balloon bobbing like an extra person, opts to travel with Colin, wondering if he feels as odd about being invited to his twin's eighteenth by some other family as she does.

'I sort of imagined a party at the football club, you know? With the lads and Carol and all that,' he says when she asks him. He's facing forward, features flashing in and out of illumination by the streetlamps as they travel. The houses grow bigger and further away from the road the more distance they put between them and their colliery cottage.

Her boy is a man now: a man with a factory job and a car. He'd hoped to start at the garage when he left school, but it just wasn't making enough money to pay him. 'Maybe later,' Ron had said, but two years on and it still hasn't happened and is starting to look like it never will. He's a grown-up now, too old for an apprenticeship, and maybe, in the not-too-distant future, he might be ready for a home and a family of his own. It makes Edie dizzy to think about it, so she blocks it instead and focuses on his soft cheeks that still carry the hint of the baby he was in their pouchy pockets.

'Is he happy?' she asks, not sure if she wants to know the answer.

Colin shrugs. 'We don't talk all that much any more,' he says. 'Says he's just busy with exams and things.' Edie looks for signs that he is as broken as her while he checks his mirrors like Ron showed him how to, indicates and overtakes a yellow Fiat Uno, but all she can see is the concentration of driving on his face.

There are so many cars parked outside the Pike-Oberons' that both Ron and Colin have to park a street away.

'This is ridiculous,' says Hilda. 'You didn't tell me I should have worn hiking boots.'

'No matter,' says Ron, looking back at the big bow. 'We'll just bring him out here to show him. It'll be nice. Just the five of us.'

Two teenage boys with well-cut hair are walking up the garden path just ahead of them. Nathaniel Pike-Oberon greets them at the door.

'Whiffles and Stubby! You dirty old beasticles!' he cheers enthusiastically. He pumps their hands in an energetic greeting before spotting the McVeys on the path and straightening up. 'Good evening, Mr McVey, Mrs McVey, Colin, um madam.' He pronounces Colin's name as Cole-in, and Edie wants to correct him, but thinks better of it. 'Sean will be delighted that you made it.'

Inside the house, teenagers and adults lean against walls sipping wine and laughing with their heads thrown back. There's a scent of something spicy in the air, sweet and cloying, and the house is too hot. The McVeys move en masse towards the kitchen in the hopes of depositing their bottle of cava in the fridge.

'So many people here,' says Colin. 'Where is he?'

'Darlings!' says David Pike-Oberon. 'There you are.' He kisses them all on both cheeks, even Ron, who grows stiff and unyielding as a cupboard under David's winey lips. 'Let me get you all a drink.' David throws his arm around Edie's neck and drags her towards the kitchen. *He's drunk*, thinks Edie, and she turns around to check Ron and Colin are following.

'Where's Sean?' she asks.

David flaps a limp hand towards the stairs. 'Up there, I suspect, showing off the Mac.'

Edie pictures Sean twirling around in a new rain mac and wonders when he suddenly became a person who cared about rain attire.

'He can take it with him to uni, of course,' says David.

'Yes of course. It might be quite rainy in September.'

'What?' Then he bursts out laughing. 'Of course, of course. I forgot for a minute.'

'Forgot what?'

He chuckles again. 'You should go up,' he says, pouring a glass of wine that Edie hasn't asked for. 'Have a look.'

There's a circle of glowing boys around Sean when they push open the door to his room. He's holding court in a navy blue satin shirt, and the boys are hanging on his every word.

'So you see, they went for the colour display, and look at the quality!'

In front of him is a computer and he types something with great speed.

'Hello, son,' says Ron, and all of the boys turn. Hilda and Edie are still in the doorway, Edie's balloon threatening to escape to the ceiling of the hallway.

'Hello,' says Sean, almost shyly. He nods to the other boys. 'My family,' he says.

'Let's go get some drinks,' says a boy, and the computer audience troop away.

'Happy birthday,' says Colin.

'Same to you,' says Sean.

'Well, it was last week,' says Colin, 'but who's counting?' Colin suddenly flings himself at Sean, swallowing him in a tight bear hug. Their differences have never been so marked. They're both tall – grown man height – but Sean suddenly looks so much younger than his brother. Edie trimmed Colin's hair last week so it was neat for the party, and it has given him the same look all the factory boys have. Sean's on the other hand has grown and is curling lightly around his ears. He looks a bit like Ron did that first night, like a kid playing grown-ups when he should have been tucked up in bed with a hot cocoa. She wishes that she could just pull Sean into his computer chair and say 'Shall I give that a little trim for you, pet?' but it would be unfathomably awkward and her cheeks go hot at the thought.

Sean pats Colin's back, clears his throat and untangles himself from his twin.

'Look at my present from David and Bianca.' Sean places his hand on top of the computer as though presenting a high-achieving child. 'It'll be marvellous for uni. You know, assignments and stuff.'

'Don't you just use a pen and paper?' asks Hilda. 'What's wrong with pen and paper, Sean?'

Sean smiles indulgently. 'It's just different now, Nanna.'

'I got a set of spatulas for my eighteenth,' she says. 'Some people have got more money than sense.'

'Well.'

They stand for too long, before Edie says, 'We got you this balloon.'

'Lovely, thank you.'

'But your real present's outside, isn't it, Dad?'

Sean takes a long look at his computer, as though leaving it behind will be too painful, and Edie is annoyed that she's jealous of a metal and plastic machine.

Sean does funny handshakes with people as he passes. 'Be back in a minute, man,' he says. Or, 'Won't be a tick.'

'Seany,' says Bianca, sweeping her arms back, almost taking a teenage girl's eye out with her chunky silver bracelet. 'Where are you going? We're doing cake soon.' She spots Edie, Ron, Colin and Hilda, tilts her head to the side and says 'Ah, that's nice. So good of you to come.'

'There's a present for me outside,' says Sean.

'Oooh, is it a whippet?' she chuckles, clearly drunk too. 'Ahem, sorry,' she says, catching sight of Edie's puzzled frown. 'That was uncalled for.'

Edie has no idea what she meant by it, so shrugs, but Ron is scowling.

'We're just going to take Sean to see his present,' says Edie. 'We'll all be back soon.'

'David! Nate!' she shouts. 'Come on outside with us. Seany's got a present!'

Sean flashes them a look of guilt, but doesn't say anything.

Ron leads, hand on Sean's shoulder with Edie, Colin, Hilda, Nathaniel, David and Bianca in tow.

'Where are you taking us?' asks David. 'Gateshead?'

Bianca titters and they walk along the street and round the corner to where he parked the car.

'Oh!'

The bow has come loose and is flapping around like an octopus tentacle. Ron steers Sean towards the Fiesta.

'Here you go, son.' He grins proudly. 'Your very first car.'

Sean smiles. 'Aw, thanks Dad. That's lovely.' He turns to Colin. 'Did you get one too?' Colin nods. 'Lovely. That's just so nice of you.'

'Did it up meself,' Ron says. 'Been working on them since Easter.'

'How lovely,' says David. 'Looks like you're going to have the Montego all to yourself now, Nate.'

'The Montego?' asks Ron.

Bianca waves a dismissive hand. 'Just a little runaround we got for the boys. Just to share.'

Ron is standing very still, his face pale under the street lighting. Edie notices a ticking in his jaw and her belly plummets.

'But, yeah, Dad. My own car. That's brilliant.'

'Brilliant,' says Nate.

Edie doesn't realize that she's let go of the balloon, until it hits the streetlamp, before dancing off into the navy-and-silver night.

The McVeys are silent on the walk back to the house. Colin and Sean have their hands pushed into their pockets, heads down. They're walking in perfect step with one another, but there's a gap about a Ford Fiesta wide between them. The Pike-Oberons provide a grating soundtrack to the walk, David laughing about something with Nate, and Bianca's voice sharp as splintered glass, twittering about some lecturer she knows at York who's going to show Sean around the city. Edie wants to shout 'Shut up!' in her face and, for a moment, pictures shoving her into the damp road, but instead she keeps her eyes on Ron, poker-spined and striding ahead. Beside her, Hilda's mouth is pressed into a squiggle, her eyebrows raised.

'And of course,' says Bianca, 'he'll get a full means-tested grant, based on your incomes.'

'Excuse me,' says Edie, jogging to catch up with Ron. She follows him into the house, weaves behind him through the knit of bodies and wine glasses. A man in a beret is smoking something that smells like Christmas and Edie coughs her way through the hallway, into the kitchen and straight out the back door. Halfway down the garden, Ron stops.

'Ron,' she says. He is looking up at a well-established elm that looms across the garden, dwarfing him under a canopy that whispers in the August night. Behind, the noise of the party is muted behind closed windows and doors.

'Ron,' she says again. She steps closer, reaches out and touches his arm.

'I just wanted this one thing,' he says quietly. 'One thing.'

Edie closes her eyes and rubs the pilled sleeve of his best jacket. 'I'm sorry,' she whispers.

Ron shakes his head. 'This is my thing, you know. The one thing I can do.'

She circles in front of him, looks up at his strong, beautiful face contorted in the light of a fuzzed hangnail moon. She pulls him close, leaning her ear against his thudding heartbeat. Her rock, her pillar is crumbling and her belly dips. If he falls apart, what is to stop them all tumbling into the sea? Ron lets himself be hugged, and when Edie spots Sean's pale face watching them from his softly lamplit bedroom, the rolling in her stomach turns hard, clenching like a fist.

'Excuse me,' she says to Ron.

55

After

Edie is alone on the fourth day of her vigil, mid-monologue by Colin's side, when she spots a flicker.

It's just the shadow of a movement in his eyelid, and she presses her hands together in a desperate prayer, afraid she might have imagined it.

Do it again, Col, please.

She holds her breath and then it happens again.

'Quick,' she yells out into the hallway. 'Quick! There's a flick, a flick.'

'Very poetic,' says Rebecca calmly, checking something on a chart.

Doctors drift in and out for the next few hours and there's no sign of Ron. She gets Rebecca to call his mobile phone, but to no avail. Edie has the sudden, wild image of him and Sean laughing together in a bar.

She strokes Colin's face and says, 'Can you hear me, pet?' and claps her hands and laughs when the eyelid flickers again and again.

'Is that a response to me?' she asks Rebecca.

'Could be,' says the nurse. 'Or he might be winking at me cause I'm too damn sexy in my scrubs!' She smiles, drops her voice. 'Probably responding to you. I've seen how much you've been talking to him.'

When Ron does come, he looks only at the doctor who explains that this is a good sign, but not to get their hopes too high. That Colin has moved from coma into minimal consciousness.

Edie watches him nod thoughtfully in response to the doctor and feels an irrational surge of jealousy.

Colin is responding. Focus on that. The rest will have to wait.

By the next day, he can blink in response, lift a finger for yes, shake it for no.

'Oh, Colin!' she says. 'Do you know where you are?'

It's somewhere between a lift and a shake. *Yes no.*

'What's my name?' asks Jade, who has taken Ron's spot while he goes for some lunch.

'He can only do yes no,' says Edie.

'Right,' says Jade. 'Is my name Jade or Honeysuckle?'

Edie allows herself a little smile. 'Yes or no, Jade.'

'Ah yes. Erm, shall I call the baby Daniel or *ooff!*'

'What?' says Edie, then realizes that Jade has folded over her belly. 'Oh god, are you okay?'

Jade straightens up, blows out a stream of air. 'I think so. That was just a bit . . .!'

'Doctor,' Edie yells. 'I think she's going into labour.'

56

Before

He's waiting for her in the computer chair. The light from the screen is making his face a strange shade of blue, like he's a being from a dream or another planet. He looks so like a stranger, sitting here, not the boy she raised, not the comingling of her and Ron, their best and worst bits.

'You've changed,' she says. She doesn't mean it to come out as an accusation, but it does.

Sean sighs, as if she has confirmed exactly what he thought would happen when she came in here. 'Look,' he says, 'I'm sorry Dad's disappointed, but what did you want me to do? Say to Bianca and David "No thanks! I'd rather suffer and keep getting the bus"? We're not all martyrs like you.'

Edie glances at Ron outside, still now, resting one hand against the tree, the other shoved deep into his pocket. His head is curled over like a shepherd's crook in the old fairy tales and she breaks a bit.

'No.' She shakes her head. 'You know Dad's always looked forward to teaching you how to drive.'

'He got to teach *Colin*, didn't he?' There's a lemony note, a bitterness when he says Colin's name that she's never heard before.

'Yes, but . . .'

'Yes but nothing.' He stands now, stops in front of her. For an absurd moment, she thinks that he might hug her, but when she tilts her head to look up to meet his eyes, they're blazing. 'You're never happy, are you? You're the only person I know who's inherited a house and whinged about it. You pushed me into a fancy-arse school and then complained when I tried to fit in. You complain about not having stuff all the time, but then you go to your grubby little job and scrub other people's filth for a pittance and don't bother doing anything about it. You went on and on about *opportunity* and *potential*, but what have you ever done with your life? Sat around crying about not having babies, then sat around feeling sorry for yourself after you had some. It's pathetic, actually.' He stomps to the door, then turns. 'Have you ever stopped to consider that you are, in fact, the problem?'

Her heart is thudding so hard she puts her hand to it to muffle the sound. Sean tuts, is about to leave, so Edie springs in front of him. She can't let him go, she can't. Because even though his words are piercing her and shredding her heart to pieces, this is the most he has spoken to her in months – years even. There is so much she needs to say and she is not about to pass up the opportunity without Bianca or David or Nate here to ruin the moment.

'Listen, Sean. I get it. You're angry with me, for whatever reason, but please, please, don't take it out on your dad and brother.' There are tears springing, and she blinks hard to keep them at bay. 'They love you, Seany. They need you. Sweetheart, we all do.'

'"For whatever reason"?' he mocks. '"For whatever reason"? Are you that dense that you don't know why I needed to get away from you?' He sticks his face right in hers. 'You left us, remember. Left us when we really needed you. I had this huge thing to navigate, this new school far from all my friends, away from my brother who I'd never been apart from, and you said you'd be there. But you weren't.' He straightens up. 'You know, it took me a while to realize how much that hurt me, but working on it with Bianca has made a lot of things much clearer.' He moves her aside. 'Let me go,' he says, and she doesn't know whether he means now, from this room, or forever.

'Sean, wait . . .'

She follows him out onto the landing, where below, the tops of party-goers' heads dance to music that she can't hear and the chatter and supercilious laughter and clinking of glasses roar louder than church bells.

He's practically stomping and she runs to catch up, hitting her knee on a bookshelf and swearing under her breath. Her knee throbs, but she pushes on regardless.

'Sean, please . . .'

Sean doesn't wait, not for her, but when he stops to high-five someone heading into the bathroom at the top of the stairs, she grabs him and wheels him around to face her.

'Listen to me, Sean,' she says. 'I'm trying, I've never stopped trying, but you have to talk to me. You have to.' Now, the tears come properly, slimy, snaking down her cheeks through her carefully applied make-up and onto her new blouse. 'Please, Sean!'

'That's right,' he snaps and his face is redder than the wine they're all quaffing downstairs. 'That's right, turn on the waterworks like you always do. Poor, sad Edie with the crazy mother. Let's all feel sorry for Edie, shall we?' He grabs her, long fingers that are so like Ron's encircling her upper arms. 'I'm sick of your shit. I'm sick of you always playing the victim. You're crying here, pretending you're upset for Dad, for Colin, for me. But you're not, are you? This is all about you. It always is.'

'You're hurting me, Sean,' she says and she grasps for the front of his shirt. 'Stop it!'

'You stop it,' he hisses. 'Making a scene at my party. How dare you.' He gives her a shake and her brain makes a thump against the side of her skull. She pulls at the front of his shirt, trying to make him let go. 'I hate you!' he screams in her face.

She screws tight her eyes, and for a moment, there is the blessed relief of darkness and silence. Her fingers make contact with his chest, and then Sean is falling away. He lets go of her arms and she takes the opportunity to cough out the breath she was holding. She opens her eyes, and Sean is tumbling from her, plummeting down the stairs.

She screams, a shrill, curdled sound jarring across the jaunty music.

He lands with a sickening crash, hitting a table with his head, sending a lamp and a telephone skittering across the floorboards.

'Oh my god,' says someone.

'Is he all right?'

'He's breathing,' says someone. 'Is he unconscious?'

'Call an ambulance.'

Bodies gather around the crumpled figure of her son on the floor, covering him like ants over a fallen apple core. She is shaking, trembling from head to foot, and so she sinks to the top step and wraps her hand around the spindle of the bannister. She sobs now, sobs hard and loud.

'Let me look at him,' says a voice Edie recognizes as Bianca's. 'He's conscious. Poor baby. Can you move?'

'What happened?' someone says.

'She pushed him,' says someone else.

Everyone at the foot of the stairs looks up. Guests spilling out of the rooms crane their necks to condemn her. Some shake their heads, some mutter, though Edie sees them all through the smear of her tears.

The music has stopped, and she makes a sound like something hydraulic. She blinks hard, and they are just a blur of faces, until she picks out Ron's.

'She pushed him,' the person repeats, and Edie realizes that it is David.

Ron tilts his head to the side. *Did you?* he seems to say.

Then Sean sits up, slowly, clutching his head in his hands.

'Did she? Did she push you?'

Sean winces, then it happens. A tiny nod. Condemnation in that barely-there drop and rise of a head.

Did I just push my son down the stairs?

And she knows that she is wearing the answer on her face.

I don't know if I did.

57

After

It's been hours.

Jade is on all fours with her clothes mostly off, wearing only a man's shirt with a torn breast pocket. A monitor attached to the bulb of her belly sends indecipherable messages to a screen that at least seven different people have peered at in the last hour. Midwives and doctors dart in and out of the room, conversing with each other, but not Edie and Jade.

Edie's throat feels as though she's swallowed dry Weetabix. She wants to race over to the dripping tap in the corner and lap the water straight from the tap, but doesn't dare leave Jade's side.

An older man in a doctor's white coat sweeps in, flanked by three people with clipboards. He looks at the screen, taps his chin and then points at something. The clipboard people nod, one of them taking in a sharp breath. The man grabs the current midwife by the arm and Edie can just make out 'prep her for surgery'.

'Edie, what's happening?'

Edie pats Jade's arm. 'I'll find out.' She releases Jade's hand and accosts the doctor at the door. 'Doctor, what's going on?'

He looks right through her, turning instead to one of the

clipboard people and murmuring something about the placenta. Edie is hit by the sudden memory of herself giving birth. 'What's happening?' she kept asking. 'What are you doing to me?' Suddenly, she is furious, for Jade and for young Edie.

'Answer me!'

All of the chatter in the room stops. Everyone stares at Edie, apart from Jade, who keeps on panting.

The doctor folds his arms. 'Placental abruption,' he says. 'We need to take her down for an emergency caesarean.'

'Right.' Edie's hands are shaking. 'Then why haven't you bothered to tell her that?' He flaps his arm dismissively. 'Don't you flap your arm at me, doctor! Get over there and have a proper conversation with the woman.' She pushes him towards the bed. 'Go!'

The midwife is biting her lower lip. She catches Edie's eye, smiles briefly, then looks away.

The bewildered doctor stands by Jade and starts a halting explanation.

Edie blows her hair out of her eyes and clenches her fists.

'I'm scared, Edie.'

Edie nods. 'Of course you are. But listen, Jade. You were made for this, okay. Us women, we just are. And look at all you've got through so far.' She cups Jade's cheeks in her palms, swipes a tear with her thumb. 'Listen to me. You're one of the most resilient, fantastic women I know, and you just have to be brave for a little bit longer.'

They're in the theatre, Edie stroking Jade's hair. The epidural has kicked in, and Jade is now entirely at the mercy of the surgeons.

'Were you this frightened?'

'Yes,' says Edie truthfully. 'I was. But I had someone who loved me holding my hand and telling me I was doing great, and so do you.'

'Almost there,' says the surgeon.

There's a low song playing in the background. Edie recognizes the tune. Something about loving someone who doesn't love her back.

A red thing is wrenched out of Jade's body. As the surgeon holds it up, it uncurls two skinny arms and two skinny legs, letting out a piercing scream. Jade cries out and Edie's legs turn to water. She staggers, but keeps clinging to Jade's hand.

The lights above are blinding her, Ron's hand stroking her hair. He stiffens.

'Quick, he's not breathing' . . . 'Resus' . . . 'This one's all right' . . . 'Come on, little man, come on' . . . 'Oh, god, oh god, we might have to call it . . .' then everything going black.

There's a hand on her shoulder.

'It can be a bit overwhelming, can't it, Gran?' A kind face smiling at her. 'First grandbaby? Come over, come see him.'

A tear-drenched Jade gives her a nod. Edie lays a gentle kiss on her forehead.

She allows herself to be led to the back of the surgery, where the baby is being weighed, his midnight-black hair slick against his head.

'Edie! Can you see him? How is he?'

The tiny little boy on the scales opens his scrunched-up eyes and looks at Edie. The eyes are dark, earth brown – practically black – and he flashes her a glimmer of recognition.

'He's perfect, Jade.' Her heart contracts. 'Just perfect.'

58

Before

It's early December when Ron confesses that the garage isn't making any money.

'Actually,' he says, face aflame, 'it's costing me just to keep it going.'

None of them have heard from Sean since the party. He'll be off at university now. For weeks after the party, Edie had called the Pike-Oberons every day.

'He's not ready,' Bianca said. 'Give him time. He has a lot to unpack here.'

David was less polite. 'Perhaps it's all a bit too little, too late, Mrs McVey,' he said, or variations on the theme.

Even Nathaniel dropped the veneer of politeness and said 'No. Not here. Please leave,' when she called over there with a *Good Luck* card and a teddy.

She's clinging onto him showing up for the Christmas holidays.

Colin's been off work for a few months with a finger injury, so the pittance Edie gets from cleaning the Queen's Head is all they have.

The phone goes first. Edie has to use Carol's to call BT and beg for some kind of leniency, the embarrassment gnawing at her the whole time she sits in Carol's comfy armchair on the phone while Carol discreetly pretends that weeding in December is part of her annual routine. But the customer service man is having none of it, and the McVeys are cut off.

'They're not like the adverts make them out to be,' she complains to Ron later. 'What if Sean needs us?'

Next, it's the gas. They haven't paid the bill in nearly four months and British Gas are also having none of it.

'You might be better going up to Harry's for Christmas lunch, Mam,' Ron says to Hilda. 'We're having a bit of trouble with the boiler.'

They keep warm by layering up their clothes and wrapping themselves in blankets. Edie finds some hot water bottles in the shed and she, Ron and Colin watch *Noel's House Party* with the scent of hot rubber in their nostrils.

'Still,' says Edie, 'Sean'll be back soon for the holidays.'

Ron and Colin exchange a wince.

But if there's a smidgen of doubt that Sean will come, she hides it from herself scarily well. She lets herself have something to look forward to. She raids the jar where she keeps the spare change she finds when she's cleaning the pub, takes it down to Woolworths and gets some new tinsel for the tree. She gets Colin to crawl into the tiny attic space and retrieve the plastic tree that sat only semi-dressed for the last few Christmases. 'Looks like a sad fairy,' said Hilda last year. She puts on the Christmas *Top of the Pops* and drapes tinsel to a soundtrack of Elton John and Paul McCartney.

'It doesn't matter that the gas is off,' she says. 'Weird Albert says we can use his, as long as we do him a turkey sandwich.'

When the toilet springs a leak, a week before Christmas, Ron patches the floorboards around it with bits of old tyres that aren't fulfilling their purpose in the garage.

'It's no good, Edie,' says Ron. 'This thing's buggered.'

On Christmas Eve, they shut off the electricity, so they're flickering in a Dickensian candlelit glow by three p.m.

'He's not coming, is he?' says Edie quietly into the dark.

Come Christmas morning, Edie has to put three pairs of socks on just to get out of bed. She trudges downstairs to where Ron and Colin are sharing a packet of custard creams on the carpet by the sad tree. A selection of beautifully wrapped presents in cream and gold shiny paper lie at the foot of the tree-skirt. They've got thick gold ribbons and big bows wrapped around them.

'You did get presents.' She runs to the cupboard where she's hidden two packages in thin paper. 'Here you go.'

Ron and Colin exchange a look, then take their parcels.

They unwrap identical Guinness promotional scarves that the pub manager said Edie could have. She's sent one to Sean at the Pike-Oberons' too, but she doubts he'll get it.

'Lovely,' says Colin, wrapping his around his neck. 'Toasty.'

'I got you this,' says Ron. Edie opens a box to see a small gold necklace with a little cameo pendant hanging from it.

'It's beautiful, Ron,' she says. When she takes it out to put on, she realizes the clasp is broken.

'Ah,' says Ron. 'It's from the charity shop.'

'No problem,' she says, disappointed. 'I can get it fixed in the new year.'

Colin has got her a box of Quality Street and some socks, which she puts on top of the other three pairs.

'What's all this stuff then?' Edie asks.

'It got delivered last night. Taxi driver said the Pike-Oberons sent them.'

They contemplate the mound of gifts which look like they'd be better placed in Fenwick's Christmas window on Newcastle's main shopping street than in a draughty living room in Boldon Colliery.

'Shall we have a look?' asks Colin.

The card says *Christmas is a good time to reflect and reassess. Wishing you a time of quiet introspection this festive season. Bianca, David and Nate.*

Edie wants to smash the presents with a hammer, but Ron says 'Don't knock a gift horse in the mouth. You never know, there might be something useful in here.'

There are tickets to a performance of *Cats* in Newcastle, an Amstrad cordless telephone with an answering machine for them all, a computer for Ron, a Philishave for Colin and for Edie, a Moulinex microwave with a gift tag that reads, *Heard you always wanted one.*

'A microwave, Mam!' yells Colin. 'Oooh, we can microwave lunch.'

Edie stares at the useless box, the dark living room with no twinkling Christmas lights and Colin's hopeful face. Ron shakes his head grimly. 'Do you remember how electricity works, son?'

She sighs. Weird Albert is nowhere to be found, so lunch is Dairylea sandwiches on curling bread, served with a side of salt and vinegar Discos.

'I miss the Queen's Speech,' whispers Ron.

'Blimey, it's freezing in here,' moans Hilda when she comes with mince pies in the evening. 'You should've come up to Harry's instead. His new place is lovely.'

She's coughing. Long, wheezing coughs and protracted inhales where Edie panics that her mother-in-law is not going to breathe out again.

'I don't think you should be here, Hilda. Not with that cough. We've got no heating. I can't even get you a tea.'

'Stop fussing,' she says, flapping Edie away while she tries to drape a blanket over her. 'It's a cold, that's all. You'd think no one ever had a cold before. Get me an onion.'

Three weeks after Christmas, and it's still lingering.

'You have to take her to the doctor, Ron.'

'She's a tough bird, my old mam,' he says proudly. 'Nothing knocks her around for too long.'

'It might be bronchitis,' she tells Ron and eventually has to get Carol to call Harry to talk Ron into taking her.

'I'm fine,' she keeps saying stubbornly, but the doctor insists she needs to get to hospital sharpish. 'This is stupid,' she says in the back of Ron's car. 'A whole lot of fuss about nothing.'

When she's safely ensconced in a bed, fluffed against a stiff pillow, she sends Ron home to pick up her nightdress and clean underwear.

'If anything's going to make you ill, it's being in a hospital,' she says to Edie when it's just the two of them, and the woman in the bed opposite yowls like a cat.

'You'll be okay, Hilda,' says Edie, avoiding Hilda's eyes. 'You're strong as an ox.'

'An ox who spat a lung on the floor!'

She has been diagnosed with pneumonia, and only Edie seems to be fearing the worst. It is Edie everyone turns to with their questions: *Will Nanna be okay? Has that doctor said anything else? Will you hold me, Edie?* She has no answers, just blind hope and she squeezes hands, nods her head, fetches hot drinks from the vending machine and mutters something like a prayer whenever she's alone.

Edie is changing the flowers by a dozing Hilda's head when she mumbles something.

'Are you sleep-talking, Hilda?' she asks. She brings her ear close to Hilda's mouth.

'Look after my boy,' she whispers.

Two days later, Hilda is on a ventilator. Ron, his brothers, Edie and Colin gather by her bedside.

'She'll pull through,' says Ron. 'She always does.'

Edie has to look away when Harry puts his hand on his shoulder.

They're all there with her when she goes. They take it in turns to lay gentle kisses on her head, whisper *'Goodbye,'* drip clean tears onto her cheek.

When it's Edie's turn, she says *'I will.'*

She grips the receiver of Carol's phone to her ear as the tinny, empty sound of the ringtone echoes down the line. David Pike-Oberon, the administration office at York University, but nobody is answering, and though she leaves messages on blank answering machines, nobody returns her calls. The Pike-Oberons send a green and cream arrangement of lilies and ivy, as big as a shield, with a bland condolences card.

'Did you get hold of him yet?' asks Ron. His back rounds and the beautiful spine he's always held so well starts to resemble a snail shell: like he's carrying too much on his back.

Edie suddenly finds herself with a million questions she needed to ask Hilda. Stupid things like *Should I switch to semi-skimmed milk?* or *Why is this pastry too crumbly?* to the real things she meant to ask, like *How can you live with all of this sadness and loss inside your body?* Sometimes she says them aloud, other times, she sits under the apple tree just thinking them and waiting for answers that are never going to come. *We do it all*, said Hilda once. *We're like swans, floating along on the surface looking like we're keeping it all together, when under the surface, it's paddle paddle paddle just to keep afloat.* Edie is hurting, but she tucks it away in a box. This is Ron's pain, and she needs to be there for him like he always has been for her. His brothers and their wives rally round to pay for the funeral, leaving Ron to focus on missing his beloved mother.

It's stupid and selfish when Ron is suffering so much, but she can't help but hope that Sean will at least come back for the funeral. They were close, Hilda and Sean. Thick as thieves throwing bread for the swans in the Marine Park, her holding his hand as he jumped in the puddles along the Lawe Top.

Because she couldn't manage more than a few garbled words at her own mother's funeral, she offers to do a reading at Hilda's. 'It's the least I can do.' She steps up to the altar, right by the spot where Ron and Edie promised to love each other forever, and she's shaking, but she wants to do this for Hilda, for Ron.

'Remember me when I am gone away,' she starts and then she's thinking about Sean too and her mother and everyone she's lost, and the words are blurring on the sheet in front of her. She takes a big breath, then another and she can't find where her voice is gone.

She is about to turn to the vicar, to say, *I can't do it*, when Ron is beside her, his arm wraps around her shoulder, the reassuring squeeze of his fingers. She looks at his beautiful warm eyes and sees only love and pride and knows that she can.

She wipes her eyes, clears her throat and carries on. By the time she gets to the part about forgetting and smiling, Colin is at her other side, and it is not clear whether they are holding her up, or whether it is her supporting them.

When they walk through the front door, still jet-clad with the scent of chrysanthemums in their noses, there's a card on the doormat. No stamp, no postage, just pushed through the letterbox.

Dad. I'm sorry about Nanna. Sending my deepest sympathy. S x

After Ron has slipped off his jacket and gone to bed, Edie reads and rereads the card, running her fingers across the neat sloping handwriting he cultivated at Dame Allan's. She's tired of being bitter and sad, but it just won't seem to go anywhere. It's hanging around her like a stubborn fog.

'Are you all right?' Edie asks Ron the next day.

'I'm hurting,' he says and it stings like a nest of hornets.

'I'm still in my dirty work stuff,' says Edie when Ron suggests that they go down to the fair. 'Why? Why aren't you at work?'

They drive in silence, Edie examining the side of Ron's face, the little tuft of hair that's started growing inside his ear. She can't remember the last time he took time off work in the week.

'Is everything okay?'

He gives her a sad little smile and winds the window down so that she can't hear his answer over the rush of wind.

It's February and she shivers as they park up by the fairground. In the off-season the roller coaster stands like the excavated spine of a dinosaur flanked by shuttered booths and waltzer carts covered over with tarpaulin. Ron takes her hand as they stroll through the empty funfair marvelling at how grey the place is without the laughter and music and spun sugar scent of toffee apples.

'Why are we here, Ron?' she asks.

They stop under the legs of the Ferris wheel. Ron looks up.

'Do you remember the first time we went on this?'

Edie smiles. 'I could never forget.'

'I knew I loved you then.'

'You're scaring me, Ron. Are you ill?'

'I'm not ill. But I am sorry.'

Edie's heart plummets. It sounds as though he's leaving her. Sounds like he's had enough. *I should have stayed in Greece. I've brought him nothing but problems.*

'Sorry for what?'

'The garage,' he says. 'It's gone.'

'Gone?' Edie frowns. She could see it from the pub this morning and it was definitely still there. It looked all sad and saggy, a bit like the pair of them. 'What do you mean, gone?'

'I've lost it.' He drops his eyes to concrete, washed clean by the stinging rain that fell for nearly a month. 'As in, they repossessed it this morning.'

'Oh.'

A seagull screeches overhead and they follow its progression across the grey horizon.

'I failed, Edie. I started going down and I thought I could manage it alone. Thought I'd be able to figure it out.' His voice cracks.

'I could have helped,' she cries. 'Could've—'

'I know,' he says, cutting her off. He pushes his mouth into a hard, grim line, balls his fists. 'I know. But it's my job, Edie. I just wanted to give you the life you wanted.'

'You are the life I wanted! You, the boys. That's it. That's the life I wanted.'

'Do you hate me?' he says in a small voice.

'Hate you? How could I hate you?' She presses her hands against his chest. 'It should be you hating me. After the party. After Sean.'

Her words hang between them in the cold air.

Eventually, he pulls her close, chin resting on her head. 'I thought you'd be ashamed of me.'

They stand in an embrace under the Ferris wheel while the sky darkens. An old man swishes by with a sweeping brush whistling something too cheerful for a cold February day in a closed-down fairground.

'What are we going to do, Ron?'

The zip on his coat is pressing into her cheek. She burrows further into him, the bite of the teeth a welcome relief against the numbness of the rest of her. 'I've got an interview at Kwik Fit next week. They're looking for tyre fitters.'

'Oh,' says Edie.

'Yeah,' he says. 'They give you a uniform. Proper hours.'

'Well that's something.'

The Kwik Fit in Boldon is full of school-leavers and twenty-somethings. She can't imagine her big, capable Ron taking orders from someone who was at school with Colin. The skilled mechanic spending his days on tyres instead of engines. She pictures him in that blue uniform and her lungs contract. The man with the brush sweeps closer to them, and she imagines that he's sweeping up the fallen fragments of their dreams.

'You'll be great,' she says. 'We'll figure things out.'

*

Her first attempt at figuring things out is Sean. Maybe if she can bring him home, the garage, the past won't matter as much. If she can fix things, perhaps Ron will start feeling better. Sean knows how much the garage means to his dad. Would understand how hard it is going to be for him to watch years of blood, sweat and oil wash away down the drain. Edie sends letters to York University, but they're all returned, unopened. She calls all of the halls of residence in York, but either nobody has heard of him or he has asked everyone to keep quiet, which doesn't seem very plausible.

'I think you should maybe just stop for a bit,' says Colin. 'Give it space.'

But Edie can't let it go.

Her phone calls to the Pike-Oberons still go unanswered. She has tried at different times of the day, different days of the week. She wonders if they've stopped answering their phones entirely. She pictures them smirking around their kitchen table, their narrow, judgemental eyes meeting over a glass of posh wine. *Well done us*, their look will say. *See what we saved that boy from.* And then they'll chink their glasses in self-congratulatory pleasure and move on to find other ways to fan their superiority around.

'They could have changed their number,' says Carol. 'Posh people are always getting new things.'

Of course!

She hops on the Metro and goes to their house in Jesmond.

David rolls his eyes when he answers the door.

'Listen, Edie,' he says. 'I'll be as delicate as I can. He just doesn't want to talk to any of you.'

'Well, can you get a message to him?'

David sighs as though she's asked him to scale Mount Snowdon in stilettos. 'One message, Edie. Then it's out of my hands. You need to respect that he's an autonomous adult trying to heal from his childhood.'

What are you talking about? she wants to scream. He doesn't need to *heal* from a childhood where he was loved and nurtured and encouraged to grow wings. *You want to see a childhood that needed healing? Take a look at mine!* She hates David profusely at this moment, but he feels like her only chance to connect with her son.

'Could you tell him that . . . Ron lost the garage.'

'How very careless of him,' says David, barely suppressing a smirk at his own wit.

'Will you tell him?'

David folds his arms. 'And what exactly do you think that will achieve? That it'll drag him away from his glittering future so he can help you cry over a bunch of orphaned exhaust pipes?' He starts closing the door. 'Really, Edie, you don't know him at all, do you?'

The flat of her palm meets the hardwood just as the latch bolt catches the strike plate and the number 49 is firmly closed in her face. She hammers on it.

'Please, please, will you tell him?'

But there is no response from beyond the stiff, unyielding door.

59

After

Edie practically skips back to Colin's ward, the scent of the baby's coppery, waxy skin still in her nostrils. Rebecca isn't there, nor is the desk manned, and when she heads into Colin's room, he is alone. It is late: after midnight, and even inside the hospital, there's just the hushed, muted tones of life after dark.

He is awake, and she kisses him on the head. His lips are moving, trying to form shapes and words.

'It's okay, sweetie,' she says. 'Take your time. Hey, guess what? Jade's boy was born. Beautiful little thing he is. All tawny and squishy and delicious!'

Colin moves his mouth again. Some air comes out and a sound like a *shhh*.

She brings her ear to his mouth, the breath tickling the little hairs, and for a moment, she's back on the bed at Hilda's listening in the dark to the gentle exhalations that told her she was still managing to keep her babies alive.

'Seany.'

'Oh, sweetheart!' says Edie, flinging her arms around his

neck. 'Your voice is back! Your voice!' Ron comes in with a gruff cough and she forgets that he's spent the past few days ignoring her.

'He's talking, Ron! He's talking!'

Ron rushes to the other side of the bed and takes Colin's hand in his. 'Oh, Colin!' He presses Colin's hand to his forehead and subtly swipes a stray tear from the corner of his eye.

'Seany,' croaks Colin again. 'Seany, Seany.'

Edie glances at Ron. 'Your dad got in touch with him, I think?' She adds the question mark because she doesn't know.

'Not yet,' says Ron. He shifts his eyes from Colin to Edie and back again. 'I wanted to wait until there was news.'

Colin coughs. 'Was here,' he says. 'Sean.'

Edie stiffens.

'Not yet,' repeats Ron as though Colin has lost most of his hearing, even though they've been told his hearing should be fine. 'I'll call him soon.'

Colin balls his fist. 'He was here,' he says. 'Already.'

'Sean was here?' Ron asks.

Colin raises his finger, then remembers that he can speak. 'Yes,' he says.

'Stone,' says Colin, tilting his head, wincing slightly at the effort.

They both look to the bedside table, where something little and bright sits next to the water jug, a jewel against the flat grey of the rest of the room.

A stone, painted to look like a ladybird.

Ron picks it up. It's brightly lacquered, a pillar box red – and it is almost identical to the one Edie carries in her handbag.

'Is this yours, Edie?' he asks.

'No,' she breathes. 'No, that one's—'

'Mine,' says a voice. Edie turns, as a face so similar to Colin's dips through the doorway. 'It's mine.'

'Sean!' cries Edie. She stands so quickly that all of the blood rushes from her head and she staggers, gripping the metal rail on Colin's bed to right herself. She tries to take a deep breath to steady her hammering heart, but her throat is constricting, like there's a hand wrapped round it.

He's taller than last time she saw him, or at least that is how it seems. Almost as tall as Ron, wearing a pinched version of Colin's face, and with more hair. She can't stop staring and she's desperate to touch him, but he still has that invisible shield around him.

'I should go,' he says, not meeting her eye. 'I can come back another time.'

'No!' shouts Colin. He struggles to push himself up. Ron helps him sit. 'This stops now.' He coughs, splutters and then says through gritted teeth, 'Sit down, all of you. I've got no more room for secrets and lies.'

Edie closes her eyes.

Everyone at the foot of the stairs looks up. Guests spilling out of the rooms crane their necks to condemn her. Some shake their heads, some mutter, though Edie sees them all through the smear of her tears.

The music has stopped, and she makes a sound like something hydraulic. She blinks hard, and they are just a blur of faces, until she picks out Ron's.

'She pushed him,' the person repeats, and Edie realizes that it is David.

Ron tilts his head to the side. Did you? *he seems to say.*

Did I push my son down the stairs?

And she knows that she is wearing the answer on her face.

I don't know if I did.

She tries to rewind time, to that moment again. Remembers her palm on his shirt, remembers the grip of his fingers on her arms. He wavers, opens his eyes wide, then he's losing his balance.

'*She pushed him,*' says David.

All eyes volley back to Edie at the top of the stairs, crouching against the spindle.

'*I didn't,*' she whispers. '*I didn't.*' *Did I?*

Then Sean sits up, slowly, clutching his head in his hands.

'*Did she? Did she push you?*'

Sean winces, then it happens. A tiny nod. Condemnation in that barely-there drop and rise of a head.

Even now, Edie burns with shame at that simple nod. But there's something else there. Something she has spent nearly sixteen years trying to reach for, but all the eyes and Sean's nod, Ron looking at her and the muttered condemnation from the foot of the stairs have always chased it away.

A fragment of a memory, her hand on his shirt. *Was her palm flat or curled around a fold of material? The slip of satin against her hand then sliding from her grasp and he's falling, falling and she's screaming—*

'Was it me, Seany?' she asks now. 'Did I push you?'

They stare at one another for the first time in nearly sixteen years, and his face is a timelapse video, the baby cheeks, him grinning from under the *Scooby-Doo* hat, the soft concentration lines on his teenage forehead and—

'No.' His voice is rough, scratchy, sixteen years too late. 'No, Mam, you didn't push me. You were trying to catch me.'

Reading the room in the way that only a critical care nurse can do, Rebecca had waived the two visitors rule and fetched them all tea. Ron and Sean are nursing theirs, staring into the fathomless depths of too-hot liquid in a plastic vending machine cup while Edie examines the years that she missed etched onto Sean's face.

There is so much to say, but Edie is afraid that if she opens her mouth, the words – and the tears – will never stop tumbling out. That she will fill the room with things smothered by sixteen years of self-doubt, self-punishment. Like being jailed for a crime she didn't commit, she has served someone else's time, and where do you go from there?

She glances between her husband and her two sons, fingers quivering. She jams them under her legs, lets her voice push past the pulse battering her throat.

'Somebody needs to start talking,' she says.

Colin looks at Sean, who looks at Ron, who looks back to Sean. Sean clears his throat, looks back into his tea.

'I fell,' he says. 'I fell. Your fingers were trying to grip my shirt and I slipped through them and I fell.'

'Did you think I pushed you, even for a second?'

He looks at her now and her breath catches in her throat. 'No.'

Edie closes her eyes. 'Then why did you nod?' she whispers. When he doesn't answer, she opens her eyes, views him through the steam rising from his cup. His cheeks are pink.

'Because I was angry,' he says eventually. 'And David said it. I just jumped on that.'

'You were angry?' she asks.

'With you,' he takes a tiny sip, winces. 'With me.' He puts the cup down on the floor and presses the tips of his fingers into a prism. 'I was ashamed of you, all of you. I was ashamed of me. How working-class we all were. How low, how common. I wanted to be somebody, and I was struggling to shake off who I was.' He gives a short, humourless laugh. 'No matter how hard I tried to convince myself I was like those boys, they could smell the working-class coming off me like a stench.' He stands, walks over to the window and stares into the darkness. The moon tonight is a crisp half wearing a smudged halo, and wispy dark clouds snake tendrils across its half-face like hair.

'All these years,' says Edie, staring at the hand she's spent sixteen years believing was capable of harming her own child.

'I thought you knew. I didn't think for a second you'd have doubted your own memory of it all. I just thought you wouldn't want to know me. This awful son who would lie to all those people about his mother.' He digs the heel of his hands into his eyes, voice cracking. 'I've thought a lot over the years about what I did, and to be honest, I look back at that desperate kid with shame.' He glances at Ron. 'But I'm working on it.'

'I knew,' blurts Colin. 'He told me.'

Sean and Colin stare at one another and it is like looking in a fogged mirror. They are different certainly, and the years have left their marks independently, but the similarity is still there, the fibre that connected the two before Edie even knew there were two of them.

'I told him,' says Sean. 'I told him and he hit me. Told me he never wanted to see me again. Told me to stay away from you.'

'That's why you wouldn't help me find him,' says Edie. It's a statement, rather than a question. Her beautiful, loyal boy, who has been there for her through all of this. Who had a space by his side where a best man should have been, a gap that only Sean could have filled, and all to protect his mother.

A sob escapes, and Edie presses her hand to her mouth to push it back in. *Don't crack now, Edie. Hold it together a little while longer.*

'Why didn't you tell me?' Ron asks Colin.

'Nanna died, you lost the garage. You were falling apart.' Colin closes his eyes for a moment and fixes them on Ron when he opens them. 'And you seemed like you were standing by Mam anyway. I thought maybe we could all just move on.'

Sean clears his throat. 'I've learned more in the hollow spaces where you all should have been than I ever did at that school or at university,' he says. 'It took me far too long to figure out that I was some trifling little social experiment to the Pike-Oberons. Well, until Bianca got strange and started coming on to me.'

That Nathaniel Pike-Oberon had said something about Sean ruining their family. She wants to ask more, but that can wait.

'And the phone calls? On my birthday.' She swallows. 'That was you, wasn't it?'

He nods, mouth pressed into a thin line. 'I didn't know where to start, how to even begin to get over what I did to you. But I wanted to hear your voice. Thought maybe if you knew that I was thinking of you, you might be able to forgive me for what I did.'

'So what changed?' says Edie. 'Why did you suddenly get back in touch with Dad after all these years?' She wants to add *And why Dad and not me?*

Sean looks back at Ron. 'My new therapist wanted me to have some joint sessions with you all. I thought Dad would be the best starting point.' Ron's gaze returns to his cup. 'I thought if Dad could forgive me, he could help figure out where to start with you two.'

Edie watches the Adam's apple in his neck going up and down like a lift. She presses a finger to the racing pulse point in her own throat, a stomping rhythm of love and fear on the brink of thrashing its way out.

'I'd forgive you anything,' she says at last. She slides her hand down to her chest and rests it on her thumping heart. 'This thing beats for you three,' she whispers. 'Even when you weren't there, Sean, it never stopped hammering for you.'

Sean's face crumples, then erupts into a flood of tears. 'I don't deserve you,' he says. 'I don't deserve any of you.'

Ron, Colin and Edie's eyes follow as he streaks from the room. She's watching him leave again, but she couldn't chase after him, even if she wanted to. Something settles around Edie, soft, like being cloaked in a cloud, and for the first time in years, or perhaps even the whole of her existence, the blood in her veins ebbs to a cool, easy flow.

Part 6

Ball Number 33: The Twins' Age

60

After

There had been talk of them all travelling together. But that was before Colin decided he was feeling well enough to drive again.

'Got to get back behind the wheel eventually,' he said wisely.

All three of them are a study in scrubbing up well. Ron has donned a beige linen jacket and Edie wants to rub his sleeve and rest her head on his broad shoulder, but she can't do either of those things at the moment. Last week, she accompanied Ron to a solo session with Renata, his and Sean's therapist. She sat in the waiting room enjoying a *Hello!* magazine, and when he emerged, he gave her a soft smile and reached for her hand. They're taking baby steps, but last night he turned up at her bedroom door in his dressing gown, said 'Can I sleep with you, please?' Under the soft bedding, unaccustomed to the warmth of two bodies, he whispered, 'Just tell me Edie-Eves. Tell me what you need in order to forgive me.'

She'd allowed him to fold his chest into her back and said, 'Let's just start here, okay?'

Jade, in the pew in front, turns to grin. The baby is sleeping soundly on his mother, mop of dark curls springing from a white wrap. Edie strokes the baby's head and pats Jade on the shoulder.

The order of service that Jade had printed features a photo of her and the baby taken just hours after his birth. Both Jade and the little one are wearing heart-shaped green plastic sunglasses, like something Elton John might wear. Jade has two thumbs up and a mouth open like she's riding a roller coaster. His name is printed underneath:

Silas Orion Churchill Kelly

'His initials are SOCK,' whispers Colin.

The pudgy-faced vicar winds up the sermon that no one was really listening to and gets the congregation to stand. He gestures for Jade and Edie to come forward and join him at the font and the vicar hands Edie a candle, yelping as he dribbles wax all down his arm.

Later, the assembled cram in Jade's house. Edie marvels that they all fit and wonders why she never thought to have everyone she cared about over. Some gangly teens attempt to extract the last squeezes from a box of wine, while competing to see who can be the loudest. Across the room, Carol pretends to be interested in whatever a pinstripe-trousered man is talking about. She catches Edie's eye, raising a stubby bottle of beer in cheers.

All the aqua aerobics ladies are there, mingling with Jade's old school friends and Edie's old friends, who have rallied around to form Jade's village, cooking her food and soaking up snuggles from baby Silas while she grabs some shut-eye here and there.

'You will come. No car. We send bus. No question,' Verushka promises Brenda. 'Our class will be better than Jooty's.'

'Tooties?' asks Brenda.

'No, Jooty. This pool lady you had at *leisure centre*.' She says *leisure centre* with the same disdain as someone might say *puppy abattoir*, disgusted that such a place exists. 'Edith's class is better.'

'It is,' says Sarah Moss. 'I made a video on my computer. Look!'

Even Jade's mother, the infamous Kerry Kelly, has made it. Her face reminds Edie of a leather satchel Sid left behind, though she can't be much more than forty-five. She's leaning on the fridge beside Ron.

'I'm just a very sexual person, Ronald,' she tells him, warm wine sloshing out of her glass and onto the lino. Ron has gone all rigid and twitchy. Edie stifles a giggle.

Patricia is there too, tanned and happy with her very own Jimmy Mack. She presents Edie with a genuine postcard from the trip to Bali that Edie gifted them.

'I can't thank you enough,' she says. 'How will I ever make it up to you?'

'Oh, I reckon I can milk you for a couple of cream teas and a trip to Minchella's,' says Edie.

Colin cradles baby Silas whispering something inaudible. He stops from time to time to glance around the familiar room. Perhaps he's seeing what she is: a lifetime of breakfasts, dirty dishes and squabbles overlaying the current scene. Sean, legs crossed on the table, yammering about revision plans and sailing, while Colin sneaks a peek at his dad's car magazines that poke out from behind cushions and chopping boards. She smiles at her son.

If only Sean was here too.

'Edie! Come with me.' Jade grabs her hand and pulls her towards the back door.

'Wait!' says Edie, grabbing a bag on the way out. 'I've got something to give you in private, anyway.'

They make their way down the garden and away from the noise of the kitchen and stop at the tree.

'Look!' Jade points at a wooden house hanging from the apple tree. 'It's an insect hotel,' she says. 'I thought little Silas would like it. Look at all the ladybirds.'

A tear springs in the corner of Edie's eye.

'I know, I know. It's portable, so it's okay. I'm sure we'll have to move soon, but listen: Mam's seeing this gardener guy so I was going to see if he can dig the tree up and transport it to yours,' says Jade. 'I know you're fond of it, and I won't be here to look after it when I get evicted.' She sags a little, then pastes on a bright face. 'I know you said your friend would help, but they'll be here to turf me out on Wednesday.'

Edie's heart thuds. 'Jade, I've got a little christening gift for you. Well, for Silas, actually.'

Edie pulls a fat envelope from her bag and hands it to Jade. Gemma had everything finalised and couriered back to her this morning.

Jade roots through the papers. 'Edie, what's this? I don't understand.'

Edie is shaking. 'The deeds. To the house.'

'What? Why?' Jade shakes her head. 'I can't accept that.'

'See, I thought you might say that.' Edie takes one of the pieces of paper from her and scans it. 'So *you* don't have to. Ah, here, look.' She points at Silas' name. 'You don't own the house, Silas does. I mean, I'm sure he'll let you live here, but it's his.'

Jade stares at Edie. A breeze rustles through the apple tree, leaves preparing to crisp from green to a brittle brown in their cycle of regeneration.

'You did this? For me?'

'Well, for you and Silas,' she says.

'Thank you.' It's barely a whisper.

They contemplate the bricks imbued with a lifetime of memories. The love Edie poured into making it a home for their family. The echoes of times they were happy here. Hilda, the boys, a younger Edie wrapped in Ron's loving arms.

It is Jade's now to fill with love and things that Silas will want to return to when he's older. And she will, because his little cup is already brimming with love and a ready-made chosen family to provide everything he could need.

Edie sits down on the grass beside the tree. A cluster of yellow-green fruits huddle together, semi-hidden by the foliage. By next spring, the tree might provide Silas with home-grown nourishment planted thirty years ago, and this makes her smile.

Through the open window, baby Silas wails, seeking out the comfort of his mother.

'Best go see to the landlord,' Jade says. She smiles as Ron appears framed by the back door. 'Someone else wants you now.'

Ron walks slowly across the little garden. 'Do you remember when we planted this?'

'All that hope,' says Edie. 'Fresh starts and all.'

'Do we need a fresh start, Edie?' He sits beside her on the grass. 'You're probably going to have to help me get back up.'

A ladybird settles on Edie's finger. She squints to count the dots, but he flies away before she can. *Ladybird, ladybird, fly away home.* She hopes he has a nice home to go to. A family waiting for him in his little insect hotel room.

'I saw you,' says Ron, and his eyes are focused on her cheek. 'I saw you at the hospital yelling at the doctor.' She glances at him sideways. 'I saw you there taking charge. Fighting for someone who needed you, and it made me angry. Why were you fighting for someone you barely know when you never fought that hard for our family? That's what I was thinking.' Edie shakes her head softly. 'But you were, weren't you?'

'I never stopped fighting,' she whispers.

Ron reaches for her hand. 'I doubted you, Edie-Eves. I doubted you and I'm sorry.' He shakes his head. 'You are the kindest, strongest, bravest person I know, and I let myself forget that. Can you forgive me?'

She hesitates. This could be it. Their moment to go back to what they were. But there are still some things she needs to know.

'Why did you let them tie my tubes?'

His face contorts. 'They said you'd die, Edie. Said you'd die if you had to go through childbirth again.' He laces his fingers through hers. 'I couldn't risk that,' he whispers. 'Couldn't imagine life without you.'

She stares down at her belly, long past its sell-by date. How angry she was that he was making decisions about her. It dissipates now, steam into the late September air.

One more thing. She takes a deep breath.

'The woman with the long hair,' she starts. 'Back in Boldon. The after-hours visits to the garage. Who was she?'

Ron takes a deep breath. 'Lillian. Old school friend. I took out a loan from her husband. Real dodgy bugger. Nasty. Lillian saved my fingers.'

'Did you . . .?'

'What? Edie, no! You can't possibly think . . .?' He pulls her to him. She's stiff, feels awkward in his arms. He presses his lips to her hair. 'There's only ever been you, Edie-Eves. Always. Forever.'

Edie closes her eyes, lets herself melt into his chest.

61

After

The smell hasn't changed in fifty years: buttery vanilla smothered in strawberry, banana and caramel. Edie sniffs and closes her eyes and Minchella's fills her lungs and the dusty corners of her memory.

At the same table where she started to fall in love with Ron all those years earlier, Edie hovers over a postcard of the Marine Park.

Come home. That's all she can write.

She doesn't have an address – since Sean ran from the room, none of them have heard from him – but for the first time in years, she is confident that it's going to be okay. Now they've seen him, now that they know he's safe, if not entirely well, it is only a matter of time before they can start properly rebuilding their family.

'Did I ever tell you, me and Dad had our first ever date right here?'

Colin smiles with a weirdly moony expression. She was surprised when he said he wanted to take her out for the day, even more surprised when he brought her here.

'What? Why are you looking at me like that?' Edie dabs her mouth with a napkin.

'I love you, Mum. I love you and know that you have always loved us. And that's all that matters.' He nods his head. 'There.'

Edie tussles him into an embrace that he's far too big for, dots kisses on his pillowy cheeks. 'You're a fantastic boy, Colin McVey. You're my greatest achievement. And thank you. For always being in my corner.'

Colin blushes. 'Enough of that, Mum. Finish up your ice cream and then I've got a surprise for you.'

This part of town has been pedestrianised, so she and Colin make their way slowly to the car park behind Kirkpatrick's. There's a sputtery noise and a funny little car chugs around the corner.

It's a familiar car. Little, low, a smart racing green.

'Vintage,' she says pointing at it. 'I wish we could take a picture for Dad. He used to have one like this.'

Colin wraps his arm around her shoulder. The car pulls right up to where they're standing, the passenger window down.

'Hop in, Edie-Eves!'

Ron grins from behind the wheel. His cheeks are flushed and he rests one elbow out of the open window.

'Oh!' says Edie. 'Oh, my goodness, Ron! How did you— This looks a bit like—'

'It is! Not the same one, but same model, same year.'

Edie laughs and claps her hands. 'Did you know about this, Colin?'

'Come on, Edes. We haven't got all day.'

'Have fun!' says Colin. He closes the door behind Edie as she settles into the passenger seat.

'Aren't you coming?' asks Edie.

'You want me to?'

'Of course!'

The car is a shiny Ford Prefect, the 1961 model that Ron drove her in on their very first date. The driver's window doesn't quite shut and there is even a freshly sewn patch of denim on the passenger seat.

'I wanted it to feel exactly right,' he says, watching her fingers gently brush the patch.

'You did all this?'

Ron nods. She closes her eyes to keep the tears from leaking out.

Ron manoeuvres the car slowly out of the car park and into the gentle stop-start of town centre traffic. Past the white and blue painted Victorian guest houses on Ocean Road with their neon Vacancies signs, past the aromatic row of Indian restaurants that now stand in the shells of businesses gone by, past the old lifeboat model painted red and white and blue, signifying the tumultuous history of the town on the tides, and down to the sandstone pavilion housing the Westovian Theatre, they drive in silence. This place that has formed the backdrop of their lives together glows with the burnished golds of early autumn and Edie pushes down the window to savour it.

Ron indicates right at the junction, but pauses before turning.

'Press the blue button,' he says.

In place of the confusing radio dials that used to suddenly jump between stations is a sleek digital console. Edie presses it as they turn into a wide traffic gap. A familiar drumbeat fills the car.

'Jimmy Mack,' sings Martha and her Vandellas.

Laughing, Edie flings an arm around Ron's shoulder and sings at the top of her voice. The car picks up speed on the coast road past the fair and the beach and they're flying, flying and singing and laughing.

'My Jimmy Mack!'

The red and white striped body of Souter Lighthouse beckons them towards the windy tops. Edie can't remember the last time she was here, gulping down fresh salty balloons of air. Solid, lovely Ron, still there, like the lighthouse, guiding her home when she was lost.

They pull into the lighthouse car park and Ron stops where just a rolling vista of cloud-punctured sky fills the windscreen. Another car, something grey and nondescript, idles in a space nearby, a lost driver perhaps, dipping his head low against the steering wheel.

'Edie, I've got a little surprise for you.'

'I thought this was the surprise,' grins Edie.

Ron rolls up his shirtsleeves. Where once a scrawled heart clasped the name Eva across its body, there now sits a beautiful, perfect heart in a deep claret. A banner crossing the middle reads 'Edie-Eves'.

'You two!' jibes Colin gently from the back seat.

'I should have known, Edie-Eves. Known that you were only ever trying to do the right thing. Trying to keep us afloat when the seas were rough.' Ron swallows hard. 'You know that I couldn't be without you, pet? It's always been you, Edie. Even when Joan Collins tried to kiss me. I told her no, told her she wasn't the one for me.'

'You never told me she tried to kiss you!' Edie folds her arms and frowns.

'Edes, I'm sorry, I . . .'

'Get out of this car, Ron McVey.' She leaps from the passenger seat and strides around the front of the car. Ron is still struggling with his seatbelt as Edie wrenches open the door.

'Edie, please don't be upset.' He gets out, stands by his wife. 'I didn't do . . .'

She flings her arms around his neck, pulls him close. 'Do you think it's too late?' she whispers.

'Too late for what?'

'For us.'

His arms tighten around her waist and they hold one another, matching up the rhythms of their heartbeats once more. Edie breathes and fills her lungs with that familiar Ron smell – a faint hit of petrol and plain soap – along with the tang of the sea. Home.

She pulls back, smiles. 'And another thing: I think it's time you taught me how to drive.'

Ron helps her slide into the driver's seat, then scoots round the car as she runs her hands across the steering wheel.

'Come on, Ron.'

His door is barely shut before she turns the keys, feels the car, thrumming and alive, beneath her.

Ron shows her how to press the clutch, how to guide the gearstick into first. Slowly, she puts the car into gear, presses the accelerator, brings it around in a tight circle.

It bumps a bit but Edie brings the car around the side of the lighthouse keepers' centre and to where the car park meets the narrow entrance road in one piece. She pauses, looks down at the gearstick and the pedals to remind herself where everything is. To her left, there's nothing coming, but when she turns to look right, there's a person blocking her view. A knuckle raps on the window and Edie winds the lever, letting a cool breeze in.

Sean pokes his head through the window.

'Room for one more?' he asks.

That's the skin she kissed, the cheeks she wiped, the mouth she fed for so many years. Her heart is about to leap straight through her ribcage.

'Hop in,' she says, her voice thick with the weight of a thousand missed conversations.

There's talking to do – so much talking – but talking can wait. For now, Edie has all of her boys in one place for the first time in too long, she just wants the luxury of them breathing the same air at the same time in the same place.

Sean hops in the back seat beside his brother. Edie eases the car into gear and guides the McVeys back onto the road.

Acknowledgements

Thanks go to my amazing agent Hellie Ogden, who spotted something more in the doom sandwich I initially presented you with, and helped me craft it into something palatable. Your faith in the book and in this insomniac Geordie weirdo has been incredible and humbling. Enormous thanks too for the ongoing eyes, ears and support of Ma'suma Amiri. Thanks to the wonderful and immeasurably talented Martha Ashby for loving Edie as much as I do and helping her find her way.

Thanks to Florence Dodd – I always get excited when I see your emails! And Rhian McKay for your excellent eye for detail.

A huge thanks to Cathie Hartigan, Sophie Duffy, Margaret James of Creative Writing Matters for giving new writers the chance to put their books in front of agents. I am so grateful for the door you opened for me. To my Binklings: Susan Perrow, Vicky King, Jenni Cargill-Strong, Lynton Francois Burger, Ana Davis and Mitchell King for being a writing group so great that I boast about you in my dreams. Thanks to the Blue Marble crew for building a supportive and inspiring international writing company, especially Russell Norman and Deidra Whitt Lovegren for making it happen. To Meg Biddle in the middle, for teaching a technosaur how to do things! To Seán McNicholl for being a fab beta-buddy – *by drug!* To Malcolm Davison, the best English teacher in the world – you inspired so many and are sadly missed.

I am lucky to come from a family of amazing and strong women, some of whom are no longer with us but deserve credit, some of whom inspired characters in this book: Iris Crawford, Brenda Hunter, Surajah Hunter, Julie Coulson, Mary Jorgensen, Veronica Sewell, Anne Marie Parker, Lucy Hughes, Ann, Sharon, Nic and Aelish Corr, Kari Ausobsky, Vera McKenzie and Lily Peacock.

I am incredibly lucky to have a great pair of parents-in-law who have kept me in coffee and looked after the bub (and the dog!) when I needed to write. Thanks so much Anne and Les Kranicz.

My fabulous parents, Tom and Carol McKenzie, instilled in me a love of reading and stories. Your love and support means everything. Thank you for all you have done for me, and for generously letting me use bits of your own hilariously cute courtship for Ron and Edie.

Yes, I am going to be that person who thanks my dog, and I'm not even sorry! Ducky, you are the goofiest, silliest girl. Thanks for keeping me company in the lonely writing hours.

And to the most wonderful two humans in the world. My fantastic husband Mick and my incredible daughter Abigail. I love you both more than anything. Thank you for inspiring me to be the best version of myself every day.